SEARCHING FOR A KILLER

Zac shoved his fingers through his hair, his tension vibrating around him like a tangible force field.

"This tape proves that Jude murdered Staci Gale. Probably in his brother's morgue."

Rachel nodded. "And then buried her in his own grave," she added.

"That seems the most likely scenario," Zac agreed. "Do you think Jacob was involved?"

"My gut feeling is that Jacob helped his brother fake his death for the life insurance money, but he didn't know that Jude intended to use the grave to dump the body of a woman he'd just murdered. Fifty thousand isn't worth the death penalty."

"I wonder how many other women he killed?" She spoke her fear out loud. "Why didn't I follow up on that fingerprint?"

Zac grabbed her shoulders, turning her to meet his steady gaze. "Because Jude was officially dead. Why would you waste resources chasing a ghost?"

"Yes, a ghost." She muttered a curse. "He managed to become invisible. The perfect way to hunt his victims without concern for leaving behind clues . . ."

UNSTABLE

ALEXANDRA IVY

ZEBRA BOOKS
KENSINGTON PUBLISHING CORP.
www.kensingtonbooks.com

Chapter 1

Zac Evans pulled the square plastic tray out of the microwave and headed to his desk. Once seated, he removed the clouded film to reveal the limp noodles covered in a weird red sauce and splotches of white that was supposed to be cheese. He grimaced. Was there anything sadder than spending a Saturday night at his desk, eating mystery lasagna?

Not that his evening would have been much different if he'd been home. He was just thirty, but his days of crazy party weekends had ended when he was eighteen.

The cost of marrying his high school sweetheart just days after graduation. And divorcing her just four years later.

Working up his courage to take a bite, Zac was thankfully distracted by the sound of a buzzer that shattered the silence. Shoving himself to his feet, he crossed the planked floor to the monitors that were mounted on the wall over the old wooden filing cabinets. Technology mixed with history. It was a deliberate choice he'd made when he'd taken over the position as interim sheriff in Pike, Wisconsin.

A quick glance at the monitor revealed a tall, slender man who was looking directly into the camera to reveal his golden blond hair and blue eyes. He was wearing a heavy leather jacket to combat the early November chill and black slacks.

Kir Jansen.

Surprised by the unexpected visit, Zac glanced at the old-fashioned clock on the wood-paneled wall. Seven thirty. Odd time for a social call.

Pressing the locking device that he'd had installed on the front door, he spoke into the intercom. "Come in."

Kir disappeared from view, and Zac moved to pull open the door to his office. The sheriff's department took up most of the old courthouse, but he was located at the front of the building. Within a few seconds his friend was strolling through the reception area and into his private space.

Coming to a halt in the center of the floor, Kir lifted his brows as his gaze swept the recently remodeled space. Kir's father, Rudolf, had been sheriff in Pike until a shooting had forced him into an early retirement. Kathy Hancock had taken over and done everything in her power to wipe away any trace of Rudolf. And the temporary sheriff who'd briefly taken over after Kathy's abrupt departure had left it, no doubt realizing there was no point in making any changes when he was going to return to Madison in a matter of weeks.

"Wow. You've made some changes."

Zac shrugged, moving to lean on the corner of his desk. Over the past six months he'd donated the plastic and rubber furniture to the local school and removed the carpeting along with the heavy curtains that blocked the windows that offered a beautiful view of the town square. He'd also raided the storage rooms to find the previous handcrafted wood furniture that had been there since the courthouse was built a hundred years ago.

He didn't ask himself why he'd been determined to create a style that suited his taste when he was just the interim sheriff, especially when he hadn't done a damned thing at his parents' farmhouse in the eight years he'd lived there, but he was glad that he'd gone to the effort. There was a sense of comfort each time he walked into this room.

"I wasn't really into the whole Ikea vibe," he told his friend.

A wistful smile touched Kir's mouth. "It looks like it did when my father was sheriff."

"Is that good or bad?"

"Perfect." Kir turned to face Zac, his brows arching at the sight of the steaming container on the desk. "Am I interrupting dinner?"

"If you wanna call it dinner." Zac smiled wryly. As tall as Kir, he had thicker muscles from his years of working on his father's farm. Even after he'd sold off the dairy cattle and rented out the fields to his neighbor, there was an endless number of chores that demanded physical labor. His hair was also a darker shade of blond and his eyes were green with flecks of gold. His mother claimed the gold was the result of being blessed by a fairy when he was a baby. Of course, his mother also said that God had given her only one child because he was so special, so her belief system was suspect. "My father would have called it hog slop."

"He wouldn't be wrong. That's . . ." Kir shuddered. "Disgusting."

"Not all of us have the Kir Jansen's magical skills in the kitchen," Zac pointed out. The older man had made a fortune in Boston by creating a company that would take care of any tedious task. Washing a car, picking up laundry, cleaning gutters, or cooking dinner. Which meant he had a wide variety of talents, including the ability to create a cordon bleu meal.

He'd recently sold his multimillion-dollar corporation to marry the local vet, Lynne Gale, and settle down in marital bliss.

"My skills aren't just in the kitchen." Kir wiggled his brows. "Just ask Lynne."

Zac held up his hand. "Hard pass."

"You know, if you want to learn a few basic skills I'll be happy to stop by and give you a cooking lesson," Kir offered.

"A true friend would invite me for dinner."

Kir smiled. "You can feed a man a fish or you can teach him to fish . . . something like that. Anyway, you can have a fish for a night or fish for a lifetime."

Zac folded his arms over his chest, the heavy utility belt that went with his uniform rattling at the movement. "Yeah I can fish, I just can't cook it."

"You don't *want* to cook it."

"That too."

Kir glanced back at the lasagna. "Does your mother know you're eating cardboard dinners at your office?"

Zac's mother had moved into a small house in Pike after his father had died five years ago, but she still stopped by the farm to keep his freezer filled with home-cooked dinners.

"My aunt Val in Omaha broke her leg, so Mom is there taking care of her for the next few weeks."

"Ah." Kir dipped his head in a wise nod. "That explains it."

Zac grimaced, realizing that Kir assumed he was helpless without his mom. And worse, he couldn't argue. He'd been so busy over the past six months that he'd come to rely on his mother taking care of his day-to-day needs.

"Christ," he muttered. "I thought I felt awful eating crap at my desk. It's worse knowing I'm one of those guys who depends on his mother to survive."

Kir shook his head. "There's nothing wrong with being a good son."

"It's pathetic."

"No." There was a harsh edge in Kir's voice. "Count each day with her as a blessing. I wish I had."

Zac understood Kir's fierce reaction. He'd recently lost his father, and he still blamed himself for the years he'd spent away from Pike.

"You're right," he agreed, although he silently assured himself that he was going to spend fewer hours at the office and more hours taking care of his home.

The smile returned to Kir's face. "And you know there is another solution."

"Don't say takeout," Zac warned. "There's nothing in town that delivers and I'm not driving to Grange." He mentioned the town fifteen miles away. It was the nearest place with fast food.

"I was going to say you should find a wife who loves to cook," Kir said dryly.

"I have a wife."

The words left Zac's lips before he realized they were even there. As if they'd been formed in the depths of his primitive brain.

Kir blinked, as if puzzled by Zac's response, then hastily cleared his throat. "Okay."

Embarrassed, and uncertain why he'd claimed a wife he'd divorced eight years ago, Zac pushed away from the desk. "Is there a reason you stopped by?"

Kir nodded, trying to hide his relief at the change in conversation. "I came into town to meet with a potential buyer for Dad's old house," he told Zac. Kir and Lynne had recently built a house on his father's land a few miles outside Pike. "I was headed home when I noticed a truck parked on the side of the road near the entrance to the cemetery."

"Was someone inside it?"

"Nope."

Zac wasn't sure what had alarmed Kir. Pike was small enough that people parked wherever they wanted. Hell, sometimes they stopped in the middle of the street to chat with a friend. If he gave out tickets to everyone who violated the parking rules, he'd never get anything else done.

"Are they blocking traffic?" Zac asked. "Or broke down?"

"I'm not sure what's going on," Kir admitted. "The engine was running with the headlights on bright and the driver-side door was open. I stopped to see if they needed help, but there was no one around."

Zac frowned, searching his brain for an explanation. "They could be looking for a lost dog."

"Could be." Kir held up his hands. "It just seemed odd and . . ."

"What?"

Kir hesitated, as if not sure he wanted to reveal what was on his mind. "That spot has a dark history," he finally forced himself to say. "That probably made it seem a bigger deal than what it really is."

Zac nodded. Last year, Pike had gone through some troubled times, and Kir had been at the heart of the evil. It was no wonder he was a little antsy.

"No problem. I'll run over and check it out." Zac nodded toward his dinner, which had congealed into a red, gooey mess. "It gives me an excuse to avoid that."

Kir frowned. "Don't you have a deputy to deal with it?"

"It's Lindsay and Greg's weekend off. And Anthony called in sick," Zac told him, referring to his deputies. "Again." Zac rolled his eyes. At some point he was going to have to deal with Anthony. Unfortunately, the younger man had served as deputy the longest of the three, and he was a second or third cousin to Zac. Firing him was going to take an effort he wasn't willing to put in. Yet. "It's just me."

"I'll go with you," Kir instantly offered.

"There's no need," Zac assured him, moving to grab the brown jacket that matched his uniform. Being sheriff wasn't about being stylish. Actually, he was a walking fashion disaster. But hey, he had his weapon strapped to his hip and his official ID clipped on his shirt. That was all that was important. "Go home to your beautiful wife."

Kir wrinkled his nose. "She called just before I arrived. We were supposed to meet for dinner but she has an emergency farm visit."

"You've been stood up for a goat?" Zac teased, leading his companion out of the office and to the front door. Once they were standing outside, he locked the door and set the alarms.

"Nope, for a bloated cow," Kir corrected him, walking down the shallow cement steps to the sidewalk.

"That makes it so much better."

"The hazards of marrying a vet." Kir shook his head. "They have worse hours than cops."

"Hard to believe." Zac glanced around the town square and nearby city park. The stores were dark and Main Street was nearly empty. The good citizens of Pike were home with their families or out of town enjoying a movie or nightclub.

Zac headed to his black truck with a sheriff's star painted on the side, while Kir climbed into a shiny SUV that no doubt cost more than Zac's yearly salary.

Together they pulled away from the courthouse and headed toward the cemetery on the edge of town. There wasn't much in the way of traffic, and they were soon turning the corner onto the street. Instantly, Zac caught sight of the pickup and pulled behind it.

Climbing out of his truck, he waited for Kir to join him and together they circled the abandoned vehicle. It was just as Kir had described. The engine was still running, although there was a distinct sputter that warned it was running on fumes. The headlights were blazing. And the driver-side door was wide open.

Zac paused at the back of the beige truck, examining the rust and grime that coated every inch of it. Not the usual layer of dust that came from living in an area with gravel roads. No, this had taken years, maybe decades to accumulate.

"Do you recognize it?" he asked Kir.

"No."

"Neither do I." Zac would have noticed this vehicle if it'd been driving around town. He glanced down at the dented bumper. "No license plates. It might be stolen."

Kir moved to stand next to him. "Who would steal it? It's a piece of junk."

Kir wasn't wrong. If a thief was going to steal a vehicle this would be last on the list. Zac leaned into the cab to shut off the engine along with the lights. Then he reached across the dash.

"There might be something in the glove box." He pulled out a stack of papers that were brittle and yellowed with age. Laying them flat on the driver's seat, Zac pulled his flashlight from his belt and studied the forms. "Registration and insurance," he murmured, leaning forward. In this area of town the streetlights were few and far between, creating a blanket of darkness that was somehow fitting for a graveyard. "The ink is faded, but it looks like the pickup is registered to a Jude Henley."

Kir furrowed his brow. "Why is that name familiar?"

Zac returned the papers to the glove compartment and shut the door before turning toward his friend.

"The only Henleys I know used to own the local funeral parlor," he said. "It shut down five or six years ago."

"Is there any family left in town?" Kir asked.

"I don't know." Zac tilted his head back, glancing at the night sky that was splattered with dazzling stars. It was one of the reasons he stayed in Pike. Nowhere else had a sky like that. Tonight, however, he barely noticed.

There could be a dozen different reasons the truck had been left there. Some kids could have stolen it to take for a joyride. Jude could have been drunk and wandered off. There could be something wrong with the vehicle and he had hitched a ride home, intending to return. But Zac had a bad feeling in the pit of his stomach. He never ignored his bad feelings. "I'm going to have a look around," he abruptly announced.

With a nod, Kir walked beside him as he headed toward the line of cedar trees that marked the entrance to the cemetery. They stepped through the open gate and Kir paused to pull out his phone and hit the flashlight app.

"I'll go this way," the older man announced, pointing toward the east side of the graveyard.

Zac watched his friend disappear into the darkness before he headed up the other side. It wasn't a large space. In the more rural areas people preferred to have family plots on their land, but it was big enough to take some time to do a thorough search. And the sharp chill in the air was going to make it seem even longer.

Swinging his flashlight in a zigzag pattern, Zac walked through the lines of headstones. He was no doubt wasting his time, but he wasn't going to be able to concentrate on anything until he solved the mystery. And that was what made him a good sheriff, he acknowledged without boasting. He wasn't flashy, he didn't have a photographic memory or psychic abilities like the detectives on television. But he was ruthlessly stubborn, and once he set his mind on a task, he was like a bulldog with a bone.

The tortoise won the race, not the hare, right?

He was nearing the center of the graveyard when his light flashed over a lump of darkness lying on top of a grave. Hurrying forward, he was able to make out the shape of a human body.

Placing his fingers in his mouth, he released a sharp whistle to attract Kir's attention. Then, halting next to the unmoving form, he crouched down. He was guessing this was Jude Henley. No doubt the man had decided he was too drunk to drive so he'd wandered into the graveyard, either in confusion or because it was a shortcut to his house, and had passed out. Lucky for him, he'd left the truck running so Kir would notice it when he drove past.

A good, solid theory. At least until Zac aimed his flashlight at the man's face. His eyes were wide-open, staring at the sky above, and his lips were parted, as if he was about to speak. That wasn't what caught and held Zac's attention. It was the dark blood that coated the pasty white skin. And the perfect hole in the center of his forehead.

Shaken by the unexpected sight, Zac surged upright, the light from his flashlight jerking toward the headstone. The glow illuminated the name etched in the dark granite.

"Christ," he muttered, just as Kir jogged up to join him.

"What is it?"

"The question is *who* is it," Zac said in grim tones, returning his light to the man's face.

Kir hissed. "Dead?"

"Yep, he's dead."

Zac didn't have to check for a pulse to know the man was well and truly past saving. And he didn't want to touch anything before he could properly set up his crime scene. He might never have had reason to use his four-year criminal justice degree until recently, but he'd been well trained.

Kir sucked in a deep breath, as if trying to steady his nerves, then he leaned over the body to study the wound.

"A suicide?"

"Possible," Zac said. He'd already noticed the Glock G19 that was lying next to the body. He'd have it tested once he'd collected all the evidence. He swung the light toward the headstone. "But check this out."

Kir turned his head, clearly confused. Then Zac could see him stiffen in surprise.

"Jude Henley. Beloved son and brother. Born April 21, 1966. Died November 12, 1994." Kir glanced back at Zac. "That can't be a coincidence."

"No." The fact that the truck was registered to a Jude Henley, and this body was found on the grave of a Jude Henley had to mean something. He was guessing they were related. Reaching up, he grabbed the walkie-talkie attached to his jacket. "Time to call in the calvary."

Chapter 2

The Dane County medical examiner's office in Madison, a couple hours south of Pike, was built on an isolated plot of land between a storage facility and a golf course. If Zac hadn't gone to college in the area he would have driven straight past it.

Parking his truck, he entered the reception area and was led to an office where a small man with thick black hair and shrewd brown eyes was seated behind a large desk.

"Dr. Woodward?" he asked, waiting for the man to nod before he crossed the silver carpet, which matched the two chairs and the pale gray walls. "I'm Sheriff Evans." The two men shook hands over the desk and Zac stepped back. "I hope you have some answers for me."

"I do." The middle-aged man laid his bony hand on a stack of files. "But I'm not sure you're going to like them."

Zac's heart dropped. He'd spent the past two days trying to convince himself that the autopsy would prove that John Doe was some relative of Jude Henley who had decided to end his life at the graveyard. Perhaps to make a statement to his family. Or just because he felt a connection to the long-dead Jude Henley. The grim expression on Dr. Woodward's lean face warned it wasn't anything that uncomplicated.

"Maybe I should stay standing," he muttered, folding his arms over his chest. "At least tell me you have an ID." It was going to be a difficult investigation if the body remained a John Doe.

"I do." Woodward opened the top file to read from an official form. "Jude Henley, fifty-six years old. Formerly of Pike, Wisconsin. Current address unknown."

"Jude? You're sure?" Zac frowned. The dead man was too old to be a son to Jude Henley, but they could be related. He knew families who used the same names over and over. There were at least a half dozen Steven Bateses in Pike. All cousins.

Woodward shrugged. "According to both the DNA and fingerprints."

Zac was surprised the reports had already come back. "They were on file?"

The doctor nodded. "He was arrested for petty theft in 1984 and for breaking and entering just a year later. Plus, he was a suspect in an armed robbery in 1992 that resulted in the death of a convenience store clerk. That's when they took his DNA."

"Is he related to the Jude Henley that's buried in Pike Cemetery?" He spoke his thoughts out loud, not really expecting an answer.

"From what I could figure out, it's the same Jude Henley."

Zac stared at the older man. His expression was still grim, but Zac suspected it always looked like that. A resting bitch face for medical examiners who spent their days wading through dead bodies. It made it impossible to know if he was joking.

"The same Jude Henley?"

"Yes."

"Am I being punked?" he demanded.

"Not in this office."

There was a hint of chiding in the medical examiner's voice, assuring Zac this was no joke. His brows drew together as he considered the implications.

"Unless he's a zombie there has to be a mistake."

"I'm just sharing what the body tells me. The fingerprints match Jude Henley who was pronounced dead and buried twenty-eight years ago."

Zac swallowed the urge to insist that it was impossible. He'd worry about the identification later. "What else?"

"He was shot at close range with a nine millimeter. The bullet entered his forehead and shattered through the back of his skull. Death was instantaneous."

Zac nodded. Nine mm. That fit with the Glock G19 he'd found next to the body. It was likely the forensic report would confirm that it was the weapon that killed him.

"Could it have been suicide?"

Woodward shook his head. "There was no powder residue on his hands." He pulled out a plastic bag that held a sheet of paper. Even at a distance Zac could see the wrinkles. As if it'd been crumpled into a ball before it'd been smoothed out. "And this was shoved in his mouth."

Zac read the words scribbled on the paper. *The student becomes the master.*

He glanced toward the man across the desk. "The student becomes the master. What the hell does that mean?"

"I have no idea. But it was put in the mouth after death." Woodward reached across the desk to turn the plastic bag over. He pointed toward two dark smears. "There was blood from the wound on it."

"Any fingerprints?"

"I'm going to send it to the forensics experts," the doctor promised. "If there's something on the paper or in the ink that can help pinpoint the killer, they'll find it."

Zac felt as if his head was spinning. He'd come here expecting a suicide. Now he felt as if he'd been dropped into a horror show. Complete with zombies.

Trying to maintain his professional composure, Zac reached into the pocket of his brown jacket to pull out a small pad and pencil. "Can you give me a time of death?" he asked.

"Between five and ten p.m."

Zac jotted down the numbers. He'd been at the grave-yard before eight so that narrowed the timeframe.

"Anything else?"

Woodward reached for the second file, reading off another report. "He was well fed. His last meal was just an hour before his death. He'd recently showered and shaved. His clothes were worn, but clean."

"So he wasn't homeless," Zac concluded.

"No."

"His clothing and shoes are with forensics," the doctor told him. "They might be able to give you an idea of where he's been staying."

"Any tattoos or scars?"

"He had a fractured shoulder when he was young that healed at an awkward angle. It would have noticeably impeded his movements and caused him pain."

Zac tapped his pencil on the notepad. The injury would help in the identification. People tended to notice physical handicaps.

"Anything else?"

"I've just done the preliminary autopsy." Woodward closed the files and stacked them in a neat pile. "The blood and biological samples will take a few days. I'll have the reports sent to you as soon as they come in."

"Thanks."

Zac headed out of the office. There were probably questions he needed to ask, but they would have to wait until he cleared his brain. Right now, it was clogged with the doctor's announcement that his John Doe was in fact Jude Henley. A man who had died twenty-eight years ago. And that his body had been left on his own grave.

Lost in his distraction, Zac failed to hear the footsteps hurrying down the hallway behind him. It wasn't until he heard someone calling out his name that he realized he wasn't alone.

"Zac."

Zac froze in his tracks. That voice sounded familiar. Too familiar.

No. It had to be stress. There was no way in hell she could be here. No. Way.

Slowly turning, he told himself he would see a stranger. Perhaps Woodward's assistant who had a question or wanted to give him further information. Instead, his hunch was confirmed.

It was his wife, Rachel Evans. No wait. Not Evans. She'd changed her name back to Fisher before the ink had dried on their divorce papers.

Because she's my ex-wife, he fiercely reminded himself, his gaze skimming over her in disbelief.

He'd seen Rachel over the past eight years, of course. Her parents still lived in Pike and she occasionally visited. But his glimpses had always been at a distance. Now he absorbed the sight of her with a sharp pang.

She'd never been a traditional beauty. Her features were strong rather than pretty, with a bold nose and a wide mouth. Her jaw was firm and her cheekbones sharply chiseled. She'd cut her glossy black hair, and instead of tumbling down her back it brushed her shoulders, but her dark blue eyes were as piercing as ever.

His gaze moved down to her tall, sleekly muscled body covered by a thick ivory sweater and black slacks. She'd been an athlete in school and her years as a cop had kept her in top physical shape.

Everything about her revealed a strong, assertive woman who didn't take shit from anyone.

He'd always loved that about her.

"Do you have a few minutes?" she asked, her voice low and husky. The sort of voice that made him think of sex . . .

Shit. Zac slammed shut the door on his treacherous thoughts. He'd given up the right to imagine Rachel naked years ago. A damned shame, but there it was. "Are you here for a case?"

"Actually, I was looking for you."

Zac stiffened. "Is anything wrong? Your parents—"

"They're fine," she hastily interrupted. "I want to talk to you about Jude Henley."

It was the last thing Zac had expected her to say. He stared at her in confusion. "How do you know that name?"

In answer, she crossed the hall to push open a door. "We can talk in here."

Zac followed her into the narrow conference room with a long table and a dozen chairs. She sat down at the end of the table, and after a second's hesitation he moved to take a seat on the corner next to her.

"I don't understand." He placed his hands flat on the table. "I thought you worked for the cold case files?"

"I do."

"Then why are you at the medical examiner's office?"

"The name Jude Henley popped up in my computer after Dr. Woodward ran his prints."

He furrowed his brow. He didn't know if it was the shock or his sleepless nights since he'd found the body, but his brain refused to function. As if it'd been knocked off-line. "I still don't understand why."

She settled back in her chair, as if choosing her words with care. He hid a wry smile. That was a change. Usually she was fearlessly confident that she knew exactly what was best in any situation. He, on the other hand, preferred to consider all angles before he came to any conclusion.

"I tried to locate Jude last year," she told him.

"Last year?"

"His name was linked to one of the cases I was investigating."

Zac leaned forward. Now they were getting somewhere. If Jude had been investigated after his supposed death, there would be a trail to follow. "Did you locate him?"

She shook her head, shattering his brief flare of hope. "No. When I searched his name, I found a death certificate with a record of his burial in Pike Cemetery. There wasn't any reason to dig deeper."

Zac sat back. "Until now."

"Until now," she agreed.

Zac tapped his fingers on the table, trying to concentrate on the case. Not an easy task when being this close to Rachel was rubbing his nerves raw.

"What was the case?" he forced himself to ask. Even if Rachel never interviewed Jude, it might give him a starting point to retrace the man's steps.

"Kim Slade," Rachel responded, her words crisp as if she was reading from a report. She had clearly devoted a lot of attention to the case. "She was a twenty-three-year-old woman from Wausau who disappeared from a campground in Devil's Lake State Park in 2004."

"Why did your inquiries include Jude Henley?"

"When I reopened the case I had all the belongings from Kim's tent examined for DNA and fingerprints," she said. "A partial thumbprint was found on an ax handle. It was placed high on the shaft and I theorized that Kim might have grabbed the ax as a weapon and he wrestled it away from her."

"The print belonged to Jude?"

She raised her slender hands in a gesture of uncertainty. "His name came up in the system, but as I said, it was only a partial print and it was eighteen years old. When it seemed that he was already dead when the crime was committed I didn't pursue him as a suspect."

Zac nodded. She was warning him that nothing had been conclusive. Still, it was an avenue of inquiry he couldn't ignore.

"The initial investigators hadn't checked for prints?" he asked.

Rachel's jaw tightened. A sure sign she was frustrated with how the original case had been handled.

"Kim was at the lake with her boyfriend," she said. "He claimed that they had a fight and he left her at the campground while he went into a nearby town to get drunk at the local bar. When he came back she was gone."

Zac could easily imagine what had happened. When there was a couple, a fight, and access to alcohol or drugs, the results were predictably tragic.

"The cops assumed he killed her."

"Yep." There was an edge in Rachel's tone. She wasn't nearly as certain. "They were convinced the boyfriend ended the fight by killing her. Then he dumped her body somewhere in the park and headed into town to establish his alibi."

"Did they arrest him?"

"No, they never had any solid proof. And without a body they finally packed everything away in the back of the evidence room."

Sounded like sloppy work, but Zac wasn't going to point fingers. He'd discovered since becoming sheriff there was too much work and too few hours. He was constantly juggling tasks, praying that nothing was slipping through the cracks. And that was without a murder case added to his to-do list. How many hours could he spare to solving the crime before it began to affect his other duties?

He was about to find out.

"Why did you open the case?" he asked Rachel. She'd moved to cold cases after they divorced. He had no idea what criteria had to be met before they decided to investigate.

"The boyfriend spent the past eighteen years returning

to the campsite to search through the woods," she revealed. "He always felt guilty for leaving her in the tent alone."

"Or for killing her." It seemed excessive for a killer to spend eighteen years pretending to search for his victim, but people were strange. They did all sorts of crazy things. Especially when in the grips of a powerful emotion.

You didn't have to be a cop to know that.

Rachel pursed her lips, as if he wasn't the first one to point out the boyfriend might be trying to play her.

"Last year he found an earring he swears she was wearing that night she disappeared."

"You believed him?"

She shrugged. "I was willing to give him the benefit of the doubt. That's when I had the belongings in the tent tested for DNA. There was only one print that I couldn't match to those who were known to have used the camping equipment."

"And Jude's name popped up."

"Yes."

Was it possible? Had Jude been at Devil's Lake State Park in 2004? And if he had, why did he have a gravestone in Pike Cemetery that claimed he died in 1994?

The most obvious answer was that this was all a bureaucratic mix-up, but he had that bad feeling in the pit of his stomach again. Shoving himself to his feet, he squared his shoulders.

"I have to open that grave," he abruptly announced. "Either to prove it's empty, or to find out if Jude is buried there. This still might be some terrible mistake."

Rachel smoothly rose out of her chair, her expression impossible to read. "While you get started, I'll clear up a few things at my office and get my bags packed. I should be there by the time you have all the paperwork filed."

He sent her a confused frown. "You'll be where?"

"In Pike, of course."

"Why?"

"My boss wants me to take a look at the crime scene and if possible to inspect his truck."

Zac grunted. As if he'd taken a punch to the gut. And that was exactly how he felt. It was one thing to catch an unexpected glimpse of Rachel out the window of his office as she walked down the street. But to know she was there in her official capacity, actually working the same case as him . . .

Christ.

"Again, why?" he demanded.

Her brows arched at his harsh tone. "Jude Henley is a suspect in an open cold case. I need to find out if he could have killed Kim Slade."

Zac narrowed his eyes as Rachel reached up to tuck her hair behind her ear. He'd known this woman since she was a five-year-old who jumped off roofs and refused to cry when she skinned her knees. She wasn't telling him the truth. At least, not the full truth.

"And that's the only reason?"

"There's the potential that Jude might solve more than one cold case. And since I'm from the area, it only makes sense for me to check it out."

Her explanation was smooth. Had she practiced the words? His vague suspicion became a certainty. "You're doing this because you think I'll need your help."

"Why would I assume that?"

His lips twisted into a mocking smile. He didn't know

whether to be annoyed by her assumption he needed her, or pleased by the thought she still cared enough to worry about him.

"We both know I've only been on my job for six months. And this is my first . . ." He grimaced, the memory of Jude's wide, sightless eyes searing through his mind. "And hopefully last murder investigation."

"I don't doubt your skills, Zac." She held his gaze without flinching, a fierce sincerity in her voice. "I've never doubted you."

"But?"

"But I bring something with me you don't have."

"Experience?"

"Resources."

"Ah." Zac couldn't argue with that.

Chapter 3

Rachel pulled her SUV to a halt near the gates of the cemetery. It'd taken her longer than she expected to clear her desk in Madison so she could make the journey north to Pike. Still, she'd been surprised when she'd arrived at the courthouse to discover that Zac was already in the process of digging the grave. It usually took at least a week to get the paperwork in order.

Pulling a leather jacket over her teal sweater that she'd matched with a pair of black slacks, she grabbed her satchel. Her boots crunched against the frozen ground as she passed through the gate and the icy wind whipped her hair over her face. It was early November, but Old Man Winter was making his presence felt. Thankfully, she'd put on a pair of thermal long johns before heading out.

Other women might spend their money on frilly undies, but she wasn't going to freeze just to have some lace and satin hidden under her clothes. And she certainly wasn't going to wear anything that didn't cover her vulnerable bits and pieces.

She was a comfort over style kind of gal.

Heading toward the group of people who were spaced around a small backhoe, she easily made out Zac.

Not only was he taller than those around him, but he also carried himself with a natural authority that didn't come from his uniform, or the gun strapped around his waist. He'd always been a leader, even when they'd been kids on the playground. That was one of the things that had initially attracted her to him. Or at least it had after they'd gone through their childhood years. When they were in grade school she usually wanted to punch him in the nose for being bossy.

A pang tugged at her heart. For the past eight years she'd managed to avoid the man who'd walked away from their marriage. Oh, there'd been quick waves from the safety of her car as she drove through town. Or a glimpse of him across a store or the local café. But until she'd sought him out at the medical examiner's office, they hadn't spoken more than a dozen words.

When Jude Henley's name had popped up in her computer, along with Zac's name as the investigating officer, she hadn't hesitated. She was going to pursue the case. Not just because she was anxious to discover if Jude could be connected to Kim Slade's disappearance, but because this was Zac's first murder.

It hadn't been a lie when she'd assured him that she believed in his skills. He'd been destined for a stellar career in law enforcement before his father had a stroke and he'd felt obligated to return to Pike to take care of the farm. But he'd sacrificed his future for his family, and now that he had an opportunity to prove his worth as a sheriff, she intended to make sure he had all the resources necessary. Including her own years of experience.

Thankfully, her supervisor had agreed.

She'd prepared herself to feel awkward during the encounter. There was no way to ignore the past they shared. Saying it was complicated was an understatement. Oddly, it'd only taken a couple minutes to fall into a comfortable exchange. Perhaps because they'd both been there in a professional capacity. It'd meant they'd been focused on the case, not on their personal feelings.

All they had to do was maintain that detached relationship, and the next few days should be fine. Right?

Halting next to Zac, she immediately caught the tang of his cologne. It was a crisp male scent that was painfully familiar. Against her will, her gaze traced the chiseled lines of his profile and the stubborn angle of his jaw.

Detached and professional, she silently reminded herself, pretending that she didn't notice the awareness tingling through her.

Slowly turning his head, he sent her a small smile. The dimples made a fleeting appearance. Long ago those dimples made her heart sputter and her stomach clench with excitement. Now they . . . well, they still caused sputtering and excitement, but she was adult enough to pretend she didn't notice them.

"Perfect timing," he said.

She reached up to brush her hair from her face. It was days like this that she wished she had kept it long enough to pull into a braid, but then again, it was short enough now she didn't have to fuss with it. Her job was too demanding to waste time in the mornings.

"I didn't expect you to get the court order to exhume the grave so quickly," she said, forcibly turning her attention to the backhoe that was carefully scraping the first layer of frozen dirt.

"Jude only has one living relative," Zac told her. "A brother who is currently in the Pike Nursing Home. He suffers from early stages of dementia."

"Ah. Diminished capacity?"

"Yep. He hasn't been able to sign legal documents for the past year. I got Judge Armstrong to sign off on the paperwork."

"He's still around?" Rachel asked in surprise. Armstrong had been a circuit court judge when she lived in Pike. He must be at least seventy.

"Not only around, but he's the current president of the Chamber of Commerce," Zac said dryly. "He's as anxious as I am to clear up this mess."

Rachel nodded. Last year Pike had been tormented by a killer. Everyone in town was desperate to return to their peaceful existence.

They fell silent as the backhoe turned to take another layer of dirt. Rachel's gaze moved to the three uniformed deputies who were standing near the grave. They were watching the digging with various levels of interest. One short, heavyset male was scrolling on his phone, a second male, this one tall and skinny, was helping direct the driver of the backhoe, and a young woman who was keeping her gaze locked on the dirt being exposed. Her attention moved to the marble headstone.

JUDE HENLEY
Beloved son and brother
Born April 21, 1966
Died November 12, 1994

"So bizarre," she muttered. She'd seen a lot of crazy things since becoming a detective. But she'd never had a suspect return from the grave. She glanced around the area. There were a few older graves nearby and a large tree that provided shade during the summer. "Was there anything of interest around the crime scene?"

"The ground was frozen so no footprints. And no security surveillance in the cemetery," Zac told her. "I'm pulling the footage from the businesses along the nearby streets. One of them might have caught the truck driving past."

Rachel didn't miss his lack of enthusiasm. Pike was a town that had been created by the local dairy farmers. Over the past fifty years it'd been brutalized by the changing economy. Any businesses still open might invest in security cameras inside their building, but it was doubtful they would cover the parking lot or nearby street.

"Where is the truck now?" she asked. She wanted to take some pictures to upload. From the report that Zac had filed, the vehicle was old enough to have been around when Kim Slade disappeared. There was a small chance someone might remember seeing it.

"At the station," Zac answered.

"I'm assuming you didn't find any clues?"

"I'm still waiting on fingerprints and DNA, but the vehicle hasn't been registered or insured since 1994." Zac shrugged. "I would guess it's been in a garage or a barn for the past twenty-eight years."

Rachel frowned. A man appearing after twenty-eight years, only to die on his own grave. And a truck that hadn't been used in twenty-eight years. It was almost as if this case had been trapped in a gruesome version of *Back to the Future*. "I logically know he didn't return from the grave, but . . ." She turned her head to meet Zac's steady gaze, the golden flecks in his eyes glowing in the late afternoon sunlight.

His lips twisted. "It's giving me nightmares."

Their gazes locked, but even as Rachel was telling herself to look away, there was a sharp whistle.

"Boss," the female deputy called out.

Zac hesitated, as if he was about to say something to Rachel. Then, with a sharp shake of his head, he was striding toward the grave. "You got something?"

"Looks like it."

Rachel watched as Zac crossed to join his deputy, her eyes lowering to take in his very fine backside. A wry smile touched her lips as she realized what she was doing. She'd done the exact same thing fourteen years ago. One day Zac had been another classmate, and the next she'd been ogling his butt as he walked down the hallway in a pair of faded jeans. Nothing had ever been the same after that moment.

Halting next to the grave, Rachel was surprised to discover that only a few feet had been dug away. Less than three. Certainly not a traditional burial. A fact confirmed when she realized there was no coffin. Instead, there was a black tarp that had rotted away to reveal a glimpse of a skull.

Zac held his hand toward the backhoe. "You can take off, Vic," he called out. "We'll have to dig the rest of the grave by hand." He waited until the middle-aged man bundled in coveralls and a ski hat backed away and chugged toward the nearby trailer attached to an old truck. "Anthony." Zac snapped his fingers, attracting the reluctant attention of the heavyset deputy. "Contact the M.E. and tell them we have a body. Then get some sort of barrier we can put around this area. I don't want a bunch of gawkers contaminating the crime scene."

"That isn't Jude," Rachel said. Not only was the body left in a way that suggested it had been hastily tossed in the grave, but she could see a handbag next to the tarp.

He turned toward the deputy next to him. "Lindsay, start photographing what we have uncovered." He pointed toward the handbag that was lying next to the tarp. "Start with the purse."

Rachel leaned forward as Lindsay pulled her phone out of her pocket and began a careful, detailed documentation of the grave. The deputy looked as if she was barely out of high school, but she handled herself with a confidence that Rachel silently applauded. This woman was going to go places.

Once she'd meticulously photographed every inch of the grave and surrounding area, she nodded toward Zac.

"Done."

Zac reached into his pocket to pull out a pair of rubber gloves. Then, going to his knees, he carefully reached to grab the purse out of the frozen ground. Rachel knelt next to him, studying the scene.

Someone had used the grave to dump a body. The question was whether it had been Jude who'd used his empty grave to get rid of a victim, or someone else. And, of course, if there were any other bodies hidden in the frozen dirt.

"Shit," Zac suddenly muttered. "This can't be right."

Rachel glanced in his direction to discover that he'd opened the purse and pulled out a matching wallet. They were both made of a cheap faux leather that had cracked and faded. The sort of handbag that came from a box store, not a designer shop. From inside the wallet, Zac had removed a yellowed driver's license.

"Can you read the name?" she asked.

He turned it so she could see the front. "Look for yourself."

Rachel first studied the small, faded picture. She could make out a brown-haired young woman with a round face and petulant expression. She didn't recognize her, but there was something oddly familiar about the curve of her face and line of her jaw. Next she read the name typed next to the photo.

"Staci Gale," she read out loud. She glanced up at Zac. "Is she related to Doc Gale?"

"I think it was his wife."

"Wife?" Rachel frowned, trying to remember back to what she'd heard about Staci Gale. There wasn't much. "I remember asking Lynne one time why she didn't have a mother." Rachel grimaced. "Little kids have the subtlety of a charging rhino. I think she said that her mom had moved away when she was just a baby. But . . ." Rachel shook her head. "Surely they would have known she was dead or at least missing?"

Zac straightened, tucking the license and wallet back into the purse. Then he held the purse toward Lindsay.

"Have this bagged and sent to the lab in Madison."

The deputy was careful to pull on gloves before taking the piece of evidence. "Got it."

Zac glanced toward Rachel, nodding at a spot away from the deputies who were scurrying to complete their various duties. Rachel pushed herself upright and moved toward the nearby pathway. Once they were out of earshot, he gazed down at her with a grim expression.

"We can't be sure that this body is Staci."

"True." It would take days to get an official ID. Until then they needed to keep an open mind.

"But working on the hypothesis that this is her, do you remember how old you were when you asked Lynne about her mother?"

Rachel dredged through the recesses of her brain. "I'm not really sure, but it was before we started school," she finally concluded. "We lived just a couple blocks apart and I used to spend the night at her house. After we started school we drifted apart. She was into animals and I liked to throw a ball around."

His expression softened as he gazed down at her. "You were pretty good at throwing that ball around."

Heat touched her cheeks. Not all the guys in school appreciated her athletic abilities, but Zac had urged her to take pride in her competitive nature. It'd been only one of many reasons she'd loved him.

Unnerved by the giddy pleasure that raced through her, Rachel forced herself to glance back at the open grave, where the two male deputies were hammering poles in the ground to stretch a tarp over it.

"Someone had to know," she murmured.

"Know what?"

"That Jude was alive and that someone else was in this grave. That's why his body was left here."

Zac nodded. Obviously he'd been thinking the same thing. "My first guess would be his brother Jacob. He was a local mortician. If anyone could have faked his brother's death it would be him."

"I suppose," Rachel agreed. "Still, to forge a death certificate you would need the signature of a doctor or M.E."

"I have a copy of the death certificate in my truck," Zac

said, speaking more to himself than her. "I'll have a look at it before I talk to Jacob."

"I thought you said the brother suffers from dementia."

"He's legally incapacitated," he agreed. "But that doesn't mean he can't remember the past."

Rachel shrugged. "It's worth a shot."

She turned to head toward the front gate. There was nothing left here to do until the M.E. had completed their investigation and removed the female body and the rest of the grave was uncovered.

The sound of boots crunching against the gravel path echoed through the air as Zac hurried to catch up with her long strides. "Where are you going?"

"To talk to Jacob."

"Why?"

"Anything or anyone connected to Jude is a part of my cold case."

She studied his profile. Was he unhappy that she was there? Relieved? Indifferent? The last thought made her flinch.

There was a long silence, then, as if recalling how stubborn she could be when she dug her heels in, he shrugged. "Okay. Do you want to ride?"

"Sure."

Although she'd been born and raised in Pike, it'd been years since she'd lived there. And according to her parents the citizens of Pike were delighted to have Zac as their sheriff. The locals would be more likely to answer her questions if they realized she was his current partner.

Leaving the cemetery, Zac led her to the truck with a sheriff's star painted on the side. He paused to unlock her door before rounding the hood and climbing behind the steering wheel.

"Are you staying with your folks?" he asked as he switched on the engine and pulled away from the curb.

"Good God, no!" Rachel smiled as he sent her a startled glance. "Um, that came out more emphatic than I intended. I love my parents, but . . ."

"Distance makes the heart grow fonder?"

"Something like that." She glanced out the frosty side window, swallowing a sigh. If her past with Zac was complicated, her past with her parents was the proverbial Pandora's box. Better left closed.

"Where are you staying?" Zac turned onto Main Street, passing the park and the town square.

"At the local motel."

"Yikes."

Rachel chuckled. The place had been built in the seventies and had never left the psychedelic decade.

"It's just for a few days," she said, more to reassure herself than him. "What about you?"

"What about me?"

"Are you still at the farm?"

His fingers tightened on the steering wheel. "Still there."

Hmm. It felt as if she'd touched a sore nerve. Was his mother still putting pressure on him to follow in his father's footsteps? It'd been a main source of disagreement between Zac and Rachel when they were married.

Or perhaps it was just the one fight they were prepared to have. They fiercely pretended their other troubles didn't exist. As if they would magically disappear.

Shoving away the unhappy memories, she reminded

herself it was all in the distant past. "How are you managing to take care of the chores and still do the job of sheriff?"

"We sold off the cows after my dad passed. I only kept them until then because it would have broken his heart to know they were gone." He turned onto a narrow road that led to a dead-end street. "The dairy industry tanked and it cost more to feed the herd than they could bring in. And last spring, I rented the fields to Carl Anstead." He lifted one shoulder. "I try to stay on top of the daily chores in the morning before work and on the weekends."

She tried to hide her stab of satisfaction at the knowledge the bulk of the work had been handed over to someone else. Zac had never wanted to be a farmer. That had been his parents' dream.

"How's your mother?" she forced herself to ask.

"Good. I finally convinced her to buy a small house in town so she can easily drive to church and the store. Right now she's in Omaha taking care of my aunt."

She arched her brows, unable to imagine Joyce Evans leaving her son to cope on his own. She was the definition of a helicopter mother.

"So who's taking care of you?" she teased, then immediately regretted the words. She clenched her hands, wishing she could sink into the soft leather seat. "Never mind. It's none of my business."

He slowed as they reached the L-shaped brick building at the end of a cul-de-sac. It was one story with industrial windows and a tin roof. Even from a distance it was a dreary place, framed by a gravel parking lot on one side and a barren field on the other. Pulling into an empty space, Zac shut off the truck and sent her a wry smile.

"I'm taking care of myself," he said, his tone deliberately

light. "And if you ask Kir Jansen he'll tell you I'm doing a piss-poor job of it."

"I heard Kir moved back to town." She pounced at the opportunity to change the conversation. "Although I was sorry to hear about Rudolf."

"A bad business." Zac shook his head. "But I'm glad Kir's back in Pike."

"He married Lynne Gale, didn't he?"

"Yep."

Rachel tried to imagine the two of them together, but her mind wouldn't obey. During school Kir had always been the bad boy. In contrast, Lynne had been an A student who never caused trouble.

"I would never have seen that coming," she said. "They were so different."

"I suppose we all change as we get older." Zac sent her a glance that she found impossible to read. Regret? Maybe.

She reached for the door handle. That was a smile that a smart woman avoided.

"If it is Staci Gale in that grave, it's going to be a nightmare telling Lynne her mother is dead," she said, slipping out of the truck.

She walked to stand in front of the nursing home. There was a covered veranda with a few folding chairs and cement pots filled with dead plants.

Zac joined her, a file folder in his hand. "This place never changes."

"No crap. It looked exactly like this when my grandma was here twenty years ago," Rachel agreed with a shudder. "Even those pots. I swear those are the same dead plants in them."

"You worked here, didn't you?"

She rolled her eyes. "For one memorable week during my summer vacation. My mom was hoping she could persuade me to become a nurse instead of a cop." Rachel shuddered again. This time it was from the memory walking down the silent halls late at night, the stench of antiseptic and creamed corn clinging to her uniform. "All she managed to accomplish was to convince me to get my criminal justice degree."

"They were worried about you."

"Yeah, I know."

It had taken years, but she'd finally accepted that her parents' acute hatred for her job wasn't a reflection of her choices. It was simply an aching fear she might be hurt.

He studied her for a long moment, as if waiting for her to continue. Then, when she remained silent, he walked up the narrow path and across the veranda. Entering the small lobby, Zac pressed a button near the double glass doors. Rachel raised her brows. The security was new. A good idea, no doubt, and a timely reminder that not even this small town was immune to evil.

A few seconds later a nurse in white scrubs pushed open the door to wave them inside. She was close to Rachel's age with a thin face and brown hair pulled into a knot on top of her head. She seemed vaguely familiar as Rachel walked past her and into the public lounge, but it wasn't until she reached out to lay her hand on Zac's shoulder that she realized it was Bailey, Zac's cousin.

"Hey, Zac." The woman sent Rachel a curious glance. "Rachel. I didn't know you were back in town."

"Just temporarily," Rachel murmured. Bailey had been

a few years younger and they hadn't really been friends, but they'd always gotten along.

"She's here to work on a case with me," Zac added.

Bailey pursed her lips, as if not entirely convinced there wasn't more to Rachel's return to Pike, but she was clearly too distracted to pursue the issue.

"Is it true that it was Jude Henley you found dead in the graveyard?"

Zac tried to look stern, but the frown he sent toward his cousin was affectionate. "Can't discuss the details of the case. Especially not with the town's biggest gossip."

She stuck out her tongue, but she didn't press for details. "What are you doing here?"

"Can we see Jacob Henley?"

Curiosity sparked in her dark eyes, but her expression was professional. "He's allowed visitors, but he's not always capable of recognizing people, or even where he is. I think he's been better than usual this morning. At least he didn't spit on me when I brought him breakfast." She turned to lead them through the wide door and into a narrow corridor. "Follow me."

Rachel grimaced, the familiar smells hitting her nose like a punch. She thought her job was tough. It was nothing compared to poor Bailey's.

Chapter 4

Zac followed Bailey to the end of the hallway and into a long room lined with windows. At one end a folding table was set up with cards stacked in the center. Next to it was a matching table. This one had a half-completed puzzle on it. And a third table had a stack of board games. At the other end was a grouping of worn leather furniture. This was presumably a gathering place for the residents.

Glancing around, Zac could only see one person seated in a chair next to the windows. Obviously, late afternoon was not a hopping time at the nursing home.

"That's Jacob," Bailey said next to his ear.

"Thanks."

Zac waited for his cousin to reluctantly turn to leave the room before crossing the linoleum floor that was cracked and peeling. Like the rest of Pike, this place was suffering from the depressed economy and rapidly shrinking population.

He halted in front of the man who was slumped in the chair, seemingly lost in his thoughts. At a glance it would be difficult to see any family resemblance between him and his brother. Perhaps it was the ten years that separated them. Plus, Jacob had been a large-framed man who'd trended to fat as he aged. He'd also lost most of his hair to reveal a shiny scalp with a liver-shaped birthmark on the side of his skull. He looked weirdly like a squished mushroom.

Chiding himself for his unkind thoughts, Zac pushed a short sofa until it was near the older man. Then, waiting for Rachel to take her seat, he settled on the cushion next to her.

Since becoming the sheriff, Zac had worked with his deputies. But he was the boss and they took care of the duties he didn't have time to do. Having Rachel at his side was like having a partner.

Weirdly, it felt good. Even if it was his ex-wife.

Or perhaps because it *was* his ex-wife.

Whatever had happened between them, he trusted Rachel. With his life. And he fully intended to take advantage of her experience as an investigator. Only an idiot—or an egotistical jerk—would look a gift horse in the mouth.

Leaning forward, Zac grasped the arm of Jacob's chair and gave it a small shake. "Hello, Jacob, can we talk to you?"

The man blinked, slowly turning to eye them with a sour expression. "Are you a doctor?"

"No, I'm Sheriff Zac Evans." Zac touched the badge clipped to the pocket of his jacket.

Jacob looked confused. "Rudolf Jansen is sheriff."

"He died last year."

"Did he?" Jacob blinked, then a scowl furrowed his heavy brow. "I didn't do the funeral."

Zac hid his grimace. The older man obviously didn't remember he'd closed down the family business.

"It was just a graveside service," he assured the man.

"Cheap." Jacob snorted in disgust. "A shame for a man like Rudolf." The faded brown eyes narrowed. "Do you have a burial plan? Sheriff's work is dangerous. Never too young to get things organized."

Zac hesitated. Did he humor Jacob? Or did he try to snap him back to reality? He felt Rachel's hand brush down his back. A familiar touch of reassurance that she'd offered a thousand times before.

A tiny ache opened in the center of his heart as he realized just how desperately he'd missed that light touch.

He squared his shoulders, concentrating on the man in front of him. This had gone beyond Jude Henley. They had at least one more dead body. He needed answers. ASAP.

"I'll stop by later to discuss the issue," he assured Jacob.

Jacob leaned forward, a sly glint entering the dark eyes. "You'll want top-of-the-line. Nothing shoddy for such a distinguished man."

"Right." Zac forced a tight smile. "But today I'm here to discuss your brother."

The man flopped back in his chair, his expression hardening. "I don't have a brother. Not a living one anyway."

"I suppose he died in a car accident, right?" Zac asked, testing the man's ability to recall the past. If it was lost in the haze of his dementia, then they were wasting their time there.

Jacob gave a sharp shake of his head. "He fell and busted his skull in his apartment. Terrible accident."

"Tragic." Zac flipped open the folder in his lap. "You

know, I can't seem to find a police report. He was living in Grange, wasn't he?" Jude's last known address was from the town fifteen miles away. "Was it filed by the local authorities?"

There was a noticeable tension in Jacob as he clenched the arms of his chair. "Why would there be a police report? As I said, it was an accident."

"And you identified the body?"

"Course I did. It was just the two of us after our parents died. He was more of a son than a brother."

Zac tucked away the information. It might help explain Jacob's willingness to break the law to protect his brother.

"And you performed the funeral?" Zac pressed.

"Who else would do it?" Jacob leaned forward, grunting as his joints loudly popped in protest. "Why are you asking these questions?"

"I think you're lying to me."

Jacob hesitated, his hands tightening on the chair as he licked his lips. This man might suffer from dementia, but he knew that Jude hadn't been in that grave. Zac could read the guilt on his flushed face.

"Lying about what?" he at last demanded.

"Jude didn't die twenty-eight years ago." Zac held up the death certificate he'd pulled from the folder. "Did he?"

The man paled, clearly unnerved by Zac's questions. "You got a paper that says he did, don't you?"

Zac shrugged. "That's easy enough to fake, especially when you're the funeral director."

"I wasn't the only one to sign the paper. There was a doctor in Grange who pronounced him dead," Jacob tried to bluff.

Zac had noticed the doctor's signature at the bottom of

the death certificate, but he'd assumed it had been forged by the brothers. Without warning, Rachel held out her hand and he readily gave her the death certificate. She had resources to search for the doctor who might or might not have existed in Grange twenty-eight years ago. Rising to her feet, she silently moved toward the far end of the room, her phone already pressed to her ear.

Jacob ignored her departure, his gaze never wavering from Zac's face. "Why are you trying to make me out to be a liar?"

Zac was done playing games. This man might be confused about some things, but he knew what had happened to his brother.

"Because Jude returned to town."

Jacob sucked in a sharp breath, the blunt words shocking him out of his pretense of innocence. "He's here?" he rasped. "In Pike?"

"Why did you forge the death certificate?"

"Where's Jude?"

"I asked you a question, Jacob—"

"Where's my brother?" Jacob interrupted, his voice echoing loudly through the room as his face flushed with anger. He was a man used to giving orders, not taking them. "Tell me."

"He's dead," Zac retorted. There was no way he was going to get any information until he'd told the man what he wanted to know.

Jacob flinched. "You're sure?"

"The fingerprints match," Zac said. "As well as the DNA. There's no mistake."

Jacob glanced away, as if trying to process the shocking news. "Where? How?"

"It's an ongoing investigation." He studied the man's profile, unable to determine if Jacob was mourning the loss of his brother or figuring out how much trouble he might be in. "Why did you lie?" Zac demanded.

"Dead." Jacob shook his head.

"Jacob, why did you lie?"

Jacob turned back toward Zac, his expression troubled. "He was supposed to stay safe. That was the plan."

"Safe from what?"

"None of your business," the man snapped.

"Actually it is my business," Zac warned. "Someone murdered Jude."

Jacob frowned, his eyes unfocused, as if he was beginning to drift away. "No. You've made a mistake. He's not dead . . . he's hiding."

Zac suppressed his smile of satisfaction, sternly reminding himself not to spook the man. "Who is he hiding from, Jacob?" he asked in soft tones.

Jacob hunched his shoulders. "I can't tell you. I promised."

"You promised Jude?"

"Yes."

"Was he in trouble?"

The man pressed his lips together, as if remembering back to the years when Jude had been his responsibility. "My brother was always in trouble," Jacob groused. "He got kicked out of school a dozen times. Smoking, cheating, stuffing some girl in her locker. His senior year they told me they wouldn't take him back. How was he supposed to get a job if he didn't graduate? It was no wonder he ended up in jail." Jacob banged his hands on the arms of his chair. "I warned them that he was going to get in over his head, but no one would listen to me. Not until it was too late."

"So what was he into? Drugs?"

Jacob shrugged. "He never said. He just showed up at the funeral parlor one night and said that there were bad people who intended to kill him."

"Did he tell you who was threatening him?"

"No."

Zac leaned forward, sending his companion a stern frown. "Jacob, I'm trying to find the people who hurt your brother," he chided. "I need a name."

"I don't have one. Jude never said. He only told me he needed to disappear."

Zac tried to imagine what had happened. Jude no doubt had arrived in a panic, expecting his older brother to solve his latest problem. A familiar situation. But faking a death seemed extreme.

"Why didn't he just move away?" Zac asked. "People vanish all the time."

"That's what I said." Jacob lifted a shaky hand to rub his bald head, as if it was aching. Was it grief for Jude? Or the strain of trying to dredge up the memories? "He said they would never stop hunting him. He insisted we had to convince them he was dead."

"So you faked his funeral."

Jacob continued to rub his head, his expression petulant. "I didn't do nothing wrong. There was no funeral. I bought a plot and put up a headstone."

"And dug a grave," Zac added.

The man blinked, his hand slowly lowering as he regarded Zac in confusion. "I scraped up some ground. Just enough to make it look as if someone had been recently buried. I wasn't going to the time and expense to hire someone to dig an empty grave."

There was a sincere horror in Jacob's voice at the suggestion of wasting money. Zac made a mental note to check the man's finances. Had he benefited from Jude's death? He wouldn't doubt it. On the other hand, Zac was willing to accept that he hadn't known about Staci Gale. Or whoever it was they'd uncovered. The man might not be as sharp as he'd once been, but he was a cagey salesman who would have a ready lie to explain any stray bodies found in the grave.

"It wasn't empty," Zac said.

Jacob frowned. "What wasn't empty?"

"There was a body in the grave."

A long silence settled between them. As if Jacob was waiting for him to continue. Then he made a sound of impatience. "So? That happens. The graveyard didn't keep records until the 1880s. They accidentally dig up old coffins all the time."

"It wasn't an old coffin." Zac carefully watched Jacob's face. "The body was wrapped in a tarp and tossed into the ground you disturbed twenty-eight years ago."

"What?" The man jerked back, his eyes darting from side to side. "That's impossible."

"I have the body to prove it."

"Stop it." Jacob struggled to his feet, spittle forming at the corners of his mouth. "You're trying to confuse me. I put up a headstone and scraped up some ground. I didn't put any damned body in there."

Zac shoved himself upright, eyeing the strange color that was crawling beneath the man's face. "I'm not accusing you, Jacob. I'm just trying to figure out what happened."

"What happened is my brother is dead. I want to know who did it. Why aren't you out there finding his killer?" The man's voice was spiraling toward a harsh shout as he worked himself into a rage. "I want Rudolf in charge of his murder." He faltered, glancing around in confusion. "Where's Rudolf?"

There was the squeak of footsteps on the tiled floor before Bailey abruptly appeared in the doorway. "Is anything wrong?"

"I'm late." Jacob rubbed his head, his expression troubled. "What time is it?"

"Everything is fine," Bailey assured him, moving to take his arm in a gentle grip.

"The funeral . . ." Jacob sent her a pleading glance. "I need to get to work. I can't be late."

Bailey grimaced. "I think he needs to go back to his room and rest."

Zac nodded. It was obvious they weren't going to get anything else out of Jacob. Not today. "Can you let me know when he's feeling better?"

"Sure."

Bailey led Jacob toward the door, his steps shuffling and his shoulders stooped. He looked old and tired.

With a grimace, Zac crossed the room to where Rachel was tucking her phone into her leather satchel.

"Anything?" he asked.

She nodded moving to stand next to him. "I had my team do a quick search for the Dr. Dickerson that signed this." She waved the death certificate.

"And?"

"There was a Dr. Dickerson in Grange on the date that Jude was pronounced dead at his apartment."

His eyes narrowed. There was an expression on her striking features that he easily recognized. Satisfaction.

"Please tell me he's still alive."

"Nope." She handed him the death certificate. "He was killed by a hit-and-run driver. Two days after Jude's death."

Zac pursed his lips, releasing a low whistle. "Damn."

Paige Carr stormed out of the small trailer she shared with her husband, Joe, and their two-year-old daughter, Zoe. After a day dealing with Zoe's ear infection, a broken toilet, and babysitting the next-door neighbor's kids after school to make some extra money, she was done. Done with a capital D.

Yanking open the door of her battered secondhand car, she tossed in her purse and did her best to ignore the large man who was following behind her, his chest bare despite the icy bite of the night breeze.

"Damn it, Paige," he rasped. "Where are you going? It's my Friday night bowling league."

Reluctantly she turned back to glare at the man who'd been her husband for the past three years. He was still handsome with reddish hair cut short and a broad face that was freshly shaven. And while he was starting to put on a small gut, he was still muscular from his hours working at the farmers' co-op. She, on the other hand, couldn't claim to be aging with the same grace. She kept her dark hair cut short so she didn't have to bother with it and she'd never fully taken off the baby weight. Plus, she had dark circles under her brown eyes from spending the past two nights trying to soothe a crying child. She was starting to look and feel like an old woman, and it scared the hell out of her.

"And last night you had to meet the guys for a beer after work," she reminded him in tart tones. "And this weekend you plan to go hunting with your dad."

Joe grimaced, but he refused to concede he'd been a total jerk lately. "I work hard at the co-op," he whined. "What's the big deal if I let off some steam with my friends? Their wives don't nag at them."

Of course they didn't, she thought bitterly. They were all off having fun with the delivery man, or neighbor, or local bartender. She didn't want another man. There'd never been anyone for her but Joe.

All she wanted was a break.

"Well I work hard too," she reminded her husband. "And then I spend every night alone with a squalling two-year-old. Tonight I'm going to let off steam and you're staying home."

"Can't you get your mother—"

"No," she hissed, glancing toward the open door of the trailer. "I've made dinner and given Zoe her bath. All you have to do is read her a bedtime story and tuck her into bed. Seriously, how hard is that?"

He stepped toward her, reaching out to cup her face in his hands. "Come on, Paige," he wheedled. "Tonight we're bowling the first-place team. The guys will shit if I miss." He leaned down to brush a kiss over her mouth. "I promise next week I'll be home."

How many times had she melted when this man kissed her? How many times had she given in to whatever he wanted? Even when she knew he was manipulating her.

Well, not tonight.

Lifting her hands, she shoved him away. "I'm not sure I'll be here next week."

He scowled as she climbed into the car and switched on the engine. "What the hell is that supposed to mean?"

"Figure it out." She slammed shut the door and put the car into reverse.

The engine sputtered, as if it was going to betray her, then with a loud rattle she was rolling out of the driveway.

"Wait!" Joe dashed into the road as she stopped to put the car in drive. He pounded on the window. "Dammit, at least tell me where you're going."

Rolling down the window, she sent him a defiant glare. "I'm going to the Bait and Tackle to meet Pam," she said, not caring if her nosy neighbors heard she was headed to the local bar. Living in the trailer park was like living in a fishbowl. "Don't wait up for me."

Gunning the engine, Paige squealed away. A part of her knew she was acting childish. Her mother would happily have taken care of Zoe. She adored her only grandchild. And it wasn't even like she wanted to go to the bar. She'd been a party animal when she was in high school, but since getting married, she preferred to spend time with her family.

But after weeks of having Joe devote more and more time away from home, she decided if she didn't take a stand, nothing was going to change. She needed to teach Joe she wasn't his maid, or babysitter, or convenient body in his bed. If he wanted to keep her, then he'd better start paying attention.

Driving across town, Paige slowed as she reached the plain brick building with large windows that was framed by the dentist's office and laundromat. The narrow street was already lined with cars. Paige sighed. Since the new owner had taken over, the place had been cleaned up and a local band had been hired to play. There was always a crowd on Friday night.

Circling the block, Paige pulled into the alley behind the bar and switched off the engine. She wasn't going to park blocks away. Not when she was wearing her only good pair of heels. If the cops wanted to tow away the piece of shit car, then they could knock themselves out.

She paused long enough to tug at the hem of her dress. It was shorter than she remembered. Or maybe she just filled it out more, she conceded. Then she headed toward the back door. She thought she heard the crunch of footsteps against the icy pavement behind her, but she didn't bother to turn.

Lots of customers came out here to have a quick smoke.

She was reaching for the doorknob when a hand appeared from behind her, as if it was going to keep the door pressed closed. For a second, she assumed that Joe had followed her. How dare he bring Zoe to this place?

She'd started to turn, when the hand slammed over her mouth and something soft was pressed against her face. A shirt? A towel? She reached up to grab the wrist, gagging at the chemical scent that was flooding her nose.

Was Joe playing some sort of game? Was he trying to scare her from going to the bar with her friend? It didn't seem like something he'd do. But he'd been pissed when she'd left. Desperately yanking on the attacker's wrist, she lifted her foot and brought it sharply down on the foot behind her. She heard a muffled grunt and she felt a burst of satisfaction. That would teach Joe to . . . to . . .

To what? Paige blinked, trying to concentrate. She needed fresh air. That acrid stench was clouding her brain. And worse, her knees were suddenly refusing to hold her weight. Clutching the wrist, Paige no longer tried to shove the attacker away, she struggled to keep from falling to the ground.

It was a losing battle as the world condensed to a small pinprick of light, her head falling backward as arms wrapped around her limp body.

She is perfect. The right age, the right family. The right looks. The right amount of bitch. A shame her hair is so short but otherwise she fulfills my needs.

I study her in satisfaction. She has been stripped naked, revealing the pale, perfect body that I had enjoyed. More than once.

Now that my physical hunger has been sated, I've arranged her on the narrow gurney with her arms stretched over her head and her legs bound together.

I allow myself a smile as anticipation curls through my gut. My blood is hot as the flames that used to burn in the nearby crematorium. I've waited for the moment for so long. A part of me longs to give in to my savage desires. There's a devil inside that's ready and eager to be released. But I remind myself that I'm not a savage. Unlike my master I possess an appreciation for artistry. Anyone could be a brute. I am a maestro. An artist. A master of my craft.

I'm not going to ruin my first kill with sloppy haste. I force myself to take a deep breath, easing my grip on the crowbar I hold in my hand. It isn't the most elegant weapon. In fact, it's tediously cliched, but I promised myself to walk in the same footsteps. How else can I prove I am superior in every way?

I move to stand over the woman. She's beginning to regain consciousness. Good. I long to hear her screams. Lifting the weapon I wonder how many ribs I can break before puncturing a lung.

"Welcome to the game, Paige . . ."

Chapter 5

Rachel pulled her SUV into the driveway and switched off the engine. In front of her was the house where she'd been born and raised. It was a white two-story home built on the edge of town with black shutters and a sharply angled roof. There was a wraparound porch complete with a wooden swing and ceramic pots that were filled with flowers during the summer. Behind the house was a large open field where Rachel had organized neighborhood games of hide-and-seek and baseball and swimming in the shallow creek. So many fun memories.

But it was also where the greatest tragedy of her life had occurred. With a grimace, Rachel jumped out of the car and climbed onto the porch. She didn't know if there would ever come a day when she could return home without it being tainted by the past, but it seemed doubtful.

Rachel shoved away her dark thoughts even as a shiver snaked down her spine. She told herself it was from the cold. The sun was cresting the horizon, but the air was still frigid enough to coat the wooden planks of the porch in frost.

Lifting her hand, she rapped her knuckles against the

door. Less than a second later it was pulled open, revealing that her mother had been watching out the window for her to arrive.

"Come in." The slender, dark-haired woman stepped aside. She was wearing gray pants with a patterned silk blouse, and her hair was pulled into a sleek bun at the back of her head. DeeDee Fisher always looked perfectly polished. As if she were a doll, not a flesh-and-blood woman. Rachel assumed it was because she was married to the manager of the local bank and she felt she had a social position to maintain, but it was also possible that she used her perfect exterior to cover the broken woman underneath. "I've told you there's no need to knock." DeeDee closed the door. "This is your home."

Rachel ignored the chiding, glancing around the living room that had been recently redecorated in cool shades of silver and gray. The furniture was low and sleek and looked extremely uncomfortable, but Rachel knew it made her mother happy. Or at least the renovations kept her mind occupied.

"Something smells delicious," Rachel said, sucking in a deep breath. "Bacon? And pancakes?"

"Yes." Her mother smiled, pleased by Rachel's dreamy expression. "Eggs and bacon, with your favorite blueberry pancakes."

"I told you not to go to a lot of bother."

"When does your mother ever listen to what anyone says?" a male voice tartly demanded.

Swallowing her rueful sigh, Rachel glanced toward the entrance of the hallway where a tall, solidly built man with silver hair was standing, wearing dark slacks and a crisp white shirt.

Wilson Fisher was close to sixty, but he looked forty from a distance. He worked full-time at the bank, and golfed on the weekends when the weather was fine, and jogged at the local high school gym when it was cold.

Walking across the silver carpet, Rachel brushed a kiss over his recently shaved cheek. "Hello, Dad."

"Good to see you, Rach." He stepped behind her to help her slip off her leather jacket to reveal her jeans and casual sweatshirt. It was Saturday morning, and while she was never truly off duty, she was planning to spend most of the day at the motel going over her file on Kim Slade, while searching for additional information on Jude and Jacob Henley. "It's been too long." Her father got in his own subtle rebuke. "You look skinny. Are you eating?"

"Like a horse," she assured him.

"Come into the kitchen and prove it," DeeDee commanded, headed toward the opening across the living room. "I want your plate cleaned."

Obediently following her lead, Rachel entered the long room with white cabinets, a ceramic-tiled floor, and stainless steel appliances. Unlike the living room, the kitchen was warm and inviting. Her mother loved to cook and it filled the atmosphere with an infectious joy.

Taking a seat at the large wooden table, she watched DeeDee efficiently filling three plates while her father poured her a mug of coffee and set it in front of her.

"Don't worry, I made it," he said with a wink.

It was a running joke in the family that DeeDee could cook like an angel, but her coffee tasted like sludge.

Rachel reached for the mug, taking an appreciative sip as her mother placed a plate in front of her. Grabbing her fork, she dug in, her stomach rumbling in pleasure at the sticky sweet taste of pancakes slathered in warm maple syrup. She rarely had time to make a homemade meal, and even if she did, it wouldn't taste like this. Cooking was a talent she'd never bothered to acquire.

DeeDee sat next to her, eating with far more decorum than her daughter. Of course, everything DeeDee did had more decorum.

"Before I forget, Aunt Trina wants you to come to dinner on Tuesday," the older woman told Rachel. "And the church luncheon is on Thursday. The ladies will be expecting you to make an appearance."

Rachel polished off a piece of bacon before answering. She'd already braced herself for this argument. DeeDee would organize every second of Rachel's life if she allowed her.

"This isn't a vacation, Mom. I'm here to work."

"You can't work every second of the day."

"No, but my hours are never regular. I can't make plans when I'm on a case."

DeeDee clicked her tongue. "Everyone should have time off. And it's not like we ever get to see you. When was the last time you were home? Six months at least."

"Don't pressure the poor girl." Her father intruded into the familiar lecture.

Her mom glared in his direction. Like most couples, her parents bickered, but there was a brittle distance between them that came from a pain they all kept buried deep inside. In her family, you didn't discuss loss or grief or guilt. You pretended it didn't exist. It was a legacy she'd taken into her own marriage.

Unfortunately.

"Is it wrong to want to spend time with my only child?" DeeDee snapped. "It's not like she's staying here."

Rachel ate another slice of bacon. "I told you, it's more convenient to have my own space. I work crazy hours and grab sleep whenever I can. I would be constantly disrupting your routine."

DeeDee's thin hands clenched into tight balls. "Perhaps we could use a few disruptions."

Realizing that her mother was never going to accept her insistence on staying at the motel, Rachel held her plate toward the older woman. "Is there more bacon?"

DeeDee was instantly distracted as she jumped to her feet to take Rachel's plate. "Of course."

Her father waited until his wife was busy at the stove before he sent Rachel a curious glance. "I know you're not supposed to talk about the case, but the rumor around town is that the body found in the graveyard was Jude Henley."

Rachel nodded. The ID was official so there was no longer a need for secrecy. "It was."

"I don't understand," her mother said, reclaiming command of the conversation as she placed Rachel's plate in front of her and took her seat. "Didn't he die years ago?"

"He had a grave, but he wasn't dead." Rachel narrowed her gaze, abruptly realizing her mother would have been close to the same age as Jude. They had to have gone to school together. "Did you know him?"

"Not really. He was in the class below me, but we didn't have the same friends." The older woman wrinkled her nose. As if her memories of Jude weren't pleasant. "I don't think he even graduated."

Rachel shoved aside her plate, folding her arms on the table. "What did he do?"

"Do?"

"Did he have a job?"

DeeDee tapped a manicured fingernail on the table, her brow furrowed as she tried to recall what she knew about the man. "I think he was arrested not long after he left high school. Petty theft or something." She shrugged. "Once he got out he might have helped his brother at the funeral home." She paused, as if struck by a sudden memory. "Oh. I think he worked as a handyman around town. I remember my father hired him to help paint the outside of our barn one year." Rachel's grandparents had owned a dairy farm before it had to be sold after her grandpa had died of a heart attack and her grandmother had gone into the nursing home. "Eventually I heard that he moved to Grange."

That tracked with what Jacob had told Zac.

"What about girlfriends?" Rachel asked.

"I do remember the girls at school talking about him in whispers." A delicate shudder raced through DeeDee. "I suppose he was good-looking and a lot of girls like the bad boys. I thought he was a jerk."

Rachel agreed with her mother's sour opinion about bad boys. Her years as a detective meant she'd seen the tragic results when women thought they could change a man.

"What about after high school?" she asked. "Did he have a steady girlfriend around town?"

"I . . ." DeeDee's words trailed away, her gaze surprisingly moving toward her silent husband. "I remember now."

"You know something," Rachel said.

"Not me." DeeDee nodded across the table. "Wilson."

Rachel swiveled in her seat, her brows raised in surprise.

Her father had lived in Wausau until he married her mother and moved to Pike to start working at the local bank.

"Dad?"

He scowled, obviously unhappy to be a part of the current conversation. A man didn't become a trusted manager of a bank without understanding the value of keeping his lips shut. "That was all malicious gossip."

"Tell me."

His jaw tightened and Rachel knew that it was only because he loved her that he forced himself to answer.

"There were rumors that Evie Parson was having an affair with Henley."

It took a second for Rachel to place the name. "Wasn't she married to your boss?"

"Yes." The word was clipped. "I believe that Jude did some handiwork around the house."

"Is that what they call it? Handiwork?" DeeDee drawled.

Her father's features tightened. He'd always been absurdly loyal to Russell Parson, the owner of the bank.

"It was nothing more than ugly stories spread by people with too much time on their hands," Wilson said in stiff tones.

DeeDee snorted. "I know it's not polite to speak ill of the dead, but I heard Evie had a breakdown after her husband threatened to divorce her. She went to a facility in Chicago to recover."

"That's not true," Wilson snapped. "She went to Green Bay to take care of her dying cousin."

"Well I heard she was seen in Chicago by Vonda Howell."

Sensing a brewing argument, Rachel hastily distracted her mother. "Any other rumors about Jude having affairs?"

"Dozens." She sniffed. "As I said, there are always women who like bad boys."

Her father ignored his wife, his gaze focused on Rachel. "I still don't understand how Henley died twice."

"Me either." Rachel heard the muffled sound of a phone ringing and she jumped out of her chair. "I have to answer that. It could be work."

"At this hour?" her mother complained.

"I warned you my schedule was crazy." Rachel scurried into the living room, grabbing the leather satchel she'd dropped next to the door. Pulling up the flap she dug out her phone and glanced down at the screen.

Her heart did a crazy zigzag, her breath stuck in her lungs. *Zac.* Once upon a time, she'd taken calls from her husband for granted. Now she felt frozen at the unexpectedness of his name popping up.

Pressing the screen, she lifted the phone to her ear. "Hello?"

"Sorry to call so early." Zac's familiar voice echoed through the speaker and curled through the pit of her stomach.

She licked her lips. Why were they so dry? "No problem. What's up?"

"I'm at the old Henley Funeral Parlor." There was an unmistakable tension in his voice. "Can you join me?"

Rachel cleared her mind as she automatically shifted into cop mode. "I'll be right there." Ending the connection, she tossed her phone back into the satchel and pulled on her leather coat. Then, moving to stick her head into the kitchen, she sent her parents a tight smile. "Sorry, duty calls."

DeeDee rose to her feet, her expression pinched. "When will you be back?"

"I'll call you."

"I have a pot roast for dinner."

Rachel swallowed her reflexive urge to refuse the incessant demand for her time and attention. Her mother couldn't help herself, she silently conceded. DeeDee had lost her son; the grief made it impossible for her not to cling to her only remaining child.

"I'll try to make it," Rachel promised. "But don't wait dinner for me. I'll eat whenever I can get here."

Spinning away before her mother could protest, Rachel hurried across the living room and out the front door. Once on the porch, she paused to take a deep breath, tilting back her head to feel the morning sun on her face. She loved her parents, but when she returned home it always felt as if she was being mired in the lingering sorrow that infected their lives.

With a burst of eagerness to be away, she jogged down the steps and climbed into her SUV. Once driving down the narrow residential streets, however, she was forced to backtrack and circle blocks as she struggled to recall exactly where the funeral home was located. It wasn't a place she'd noticed when she was young, and the few funerals she'd attended over the years had been held at their local church or in other towns. She'd never had a need to visit the place.

At last she managed to turn onto the right street, her brows rising at the sight of the fire truck, along with a half dozen other vehicles, parked in the large lot.

Pulling to a halt next to the curb, Rachel climbed out of her SUV to study the long brick building with a portico and a detached garage with five bays. At one time the expansive yard must have been charming, with large oak trees and a sunken garden. Now it looked neglected, with ugly patches of bare ground in spots, and other places overgrown with dead weeds.

Just one of a dozen former businesses in Pike that were decaying into a pile of rubble.

She was distracted from her dark thoughts as Zac appeared around the corner of the building, waving her to join him. With quick steps, she crossed the uneven lawn. As usual he was wearing his uniform with a heavy jacket and leather boots. His hair was covered by a baseball cap with *Sheriff's Department* embroidered across the front and his weapon was holstered at his side. But she didn't miss his unshaven jaw and the hint of shadows under his eyes.

She was guessing he'd been called out of bed at some ungodly hour.

Resisting the urge to wrap her arms around him and offer a comforting hug, she instead turned her attention toward the nearby funeral home.

"Was there a fire?" she asked, catching the acrid stench of charred fabric from a side door that was propped open.

"More smoke than fire," Zac assured her, turning to lead her inside the building.

They stepped into what appeared to be a storage area with long metal shelves and an opening that revealed narrow steps going down to a dark basement.

"Do you think it's connected to Jude Henley?" she asked in confusion.

"The fire was a way to get our attention." His expression was grim as he grabbed a pair of disposable shoe coverings and gloves off a nearby shelf. "You'll need these."

Rachel efficiently slipped on the booties and gloves. She'd been to enough crime scenes to know what they meant.

"There's a victim." It was a statement not a question.

"Yes." He headed down the steep stairs. "Careful, there's no electricity at the moment. It should be back on as soon as the chief is sure it's safe. Unfortunately, there's no heat. The gas was turned off years ago."

They reached the bottom of the steps and entered a long, open basement with a low ceiling and cement walls with narrow windows at the top that allowed in enough light to see. A mixed blessing, she ruefully acknowledged, her gaze skimming around the embalming room.

There were cabinets built into the walls along with a deep ceramic sink. The dusty countertops were stacked with strange machines that included long suction tubes and metal instruments. The floor was cement with a large drain in the center. And most unnerving, there was a rolling table loaded with bottles of foundation, pots of blush, mascara, lipstick, and powder.

Rachel shivered, and not because of the cold. "A perfect setting for a horror show."

Zac sent her a curious glance. "Do you still watch those?"

She shook her head. When they'd gone off to college they'd shared a cramped apartment near campus and struggled to scrape together enough money to pay the bills. Their weekends were spent cuddled on the couch watching old movies and eating popcorn.

"Not so much now that I live alone."

"Me either."

They shared a rueful glance. It was one of many things they'd lost after they divorced. Their gazes remained locked together, the memories threatening to rise up and overwhelm her before she abruptly turned away. "There was something you wanted me to see?"

Zac paused, as if he wanted to say something. Then, muttering beneath his breath, he headed toward the opening at the far side of the basement. "In here."

Rachel followed behind, wrinkling her nose at the sharp stench of smoke. It was worse as they passed by the sink. But as she stepped into the small space that looked like some sort of walk-in cooler with silver walls and ceiling, she was instantly distracted. In the middle of the narrow space was a dead woman lying on a steel gurney.

"Damn," she breathed.

Chapter 6

Zac watched Rachel's reaction as she cautiously approached the corpse. He'd already recovered from his initial shock, although it was still disturbing to see the dead woman arranged on the gurney. Not just because she looked so heart-wrenchingly young. Or because she'd been stripped naked. It was the splotches of black and blue that marred her pale skin. The contusions covered her from her breasts down to her hips. And there were weird bumps where her rib cage should have been. As if the bones had been snapped and twisted by a violent beating. Her lips had been split open, as if someone had punched her in the face. And there were flecks of blood on her inner thigh that suggested she'd been brutalized before she died.

On the floor beside the gurney was a slender crowbar that he assumed was used in the attack and in the far corner was a pile of clothes that had no doubt been ripped off the poor victim.

He clenched his hands into tight fists as anger blasted through him. His shock and horror was already being replaced with a gut-deep fury as he gazed at the body.

The last few minutes of the woman's life had been one of pain, terror, and humiliation. No one deserved that. No one. And while he didn't know who was responsible for doing this—yet—when he eventually tracked down the animal, he intended to see that he was locked away for an eternity.

"Do you recognize her?" Rachel asked, her voice soft as if afraid of disturbing the dead.

Zac gave a curt nod. "Paige Carr," he said. He'd known who she was the minute he'd seen her on the gurney. She was younger than him, but he'd been friends with her family forever. "She was Paige Trent before she married Joe Carr."

Rachel's lips parted in surprise. "Lori's little sister?"

"That's the one."

Without warning, the fluorescent bulbs overhead flickered on and they both blinked as the light reflected off the polished steel walls. When his eyes finally adjusted, Zac grimaced. The sight of the battered, broken woman was even more gruesome in the garish glow. It also made the space feel twice as cramped.

Barely aware he was moving, Zac backed out of the cooler. A second later, Rachel had joined him. Her face was pale, but there was an unmistakable resolve in the stubborn angle of her jaw. She was a trained professional. He could sense that her thoughts were already turning to capturing the killer.

"There has to be a reason Paige was left in this particular spot." She confirmed his suspicion, her brows pulling together as she glanced around the empty morgue. "Was she connected to the Henleys?"

Zac considered the question before he shook his head. "Not that I know of."

"Could you tell if someone used a key to enter the building or if they had to break in?"

"The firemen were in a hurry when they arrived so they broke the door down to get in," he told Rachel. "There's no way to determine if someone had used a key or jimmied the lock."

His jaw tightened. The firemen had just been doing their job, but they'd not only destroyed the door, they'd trampled through the crime scene, obliterating any potential footprints and spraying foam that might contaminate any potential DNA.

Rachel sent him a wry smile, easily sensing his annoyance. "No one lives on the property?"

"Not since Jacob went into the nursing home."

She returned her attention to the bleak room, a visible shiver racing through her slender body.

"It's freezing down here," she murmured. "If there hadn't been a fire the body could very well have remained here until spring without anyone finding it."

Zac nodded. That had been his first thought. The building was abandoned, the air in the basement was close to freezing, and the body had been shoved into a cooler with no windows where someone passing by might have caught sight of her. If the killer wanted to keep Paige hidden, he'd chosen the perfect spot. That meant there could be only one reason for the fire.

"Like I said, someone wanted our attention," he said.

"Why?"

He'd thought about that too. "Same reason they left Jude's body on his grave."

"How can you be sure that whoever did this wasn't intending to burn down the place to get rid of any evidence?"

Zac didn't miss the fact that she didn't question his assumption that whoever killed poor Paige was also responsible for putting a bullet in Jude's head. She didn't believe in coincidences either.

He moved to stand next to the deep sink that was coated with ash. The firemen had removed the wastebasket from the building to make sure there were no lingering embers, but Zac had insisted it be kept as evidence.

"The trash can was placed in here." He pointed up. "Just below the window that was cracked open to release the smoke." He paused to let her study the small window above their heads that had been wedged open before revealing what else he'd learned from the fire chief. "Plus, whoever did it started the fire and then covered it with damp cloths to be sure it would smolder before dying out. Lots of smoke, but no flames."

Her lips parted, but before she could ask her next question there was the sound of heavy footsteps stomping down the stairs. They both turned to watch two uniformed EMTs enter the basement carrying a stretcher. He recognized both of them. Britt O'Neill, who was several years older with reddish hair and a ruddy face, and Hans Cole who was younger and twice as wide as Britt with muscles that came from hours in the gym. Zac's deputies, Lindsay and Anthony, followed close behind them.

It was Britt who spoke. "Can we take the body?"

Zac nodded toward the walk-in cooler. "The medical examiner is expecting you."

The two medics maneuvered the stretcher into the small space and Zac motioned toward his deputies to follow. It would be cramped, but he wanted to make sure he had an official observing anyone entering or leaving the location. The crime scene had already been tainted by the fire department. He wasn't going to have anyone else bungling around destroying evidence.

Once they had disappeared from view, Rachel stepped toward him, her expression troubled. "Any theories on who might be responsible for the murders?"

"A few." Zac glanced toward the cooler. "Until this morning."

"Tell me."

Wondering if Rachel was simply attempting to distract him from the grinding sadness of Paige's brutal death, Zac dredged up his earlier suspicions.

"I did some research on Jacob Henley," he said.

"And?"

"I discovered that this funeral parlor was facing bankruptcy twenty-eight years ago. It had obviously been struggling since Jacob's parents had died. Then, Jacob received a nice payment from an insurance policy that he held on his brother and his most pressing bills disappeared."

Rachel's brows lifted. "How much?"

"Fifty thousand."

"A good number back then," she said. "It wasn't enough to be suspicious but handy if you're in debt."

"That was my thought. It would explain Jacob's willingness to go along with the scheme to fake Jude's death. And it also made me wonder what would happen if his brother grew tired of his life on the run and decided to return to town."

"He'd probably panic," Rachel said.

"Exactly. No one wants to spend their golden years in jail for insurance fraud. And even if Jacob is occasionally confused, he's still able to walk on his own. He had the physical strength to lure his brother to the graveyard and put a bullet in his head." He glanced around the morgue, shaking his head. "But this . . ."

Rachel shoved her hands into the pockets of her jacket. "Hard to believe he would be capable of committing a murder like this."

They fell silent, both contemplating who could possibly have a motive to kill both Jude and Paige, until Lindsay called out from the cooler.

"Boss, there's something here I think you'll want to see."

Zac hurried into the cooler at the unmistakable edge in the woman's voice. Lindsay was proving to be a damned fine deputy and he trusted her judgment without question. The other two deputies . . . not so much.

Squeezing into the space, he discovered that Paige had been zipped into a black body bag and placed on the stretcher. But that wasn't what had captured his deputies' attention. Instead it was the black, square-shaped object that was on the steel gurney. It had been hidden beneath Paige's corpse.

"A VHS tape?" he muttered in confusion. Frowning he waved a hand toward the EMTs. "You guys can take off." He waited for them to carry out Paige's body before he returned his attention to his deputies. "Lindsay, get some pictures. Anthony, check it for prints and then bag it."

"It could have been here before Paige was murdered," Rachel suggested as she moved to stand next to him. Zac sent her a glance of disbelief and she wrinkled her nose.

"Yeah, I know. We should check it out. I have a VCR player at my office in Madison. I often have to deal with older technology in cold cases."

Zac shrugged. "We don't have to go to Madison. I have one at the farm."

She blinked. "You're kidding?"

"It's in my parents' room." Zac couldn't keep the hint of defensiveness out of his voice. He didn't know if it was because he was a thirty-year-old man living in his childhood home, or because that home hadn't changed since he'd been a child. Probably both.

Thankfully, Rachel merely nodded. "Okay. Let's walk through what might have happened here." She returned her attention to the murder. "It seems doubtful that Paige would have come here willingly."

"Unless she was meeting her lover," he pointed out. "If she was married and trying to keep her affair secret, there's not many places in Pike to get away from prying eyes."

Rachel snorted. "Trust me, no woman is going to agree to meet here, no matter how desperate she might be to keep it secret."

Zac paused before slowly nodding. There might be a few women who would be titillated by having sex in such a macabre setting, but none of them would be interested in stripping off their clothes in freezing temperatures.

"Agreed," he said, recalling when he'd first arrived at the funeral parlor. "And there weren't any cars parked in the lot. I assume she was picked up or kidnapped by her killer and brought here."

"Any cameras?"

"No. I have Greg canvassing the neighbors," he said,

referring to his third deputy. "Someone might have noticed something."

"Okay." She folded her arms over her chest, her expression pensive. "We assume Paige encountered her killer and was forced down here."

Zac nodded. "I'm guessing she was already unconscious or maybe he held her at gunpoint. There were no signs of a struggle either outside or in here."

Rachel pointed toward the door. "He forces her downstairs and into this cooler and ties her to the gurney." Her lips twisted in disgust. "He probably abused her and then kills her. Next, he lights a fire to attract your attention."

Zac attempted to put himself in the mind of the killer. Starting with the truck left running outside the cemetery so they would find Jude's body displayed on his grave. And the fire to lead the officials to Paige's shattered body. "This is a person who wants to be noticed. A narcissist."

"Dangerous," Rachel whispered.

"Really dangerous."

They exchanged a worried glance. The deaths of Jude and Paige were tragic. But they both feared that this wasn't the end of the horror. In fact, it might very well be the beginning.

"Now what?" she asked.

Zac hid a smile. Although Rachel was the more seasoned investigator, she was being careful not to step on his toes. That was why she'd always been destined to climb the ranks, he acknowledged. She was not only a great detective, but she understood the politics of every situation. He wasn't as willing to compromise. He liked to take time to consider a situation, and he rarely spoke without thinking through his words. But once he'd come to a decision, he didn't mind stepping on toes.

"I need to interview Paige's husband. He'll have to go to Madison to make the ID. Plus, I want him to give a statement before he has a chance to consider his answer," he decided, considering the most pressing issues he needed to tackle. "You want to meet at the farm around noon?"

She hesitated. "Are you cooking?"

He chuckled. "No, I'll swing by Bella's and pick up a pizza," he promised.

"Sounds good."

They moved out of the cooler and Rachel headed up the stairs while Zac waited for Lindsay and Anthony to join him. A minute later the deputies were entering the embalming room. Anthony moved toward Zac, but glancing at something over Zac's shoulder, he abruptly stumbled over his feet. Instinctively, Zac reached out to steady the younger man, grabbing the bag from his hand before the fool could drop it on the cement floor and shatter the tape inside.

"What the hell, Anthony?"

The deputy straightened, his round face flushed. "There was someone peeking through the window. It startled me."

Zac turned toward the window over the sink, which had been wedged open. "I'll check it out. You guys mark off the building as a crime scene and return to the office."

"It's Saturday. . . ." Anthony started to protest, only to have his words die away as Zac sent him a warning glare. "Fine."

Indifferent to his deputy's petulant expression, Zac

bounded up the staircase and out of the building. He wasn't as fast as he had been when he was on the track team, but he was still quick enough to catch sight of the man who was trying to scurry toward the back fence.

"Stop," Zac commanded, running behind the man. "I said stop or I'll shoot," he bluffed loudly. He wasn't going to shoot anyone in the back, but the threat had the desired outcome.

Coming to a sharp halt, the young man slowly turned to face Zac.

Keeping his hand near his weapon as he cautiously approached, Zac studied the trespasser. If this guy proved to be a threat, he wouldn't hesitate to retaliate. "Who are you?" he demanded.

The man was wearing heavy coveralls that were stained with grease and grime and there was a thick stocking hat on his head. All Zac could make out was that he was young, probably in his late twenties, with muddy brown eyes and a scraggly beard.

"Curly Bolton," the man muttered, shoving his hands into the pockets of his coveralls. "I ain't doing nothing wrong."

"You're trespassing on private property."

Curly hunched his thin shoulders. "I was passing by and noticed the fire truck. I wanted to see what was going on."

"Passing by on the way to where?"

He waved a hand toward the street. "I work at Sykes Automotive on the corner."

"The shop is opened on Saturdays?"

Curly's jaw tightened. He didn't like being questioned. "A part of my salary includes the apartment above the place. I'm headed home."

"That doesn't explain why you were peeking through the window."

"I told ya. I wanted to see what was going on," he groused. "And I knew Jacob wouldn't mind."

Zac arched a brow. He knew Jacob Henley. And well enough to call him by his first name. "Are you a friend?"

"Friend?" The man's lips twisted. Not in amusement, but in mockery. As if the thought of being friends with Jacob was unthinkable. "No. But my dad worked for him."

"He worked at the funeral parlor?"

"Yep."

"Doing what?"

"Everything." Curly sucked air through a gap in his front teeth, nodding toward the nearby garage. "He took care of the buildings, he drove the hearse, and dug the graves."

Zac narrowed his eyes. "What years was he employed?"

Curly shrugged. "I don't know. He was working there before I was born and stopped when the place closed down."

Perfect. It sounded as if the older man had been around during the years that Jude was still living in Pike, and when he was supposedly buried.

"Is he around here?" Zac barely dared to breathe until Curly nodded. It would be his luck to have discovered someone who could tell him about the Henleys' past only to find out he was living across the country. Or dead.

"Yeah."

"What's his name?"

"Curly."

Of course it was. Zac resisted the urge to roll his eyes. "Where does he live?"

The man hesitated, clearly reluctant to share the address. Then no doubt realizing that Zac could easily discover it, he grudgingly forced himself to answer.

"Pike Trailer Park," he spit the words out. "Number sixteen."

Zac stiffened. His interest had gone from mild to off the charts. Pike Trailer Park was where Paige had lived. Which meant that Curly Senior would have been a close neighbor. That seemed more than a vague coincidence. It also made him wonder how often Curly Junior visited his father. Glancing over his shoulder, he studied the spot where the man had been peeking into the basement. It was nearly hidden by the bushes that framed the back of the building. Only someone who was familiar with the place would have known where to find a perfect spot to spy into the basement. "What about you?" he demanded, turning back toward the younger man.

Curly looked confused. "Me."

"Did you ever work for Jacob Henley?"

"Not really. I mowed the grass during the summer and sometimes washed the hearse, but that's it."

That was enough, as far as Zac was concerned. This man would have a familiarity with Jacob and the funeral parlor. Which meant he would have had the opportunity to discover that Jude wasn't as dead as he was pretending to be. Plus, he could have seen Paige whenever he visited his dad. For now he was Zac's most likely suspect.

"Do you have a key to this place?" he asked.

Curly looked genuinely puzzled. "Why would I have a key?"

"What about your dad?"

Curly frowned, as if belatedly realizing the direction of

Zac's questions. Holding up his hands, he backed away. "Look, I don't want any trouble. Neither does my dad. Just leave us alone."

With that, Curly turned to hurry away, his head bent down as he picked up speed.

Zac let him go. He knew where to find him.

And right now, he had something more important to do.

Half an hour later, Zac was uncomfortably seated on a sagging sofa in a narrow living space that was littered with toys, stacks of laundry, and empty beer bottles. This was his first death notification, and it was just as awful as he'd expected it to be.

Joe Carr looked unbearably young and lost as he paced from one end of the carpet to the other. His hair was standing upright and he was wearing wrinkled jeans and a shirt that was hanging open. As if he'd slept in his clothes. Or maybe he never went to bed.

"Murdered," he muttered, dry washing his hands as he struggled to accept what Zac had just told him. "I don't believe it."

"I'm sorry, Joe." Zac didn't have to pretend his soul-deep regret. What had happened to Paige would haunt his dreams for years.

Joe came to a halt to stare at Zac with a hopeless expression. "I mean . . ." He glanced toward the corner where a small child was sleeping in a crib. He lowered his voice to a harsh whisper. "You're sure it's Paige?"

"I'm sure, but you'll have to make the formal ID at the medical examiner's office in Madison."

Joe winced. Was he going to be sick? "Now?"

Zac wanted to assure the poor man that he could take his time, but this wasn't a tragic accident. It was a murder. The quicker things could get taken care of, the quicker the investigation could get moving. "As soon as you can get there."

He grimaced, but he didn't argue. "You said she was at the old funeral parlor?"

"Yes."

"Why would she be there?"

A good question, Zac silently acknowledged. Once he answered that, he would have an insight on who killed her and why.

"It's possible she was taken there by her killer," he admitted.

"Dammit." Without warning, Joe smacked a fist into his open palm. "I told her not to go out last night."

"Go where?"

"To the Bait and Tackle."

Zac leaned forward, surprised by the answer. In the past few months the bar had been refurbished and cleaned up, but it was still a dive. Not the sort of place for a young, married mother to hang out.

"Was she meeting someone?"

"Her friend Pam Haas."

Zac recognized the name, but he didn't personally know Pam. He'd give her a call after he finished with Joe. "Did she drive there?"

"Yes. She took our old Ford Focus."

Zac pulled out a small pad and pencil from the pocket of his jacket to take notes. "What color?"

"White."

Zac glanced up. "Did she go out at night a lot?"

"No, never. That's why she . . ." Tears formed in Joe's eyes.

"Why she what?"

The man blinked, clearing a lump from his throat. "That's why she went. Lately I've been running around with the guys from work, and she was sick of staying home with Zoe." His hands clenched into tight balls, his face paling to a sickly shade of gray. "This is my fault."

Zac rose to his feet. The younger man could be putting on an act. After all, the significant other was always the most likely killer. And Joe could have been smart enough to use the recent discovery of Jude Henley's body to convince them the two murders were connected. But it seemed unlikely. At least for now.

"Joe, you can't think like that," he insisted.

"How else can I think?" he rasped, lifting his hands to shove them through his disheveled hair. "I didn't even call to report her missing."

Zac narrowed his gaze. It was a question he'd intended to ask. Joe just made it easy. "Why not?"

"Because we'd been in a stupid fight." Joe made a sound of disgust. "I thought she got drunk and stayed at Pam's just to piss me off."

Zac paused, holding the younger man's gaze. "Where were you last night?"

Joe waved a vague hand. "Here with Zoe."

"Was anyone else here?"

"Nope. I had a few beers and went to bed."

The empty bottles on the coffee table seemed to confirm the man's alibi. Zac would have his deputies canvas the trailer park to see if anyone had noticed Joe leaving during the evening.

Zac's thoughts were interrupted when the door to the

trailer was thrust open and a crowd of people rushed in, including Joe's mother, his aunt and uncle, and what seemed to be a dozen cousins.

"Joe, I just heard." His mother moved to wrap Joe in her arms. Instantly Joe burst into tears, sobbing uncontrollably as the older woman patted his back.

"I'll be back later," Zac said, weaving his way through the gathered family and stepping out of the trailer.

He paused to take a deep breath, glancing around at the nearby trailers. They were crammed close together, as if the owner of the park was determined to get as many trailers as possible squeezed in. It gave the feeling of living on top of one another. An impression that was intensified by the screaming kids playing on the swing set next door, and the rev of a loud engine from the man across the narrow street who was tinkering on an old truck. Zac leaned forward to see the end of the cul-de-sac, noting the postman who was busy filling the metal mailboxes.

It would be difficult to have any privacy in this place.

As he walked down the steps, his gaze was suddenly captured by the trailer that was catty-corner from Joe and Paige. It wasn't just that it was in better repair than the others with a recently painted porch and trimmed hedges. It was the large silver numbers on the front of the trailer.

A one and a six.

This trailer belonged to Curly Bolton Senior.

With long strides, Zac was across the street and climbing onto the porch. He rapped his knuckles on the screen door. No answer. He rapped again. Nothing. Turning, he leaned over the railing to peer through the nearest window. He could see the outlines of a couch and a recliner as well as a television that was turned off.

Assuming no one was home, Zac turned back toward the street, judging the short distance to Joe Carr's trailer. Certainly close enough to see what was happening, and probably to hear any loud arguments. It would also be easy to follow behind a woman leaving her trailer at night.

Zac grimly headed toward his truck.

He intended to drive the route to the Bait and Tackle. He might find Paige's car, or at least a spot where she might have been forced off the road. Plus, he wanted to see if the bar had any security cameras.

Paige might have left with someone. Or someone might have followed her when she exited the bar to go home.

He'd come back later to finish his questioning of Joe, and to track down Curly.

Zac sighed. The to-do list just kept getting longer.

Chapter 7

Rachel hadn't been out to the Evans farm since the divorce. It wasn't that she'd deliberately avoided the place, but it was five miles outside town and down a narrow road that ended at the old two-storied house. She hadn't had any need to drive out there.

Now she pulled her vehicle to a halt and climbed out to study the place where she'd once spent endless hours helping Zac finish his chores or fishing along the banks of the nearby river.

It hadn't changed much.

There was a new tin roof and the railing on the porch had been recently painted. Otherwise, she might have been a seventeen-year-old girl eagerly rushing to spend time with her boyfriend.

Slamming shut the door of her SUV, Rachel headed toward the back of the house where she could see Zac's truck parked. No one used the front door. She wasn't even sure it opened.

Rounding the corner, Rachel wasn't surprised to discover that Zac was waiting for her on the stoop. He would have heard her pull up.

"Come in."

He led her through the mudroom into the small kitchen, helping her to remove her leather coat and laying it on the countertop that was as battered as the old cabinets and linoleum floor. The appliances, however, were new, as was the dining table that was set in the center of the floor.

Rachel wondered if Zac's mom had taken the old table and matching china cabinet when she'd moved out. They'd probably belonged to her own mother.

Her inane thoughts were scattered when the tantalizing scent of freshly baked crust and Italian sausage teased at her nose.

"Mmm." She sucked in a deep breath, crossing to loop her satchel over the back of a chair before flipping open the top of the square box set on the table. The scent of heaven filled the air. "I haven't had Bella's pizza for years."

"Let's dig in while it's hot," Zac suggested, grabbing two paper plates and a couple beers before joining her.

They both took a seat and Rachel arched her brows when Zac shoved one of the bottles in front of her.

"You're going to need it," he assured her.

Rachel shrugged and took a swig. She was technically off duty, and one beer wasn't going to hurt. Not when she intended to eat a huge amount of pizza.

"Did you talk to the husband?" she asked, not waiting for Zac to take a couple slices. There was no such thing as manners when it came to Bella's pizzas. It was every man . . . or woman . . . for themselves.

"I did." Zac grabbed his own share, taking a large bite before he continued. "He seemed pretty tore up, but that doesn't necessarily mean anything."

Rachel nodded. "Significant others are always prime suspects."

"And he doesn't have an alibi."

Working her way through her pizza, Rachel paused to take a sip of beer. "Did he say what Paige was doing last night?"

"She was headed to the Bait and Tackle."

"Alone?" Rachel asked, a chill inching down her spine. From what she'd heard, the Bait and Tackle had been involved in the murders that had swept through Pike last year.

It felt like an ominous connection.

"No. She was supposed to meet her friend Pam Haas."

"Did you talk to Pam?"

"I did." Zac grabbed for his beer. "She went to the bar, but Paige never showed up. She told me she tried calling several times with no answer, and eventually she went home."

"Do you believe her?"

Zac shrugged. "I've sent in a request to get Paige's phone records so we'll know whether or not she's telling the truth."

Silence filled the kitchen as they concentrated on demolishing the pizza. Rachel polished off her last slice and contemplated whether she could finish a third. *Hmm. Probably not.* With a sigh, she settled back in her seat.

"So, Paige disappeared between her house and the Bait and Tackle," she said, allowing her mind to trace the route from the trailer park to the bar. It would have been less than a fifteen-minute drive. Not much distance to have something bad happen. Then Rachel grimaced. "Assuming she left her home at all."

"It appears she did." Zac reluctantly closed the lid on the pizza, as if to hide temptation. "Her car was found in the alley behind the bar, along with her purse and phone. I had Lindsay pick them up and take them back to the office." He paused, as if sorting through what he'd discovered. "It doesn't mean Joe couldn't have killed her, and drove the car to the bar to make it look like she was snatched from the alley."

Rachel nodded. It was amazing how cunning people could be when there was the chance of going to jail. Especially if it could be a life-time sentence. "Any cameras?"

Zac's features tightened in disgust. "There's a couple inside the building, but not in the alley. The previous owner had a habit of selling beer and other illegal substances to underage kids out the back door and didn't want his crimes recorded."

Rachel swallowed the urge to curse. After years in the cold case squad she'd learned that gathering evidence was like fishing. You spent endless hours casting out bait in the hopes of a small nibble. And more often than not, you went home empty-handed.

It was the nature of the beast.

"Do you think the killer followed her?" she instead asked.

"I'm checking out a man called Curly Bolton," he replied. "He used to work for Jacob Henley at the funeral parlor, and more importantly he's a neighbor to Joe and Paige in the trailer park."

Rachel leaned forward, placing her arms on the table. Connections were important. And this Curly had two links to the victims.

"Interesting." She paused before offering assistance.

This was Zac's case. She didn't want to step on his toes. "I can have my team do some poking into his past if you want."

He nodded without hesitation. "You should probably include his son, Curly Junior."

Rachel reached into her satchel to pull out her phone, sending a quick text to her staff. "Got it." She glanced up. "Do you have the tape?"

Zac shoved himself to his feet. "It's upstairs with the VCR."

She nodded, joining him as he led her out of the kitchen and up the wooden steps to the second floor. A smile curved her lips as her hand gripped the same wooden bannister she'd gripped a thousand times before and the familiar squeak as she placed her weight on the fourth step. There was a bittersweet emotion at the memory of happier times when she'd been in this house, along with pain and resentment toward the farm that had ripped apart her marriage.

"The house hasn't changed," she said.

Reaching the landing, Zac sent a rueful glance over his shoulder. "I never had the time to do anything with it."

"I wasn't complaining. Some things are better left alone," she hastily assured him.

So far they were working well together, but there was still a sensation of treading on ice around each other. Besides, there was a part of her that savored the feeling of constancy. Her own childhood home was forever being refurbished. Like a snake shedding its skin that had become too small and uncomfortable. She understood her mother's restless urge to build barriers between herself and the past, but it meant the house seemed more like a hotel than a home.

Waiting for her to reach the top of the stairs, Zac led her into the closest bedroom. It had once belonged to his parents and it looked as if it'd been modeled after *Little House on the Prairie*. There was a wrought-iron bed with a homemade quilt and matching curtains. The floor was worn wooden planks and the walls were covered in a paisley print wallpaper.

"Honestly, I don't think I bother to change anything because I can't see myself staying here for much longer."

"Really?" Rachel didn't try to hide her surprise.

Their marriage had ended because he'd walked away from their future to take care of this farm. Now he intended to sell it all?

"Dad's gone and Mom lives in town. More importantly, the fields are in the hands of my neighbor." He shrugged. "It would be better for everyone if I offer the place to a family who wants to make this a home again."

"Letting go of the past?" she demanded, a hint of bitterness in her voice.

He sent her a wry glance. "A day late and a dollar short, eh Rachel?"

"Something like that," she muttered.

"It took me a while." He deliberately paused. "You, on the other hand, were ready to move on with lightning speed."

She sent him a puzzled glance. "What do you mean?"

"Our divorce was barely finalized when you reverted back to your maiden name."

She flinched, blindsided by his accusation.

"You were gone," she reminded him, not about to admit

that it had been a burning need to erase the pain of his departure. "And since I was just getting my career off the ground, it seemed the opportune moment to have a fresh start."

"I get it." Pain, regret, and something that might have been yearning darkened his eyes. "It didn't make it any easier when I found out."

Her lips parted, but before she could speak Zac was turning toward the tall dresser where a small television and VHS player were set on top. "It should be all hooked up and ready to go."

Biting her tongue, Rachel resisted the urge to press for a reason why Zac had belatedly given up his father's dream to keep the farm in the Evans family. She wasn't here to hash over their personal choices. She was here to work.

She glanced around, locating the plastic bag set on the bed. Picking it up, she studied the black object inside.

"This doesn't look like a regular VHS tape," she said, carrying it toward Zac.

"My mom had something like it," he said, taking the bag. "It's an adapter. She used it to play the tapes from her old camcorder."

Rachel watched as Zac carefully removed the adapter and slid it into the machine. Then there was the sound of clicking and the tape whirled into motion. Together they moved to stand directly in front of the small television as the screen flickered and glowed to life.

At first there was nothing to see but a gray fuzz. Rachel frowned, leaning forward. It looked as if the camera was struggling to focus, and the sound was muffled. She briefly wondered if the tape had been erased, then abruptly an image formed, as if someone had removed the lens cap. At first there was nothing to see beyond a blank wall. The picture was so grainy it was impossible to determine anything else. Then the camera was slowly tilted down to reveal a naked woman who was lying on a narrow gurney.

"Shit," Zac breathed, reaching out he hit the pause button on the player. "It's a video of Paige's murder."

That was exactly what Rachel first assumed. The body looked the same. She was arranged the same. Even her features looked the same. It wasn't until Rachel took a second glance that she noticed the difference.

"Not Paige." She pointed at the screen. "Look at her hair, it's too long."

Zac slowly nodded, pressing play. "It's in the same place," he said. "Or at least, they're in a cooler."

"Yes," Rachel agreed as the camera light reflected off the metal wall.

"And she's lying on a similar gurney," he added.

They fell silent as the woman began to twist her head from side to side. "Please, please, please, please," she repeated the word like a mantra, or a prayer. "I just want to go home. I won't tell anyone what you did to me. Please . . . please . . ."

Rachel's heart clenched at the tragic horror in the woman's voice. She'd obviously been brutalized, and now she was staring death in the eye. Still, she begged for a miracle. A miracle that Rachel suspected wasn't going to come.

Damn. How many times had Rachel casually said that the victims talked to her? That learning who they were, where they'd come from, and what they most wanted in life could lead her to the person responsible for their death. But now she truly had a victim talking to her. And it wasn't at all the same thing.

"I like when you beg, Staci," a voice cooed before a man moved to lean over the gurney.

"Jude," Rachel choked out in shock. Although the man on the video was much younger than the corpse that had been dumped in Pike Cemetery there was no mistaking it was the same person.

"And Staci Gale," Zac added, his voice harsh as they watched Jude grab Staci's chin in a rough grip.

"Please, Jude," she pleaded, tears streaming down her pale face.

Jude chuckled in pleasure. "Yes, like that." He slowly straightened, his arm lifting to reveal the crowbar he clutched in his hand. "And now it's time for you to scream." Slashing the crowbar downward, Jude hit the trapped woman across the torso with a vicious blow. Staci parted her lips to release a high-pitched cry of pain. Jude closed his eyes, a smile curving his lips. "So sweet," he murmured, once again lifting the crowbar and bringing it down with violent force. On cue, Staci screamed. "Like music to my ears."

Rachel lifted a hand to her lips, her stomach heaving as she watched the woman being shattered beneath the ruthless beating. The fact that she couldn't do anything to stop the inevitable only made it worse.

Easily sensing her distress, Zac wrapped an arm around her shoulders and pulled her close. It was a familiar gesture that she didn't try to fight. In fact, she readily leaned against the solid strength of his body. Right now she needed to be reminded there was more than evil in this world.

"A crowbar," Zac said. "The same weapon used on Paige."

"Yes." Rachel grimaced. "It's the same murder."

Once he'd finished his frenzied attack, Jude dropped the crowbar, then with a dreamy smile of satisfaction, he leaned forward to place a gentle kiss on her lips. Then, slowly straightening, he gazed down at the dead woman with a mocking smile.

"Was it as fun for you as it was for me?"

Still smiling, Jude glanced toward the camera and, reaching into his pocket, pulled out a small remote. A second later, the image clicked off and the video came to an end.

There was a long silence in the bedroom as they struggled to process what they'd just witnessed. At last, Zac reached forward to eject the tape and replace it in the plastic bag.

Grimly, Rachel gathered control of her shaky nerves. She was a professional. It was time to do her job.

"If you don't mind, I'd like to take this to my office in Madison," she said. "I have a detective who specializes in older technology. It's possible she'll be able to tell us what camcorder filmed the video and the approximate year it was made. She can also figure out where someone local could buy it."

Zac nodded, handing her the plastic bag. "I'll need a copy."

"Of course."

Zac shoved his fingers through his hair, his tension vibrating around him like a tangible force field.

"This tape proves that Jude murdered Staci Gale. Probably in his brother's morgue."

Rachel nodded. "And then buried her in his own grave," she added.

"That seems the most likely scenario," Zac agreed.

"Do you think Jacob was involved?"

"My gut feeling is that Jacob helped his brother fake his death for the life insurance money, but he didn't know that Jude intended to use the grave to dump the body of a woman he'd just murdered. Fifty thousand isn't worth a life sentence."

Rachel's breath hissed through her teeth. The image of Jude smashing Staci with a crowbar was going to give her nightmares. But worse was the deepening suspicion that the fingerprint left in Kim Slade's tent had belonged to Jude.

"I wonder how many other women he killed?" She spoke her fear out loud. "Dammit. Why didn't I follow up on that fingerprint?"

Zac grabbed her shoulders, turning her to meet his steady gaze. "Because Jude was officially dead. Why would you waste resources chasing a ghost?"

"Yes, a ghost." She muttered a curse. "He managed to become invisible. The perfect way to hunt his victims without concern for leaving behind clues."

"You couldn't know, Rachel," he insisted, his jaw tightening. "Besides, we have a bigger problem."

"What could be bigger?"

"Whoever killed Paige was re-creating Staci's murder."

Rachel shuddered, suddenly struck by the memory of the note that had been stuffed into Jude's mouth.

"*The student becomes the master*," she quoted the chilling words.

"Someone either knew Jude and his dark secrets or they found his tape and decided to copy the crime."

Rachel glanced down at the bag in her hand. Since joining the cold case squad, she'd investigated two serial killers. After watching Jude Henley taking such perverse pleasure in tormenting Staci, she suspected she was about to investigate her third.

"If there was one tape, there has to be more," she said. "A man who goes to such an elaborate effort to stage this kind of murder doesn't stop at one victim."

Zac nodded. "And whoever it is copying Jude has decided to re-create the crimes in Pike."

"We have to stop this."

Zac brushed his fingertips down her cheek, his touch as light as a butterfly wing, but as searing as if she'd just been branded. Tingles of excitement fluttered through her stomach.

"We will," he murmured. "Together."

Chapter 8

Zac was exhausted by mid-morning on Monday. Probably because he'd worked all weekend, and then was up and in his office before six a.m. Or maybe it was the stress that was bothering him. It was one thing to break up squabbles between neighbors, or investigate petty crimes. It was another to hunt down a potential serial killer. The knowledge that he was responsible for preventing another murder weighed on him with staggering force.

Unfortunately, he not only had two murders waiting to be solved, but the daily tasks of running the sheriff's office were rapidly piling up. He was going to be buried beneath the paperwork if he didn't try to stay on top of it.

He was plowing his way through the quarterly budget report when the door to his office was pushed open.

Jerking up his head, Zac intended to vent his frustration on the poor fool who was unlucky enough to interrupt his concentration only to have the words die on his lips at the sight of Rachel.

"Am I interrupting?" she asked.

"Come in."

He dropped his pen, the budget forgotten as he watched

his ex-wife stroll into the office. She was wearing a fitted black jacket and matching slacks with a crisp white shirt that was unbuttoned to offer a hint of her firm breasts. The tailored clothing emphasized her tall, slender frame, just as having her dark hair framing her face emphasized the elegant lines of her features.

She halted in front of the desk, gazing down at him. "You look tired."

Zac grimaced. The heated awareness that was curling through the pit of his stomach at the sight of her was effectively extinguished. Obviously, she didn't have the same reaction when she looked at him.

A painful but much needed reminder that she was in Pike to work, not to rehash their complicated past.

"I've slept better," he muttered.

She wrinkled her nose in sympathy. "Me too."

He nodded. After they'd watched the videotape, Rachel had driven to Madison to deliver the evidence to her office. He'd stayed busy enough that he shouldn't have missed her absence. Hell, he shouldn't have missed her even if he hadn't been busy.

But he had.

"Did you just get back into town?" he asked.

"Yep." She glanced toward the old-fashioned clock on the wall above his head. "I had a meeting with my staff before heading back. Did you already notify Lynne about her mother?"

"I did." He grimaced. "I had to get a sample of her DNA."

"How is she?"

Zac had driven out to Kir and Lynne's new home outside town to share what he suspected and to get the sample for a DNA test. It'd been one of the hardest things he'd ever had to do.

"Stunned, and not sure if she wants the body to belong to her mom or not," he said. Lynne had sat as still as a statue for what had felt like an eternity trying to process what he'd told her. "On one hand, if it is Staci Gale, she'll have the comfort of knowing her mother didn't willingly abandon her and ignore her existence for the past twenty-eight years. On the other hand . . ." His jaw tightened as the memory of the violent assault with the crowbar seared through his mind. "She was brutally murdered."

"Understandable." Rachel heaved a small sigh. "Have you talked to Dr. Gale?"

Zac settled back in his leather chair. His shoulders ached from leaning over his desk. He'd discovered over the past months that it was easier to do a full day of physical labor than hunch over a stack of paperwork for an hour.

"I just got off the phone with him," he told Rachel. "He's preparing to return to Pike from Florida, but he won't be here until tomorrow."

Impatience flashed in her eyes. Zac sympathized. Any delay right now might be the difference between life and death. Literally.

"Did he tell you anything?" she demanded.

Zac reached for the paper that was covered in his scribbled notes. Dr. Gale had been as shocked as his daughter when Zac had called to tell him they suspected his wife's body had been discovered. Thankfully, he'd been able to answer a few basic questions.

"Dr. Gale claimed the last time he spoke to his wife was in the autumn of 1994," he read off the paper.

"He didn't have an exact date?"

Rachel perched on the corner of the desk. It was something she'd used to do when they shared a small apartment near the college. He would be finishing his homework and she would be chatting about her day or trying to lure him into taking a walk. At the time he'd been annoyed by the interruption. Now he looked back with regret. How many tiny gestures of affection had he ignored? How often had he resented instead of cherished their time together?

Zac cleared the sudden lump from his throat, focusing on his conversation with Dr. Gale. "Sometime after Lynne's second birthday was as close an estimate as he could give me."

Rachel's brows drew together. "And it never bothered him that she'd just disappeared?"

That had been his first question. It seemed impossible to believe that a woman could vanish into thin air and no one be concerned about what happened to her.

"He told me that he assumed she'd run off with her lover."

"What lover?"

"It was more a suspicion than any tangible proof," Zac said. "Dr. Gale confessed that the marriage had been in trouble for some time and that he'd feared it was inevitable that she would walk away."

Rachel's expression remained skeptical. Understandable. He didn't doubt that she would have scoured the world if he ever disappeared. No matter how rocky their relationship.

"Did she leave a note?"

"Yes." He glanced back down at the paper. "When Dr. Gale came home from work he discovered that Lynne had been taken to a neighbor and Staci had left a message saying that she was spending the weekend out of town with a friend."

"She didn't name the friend?"

"No name. When she didn't come home, he assumed she'd been with a lover and decided to abandon her life and family in Pike."

"That's a pretty big leap," Rachel muttered.

"I'm going out on a limb and guessing that he was relieved she'd walked away. It meant the end of a difficult situation without him having to take responsibility for the split."

Rachel grimaced. "Surely he expected her to request a divorce?"

Zac shrugged. "He had a small daughter to raise plus he was busy with his vet practice. I think he tried to put her out of his mind."

"True." She shook her head. "I remember my mom complaining to the other neighbors that Lynne was left alone way too often. I think she pretty much raised herself."

"She had that in common with Kir," Zac added. After Kir's dad had been shot, Rudolf had lost himself in an alcoholic haze.

"What about Staci's parents?" Rachel asked. "Surely they were concerned?"

"According to Dr. Gale, Staci's mother died a few hours after she gave birth to Staci. Just a year or so later her father remarried and had a new family. I don't think Staci and her father were ever very close. Once she supposedly left town, the older man probably didn't give her a second thought."

Rachel made a sound of disgust. "I would find it unbelievable if I didn't have endless Jane Doe files stacked on my desk. It's amazing how many people go to their graves without a name."

"I'll finish questioning Dr. Gale when he gets here." He leaned back and glanced up at Rachel. "Did you get anything on the camcorder?"

Rachel pushed off the desk and reached into the leather satchel she wore crossed over her body.

"Here's a list of the makes and models that used that particular size of video," she said, placing a stack of papers on his desk. "There were no stores in Pike that sold camcorders, but there were two in Grange. Both closed down years ago, unfortunately. I have my staff digging into their old records. There's a small chance we might be able to put a name to who purchased the camera that was used during Staci's murder." She didn't sound overly hopeful. Not many small businesses kept a list of every customer who bought an item from their store. Their only hope would be a credit card receipt. "Leslie's still studying the video. She'll keep me updated if she finds anything that might help."

Zac narrowed his eyes. Her voice was distracted, as if she was thinking about something besides camcorders and murderous videos.

"Is something wrong?" His lips twisted. "Beyond the obvious?"

"You said that Staci disappeared after Lynne's second birthday?"

Zac frowned, not sure where she was going with the question. "Yes."

She once again reached into her satchel and pulled out a file. Flipping it open, she studied the top paper.

"And that they were having marital difficulties?"

"Who doesn't?"

She stiffened at his soft words, but she kept her attention locked on the file. "We could be discussing Paige, not Staci Gale."

Zac blinked, swiftly reviewing what he knew about Paige. She had a young daughter, probably around two, a difficult marriage, and she looked like Staci.

"*The student becomes the master*," he quoted the note left in Jude's mouth. "So does that mean the killer is hunting women like Staci?"

Rachel closed the file and returned it to her satchel. "Without knowing if Jude had more victims, and if they fit a certain pattern . . . wait."

"What?"

"Kim Slade," she breathed.

It took a second to recall the woman who'd been murdered at Devil's Lake. Which was kind of crazy, considering she was the reason Rachel was even standing in his office.

"We can't be sure she was one of Jude's victims," he pointed out, determined not to jump to conclusions.

"She was young, dark-haired, and she'd just had an argument with her boyfriend."

"That part fits with the other two victims, but the murder didn't happen in Pike."

"No," she said slowly and they exchanged a worried glance.

Tracking a killer was hard, but tracking a killer who moved around the country would be next to impossible.

"I'll call my contacts and warn them to keep an extra eye on the campsites," Rachel added.

There was a tap on the door before it was pushed open, interrupting their private conversation. Zac glanced around, his brows lifting at the unexpected sight of his friend who entered the office carrying several thick files. The last time he'd seen him, he'd been comforting a shocked Lynne as she struggled to accept her mother's death.

"Kir."

"Can I come in?"

"Of course."

Rachel turned to study the golden-haired man with brilliant blue eyes and stark features. Kir had been ahead of her in school, but they'd both been avid athletes. They'd spent a lot of hours together practicing free throws in the gym or running around the track after school.

"Kir. I'm so sorry." She moved forward to give him an impulsive hug before she stepped back. "How's Lynne?"

"Struggling, but she's strong," he said. "She's already back at work."

"I don't blame her," Rachel assured him. After her divorce she'd thrown herself into her job. It was the only way to bear the loss. "There's nothing worse than sitting around and brooding on whatever is bothering you."

"It's good to see you back in Pike, Rachel," Kir said.

"It's just temporary."

Kir winked in her direction. "That's what I said. But

here I am. Happily settled and never intending to leave again."

Rachel stiffened, but before she could insist that she would never move back to Pike, Zac pushed himself to his feet.

"Is there a reason you're carrying around a stack of files?"

Kir moved to set the manila folders on the desk. "These belonged to my dad," he said, referring to the old sheriff. "He left his official reports here at the station, but he had hundreds of documents that were off the record, stuffed into his home office."

Rachel stepped toward the desk, eyeing the impressive stack. "What sort of documents?"

"Everything from his opinion on parking along Main Street to a photo that recently helped solve an old murder," Kir said. "I couldn't sleep last night so I spent the hours pulling out the files that might interest you. Most of them deal with the deaths he thought were suspicious but he didn't have enough evidence to pursue, or missing people who weren't formally reported missing."

Rachel reached for the top file, her eyes widening as she caught sight of the name neatly typed on the label.

"Staci Gale?"

"Yep, Lynne doesn't know that it was in there." Kir heaved a sigh. "There isn't much in the notes to help you, but my dad did make a few calls to try and track her down after she left town. He didn't suspect Dr. Gale of anything nefarious, but he was curious where she went. I suppose he wanted to ease his mind that nothing bad had happened to her. It's a shame he didn't dig deeper. Maybe . . ."

Rachel reached out to give his arm a squeeze as his

words trailed away. Clearly, he was still mourning the loss of his father. Plus there was the additional concern for his wife. Poor Lynne had to be going through a toxic mixture of emotions. Disbelief. Grief. Horror. Hopefully she would eventually get to a sense of closure that she knew exactly what had happened to her mother.

"Thanks, Kir. Rudolf inspired me to go into law enforcement. It doesn't surprise me that he's still helping Pike solve cases."

"Nothing would make him happier." With a distracted smile, Kir dropped a kiss on top of Rachel's head. "I'm going to check on Lynne. Don't leave town without stopping by."

Rachel watched him go, noticing the casual grace. Although he was clearly worried about his wife, there was a relaxed ease about him that hadn't been there when he was young.

"Marriage suits him," she murmured.

"It does," Zac agreed. "I've never seen him happier."

She nodded toward the files. "Do you want to take half and I'll do the other half?"

Zac shook his head. "I'll look through them later tonight. Right now I want to talk to Curly Senior."

"Oh, I almost forgot." Rachel reached into her satchel to pull out the report she'd printed off before leaving her office in Madison. "I have the preliminary background check on the Curly duo."

Zac grabbed his jacket off a hook on the wall along with a matching ballcap. "You can share it on the drive."

They walked out of the building using a side entrance that led to the attached parking lot. Noticing the long shed that had been constructed at the back, Rachel was reminded that Jude's body wasn't the only surprise left at the cemetery.

"Have you discovered anything about Jude's vehicle?"

Zac shook his head as they climbed into his truck and he started the engine. "I had Ed Hoyer come over and take a look at it," he said, referring to his cousin who'd been a mechanic since he'd left high school. "From looking at the engine he was convinced the thing hadn't been used in years. Probably not since Jude had supposedly been buried."

Rachel grimaced. "It's like both Jude and his truck materialized from a time warp. But we know they didn't. So they had to be somewhere."

"Agreed." Zac pulled onto Main Street. "It's possible the truck was stored in one of the garages at the funeral parlor. Another question for Curly Senior."

It was a reasonable hypothesis, but it didn't explain where Jude had been hiding.

With a frustrated shake of her head, Rachel reached into her handy-dandy satchel and pulled out the file on the Boltons. Flipping it open, she read from the abbreviated notes she'd written down.

"Both have a record," she told Zac as he zipped through the streets. "Senior was arrested for a DUI in 1991 and arrested again for domestic violence in 2001. Those charges were dropped. He was also sued by a neighbor for criminal trespassing and destruction of property. He was ordered to pay five hundred dollars in damages."

Zac made a sound of disgust. "Domestic violence against his wife?"

"No. His son. He supposedly threw Curly Junior out an upstairs window," she corrected. "His wife divorced him and moved to Grange. She died of an overdose when Junior was seventeen and he came to Pike to stay with his father."

"An overdose." Zac narrowed his eyes. "Convenient."

Rachel nodded in agreement. It'd been her first thought as well. The easiest way to make the death look like an accident was with an overdose. "Something to check out."

Zac turned to head to the outskirts of town. "You said they both had records."

"Yep." Rachel returned to her notes. "Junior was arrested for disorderly conduct. He was trying to break down the door to his girlfriend's house."

"Violent."

"He also was charged with carrying an illegal handgun."

"I think we should have a chat with Junior." Zac's jaw tightened as he stepped harder on the gas. "But first, Senior."

Chapter 9

Zac pounded on the door of trailer number sixteen. Just like last time, there was no answer. Was Curly really gone? Or was he hiding inside? Zac felt a stab of annoyance. It would take hours to get a search warrant. Even assuming the judge would sign it. He glanced toward Rachel, who was standing at the front of the trailer to make sure no one managed to sneak out a window. Her hand was beneath her jacket where he assumed she had a weapon. She shrugged as she met his impatient frown, then with a smooth motion, she whirled toward the side as a small postal vehicle pulled to the curb and a man stepped out.

"Are you looking for Curly?" the stranger asked.

Zac's hand went to his side, hovering over the handle of his weapon as he took a quick survey of the approaching stranger. He was young, perhaps in his mid to late twenties with gray eyes and short, black hair. His features were smooth, and vaguely familiar. At the moment, he was wearing a blue jacket with matching pants. The official postal uniform.

"Who are you?"

"Isaac Dowell."

Zac didn't recognize the name, but he assumed that he'd noticed the younger man around town as he delivered the mail. "Do you know Curly Bolton?"

Isaac shook his head. "Not really, but I live next door." He waved a hand toward the neighboring trailer. "I think he might have left town."

Zac stepped toward the edge of the porch. "Why do you say that?"

"Last night I saw him load a bunch of stuff into the back of his truck and take off."

"What kind of stuff?" Rachel demanded.

Isaac shrugged. "Suitcases, a few boxes. That's all I saw." He paused as if trying to remember what had been piled in the truck. "Oh, and his television. That's when I figured he wasn't coming back for a while."

Zac balled his hands into fists at the realization he was too late. *Dammit.* Curly had obviously been spooked into hiding. And it didn't take any guesswork to know who'd given him the heads-up that Zac wanted to talk to him.

Reaching into his pocket, he pulled out his business card. "This is my phone number. I'd appreciate you giving me a call if Curly happens to come back."

Isaac hesitated before reluctantly taking the card. "Is he in trouble?"

"I just have a few questions for him."

"Huh. I watch movies." Isaac eyed him with a curious expression. "That's cop talk for trouble."

Zac parted his lips to insist he just wanted to talk to the man only to be distracted when a car pulled into the driveway across the street and an older woman climbed out carrying a pan covered with aluminum foil. The citizens of Pike were bringing comfort to Joe Carr and his young daughter in the form of home-baked casseroles.

"Were you here Friday night?"

The man blinked, as if caught off guard by the question. "I worked that morning, but I was home a little after three."

"Did you notice anything across the street?"

He shook his head. "Not really."

Zac paused, choosing his words with care. He didn't want to lead the witness. "There weren't any cars coming or going?"

"Oh." The man looked uncomfortable. "You're asking about the argument that happened over there?"

Zac struggled not to react. "I'm just trying to get a timeline."

"So horrible," Isaac muttered. "I heard that the woman . . . Patty? No, Paige. I heard she was found in the funeral parlor. I still can't believe she's dead."

"What did you see on Friday?" Zac prompted.

"Not much." Isaac glanced toward Joe's trailer. "I happened to be in the kitchen washing the dishes when I saw the woman come out and open the door to her car. The man came out and it was obvious they were angry with each other."

"Could you hear what they said?"

Isaac was shaking his head before Zac finished asking the question. "No. I had all my windows closed. I can't even be sure they were mad at each other. It just looked that way from a distance."

Rachel moved to stand next to Zac. "Did they have a lot of arguments?"

Isaac lifted his hands in a vague motion. "I really don't pay attention to the neighbors. I have to get up at an ungodly hour to get to work so I'm in bed by the time most people are going out at night."

As the son of a farmer, Zac understood the need to be up before dawn. Still, he refused to believe the man hadn't ever noticed what was going on around him. The trailer park was too crammed together for him to be oblivious.

"What happened after the couple argued?" He returned the conversation back to the events of Friday night.

"She got in the car and drove away and the dude went back inside."

"Did he leave the trailer at any time?"

"I don't know. I finished the dishes and went back to the bedroom to play video games." Isaac's expression settled into defiant lines. He was starting to resent the questions. "Like I said, I don't pay attention to my neighbors. I live here to save money until I can buy a plot of land and build a cabin."

Zac grimly attempted to keep the frustration out of his voice. "Did you hear any cars coming or going during the night?"

"No, I was playing my games and then . . . wait." He frowned, as if suddenly remembering something. "I heard a truck returning around three a.m. It woke me up."

Zac could hear Rachel's breath catch in her throat. "Joe's truck?"

"Nah. That neighbor." Isaac nodded toward the trailer behind Zac. "His muffler sounds like a jet engine on steroids." He sent Zac a chastising glance as he turned to head toward his vehicle. "Someone should do something about it."

"Yeah, I'll be sure to mention it once I manage to track him down." Zac squashed the urge to demand the man return. He was obviously in the middle of his postal route. If he had more questions, he'd ask him to come down to the station.

Isaac drove away and Zac turned back to eye the trailer. Why would Curly be out until three a.m.? He made a mental note to check with the local bars to see if Curly had visited any of them. No other businesses would be open that late.

"Now what?" Rachel asked.

"Let's find out if Junior knows where his dad is," Zac abruptly decided, jogging toward his vehicle.

Rachel climbed in beside him. "Curly must have realized you were going to question him."

"I'm guessing Junior called." Zac shook his head in disgust as he drove out of the trailer park. "I should have known he would warn his father."

"He wouldn't have taken off if he was innocent," she murmured. "What's he hiding?"

"A good question that goes on the pile with a thousand other good questions," he said in wry tones. "At some point I'm going to need some good answers."

She sent him a sympathetic glance, sharing the frustration that bubbled through him. It was something she no doubt felt on a regular basis, he silently acknowledged. Trying to solve cold cases would be even worse than an ongoing murder investigation.

Her lips parted, but with a sudden frown she turned her head to glance out the passenger window. Zac instinctively took his foot off the gas as he realized they were passing the funeral home. Had she spotted something?

"Rachel?"

She pointed toward a form stepping out of the side door that led to the morgue. "Isn't that your deputy?"

Zac frowned as he caught sight of the short, pudgy man in a brown uniform. "That's Anthony. What the hell is he doing in the middle of my crime scene?"

Glancing over his shoulder, Anthony abruptly darted around the corner of the building, disappearing from view.

"That was weird," Rachel muttered.

Zac started to pull toward the curb, only to give a shake of his head and continue down the street. He'd allowed himself to put off interviewing Curly. And now the man had disappeared. He wasn't going to make the same mistake with his son.

"I'll talk to him later," he muttered, concentrating on the various businesses they rolled past. Reaching the corner, he abruptly turned into a narrow lot next to a white brick building with an attached garage. A large sign that was bolted to a tall pole read SYKES AUTOMOTIVE.

"This must be the shop where Curly said he worked."

Parking his truck away from the building to make sure he didn't get boxed in, Zac climbed out and waited for Rachel to join him. A second later, a middle-aged man walked out of the open bay of the garage. He was shorter than Zac and wearing coveralls with the name *Ray* stitched on a patch.

"Can I help you?" he asked, wiping his hands on a greasy rag.

"I need to speak to Curly Bolton," Zac said.

The man snorted. "Yeah, me too."

Zac stared at him in confusion. Had Curly lied when he claimed he was employed at the shop?

"He's not here?"

"Nope. He didn't show up to work today."

Zac breathed a small sigh of relief. At least he was in the right place. "Is he sick?"

"Don't know. He didn't call in." Ray didn't bother to disguise his displeasure with his employee. "Now I'm having to cover his ass."

"He said he lived above the shop."

"Yep." Ray pointed a hand toward the side of the building where a set of metal steps led to a second-floor door.

"Mind if I check on him?"

Ray shrugged. "Knock yourself out. I already pounded on his door when he didn't show up. He's either passed out or didn't bother to come home last night."

With a nod of thanks, Zac headed for the stairs, feeling the heat of Rachel's body as she followed closely behind him.

It felt good, he silently acknowledged. He hadn't had anyone watching his back in a long time. His mother leaned on him for support. His friends were great, but most had families of their own to worry about. And the town now depended on him to protect them.

He hadn't realized how alone he felt. Not until Rachel walked back into his life.

Reaching the top of the stairs, Zac paused to listen. He couldn't hear the sound of a television or voices from inside. His jaw tightened. He hoped Curly and his dad were hiding inside, but he was getting a bad, bad feeling.

Desperately hoping he was wrong, Zac lifted his hand and rapped his fingers against the door. He used more force than actually necessary, and with a loud creak, the door slowly swung inward.

Zac hastily stepped to the side, pushing Rachel out of the line of fire. She muttered her annoyance at his protective gesture, moving so she was standing next to him as they both peered into the shadowed apartment.

"Shit," Zac muttered. It didn't take any extraordinary investigative skills to see the place had been cleaned out. There was only one room that doubled as a living room/bedroom and a small kitchenette. There was one door that Zac assumed led to the bathroom, but it was open to reveal no one was hiding in the cramped space. A sagging couch and matching chair were left behind, along with a pile of empty takeout boxes, but nothing else. Zac stepped back, cursing his streak of bad luck. "I need to head back to the office. I want the Boltons found. Today."

He took the stairs two at a time and jogged toward his truck. He didn't worry about Rachel keeping up; she could run circles around most men. Together they climbed into the vehicle and he took off out of the lot at a speed that made Rachel grab her seat belt and hurriedly pull it across her body.

"Do you mind swinging by the motel?" she asked. "I need to pick up my computer."

Zac nodded, turning onto the road that would take them toward the center of town. The motel was on the way to the office and in a few minutes he was pulling to a halt in front of her room. She frowned as he shut off the engine and climbed out of the truck.

"You can wait here. It will only take me a second."

He ignored her words, stubbornly following her as she unlocked the door and stepped into the small room.

"Ouch," he muttered as he took in the psychedelic décor. It wasn't just the cheap furniture or splotches of velvet green and orange that passed as wallpaper. It was the shag carpeting that smelled of stale cigarettes and the Styrofoam beams that were stapled to the ceiling.

"No crap." Rachel grabbed her laptop, which had been

left on the end of the narrow bed. "I feel like I'm surrounded in an acid dream."

"More like a nightmare," he muttered with a shudder.

She shrugged. "It's a place to sleep."

"I have one." The words escaped before he could halt them.

"Excuse me?"

Now that he'd made the offer, Zac realized that he didn't want to take it back. "I have a place to sleep. At the farm."

"Okay," she said, clearly confused.

No surprise. He was babbling like an idiot. Giving himself a mental shake, Zac squared his shoulders and met her wary gaze. "I mean, I have an extra bed that no one's using," he clarified.

"Oh." She suddenly looked flustered. "I don't think that would be a good idea."

Zac hid his smile. He liked watching the heat stain her cheeks. It reminded him of the days when they were young and just beginning to flirt with each other. She tried to act so brash and confident, but whenever he glanced in her direction she would blush.

"Why not?" he pressed. "We're working the same case. We'll be spending time together."

"All the more reason not to stay in the same place," she insisted. "We both need our privacy at the end of the day."

"You can have that." He kept his tone deliberately casual, as if it was no big deal if she decided to come or not. The one thing he knew about Rachel was that she hated being pressured. It was the one certain way to drive her away. "The guest room has a private bathroom attached and a separate door so you can come and go whenever you want."

"Zac—"

"Look," he interrupted. "This isn't about your groovy motel room." He glanced around with a grimace. "At least, not entirely. We have a shit-ton of work to do and if you stay at the farm it will give us the opportunity to do some of it in the comfort of the kitchen and not be stuck in the office for endless hours."

He watched the tension in her shoulders slowly ease, her eyes narrowing as she eyed him. "Wait. Are you looking for someone to cook for you?"

His lips twitched at her teasing. "I promise to do the dishes."

She hesitated. "I don't know."

"Just think about it."

Zac turned to head toward the door, his heart beating too fast in his chest. He knew he would be doing nothing but thinking about having Rachel in his home . . . in his bed.

Day drinkers were the worst, Tory Devlin decided. It wasn't a moral decision. It was an economic one.

The afternoon customers ordered the cheapest beer on tap and never bothered to leave a tip. And worse, she had to drive five miles outside Pike to get to this shabby bar called the Roadhouse. It wasn't that far, but gas wasn't cheap and she was trying to save every penny to move out of her parents' basement.

Washing glasses at the end of the bar, Tory cast a jaundiced glance around the bar. It wasn't much more than an old cabin built with split timbers and a cement pad for a floor. The majority of the space was consumed by the bar, which took up one side of the public room. Currently there were four men seated on the high stools, retelling the same stories they told every day.

Tory had no idea how long the men had been coming to the Roadhouse. She'd only worked there since her rat's ass of a husband had taken off with her best friend, Connie. But she suspected they were as much a fixture as the flickering neon lights, dusty dartboard that hung at a wonky angle, and the small platform in a corner that was used when they hired a band to play.

There were three tables pushed against the far wall. They were no doubt occupied at night, but during the day the chairs were stacked on top of them. It added to the sense of emptiness.

Finished washing the handful of glasses, Tory wiped her hands on a towel and glanced toward the men who were nursing their beers. It would be at least half an hour before they ordered another round. They were nothing if not predictable.

"I'll be right back. I'm taking out the trash," she called in a loud voice.

Not for the men who were laughing and punching one another on the shoulder. They'd reached the happy drunken phase and wouldn't notice if she stripped naked and danced on the bar. She was covering her absence for the hidden camera her boss used to spy on his employees. She'd spotted the surveillance equipment within an hour of her first shift. She'd installed a similar device to spy on her husband when she was visiting her parents. That was how she'd caught him banging her supposed friend. She'd stupidly confronted the bastard. She'd demanded he choose. It was either her or Connie.

He chose Connie.

Muttering a curse, Tory headed into the storage room and pulled on her puffy coat. Then, ignoring the trash that overflowed the can, she stepped out the back door.

This was the one certain place she was out of view of her prying boss, along with any customers who might pull into the lot. There was nothing but trees as far as the eye could see.

She shivered as the brisk breeze whipped around the corner of the building. It was nearly four o'clock and the temperature was rapidly dropping. Pulling out a cigarette from the pocket of her coat, Tory turned her back to the wind and cupped her hands around her mouth. It took several tries to get the cigarette lit, but finally drawing in a deep drag she held the smoke in her lungs. She'd given up the habit when she'd gotten married. Now she took bitter pleasure in savoring the hit of nicotine that raced through her body.

Better than a douchebag husband any day of the week.

Releasing her breath, she blew out the smoke and stamped her feet. Her toes were already starting to freeze. Damned cheap sneakers.

Once she got a better job, she intended to buy a whole new wardrobe. It would include the sort of clothes that would help her attract the attention of a new husband. One who would treat her with respect, kindness, and loyalty.

One who knew how to keep his cock out of her best friend . . .

She took another deep drag, her thoughts too consumed with her burning anger to notice the soft tread of footsteps.

Not that she would have been alarmed if she had heard them.

She was standing in the middle of nowhere. A place where nothing happened. Not good or bad. Just the same boring routine day after day.

That was when the blow struck the back of Tory's head and she fell face-first into the mud.

Chapter 10

Later that evening, Rachel sat at the table in Zac's kitchen, skimming through the stack of files in front of her. It wasn't easy to concentrate. Usually she spent her evenings alone, catching up on paperwork or at the gym burning off her stress. Having Zac sitting just a couple feet away as he studied his own files felt . . .

Actually, she wasn't sure how she felt. Bemused? Yes, that was the word. She wasn't sure exactly why she'd abruptly agreed to move from the motel to this farmhouse. When she'd made the decision it was easy to accept that it was only logical. After all, she and Zac would be working late into the night together. Why not take advantage of the convenience of being under the same roof? Besides, the motel really was disgusting.

It wasn't until they were moving around the kitchen that she wondered if she was fooling herself. There was a familiar comfort as he chopped veggies and washed up dishes while she cooked a pot of chili and fresh cornbread. Like a favorite dance she'd learned years ago and never forgotten.

Was she stirring up emotions that she'd struggled to

bury when Zac had left her? *No.* She sternly shoved away the niggling fear. Long before she'd become Zac's lover, they'd been friends. There was no reason they couldn't return to that earlier relationship.

Right?

Ignoring the strange shiver that raced through her body, Rachel glanced up from the files.

Zac was bent forward, his blond hair messy from running his fingers through the short strands, and a hint of a golden stubble darkening the line of his jaw. He'd changed out of his sheriff uniform and was wearing a thermal shirt that outlined his broad shoulders and the width of his muscular chest, and a pair of faded jeans. It seemed impossible, but he'd managed to become more handsome as he aged, she ruefully acknowledged.

So why hadn't he remarried? The question barely had time to form before she was squashing it like a nasty bug. She wasn't going there. No way.

"I wish I had Rudolf Jansen on my staff," she abruptly said, as much to distract her treacherous thoughts as to break the silence. "He had a good eye for small details that most people overlook."

Zac glanced up with a wry smile. "And a suspicious mind."

Rachel nodded in agreement. The stacks of files proved that Rudolf Jansen possessed a grounded view of his fellow man. Some might even call it jaded. He clearly believed that anyone was capable of very bad things.

"That's essential for a good lawman," she admitted.

"A good lawman like you."

She blinked at the unexpected compliment. "I try."

"No false modesty," he insisted. "You were always

destined to be a great cop. I envied you the talent to have such single-minded focus on your career."

She arched a brow. During the last days of their marriage, Zac had accused her of caring more about her career than him. And he hadn't been entirely wrong. She'd used her new job to escape dealing with their crumbling relationship.

"Envied or resented?" she asked in a soft voice.

He grimaced. "Both, if I'm being honest. I wasn't so confident in what I wanted for my future. It made me feel as if I was failing both of us."

She planted her elbow on the table and cupped her chin in her hand. "You've obviously decided you don't want to be a farmer."

"I never wanted to be a farmer. I came back to Pike to help my dad."

"But you stayed."

"My mother depended on me."

She struggled not to react to his words. Joyce Evans had always been nice to Rachel, and had even welcomed her into the family, but there was no doubt that she resented having to share her son. Rachel had always assumed it was a symptom of Zac's being an only child.

"Yes," she murmured.

His lips twitched, as if sensing her reaction to the mention of his mother. "It was also a convenient excuse."

"Excuse for what?"

"Making a mess of our marriage." His jaw tightened, as if he was fighting a sudden emotion. "It was easier to pretend that I had no choice but to come home instead of staying and fighting for us." He held her gaze. "Fighting for you."

Her heart dipped, suddenly feeling too heavy. As if a soul-deep yearning was weighing it down. Shaking her head, Rachel dismissed the unwanted sensation.

"We were young. Too young. We both made a mess of it," she said, directing the conversation away from the past. "Why do you stay?"

He shrugged. "It's home."

It was the answer Rachel had been expecting. While she'd been eager to escape from Pike, Zac had never fully committed to moving away.

"Do you enjoy being the sheriff?"

"I do. More than I ever expected." His tone revealed his surprise at his pleasure in the job. "It reminds me why I wanted to get my degree in criminal justice when we went to college." He glanced down at the files spread open in front of him. "Of course I didn't expect to be tracking a potential serial killer in Pike."

She sent him a sympathetic smile. "Trial by fire, eh?"

He reached across the table, brushing his fingers down the line of her jaw before leaning back. "I'm glad I'm not doing this alone."

Her heart jumped, no longer feeling heavy. Just the opposite. It was fluttering like she was sixteen again. She awkwardly brushed back her hair, which was still damp from the shower she'd taken before changing into a casual sweatshirt and jeans.

"You were never going to be alone," she reminded him. "You have your deputies."

"Right." Zac rolled his eyes. "My top deputy left his phone at the crime scene. That's how much help he's been."

It took a second for Rachel to figure out what he was

talking about. "Oh, is that why we saw him leaving the funeral parlor?" Zac nodded, his expression one of disgust. "Okay, you might have to consider demoting him to a desk job, but Lindsay has potential," she offered.

"True," he conceded. "And Greg isn't bad, but this is just a job he's doing until he can find something that pays better."

"That shouldn't be hard."

"No shit."

They exchanged a wry glance, both painfully aware of the skimpy salary of most law officials. His lips parted, but before he could speak the phone he'd set on the table started to vibrate.

"Damn." Scooping up the phone, he glanced at the screen. "It's Anthony." Pressing the phone to his ear, he rose to his feet. "What's up?" He paced across the floor of the kitchen as he listened to his deputy, his brows drawing together in a way that warned Rachel he didn't like what he was hearing. "I'll be right there. You start tracking down her family and friends to see if anyone has heard from her."

Rachel pushed herself out of the chair, a sinking feeling in the pit of her stomach as Zac shoved the phone into his front pocket.

"What's happening?" she demanded.

"A missing woman."

Rachel felt a small stab of relief. Missing. Not dead. It was possible this wasn't related to the killer. Or if it was, they might have a small window of time to find her before it was too late.

"I'll get my coat."

She hustled through the house and into the guest room.

She hadn't unpacked yet, but all she needed was her coat and the weapon she'd locked in the gun case she always took with her. Better safe than sorry.

Wrapped in protection, she joined Zac as he headed out the back door and climbed into his truck. She waited until they'd navigated the muddy road leading to the farm and at last reached the blacktop.

"Where are we headed?" she asked.

"The Roadhouse." The words were clipped, revealing Zac's tension. He didn't believe that the woman was simply missing.

Rachel searched her memory, at last dredging up the image of an old log house outside town. It should have been condemned when she was still in high school. She couldn't imagine what it was like now. "That place is still open?"

"Yep." He wrinkled his nose, gunning the engine as they drove through the empty darkness. "And still a dive."

"Who's missing?"

"Tory Devlin, the bartender."

"Do you have any intel on why they think she's missing?"

"According to Anthony, she arrived for her shift as a bartender at noon and four hours later she stepped out the back door and disappeared."

"If I worked as a bartender at the Roadhouse I would walk out the back door too," Rachel murmured. She wasn't trying to diminish the seriousness of Tory's disappearance, but she'd been in law enforcement long enough to know that people walked away from their lives all the time. Some to escape violence. Some to be with lovers. Some to simply start over.

"Yeah, but she left behind her phone, her purse, and her car."

Ah. That changed everything.

"Okay. Her car might be explained if she ran off with the boyfriend, but not her phone and purse," she admitted, reaching into her satchel to pull out her own phone. Touching the screen, she quickly pulled up the various social media pages. "I found her Facebook page. Tory Devlin, animal lover and eternal optimist. She's twenty-seven years old, a part-time bartender and recently divorced." She scrolled down, sucking in a breath at the various memes that all had various ways of punishing a cheating spouse. Some of them remarkably graphic. "And very bitter about it."

"Did she have dark hair?"

Rachel studied the profile pic. It revealed a young woman who was thin to the point of being gaunt, with large brown eyes heavily outlined with makeup and pouting lips. Rachel didn't know if she was trying to look sexy or angry. Maybe both.

"She's blond in her picture, but who knows if it's natural. It looks bleached."

"She's about the right age," Zac murmured, turning the truck off the main road and bumping down a rough path. "And publicly feuding with her ex. Similar to Staci and Paige."

Rachel dropped the phone back in her satchel, a bad feeling in the pit of her belly.

Zac pulled into the narrow parking lot in front of the long, one-story building with a covered front porch that was lined with empty kegs. Light spilled from the large window, but they were far enough away from town to surround the place in a thick darkness. As he opened the door of his truck, the muffled sound of a karaoke machine spilled through the air.

"You're right." Rachel moved to walk beside him, shaking her head as she skimmed her gaze over the sketchy establishment with the sagging tin roof and faded logs. "This place hasn't changed."

Any other time, Zac might have reminded Rachel of the night they'd tried to sneak in and order a beer only to be caught before they got through the door by Rudolf Jansen, who'd been there to break up a barroom brawl. Tonight, he was too on edge to think of anything but the grim fear that another woman was dead. A woman it was his duty to protect.

Pushing open the door, he grimaced at the stale scent of beer that saturated the air. There was also the smell of cigarettes despite the ban on smoking. Something he'd deal with later. For now, he glanced around the sparse crowd that were huddled at the end of the room where a middle-aged man was singing Hank Williams in a drunken slur.

"Zac."

Zac turned at the sound of his name being called out, watching a man hurry from behind the bar to stand in front of him. He was shorter than Zac with the beginnings of a potbelly. His hair was brown and he kept it brushed back, emphasizing his chubby cheeks. His eyes were dark and held an unmistakable wariness.

Zac frowned, struggling to put a name to the vaguely

familiar face. At last, he recalled the younger boy who'd been on the same school bus.

"Hey, Hugh." Zac's gaze moved down the man's uniform that had the local electric company logo on the pocket. "What are you doing here?"

"My uncle owns this place," Hugh explained. "He . . . um . . . had a few things to take care of, so he asked me to come down here and wait for you."

Zac had forgotten that Hugh was related to Vann Ellison, the owner of the Roadhouse. He resisted the urge to roll his eyes. Vann was notorious for flaunting local laws, including serving to minors and paying his employees off the books. It was no wonder he made himself scarce. He'd been dodging authority figures for fifty years.

Zac didn't care. He wasn't interested in petty crimes. At least not tonight. Later he'd return and have a long talk with Vann. "Can you tell me what happened?"

Hugh stepped closer, turning his back to the gathered customers as if he was afraid of being overheard.

"The bartender, Tory Devlin, showed up for her shift, but at four o'clock she took out the trash and disappeared."

Zac pulled out his pad and pencil, jotting down notes. Beside him, Rachel was turning in a slow circle, as if inspecting every inch of the seedy bar. No doubt she was determining how easy it would be to enter and leave without attracting attention, along with judging how a lurker could watch the people inside the bar from a hidden location in the nearby woods. Those were the top two questions if Tory had been snatched by a killer.

Zac concentrated on getting as much information about Tory as possible. "Who was working with her?"

"Tory was the only employee," Hugh said, looking uncomfortable at Zac's startled glance. "The day shift is usually pretty slow. There were four of our regular customers here when she disappeared. I wrote down their names." He reached into his pocket to pull out a folded piece of paper. "I don't have the addresses, but they're all local."

"Thanks." Zac tucked away the names to study later. "If there were no other employees here at the time, how do you know Tory took out the trash at four?"

"Video." Hugh pointed toward the small camera attached to one of the open rafters. It was aimed directly at the bar area. "You can watch it if you want."

"I'll check out the car," Rachel said in decisive tones. "Which one is Tory's?"

"The white two-door," Hugh answered.

With a nod, Rachel turned to head out of the bar. Zac watched her leave, grabbing the opportunity to appreciate the sight of her slender form before it disappeared from view.

"Are you two back together?" Hugh asked, interrupting Zac's brief moment of distraction.

With a shake of his head, Zac turned back to his companion. "Where can I watch the video?"

Hugh cleared his throat, getting the message that Zac wasn't there to discuss his private life. "This way."

Together they rounded the end of the bar and stepped through a narrow door into the attached storage room. The first thing that Zac noticed was the trash that overflowed from a can near the back door. Unless the bar produced a vast amount of garbage, Tory hadn't taken it out. Why not? Had someone been hiding in here?

Hugh moved to the steel shelves that lined the walls.

They were loaded with old boxes and dusty glasses. As if no one had bothered to clean out the place in years. There was one shelf, however, with an open laptop that was currently displaying the public area of the bar.

Leaning forward, Hugh pressed a finger against the keyboard, rewinding the video.

"I watched this earlier," he muttered. "There's nothing to see until here."

The video went from a fuzzy blur to reveal the bar area. This time, however, there were four men seated on high stools, leaning together as if they'd developed a system of keeping themselves from tipping over. There was also a young, blond-haired woman who had her head tilted back to stare at the ceiling.

"I'll be right back. I'm taking out the trash," she called out before turning to disappear into the storage room.

"She's talking directly into the camera," Zac said, glancing toward Hugh. "Does someone monitor it?"

The younger man grimaced. "My uncle is convinced his employees are taking money from the till so he keeps a watch on things from his house. When Tory didn't come back from taking out the trash, he drove down here to check things out." Hugh hit another key, fast-forwarding the video. He stopped when a large man smoking a cigar entered the bar. "Tory was nowhere to be found."

Zac turned away from the shelves. He'd do a more thorough investigation of the video later. "Did she go out through here?" he asked, pulling open the door and stepping out the back of the bar.

"I assume so." Hugh joined him, shivering as a gust of wind whipped around the corner of the building. "There's just two exits. This one and the front door."

Zac glanced around. There was a small clearing with a dumpster and more empty kegs. The trees were close enough to cut off any light, shrouding them in a thick darkness. It was impossible to see anything tonight.

"Try to keep anyone from coming out here," he told Hugh, stepping back into the storage room. "I'll send one of the deputies in the morning to look for any sign of a struggle."

"You got it." Hugh closed the door and turned the lock.

"I don't suppose the customers noticed anything?" Zac asked.

"They claim they didn't. No one came into the bar and they didn't hear Tory call for help." Hugh grimaced. "Of course, I'm not sure how reliable they would be as witnesses."

Zac silently agreed. Regulars who started at noon were hardened drinkers who wouldn't have any interest in anything but keeping their buzz.

"How long has Tory worked here?"

"Around a year, but I've known her forever." Hugh shrugged as Zac arched a brow. "She was a friend of my younger sister before Angie left for college."

Zac tucked away the knowledge. Hugh seemed like a decent guy, but so did a lot of criminals. It was possible he'd had his eyes on Tory for years. Maybe he'd even tried his luck, only to have her shut him down. He would certainly know when she was working, the best time to snatch her, and exactly where to hide.

"I understand she's divorced?" He returned his attention to Hugh.

"She was married to Matt Porter. A year ago he took off to Des Moines with her friend, Connie Watson."

Zac added the husband to his list of suspects. Des Moines would be a drive, but if Matt was originally from Pike, he might be back visiting family.

"Any new boyfriends?" he asked.

"Not that I've heard, but I don't really pay attention to gossip," Hugh told him.

Zac didn't press. Anthony could tell him. His one talent as a deputy was knowing everyone in town and all their dirty secrets.

"Where was her phone?" he demanded.

Hugh headed out of the storage area. "Under the bar, along with her purse."

Zac pulled out a pair of gloves before he reached for the phone that was lying next to a red leather purse. Glancing at the screen, he wasn't surprised to discover it was locked. He would check with Tory's parents to see if they had the passcode.

His own phone buzzed and he pulled it out to see a text from Anthony.

Tory's parents haven't seen or heard from her. Worried. They gave me a list of friends. Returning to office to start the calls.

Zac slid the phone into his pocket, glancing toward Hugh, who was studying him with a worried gaze.

"You don't think she just took off, do you?"

Before he could answer, the front door swung open to reveal Rachel. She motioned for him, a grim expression tightening her features. Zac swiftly moved to join her. "What's up?"

"There's something you need to see."

Zac nodded, following her out of the bar and across the graveled lot to the compact car wisely parked well away from the customers. Noticing the open door on the passenger side, Zac leaned into the car. The interior light was on, revealing that it was littered with fast-food wrappers, empty cigarette packs, and dirty clothes wadded on the floorboard. His attention was captured by a padded envelope with his name scrawled on the front lying on the car seat, along with a note scribbled on a torn piece of paper.

Let's add some spice to the game. I'll give you 24 hours to find us. Tick tock.

Chapter 11

It was well past midnight, but ignoring his weariness, Zac stood in front of the television in his parents' bedroom. His deputies were continuing to look for Tory after they finished investigating her abandoned car while Zac had taken the envelope and note to the office. He would have them sent to the lab in Madison. They had superior techniques in searching for any fingerprints or DNA left behind. But he'd kept the VHS tape he'd found inside the envelope.

There was a chance there might be something in the video that would help him locate the missing Tory.

Grabbing the remote control, he glanced toward Rachel, who was standing next to him, a notepad and pencil in her hand. "Ready?"

"As ready as I can be."

"No crap," he muttered. "Okay, here we go."

The television screen glowed as he punched the play button, a blurry image slowly coming into focus. Zac frowned. He'd expected to see the morgue again. Didn't serial killers have patterns they felt compelled to replicate?

Instead he could make out dirt walls and a low,

open-beamed ceiling. A cellar? The video wobbled as if the camera was being moved into position, then it was slowly tilted down.

Zac clenched his teeth as a young female came into view. She looked like a broken mannequin that had been tossed into a forgotten corner. Her naked body was slumped against the wall and her head flopped forward as if it was too heavy for her slender neck. She had a cloud of permed hair that formed a bouncy halo that cascaded to her shoulders.

"A blonde, not a brunette this time," Rachel murmured, making a note on her pad. "Like Tory."

He nodded, the breath squeezed from his lungs as the woman lifted her head to reveal her pale face. Even with the blindfold over her eyes she looked tragically young. And scared. Her lips were parted as if she was struggling to breathe and her cheeks were damp with tears.

"Jude, is that you?" she called out, visibly trembling as a man with short brown hair stepped into view.

"Who else would it be, sweet Maureen?"

Jude Henley. He looked exactly the same as he did in the first video, except he was wearing black jeans and a tailored jacket with the sleeves pushed up to his elbows. There was also a shadow of whiskers on his jaw. He was obviously going for the whole *Miami Vice* vibe. He even glanced toward the camera to flash a smile of smug satisfaction.

Zac and Rachel shared a look of mutual disgust before she lowered her head to scribble on her pad. "Maureen."

Zac turned back to the television. The woman had pulled her legs up tight to her chest, as if to protect herself from the man who slowly squatted down to remove the blindfold.

"Where am I?" She frowned, warily taking in her surroundings. "This isn't your house."

"No. I never take care of my business at home." He chuckled. "It's too messy. I put a little something extra in your glass of wine so I could bring you to my private hideaway."

"I don't understand what's happening."

"Neither do I, not entirely," Jude murmured, reaching out to grab her hair. With a sharp jerk, he angled her head to an awkward position. "I just know when I look at you I want to beat you until you scream for mercy. Until I'm covered in your blood."

"Beat me? Is this a joke?"

"I find it amusing." He sneered down at her. "I doubt if you will. Not by the time I'm done."

"But . . . you just made love to me." The woman released a loud sob. "You said you cared."

"I say that a lot," Jude taunted. "I never, ever mean it."

"Please," she pleaded.

He gave her head another painful jerk. "Please what?"

"Let me go."

"We've just started."

Jude released his grip on her hair with a dismissive gesture, disappearing from view. There was the faint scrape of footsteps on cement that melded in with Maureen's gasping sobs, then Jude returned, holding a crowbar.

Lifting her hands, Maureen curled into the corner, trying to make herself as small as possible. "Stop." Her voice was shrill. "My husband will kill you."

Jude twirled the crowbar, his manner arrogant as he

strolled forward. Was he showing off for the camera? The thought made Zac's hands clench, longing to smack the smug expression off his face.

"Thankfully, he'll never know it was me," Jude assured the woman. "You're about to have a terrible accident, but first . . . we play."

Offering a taunting smile he gave the crowbar another twirl, then with a shocking force, he slammed the iron bar against her ribs. Maureen parted her lips to release a pained howl. Jude laughed, his eyes closing as if he was savoring her screams. He lifted the crowbar again, swinging it with his full strength, once again aiming at her side. Did he enjoy hearing the crack of her ribs? Or was he ensuring she was incapacitated so she wouldn't fight back?

In tense silence, Zac and Rachel watched the brutal assault, sharing a sense of helpless fury. Jude wasn't just violent, he was methodical. This wasn't a frenzied attack, it was a deliberate battering to maximize pain and prolong the torture.

Zac struggled to contain his anger. They were too late to help poor Maureen, he sternly reminded himself. But if they did their jobs, there was the possibility they could rescue Tory.

After what felt like an eternity, Jude turned toward the camera, his handsome face splattered with blood from the dead woman who lay at his feet. He posed, making sure he was in direct view of the camera before sauntering across the floor. A second later, the television went black.

The end of the tape.

Moving on autopilot, Zac reached to rewind the tape and play it again. He didn't want to see it. His thoughts were already consumed with the savage cruelty he'd just witnessed. It was inhumane. Monstrous. But right now, it was the only clue they had.

"They were obviously lovers, but he films the beating, not the sex," Rachel muttered, thankfully distracting him from the dark images replaying on the screen.

"You think that significant?" he asked.

She continued to make notes. "It shows that the woman's death was the part that he wanted to preserve. The sex was meaningless. It was the killing that turned him on."

"The preliminary medical examiner's report suggested that Paige was raped," he murmured, wondering if the copycat killer enjoyed including sex in the violence, or simply didn't want to waste the time to form a relationship with his victims.

She nodded. "I'm guessing that in both cases it was the pain and suffering they enjoyed."

"And the death," he added.

"Especially the death."

Grimly he forced his attention back to the tape, looking for anything that could help in their search for Tory.

"This looks a lot like the previous tape."

"Different location," she pointed out. "But Jude appears to be roughly the same age."

Zac reached out to touch his finger against the screen. "He's wearing the same watch, or at least a similar one."

She sucked in a breath. "Good catch. We should be able to date the year that particular watch was most popular."

He searched for any other similarities and differences. His finger moved as Jude turned his head. "No earring. In the first video he had a diamond stud."

"So this was before Staci's murder, or he took out his earring and allowed the piercing to close over."

Zac nodded, watching in silence as Jude indulged in his orgy of violence. At last the tape ended. At the same moment, he was distracted by a niggling memory.

"Maureen. That name seems familiar."

Rachel lowered her notepad, turning to face him. "Did you know her?"

"I don't think so." He shook his head. Her face hadn't looked familiar. At least not in the sense he had met her in the past. Then, he abruptly realized why the name was nagging at him. "The files."

"Files?"

Pressing the eject button, Zac carefully placed the VHS in an evidence bag before leading Rachel out of the bedroom and down the stairs to the kitchen. The stacks of folders they'd been studying earlier were still spread across the table.

Zac moved to shuffle through the papers. "There was one about a woman from Grange. I'm sure her name was Maureen."

"Why would Rudolf be interested in a woman from Grange?" Rachel moved to stand beside him.

"Because her car was found smashed into a tree just outside town." Zac at last located the file, quickly skimming through the police report that Rudolf had copied and shoved into the folder along with his own suspicions. "Her death was ruled a vehicular accident. It'd been raining the night before and it looked as if she'd lost traction and swerved off the road, but Rudolf wasn't convinced all of her injuries came from the wreck."

Rachel leaned against the edge of the table, her lips

pursed as she considered his words. "He thought she'd been beaten?" she guessed.

"Yes."

"But the coroner didn't agree?"

Zac flicked through the pages until he found the one he wanted. "Actually, the coroner noted that the wounds weren't consistent with a car crash."

Rachel frowned. "So why wasn't the accident investigated?"

Zac was as confused as Rachel. At the very least there should have been an autopsy. It wasn't until he read through Rudolf's notes that he realized that the lack of interest in her death had been caused by blatant politics.

"Her husband had been arrested twice for domestic violence," he told Rachel.

Her jaw tightened, her eyes darkening with anger. Rachel firmly believed that there was nothing more cowardly than a man who abused others. "All the more reason to investigate."

"True." Zac agreed with Rachel. Abusive men were the scum of the earth. And Maureen's husband was grade-A scum. "Amos Godwin was a prominent businessman who sued and won a lawsuit for harassment against the Grange Police Department. The prosecutor wasn't going to take risks without overwhelming evidence. Especially not back in those days."

"When did the car accident happen?"

"1986."

"Eight years before Staci."

Rachel's face paled as they both considered the implication of the date. It was impossible to believe that there hadn't been other murders in the time span. Probably several murders.

"Yes." With a grimace he glanced back down at the report, making a sound of surprise when he reached the bottom of the page. "Amos Godwin died a few weeks later."

"Really?" She leaned toward him. "What happened?"

"He was coming home from work and drove off a bridge into a river."

"A car crash, just like his wife."

Zac nodded. "And just like his wife, it was ruled accidental."

Rachel tapped her finger against the wooden table, energy humming around her despite the late hour. She'd always been like that. As if she possessed so much life it refused to be contained.

"I suppose it could have been a deer darting into the road," she murmured, perhaps trying to remind herself it would be dangerous to jump to conclusions. "Or suicide, if he blamed himself for his wife's death."

"Or Jude," Zac said, putting into words what they both suspected as he pulled out the enlarged photo of a woman with curly blond hair and turned it for Rachel to see.

Her breath hissed between her lips. "That's her."

Zac replaced the picture in the folder, his mind racing. "Let's assume that Jude somehow met and seduced Maureen. Or maybe she seduced him. Either way, they were enjoying a secret affair until Jude's madness overcame him and he beat her to death."

Rachel nodded, her brow furrowed. "But why kill the husband? Assuming Jude was actually responsible."

"Enjoyment?" Zac suggested. "He obviously savors the

power of taking the lives of others. Or maybe he was afraid Amos might have some sort of evidence. Maureen might have left something behind in her possessions that would have implicated Jude as her current lover."

He glanced down at the photo of Maureen. In the picture she was smiling, but her eyes were already shadowed, as if she'd sensed the darkness in her future. Or maybe it was the visible wounds caused by her abusive husband. Whatever the cause, it ignited a fierce determination to track down the monster who was currently stalking his town. Maureen was dead, her suffering at an end. Tory's was just beginning. "Right now I'm more worried about the note left in Tory's car," he said in bleak tones. The note was bagged and ready to go to the CSI lab in Madison, but the words were burned into his brain.

"Me too," Rachel swiftly agreed. "What does it mean that he was adding spice to the game? It feels like a challenge."

"And why did the killer change his routine?" Zac asked. "Or was this always intended to be a part of the sick game?"

She grimaced. "A good question."

"Another question," Zac continued, his mind racing with horrifying possibilities. "The note mentioned something about twenty-four hours to find them. Do we have twenty-four hours to save Tory? Or is she already dead and there will be another woman taken in twenty-four hours?"

Rachel held out her hand. "May I?"

"Of course." Zac handed her the folder without hesitation. She was the expert in cold cases. "Do you think there might be something in there that might help us?"

"Paige's murder was a fairly close duplication of Staci's death," she murmured. "Unless he changed his method completely we need to look at the past to solve the current case."

Zac struggled to contain his burst of frustration. He didn't want to look through files or dig into the past. He wanted to be out searching for the missing woman.

If only he knew where the hell to look.

"It's not like we have anything else to go on," he said, more to himself than his companion.

Rachel's expression was sympathetic. "Your deputy hasn't checked in?"

"Just to say her parents and friends haven't seen or heard from her. Neither has her ex-husband." He pulled his phone out of his pocket. No missed messages. "Anthony's probably in bed by now."

Rachel started to skim through the file. "It says here that Maureen was last seen by her husband at home in Grange at nine o'clock on the morning before her car was discovered smashed into the tree. She had a hair appointment at ten and met a friend for lunch. No one saw her or spoke to her after two o'clock."

"There's no explanation why she'd been driving through Pike?" Zac asked.

"No, she was found in her wrecked car the next morning on the old Lake Road."

Zac stiffened. There was something about what she just said that nudged at his mind. Like an insight knocking to get in.

"Ah," he breathed, lifting his phone to touch the map app.

"What is it?"

Zac zoomed in on the map. Pike had been built along an old railroad. Just outside of town was a man-made lake that had been used for the steam engines. The railroad company had eventually donated the lake to the town and it was still used by locals during the summer for fishing and swimming. Twenty years ago, they'd added a new campground and access road. "This is the old Lake Road." He dragged his finger along the trail that was nothing more than a dirt pathway. He zoomed out the map to point to a spot just a few miles north. "And here's the Road-house."

Rachel sucked in a sharp breath as she easily realized what he was implying. "Maureen could have gone to the Roadhouse to meet Jude."

"Exactly."

She furrowed her brow. "They met at the bar, and then Maureen went with Jude to have sex. The next morning her car was found smashed into a tree a couple miles away. If the killer follows the same pattern, then Tory is going to end up around Lake Road."

"Exactly." Zac shoved his phone into his pocket and grabbed the jacket draped over the back of a chair. "You wanna take a ride?"

Rachel tossed the file onto the table. "Let's go."

Chapter 12

The cellar isn't perfect. It's too large and someone has poured cement on the floor. But beggars can't be choosers, and since the original location collapsed years ago, I was forced to compromise. Annoying, but I suspected from the beginning this was bound to be a disappointing kill.

First off, the woman will never fulfill my fantasies. Not that it kept me from spending hours between her legs. Unlike Jude, I don't have any interest in wasting my time with seducing the bitches. I would take what I wanted, when I wanted and how I wanted. Any idiot with a halfway decent face and enough money to buy a few beers could get a woman in his bed. It took skill to snatch a woman from her place of employment with no one catching a glimpse of the crime.

Only a true artist could achieve such perfection.

Descending the narrow steps as the sun peeked over the horizon, I reach the wooden door. A muffled voice calls out as I remove the padlock.

"Help! Someone help me!"

Pushing open the door, I flick on the overhead light and stare down at my creation. She's huddled in a corner, her eyes covered by a blindfold. I grimace. Even at a distance she is looking wilted around the edges. Her naked body is streaked with the dust from the dirt walls and her hair is tangled from where I grasped it to drag her from the vehicle to this cellar. Plus, the duct tape I'd used to bind her wrists and ankles makes her look like a doll that had been broken and badly repaired.

Perhaps sensing my disdainful gaze, she presses her back against the dirt wall, her knees drawn up to try and cover her naked body.

"You piece of shit," she spits out. "When I get out of here. I'm going to kill you."

"Doubtful," I say in dry tones, wishing I'd put the duct tape across her mouth. She was a shrill, annoying creature. If I hadn't chosen to put an end to her, someone else would have. "Not only am I very hard to kill, but you are never getting out of here. At least, not alive."

Her bluster faded at my stark words. "Who are you?"

"Hmm." A good question. I move to position my phone on a wooden shelf filled with dusty mason jars. Once I had been an apprentice, but I'd gone beyond that role. "If you insist on a name, you can call me Maestro," I inform my companion. "The former master is gone. My time has arrived. Finally."

I smile as I hit the camera icon and start the video. Jude had one thing right. Filming each performance will allow me to perfect my craft. And I can't deny a pleasure in watching them over and over. Why not? It's sheer art.

"Okay, Maestro . . . whatever." She tilted her head back, as if attempting to see beneath the blindfold. "Just let me go. I swear I won't tell anyone what you did to me. I just want to forget this ever happened."

"Forget? You're going to hurt my feelings," I taunt, grabbing the crowbar I've left on the shelf. "I intend to remember this night forever."

The woman trembles, as if sensing death approaching. I'm suddenly dazzled by the thought.

Am I death?

No. I shake my head. I create. Pain. Terror. Nightmares. They are the tools I use to produce my masterpiece. This female is my stage. And death . . . it's the finale. The closing of a curtain at the end of a performance.

"Please, please let me go," she rasps, reminding me that the clock is ticking.

Tick. Tock.

I stroll forward, twirling the crowbar for the camera. Just as Jude loved to do.

"Surely you're not that stupid?" I demand. "We've just started to have fun."

"No, I can't bear any more," she pleaded.

"Don't worry. It won't last that long. I have a deadline to keep." I grimace, regretting the note that I left. I hoped it would add a layer of excitement. There'd been a thrill in killing Paige. She was my first, after all. But it hadn't been as . . . satisfying as I'd expected. And I'd known that Tory was bound to be even more anticlimactic. She was too dull and tedious to provide the sort of inspiration a true artist needed. Then I'd heard rumors of Detective Fisher returning to Pike. The thought intrigued me. It wasn't until I'd actually caught sight of her, however, that I'd been convinced I had to lure her into my game. She was sheer perfection. And how better to tempt her than to give her a ticking clock? "A pity. I have a feeling I'm going to enjoy hearing you scream."

Lifting the crowbar, I swing it down with enough speed that it whistles through the air. It hits Tory on the side of her torso. There's a deep thud followed by a sharp crack as a rib busts beneath the impact. For a second, the woman seems too stunned by the attack to react. Then, as the crowbar smashes against her again and again, she parts her lips to release the scream I've been anticipating.

I suck in a deep breath, my body vibrating with pleasure. What was the old song? If you can't be with the one you want . . . "Oh yes," I encourage my creation. "Louder." Another blow. "Louder."

The screams vibrate through the enclosed space, the scent of blood and tears and terror flooding my senses. Jude was right. I swing the crowbar until my arm is weary and I'm splattered in bits of flesh.

It's sweeter than sex.

On some level, Zac knew that he was driving in circles. Figuratively and literally. After all, the lake wasn't very large and the boundary road was only a couple of miles. There were only so many times he could go around in the hopes they might spot something new.

Still, the thought of conceding defeat was unbearable. Tory was depending on him. How could he drive away knowing that she was out there in the hands of a monster?

It was at last Rachel who forced him to accept the inevitable. "Zac." She reached out to lightly touch his arm. "The sun is coming up. We need to get some rest."

"I know, I just . . ." His words trailed away in frustration.

"I get it," she murmured. "But it's time to turn the search over to your deputies."

She was right. Not only was he simply retracing his steps, but he was also tired enough that his brain was beginning to fog. If he ran across an actual clue he wasn't sure he would notice. "Okay."

He turned off the dirt path onto the gravel road that would lead back to the highway. He was mentally deciding how to best split up his deputies to increase the area of the search when he noticed they were passing the Roadhouse. Expecting the place to be closed, he abruptly whipped into the lot when he caught sight of an old, battered station wagon parked next to the front door.

"What's going on?" Rachel demanded in confusion.

"I want to see if that car belongs to Vann Ellison," he said, pulling the truck to a halt and shutting off the engine.

"Who?"

"The owner of the Roadhouse." He shoved open the door and hopped out.

Rachel quickly caught up as he headed toward the front entrance. "You think he might know something about Tory?"

"No." He shook his head. He vaguely knew Vann Ellison, and while he didn't doubt that he would lie, cheat, and steal, he didn't believe he would deliberately allow one of his employees to be in danger. Not when it might jeopardize the bar he'd owned for fifty years.

"I think he might know something about Jude," he corrected.

"Ah." She nodded. "Yes."

Zac grabbed the handle, relieved when the door pulled open easily. He stepped over the threshold, halting as he carefully scanned the empty space. He couldn't be sure the station wagon belonged to Vann. If it was the killer, Zac didn't intend to get caught off guard.

"Hey," a voice called from the back of the long space, the sound of heavy footsteps echoing through the air. "We're closed. Get the hell out of . . ." The man came to an abrupt halt.

The early morning sunlight spilled through the front window, revealing a tall, large-boned man with a bald head and weathered face. Vann Ellison had to be in his seventies, but he looked twenty years younger. It had to be a case of good genes, Zac wryly acknowledged. God knew it wasn't from clean living.

"Evans." The older man muttered the name like a curse.

Zac smiled. "We need to chat."

Vann folded his arms over his chest. He was wearing a faded Black Sabbath T-shirt and jeans that were coated in dust. Why? Had he been cleaning in fear of the state inspectors making a visit? Or had he been disposing of the bootleg cigarettes and liquor he was rumored to sell off the books? Whatever his reason for being there at such an early hour, Zac would bet money it wasn't legit.

To prove his point, Vann sent him a warning scowl. "I'm not talking to the cops without my lawyer."

"This isn't about your . . ." Zac deliberately ran his gaze over the man's grimy clothes, emphasizing his awareness that something was up. "Numerous violations. We'll discuss those later."

The scowl remained. "Then what do you want?"

Zac paused, considering how best to get the information he needed. "I suppose you heard that Jude Henley's body was recently found in the graveyard?"

Vann snorted. "Who hasn't heard? That's all anyone

can talk about. My grandson was even trying to show me some stupid website or Facebookie thing that claims Jude crawled out of his grave and is ravaging the town as a zombie."

Next to him, Rachel pulled out her pad and pencil, scribbling down notes. "Not quite," he assured the bar owner in dry tones.

Vann narrowed his watery blue eyes. "If you're looking for how Jude got there, I don't have any idea. I thought he was dead the same as everyone else."

"Did you know Jude?" Zac asked. "Before he died the first time."

The older man shrugged. "Pike's a small town. I know about everyone."

"Did he spend time at the Roadhouse?"

"He liked to come in for a drink. A lot of folks did back then." A wistful expression settled on Vann's ruddy face, his eyes skimming over the shadowed space as if he was seeing the bar as it had once been. "We had a band on Friday and Saturday nights. The place was packed. And not just locals. We had customers drive all the way from Grange and Wausau."

Zac wasn't interested in the history of the Roadhouse. "Did Jude come alone?"

"Jude Henley was never alone," Vann said dryly, something that might have been envy twisting his expression. "Not for long anyway."

That matched what Rachel's mother had told her about Jude. Obviously he was a well-known womanizer. "Did he have a regular girlfriend?"

"Not really. He liked to play the field." Vann's gaze

darted toward Rachel before returning to Zac. "Usually with other men's wives."

Odd. Zac paused, then, reaching into the pocket of his jacket, he pulled out the picture of Maureen Godwin.

"Do you remember her?"

Vann glanced down, studying the picture before giving a decisive shake of his head. "Nope."

Zac frowned. Was he lying? Or was Zac grasping at straws to assume Maureen had come here to meet with Jude?

"She ran her car into a tree on the old Lake Road." Zac attempted to prod Vann's memory.

"Recently?"

"No. It was over thirty years ago."

Vann narrowed his gaze, staring at Zac as if he'd lost his mind. "Are you shitting me? I don't remember if I pissed this morning, let alone what happened thirty years ago. Why are you asking?"

Zac waved a dismissive hand, as if his interest in Maureen was insignificant. He didn't want Vann inventing information he thought might get him out of trouble for any violations he was trying to hide. "I'm working on a time-line for Jude," he said, keeping his explanation vague. "It's possible he was here with Maureen."

"Maybe. Like I said, he was here with a lot of women." He shrugged. "It was a convenient location, if you know what I mean."

Zac didn't know. "Convenient?"

Vann cleared his throat, sending Rachel another wary glance before he answered. "He could have a few drinks with a lady, and while she was still in her happy place he could take her to his cabin. No time for her to get cold feet."

Zac struggled to contain his sudden burst of excitement. He was running on fumes. He couldn't afford to waste energy on something that might be another cold trail. "What cabin?"

"The Henley cabin." Vann looked puzzled, as if everyone should know about the place. "It's just a couple miles from here."

"Is it still there?" he asked.

"As far as I know."

Rachel stepped forward, holding out her pad and pencil. "Draw me a map to get there."

Rachel leaned forward, peering out the windshield as Zac turned down the narrow path that wound through the thick woods. It was so overgrown that it would have been impossible to notice if Vann Ellison hadn't given them exact directions.

Slowly they bumped over the hard ground, both silently searching for any sign of the supposed Henley cabin. After a quarter of an hour of the bone-jarring journey, Zac at last pointed to a spot over the trees.

"There. That's the top of a chimney."

"Yes," Rachel agreed, catching sight of the crumbling red bricks just visible. Lowering her gaze, she searched for an opening in the dense trees that would lead to the cabin. "Stop."

Zac pressed on the brakes, sending her a startled glance. "What is it?"

She rolled down the passenger window, leaning out of

the truck to closely study the bushes that lined the path. They were dry and brittle as winter rapidly approached, making it easy to see where they'd been crushed beneath the weight of a vehicle.

"Someone turned in here."

Zac considered the branches that'd been dragged onto the pathway. "More than once."

Putting the truck into reverse, he backed down the road until he found a space wide enough between the trees to pull off. Then, ignoring the branches scratching against the side of his vehicle, he parked in a spot that would keep the truck hidden from view.

"Let's go around the back," he murmured, pulling out his weapon as he climbed out of the truck and carefully closed the door.

Rachel left her own weapon holstered as she joined him. Zac was sheriff here and Tory's disappearance was his case. Not that she wouldn't kill anyone who threatened him. Without blinking an eye.

Weaving their way through the aspen and red pines that carpeted the landscape, Zac made a wide arch before cautiously approaching the cabin from the back. At the edge of the clearing a wide shed blocked their path. It was built from weathered boards with a sagging roof and windows that were coated in layers of dirt. At one time, however, it'd been a substantial structure, large enough to store three or four vehicles or perhaps a fishing boat and camper.

Zac moved to push open the back door, peering inside before turning his head to give her a nod. She followed behind him, entering the shed and glancing around.

It was shadowed, but enough light penetrated the coated windows to reveal a dirt floor and high ceiling with open rafters. As she'd expected, there was an old rowboat shoved against one wall and a pile of lifejackets and broken oars lying next to it. There were also a few fishing rods and nets leaning in one corner. Directly in front of her was an empty space and on the far wall was a massive sliding door that would have created an opening wide enough for a vehicle to drive in and out.

"Looks like something was parked in here," Zac murmured softly, crouching down to study the deep indents in the dirt ground.

"Tires made these," she murmured.

Zac walked to the indents near the front of the shed. "The length of a truck."

He glanced back and she nodded. She knew exactly what he was thinking. Jude's truck that had been left at the graveyard had been stashed somewhere for the past twenty-eight years. This would have been the perfect location.

In silence they did a quick search, looking for anything that might reveal the presence of Tory. When there was nothing to discover beyond old fishing gear and a plethora of cobwebs, they exited the shed through the back door and crept toward the front corner of the building. From there they had a clear view of the nearby cabin.

It was smaller than the shed, although it was built of the same weathered wood and matching shingles. The surrounding yard was overgrown with dead weeds and there were several rusting tools and barrels littering the area in a haphazard pattern. It made it look as if the place had been abandoned for years. But a closer glance revealed that someone had washed the dust from the windows and there was fresh wood stacked near the back door.

"Someone's been here," she murmured.

Zac nodded, tilting back his head to study the red-brick chimney. "No smoke." His attention turned toward the narrow driveway at the side of the cabin. "No vehicles."

"Let's take a closer look," she suggested.

If Tory was connected to Paige's murder, the killer would be trying to walk in Jude Henley's footsteps. What better place than a family cabin within a couple miles of the place she was kidnapped?

Zac held up his weapon, quickly crossing the open space to place his back flat against the cabin. Rachel waited, ensuring that no one had seen Zac's approach before she darted forward to join him. The last thing she wanted was to spook whoever might be inside. If they panicked, who knew what they might do.

They waited, silently counting to a hundred before Rachel cautiously turned to peek into the closest window. In the dim light she could make out a tiny kitchen with a fridge, stove, and sink set between two cabinets. There was a wooden table in the center of the floor with three mismatched chairs.

"One is too big, one is too small, and one is just right," she whispered, her gaze moving to the mugs of coffee left on the counter. Again there were three. "I'm starting to feel like Goldilocks and the Three Bears."

Without warning she felt his finger brush down her cheek. "Are you looking for one that's just right?"

The heat of his finger seemed to sear against her chilled skin. She trembled, feeling the familiar awareness sizzle through her. That part had never changed. Not even when their marriage was unraveling. Deep inside she was absolutely certain she would always desire this man. No matter what the future might hold between them.

She sent him a chiding glance. "Don't distract me. I'm working."

His gaze lingered on her lips. "Later?"

"Zac . . ."

They both froze at the sound of a car approaching. Then, as it slowed and turned into the driveway, they hurried to crouch behind the woodpile. Rachel's heart pounded, adrenaline racing through her blood. She preferred using her brains to puzzle out a mystery. Nothing was more satisfying than uncovering clues and following them to a logical conclusion. But she couldn't deny there was an absolute thrill in the chase.

The car pulled to a halt in front of the cabin, the engine switching off. A second later they could hear the sound of a door slamming shut.

Zac leaned toward her, whispering into her ear. "I'll check it out."

She nodded, watching him ease past the woodpile and disappear around the side of the house before she turned to press herself against the cabin next to the back door. They didn't know who or how many people were in the cabin. She wasn't going to let anyone slip away because they were sloppy.

Reaching beneath her jacket, she touched the butt of her gun. More to reassure herself that it was there if she needed it than to prepare to shoot anyone.

"Hello, Curly," she heard Zac drawl. "I've been looking for you."

Rachel released a silent whistle. Well, well. It was one

of the Curly boys. And where there was one, she was willing to bet there was going to be a second.

"Christ. Dad, it's the cops!" Curly shouted on cue, the words echoing through the nearby trees.

There was the sound of pounding footsteps from inside the cabin, then, with a tedious predictability, the back door was shoved open and a man stumbled down the steps. Why did they always run?

"I don't think so." Rachel moved with a practiced ease, catching the fleeing man with her hip to knock him off his feet. Curly was already off-balance, and with a cry of frustration he fell heavily to the ground, hitting his head even as Rachel shoved a knee into his back. "Don't move."

Chapter 13

An hour later Zac headed down to the basement of the courthouse and entered the holding cell. It was a small, dark square that smelled of old mold and cigarette smoke that had seeped into the cement walls. It didn't matter how many times the place was cleaned, the stench lingered.

Inside the cell was a narrow table, and on each side was a plastic chair. Overhead was a bare lightbulb surrounded by a steel cage. It was a bleak, barren room. But it wasn't that way just to make it uncomfortable for the suspects. It had been stripped of comforts to make sure there was nothing in the space that could be used as a weapon.

Curly Senior was currently slumped in one of the chairs, his arms folded over his narrow chest and a sullen expression on his thin face. He was a tall, gaunt man with a bald head and a nose that consumed more than its fair share of space. His eyes were dark and sunk deep into his skull, as if they were attempting to disappear entirely. All in all, he looked like the Grim Reaper. Zac wondered if that was why he'd worked at a funeral parlor.

"It's about time." Curly intruded into his thoughts.

"You in a hurry to go somewhere?" Zac asked as he took a seat in the chair on the opposite side of the table.

"To see a doctor." The man lifted a hand to touch the swelling bump on his forehead. "I think that cow broke my skull."

Zac leaned back, folding his arms over his chest.

He'd deliberately left the man sitting alone in the cell since he'd hauled them into town. Curly Junior was in another cell just down the hall. It not only gave them time to worry about what they were facing, but he needed to get the paperwork started on a search warrant. They'd done a quick walk-through to make sure there was no sign of Tory Devlin. Or anyone else hiding inside the cabin after he'd arrested the two Curlys. But to do a more thorough investigation of the property, along with both Curly Senior's and Junior's places, he was going to need a judge to give him legal permission.

The sooner he could get it, the better.

"You're lucky she didn't put a bullet through your heart," he told Curly, not adding his pride in Rachel's ability to take down the man without ever pulling her weapon. "It's against the law to run from the police."

"Run from the police?" He made a sound of shock. "No way. I thought you were—"

"Cut the crap, Curly," Zac interrupted. "I'm too tired to play games. You disappeared from your trailer when your son called to tell you that I wanted to chat. And you tried to run when you realized we were at the cabin. Why?"

The beady brown eyes narrowed as Curly considered whether he could continue to lie. Then he gave an indifferent shrug. "I don't like cops. They give me a rash."

"Shocking," Zac drawled, studying the man's stubborn expression. He was prepared for Zac's interrogation and intended to make this as difficult as possible. Maybe it was time to shake him up a bit. "Does your dislike have anything to do with the fact they don't approve of you throwing children out of windows?"

Curly looked genuinely confused. "What?"

"You were arrested for domestic abuse against your son."

"Oh." The man reddened, as if embarrassed to be reminded of his violence toward a child. "That wasn't my fault."

Zac arched a brow. "What part? The window? Did you intend to throw him against the wall? Probably a better choice. No cops involved if you can keep the beatings private."

"There was no beating," Curly snapped. "The boy attacked me. I was just protecting myself."

"Right. It's never the abuser's fault. He provoked you. He deserved it. He—"

"I'm telling you, he came after me," Curly interrupted, his voice harsh. "Not that I blame the boy. If I hadn't been drinking, none of it would have happened."

"Why would he come after you?"

Curly hunched his shoulders in a defensive motion. "He'd overheard his mom and me fighting and he was upset."

"Fighting about what?" Zac demanded, genuinely curious now. He wanted to know if this man had graduated from beating children to murdering helpless women.

"It doesn't matter."

"It does if you want to prove you're not a violent man

capable of brutalizing a small child," Zac reminded him, his voice hard.

Curly's lips parted, as if he intended to tell Zac to shove his intrusive questions up his ass. Then, as if seeing something in Zac's expression that warned it would be a mistake to piss off the sheriff who held his future in his hands, he muttered a curse.

"I didn't know I had a son until his mother appeared on my doorstep with a two-year-old kid she said belonged to me." The older man shrugged. "I agreed to support the two of them, but I'll admit that there were times I wondered if I was being conned. I didn't have actual proof the kid was mine. And when I would get drunk I would sometimes say stuff that wasn't so nice. One night Curly overheard me saying that he didn't belong to me and he went into a fit."

Zac narrowed his eyes. "What kind of fit?"

"He started screaming and yelling like a wild creature, and the next thing I knew, he'd launched himself at me and was taking a bite out of my arm." Curly moved his hand to cover his forearm, as if recalling the unexpected attack. "It hurt like a bitch, and I swung my arm, just trying to dislodge him. I never intended to send him flying and I most certainly didn't intend for him to go through the window. It scared the shit out of me." He grimaced. "Not that anyone cared that it was an accident. I was arrested and my wife took off with the kid. End of story."

Zac didn't have the time to consider what the episode revealed about the Boltons, if anything. It was time to get to the reason the older man was currently seated in a holding cell.

"Why were you hiding in the cabin, Curly?" he abruptly asked. "And why did you run from me?"

"Like I said, I don't like cops."

Zac snorted. "Yeah, a lot of people don't like cops. It's a hazard of the job. But most folks don't pack up their belongings and disappear into the middle of the woods." He held the man's wary gaze. "Only someone who has done something illegal goes to that extreme."

His jaw tightened. "I don't know what you're talking about."

"All right. Let's see if I can explain it in words you understand." Zac spoke in a slow, concise voice. "Premeditated. Murder."

"Murder?" Fear flared through the man's eyes before he was trying to laugh off the accusation. "You're out of your ever-loving mind."

"You were hiding in the cabin of a man who was found with a bullet through his head."

"It was empty. I didn't know who owned the place."

Zac rolled his eyes. Curly Senior wasn't the most skilled liar. If he was the killer they were searching for, it shouldn't be tough to prove his guilt. "You worked for the Henleys for years."

"I worked for a lot of people around town. And I'm sure a lot of them have cabins."

With a deep sigh, Zac rose to his feet. "You should get a lawyer, Curly. A good one. You're going to need all the help you can get."

Zac headed toward the door, not surprised when Curly called out. "Wait. Wait."

Slowly turning, he sent the older man a warning glare. "Don't waste my time."

"I won't." The older man leaned forward, his expression stubborn. "But first I want your promise you'll let my son go. He wasn't involved in any of this."

Zac felt a stab of surprise at Curly's loyalty toward his son. He'd assumed he'd throw the younger man under the bus if it would divert suspicion from himself.

"If you're telling the truth, he won't be prosecuted."

Curly frowned, clearly unhappy at the vague commitment. Then perhaps realizing that he wasn't going to get any better offer, he grudgingly nodded. "Okay. It's true, I did work for the Henleys."

Zac returned to slide into his chair, leaning his elbows on the table. The session was being recorded so there was no need to take notes. "What dates?"

The older man considered for a second. "I started in the mid-eighties, a couple years after Mr. and Mrs. Henley died in a car crash. I stayed until Jacob closed the place a few years ago. I don't have the exact dates."

"You knew Jude back then." It was a statement, not a question.

Curly shrugged. "He made occasional appearances at the funeral parlor. Usually when he was hoping for a handout from his brother."

"Were you friends?"

"Barely knew him."

Zac curled his hands into frustrated fists. When he'd heard the car pulling up to the cabin he'd been convinced that this nightmare was about to end. They would find Tory and clear up both Jude's and Paige's murders.

Now he was battling a horrifying fear that he was no closer to finding Tory, or even discovering who'd brutally killed Paige. And it was pissing him off.

"Do you want Curly Junior released or not?" he snapped.

Curly scowled, but he swallowed his smart-ass comment. Did he sense that Zac's nerves were at the breaking point? Or was he actually worried about his son?

"A few times he hooked me up with some weed. That was it."

"Did you party together?"

The man snorted. "No way."

"Why not?"

"I was the hired help."

Zac frowned. He knew the sordid truth about Jude Henley. The man had been a heartless beast. But even without the videotapes, he'd gotten the impression that he was a loser. "Jude was a high school dropout and a petty criminal," he pointed out in dry tones.

"Didn't matter," Curly insisted. "The Henleys had once been a big deal in this town. My mom said that Jude's mom insisted on buying a brand-new car every year for her birthday and traveling to the beach during the winter. Even when they were barely making ends meet toward the end they thought they were better than everyone else."

"Okay." Zac tapped his fingers on the table, pretending to consider his next words. "You might not have been friends, but you knew that Jude was alive."

As he hoped, he caught Curly by surprise. His brown eyes widened, his head shaking in denial. "No. I swear."

Zac planted his hands flat on the table, as if he was preparing to shove himself to his feet. "I knew this would be a waste of time."

"I didn't know," Curly insisted, his tone sharp with an urgent attempt to convince Zac of his sincerity. "Not until . . ." His words died on his lips, and he glanced toward the door, as if wishing he could get up and walk out of the room.

"Until when?" Zac prompted, knowing he had to keep the man talking.

Curly hesitated, then with a last, longing glance at the door he returned his attention back to Zac. "Until I was coming out of the Bait and Tackle one night and Jude suddenly appeared in front of me." The older man grimaced at the memory. "It scared the bejesus out of me, I can tell you that. I thought I was seeing a ghost."

"When?"

"A couple of weeks ago."

"Be more exact."

"I can't." Curly hunched his thin shoulders. "I don't pay any attention to the passing days now that I'm retired. All I can say is that it was sometime in early October. I'd gone to the bar to watch the baseball game. It was the playoffs."

Zac ground his teeth. He'd check with the new owner of the Bait and Tackle later. "Where was Jude waiting for you?"

"I was walking to my truck I'd parked around the block and he stepped out of an alley next to the bar. At first I thought I was going to be mugged. I don't know why. Everyone in town knows I'm always broke. Then the man said my name and I realized who it was." A violent shudder shook through Curly's body at the memory. "Like I said, I thought I was seeing a ghost."

"What did he want?"

"He said he needed my help."

"What kind of help?"

"He told me that he was staying at his old cabin and that he needed someone to bring him supplies."

There was a compelling sincerity in the man's voice, and if Jude had been staying there, that would explain the three mugs on the table. Not Papa Bear, Mama Bear, and Baby Bear. But Jude Henley, who would have left his mug without realizing he would never return to the cabin. And then Curly Senior and Curly Junior, who were too lazy to clean up.

Still, Zac remained skeptical. Curly needed a convenient excuse to be at the cabin. What better justification than to say the dead man asked him to be there?

"Why couldn't he get his own supplies?" Zac asked.

"He didn't want anyone knowing he was in town. I guess because he was supposed to be dead."

"Hmm." Zac didn't disguise his disbelief. "You claimed you'd never been friends."

"We weren't."

"So why would he seek you out? Why not Jacob?"

"Haven't you heard? His brother's soft in the head." Curly grimaced. "He was caught one night walking around the streets without his pants on. By the time he was found and taken to the hospital he had frostbite on his pecker. That's when they decided to put him in the nursing home."

Zac winced, but refused to be distracted. "Why you?"

"Honestly? I think it was because I was at that spot at that time."

"What do you mean?"

"I had the feeling he'd been in the alley watching someone else," Curly told him. "I just happened to come along and he recognized me. I assumed he thought he could trust me to keep my mouth shut."

Zac tucked away the potential clue. He could go to the alley to see who or what Jude might have been watching once he was confident that Curly was telling him the truth. Right now, that was still debatable. "He hadn't seen you for twenty-eight years. Why would he trust you?"

"Because I've always been the kind of guy who will do about anything for money."

Zac believed him. He'd known lots of men like Curly. They skimmed through life, taking whatever they could and never making a contribution to the community. His own uncle had been exactly the same, constantly showing up at the farm to ask for a couple bucks to keep him going until he got a job. He'd died a few years ago, broke and alone. A shame.

"What did you do for him?" Zac asked.

"I brought groceries and kerosene so he could use the hurricane lamps at night," Curly admitted. "I delivered them each Monday morning. Three . . ." He wrinkled his nose. "Maybe four times. I can't remember. He'd leave an envelope with money on the porch to pay for the groceries and some extra cash to compensate me for my time."

Zac continued to tap his fingers on the desk. He didn't understand why Jude would ask a less than dependable Curly to bring his supplies. Even if he was afraid of showing his face in Pike, he could have gone to another town to buy what he needed. The chances of being recognized would have been close to zero.

Unless . . .

"Did he have a vehicle?" Zac abruptly demanded.

Curly considered the question, as if it'd never occurred to him to look for a car. "Not that I ever saw," he finally admitted. "But he might have had one in the old shed behind the cabin. I didn't go back there."

Zac slowly nodded. If Jude didn't have transportation, it would explain his need to approach Curly for help. Even if he did have his old truck in the shed, the license plates had expired years ago. The last thing he'd want was to attract the attention of the law.

That still left a dozen questions whirling through Zac's tired brain. "If the only thing you did was deliver a few groceries, why did you run when you heard I wanted to talk to you?"

"Are you shitting me?" Curly glared at him as if he'd lost his mind. "The dude shows up in Pike after twenty-eight years of pretending to be dead and suddenly he *is* dead. Who do you think is going to be blamed?" He slapped his bony hand against the center of his chest. "Me, that's who."

Zac knew that Curly had a point. Not that he was going to admit it. Instead, he leaned forward. "What did Junior do for Jude?"

Curly blinked at the question. As if it had caught him off guard. "Nothing. He didn't even know I was working for Jude Henley." He held up his hand as Zac's lips parted in disbelief. "Not until we heard that he'd turned up dead in the graveyard," he continued. "That's when I told the boy what I'd been doing. He was the one who decided I should keep my trap closed. He said that the cops were sure to try and blame it on me just to close the case. But he wasn't involved in anything else."

Zac made a mental note to check out the whereabouts of Junior later. It was obvious that Senior was going to insist his son was innocent. For now, he turned his attention to why he'd wanted to talk to Curly in the first place. "Do you have a key to the funeral parlor?"

The man looked confused. "Is this some sort of trick?"

Zac shook his head. "It's a simple question. Do you still have a key?"

"Oh . . . you mean because of the gal that was found there? Curly said she'd been left in the cooler. Nasty business."

"Very nasty business." Zac's voice was cold. Paige had been murdered on his watch. The knowledge was eating at him like a cancer. "Did you have your own key?"

He firmly shook his head. "I didn't need it. There was a spare key kept in the garage."

Zac frowned. Yet another convenient explanation. "Who would know that?"

"Half the town," Curly said in dry tones. "Jacob didn't want to be bothered when he was trying to pressure his customers to get the top-of-the-line funeral or was down in the morgue working on the bodies, so he left the key to the side door for the delivery people, the cleaner, the florist, the church organists. Anyone who might need to get in when he was busy. You can ask around Pike and they'll tell you I'm not lying."

That would be easy enough to prove. "Is it still there?"

"As far as I know." Curly licked his dry lips. "Is that all?"

Zac arched a brow at the stupid question. "I'm going to need to know where you were the night Jude was shot."

Curly heaved a long-suffering sigh, slumping farther down in his chair. "I was home."

"Alone?"

"Yeah, alone."

"Unfortunate."

The older man scowled. "Not really. If I'd killed Jude I would make sure I had an alibi. I'm not stupid."

Zac shrugged aside the sharp protest. The man couldn't have known his connection to Jude would be discovered. No criminal ever thought they were going to get caught. "What about Paige?"

Curly blinked as Zac abruptly changed the direction of the interview. "Who?"

"Paige Carr. And don't try to pretend you didn't know her," Zac warned. "She lived across the street from you."

"So what?"

"How well did you know her?"

"I didn't." Curly cleared his throat as Zac narrowed his eyes at the less than helpful response. "Not unless you count me yelling at her to keep her brat out of the road. Do you know how many times she'd be sitting on her porch, staring at her phone while her kid was running wild? It was a wonder the girl wasn't hit by one of the cars that drive through here like we're part of the Indy 500."

Zac swallowed the urge to remind the man that he had no right to judge the young mother. Hadn't he been arrested for abusing his son? Instead he shrugged. People were always eager to point out the faults of others while ignoring their own.

"Where were you the night she disappeared?"

Curly furrowed his brow. "When did it happen? Friday?" He waited for Zac's nod. "That's easy."

"Why?"

"I had to go to the hospital."

"What happened?"

"Couldn't breathe." Curly made a sound of disgust. "Damned cigarettes gave me COPD. I had to be put on oxygen and told to stay the night. And before you ask, my son came around six and brought me dinner. I can't stand that hospital slop. He stayed until about eight or nine."

Zac studied the narrow face. Was Curly lying? Surely he had to know that Zac would check the hospital records.

He slowly leaned forward. "What if I tell you that your truck was heard coming back to the trailer park in the early hours of Saturday morning?"

Curly nodded. "Yep. That would have been me."

Zac clenched his teeth. Was the man deliberately trying to piss him off? "You just said you were in the hospital."

"I said I was admitted into the hospital. I checked myself out around three or three thirty. Against doctor's orders." He shook his head in disgust. "You can't believe the fit they tossed. As if I'm not a grown man capable of making my own decision."

"Why did you leave?"

Curly reached up to pat the upper pocket of his flannel shirt where a square bulge was visible. "I wanted a cigarette. They said I couldn't have one, so I left."

Of course he did. Zac swallowed a sigh and leaned back in his seat. With every passing second it seemed less and less likely that Curly was the murderer. The realization settled in the pit of his stomach like a hot ball of dread.

"Tell me about your conversations with Jude," he commanded.

"I told you. We weren't BFFs," Curly growled, his impatience etched on his face. "He left a grocery list on the porch, along with an envelope with cash. I drove to the grocery store in Grange, and then back to the cabin to deliver it. That's it."

"You're claiming you never spoke to him?"

"He opened the door the first time I brought the groceries. I asked where he'd been and he said he'd been traveling. I asked where and he got real snippy. Told me to keep my nose out of his business. I wanted the money, and to be honest I wasn't that interested, so it didn't bother me when he didn't come to the door anymore. I left the stuff and drove away."

"That's it?"

Curly started to nod, only to hesitate as he caught sight of Zac's expression. There was no way he was getting out of that cell until Zac was convinced he'd revealed every detail about his encounters with Jude Henley.

"There's one question he did answer the first night he approached me," Curly grudgingly admitted.

"Tell me."

"I asked why he'd come back to town."

"What did he say?"

"That he was here to pay for the sins of his past." Curly grimaced. "I guess he was right."

Chapter 14

It was early afternoon when Rachel returned to the Henley cabin along with Zac and an official search warrant. She didn't have much hope of finding Tory. The cabin wasn't large enough to hide anyone. There was a small living room, with a sagging couch and a leather armchair along with the narrow kitchen they'd glimpsed through the back window earlier. There were two small bedrooms with a bathroom crammed between them.

It was built for an occasional weekend of fishing. Plain and functional.

Standing in the largest of the bedrooms, Rachel studied the narrow closet. It was the only one in the cabin and she'd had a vague hope it might reveal . . . something. Anything. Instead it had a few shirts and jeans that could have been purchased at any big-box store.

She reached to pull one of the shirts off the hanger, studying the cheap knit material.

"This wouldn't fit Curly Senior or Junior," she said. The two Boltons were both too skinny to wear a large.

"Nope. I'm going to go out on a limb and guess they belonged to Jude Henley," Zac said, standing beside her.

"Agreed." She hung the shirt back in the closet. "But where's the rest of his stuff?"

Zac frowned. "What stuff?"

She turned to wave a hand toward the boxes piled in the corner. They'd already been through them to discover clothes, toiletries, old magazines and letters, and a small television.

"The Curlys were here for a day and had more crap tossed around than Jude."

Zac slowly nodded. "Either he only brought a few things because he didn't intend to stay for long, or he avoids owning objects that would give away his identity. He's lived on the run for twenty-eight years."

She agreed with Zac's logic, but she wasn't sure if it explained the extreme lack of belongings. Even if you planned to be at the cabin for a short time, there were things you would have to bring with you. "There's another possibility."

He sent her a curious glance. "What's that?"

"Someone cleaned out the place after he was shot."

"Ah." Zac slowly nodded. "True."

"Did you find a wallet on him? Or a phone?"

"Neither."

"Nothing in the truck?"

"Nothing recent. The paperwork and receipts in the glove box were all from the years before he supposedly died. I assumed because it hadn't been driven since then."

His words only confirmed Rachel's suspicion that someone had been through the cabin. Even a serial killer on the run would need a phone, if only a disposable one.

So the question left was how thorough the mystery

person had been in eliminating any clue that might help them.

Returning to the main living room, Rachel walked in a slow circle. She ignored the empty beer cans and paper plates tossed on the floor. She didn't doubt those came from the Boltons. Instead, she searched for anything that might belong to Jude. "Assuming we believe Curly—"

"That's a big assumption," Zac interrupted in dry tones as he conducted his own search. "I intend to go to the hospital later to check his and Junior's alibi."

"Agreed." She'd already considered the possibility that the two men had been working together, or that Junior had kidnapped Paige and hidden her at the funeral parlor before visiting his dad at the hospital. Later he could have returned to kill her. "But hypothetically speaking, let's say that Jude has spent the last twenty-eight years on the run, indulging his evil urges and managing to stay off the radar."

"No easy task."

"Why risk it all by returning to Pike?"

Zac halted in the center of the room, his brows pulling together as he considered the question. "Curly said that Jude claimed he was here to pay for the sins of his past."

"Do serial killers possess the ability to feel guilt?" Rachel considered her own question before giving a sharp shake of her head. "My training tells me that a psychopath is like a tiger. He doesn't change his stripes."

"I agree it seems unlikely, but I suppose age might have caused him to reflect on . . ." Zac fell silent, as if he'd been struck by a sudden thought. Then, without warning, he was pulling his phone out of the pocket of his jacket. "Shit."

"What is it?"

His expression was impatient as he hit the screen. "The medical examiner sent Jude's autopsy report, but I was too focused on searching for Tory to look at it." A female voice floated through the speaker and Zac turned away to talk to his deputy. "Lindsay. I need you to go into my office . . ." His words became indistinct as he moved into the kitchen.

Several minutes passed before he walked back to stand next to Rachel.

"Got it," he announced.

"Were you looking for something in particular in the autopsy?"

"In my experience there's one time in any man's life when he reflects on the choices he's made."

She studied him in confusion. Was he talking about himself? Or maybe his father? "When is that?"

"When he is forced to confront his own mortality."

She remained confused. "Death?"

"Jude Henley was dying."

"Oh." She blinked at the unexpected explanation. "He does that a lot."

Zac's lips twitched. "No shit."

"What was he dying of?"

"Brain cancer," he said. "They missed it in the initial autopsy because of the damage caused by the bullet."

"Was he being treated?"

"There's no indication of a recent surgery or radiation therapy. According to the medical examiner he had only a few months left to live."

Rachel paused, needing a second to adjust to the latest development. Did the fact that Jude was dying change anything? Yes. She didn't believe that a monster could develop a conscience, but facing your own mortality would surely alter your priorities.

But how?

"He mentioned paying for the sins of his past, and we just assumed he was referring to the murders he'd committed." She spoke her thoughts out loud. "But it might have been for faking his own death. Or abandoning his brother. Or a dozen other things we haven't discovered."

Zac nodded. "Whatever it was, the regret was compelling enough to drive him back to Pike and risk exposing the fact he was still alive."

Rachel considered the various possibilities. He hadn't reached out to Jacob, unless the older man was a better actor than she suspected. Or anyone else in town who was willing to confess they knew he was still alive.

Did that mean he'd come to see whoever had shot him in the head? Had he suspected he would be in danger? Was that why he'd hidden in this cabin? Or was it just the fear of being seen by someone he knew?

She paced across the floor, struggling to make sense of her muddled thoughts. "Do you think Jude followed whoever killed him to Pike? Or did the killer follow him?"

"And what is the connection between them?" Zac added.

She sent him a rueful glance. "More questions without answers."

His jaw tightened. "And Tory is still missing."

Rachel sympathized with the frustration that smoldered in his eyes. Being in the cold case division meant that she rarely felt as if she had a ticking clock over her head. The pressure of trying to use the past to figure out who was stalking the streets of Pike and at the same time needing to locate the missing woman was taking its toll on both of them.

"Have your deputies finished searching the Boltons' places?" she asked.

"An initial sweep didn't turn up anything beyond a bag of weed and a bottle of prescription painkillers."

"No weapons?"

"Curly Senior had a shotgun in his truck."

That wouldn't be unusual. Everyone in town had a shotgun in their truck. Including her father, who rarely hunted. "Nothing to connect them to Tory?"

"Nothing."

"Damn." Rachel continued her pacing, passing by the rough wooden shelves that were nailed to the wall. "I . . ." The words dried on her lips as she noticed the old stack of books that were shoved at one end. There were a couple on fishing and one that offered campfire cooking recipes. It was the top book, however, that captured her attention. Not only was it free of dust, but the smooth red leather was shaped like a photo album. "What's this?"

Zac walked to stand beside her as she pulled the object off the shelf and flipped it open to reveal pages covered in news clippings.

"A scrapbook?" Zac guessed, his hand reaching out to touch the yellowed article that was neatly taped at the top of the page. "Horrific accident steals two lives," he read the headline. "James and Justine Henley, two beloved citizens of Pike, were killed in an automobile crash outside town in the late-night hours. An investigation is pending."

There were a couple more articles related to the crash taped at the bottom. Curious, Rachel turned the page, puzzled by the pictures of an unknown woman with long, dark hair and a thin face. There were at least a dozen photos of the female, taken from a distance and some so fuzzy you could barely make out her features. She turned the page to discover more pictures. This time, however, she recognized the brown-haired young woman with the petulant expression.

Staci Gale.

Lifting her head, she met Zac's shocked gaze. "A scrapbook for a serial killer."

It was midafternoon by the time Zac and Rachel returned to his office. They'd quickly photocopied the various newspaper clippings as well as the pictures in the scrapbook before bagging it up and sending Lindsay to deliver it to the CSI office in Madison. The sooner the professionals could start processing the thing for fingerprints or DNA the better. Not only to prove that the album belonged to Jude, but to see if anyone else had handled it.

Next he'd enlarged and enhanced the copies before he'd printed them out and spread them across his desk. Together, he and Rachel shuffled through them, standing close enough for her shoulder to brush his arm. He tried to ignore just how right it felt to be so close to his ex-wife, but between the stress and his lack of sleep, his defenses were at an all-time low. His awareness of her was as inevitable as the rising sun.

All he could do was savor the welcomed heat of her body and the sweet scent of soap that clung to her skin.

Rachel, on the other hand, was fully focused on the task at hand. A good thing one of them was.

"Staci." She stacked the photos of Staci Gale into a

pile. "Maureen Godwin." She stacked another pile, a hard smile curving her lips. "Kim Slade."

"Your instincts about the boyfriend were spot on. He was innocent."

"A damned shame that the cops back then didn't realize a serial hunter was hunting in the area." She shook her head. "How many women might have been spared?"

Zac waved a hand toward the photos still spread across his desk. "We have photos of at least twenty unidentified women."

"It's . . ." Rachel shuddered. "I don't have words."

"No one does." His voice was harsh. When he'd started photocopying the pictures, he'd assumed there were duplicates. His mind couldn't wrap around the possibility that there could be so many women destroyed at the hands of one man. No. Not a man. An unconscionable beast. "There are some things too awful to speak out loud."

Rachel leaned her hip against the desk, her pale face tense with a grinding fear. The same fear that churned in his belly.

"If we could identify these women, it might help us capture the monster who's walking in Jude's footsteps." She pointed out the obvious.

"Do you have a database to run them through?"

"Yes. And I've emailed the photos to the office." She heaved a small sigh. "Unfortunately, we can't be sure the women are in any system. Neither Staci nor Maureen were reported missing."

"True," he muttered.

She was right, of course. Jude Henley had been too clever to leave behind a trail of victims for them to follow. No one had ever suspected that Staci had been in Jude's grave, or that Maureen's death had been anything beyond a tragic accident. That was how he'd managed to elude the authorities for years.

"But we have another database to use." Rachel interrupted his dark thoughts.

He sent her a puzzled frown. "We do?"

"Rudolf Jansen's files," she reminded him. "The old sheriff might not have realized there was a serial killer in Pike, but he sensed something was wrong."

Zac glanced back at the pictures on his desk as he recalled the files they'd glanced through . . . was it just last night? It seemed a lifetime ago. Some were nothing more than scribbled notes that Rudolf had stuffed in a folder. But others—like Maureen—had full police reports along with Rudolf's private investigation notes.

"If we can match the photo with the file, we might get ahead of the killer," Zac murmured, assuming that was Rachel's hope. If they knew who had been murdered, and the basic details of how the women had died or disappeared, they might know where to look for the next victim. "At least it would narrow down the possibilities."

"Exactly."

Zac reached into the pocket of his slacks, pulling out his key ring. "Here's a key to the house," he said, handing it to her. "I'll meet you there later."

She looked at him with obvious curiosity. "What are you going to do?"

"Look for Tory." He glanced toward the old-fashioned clock on the wall. "We have less than two hours."

"Do you want me to—"

"Check out the files," he interrupted. He had no idea where Tory might be. There was no use in both of them wasting their time. "If I'm too late, then we can at least get a head start on the next victim."

She nodded. "Be careful."

Waiting for her to disappear from the office, Zac pulled on his jacket and considered his options. The obvious choice would be to return to the Roadhouse. That was where Tory had last been seen. But if they were right about the killer walking in Jude's footsteps, then he assumed he would want the body to be discovered in the same location as Maureen.

Driving to the old Lake Road, Zac parked his truck and walked along the edge of the narrow path. He ignored the chilled wind and low-hanging clouds that intensified the sense that he was completely alone as he turned to enter the thick cluster of trees. Would the killer simply drive by and dump Tory's body in the area? If so, he didn't have a chance of stopping the murder. His only hope was that the madman had chosen to hide her in a nearby location.

Two hours later, Zac admitted defeat.

His search had yielded nothing more than muddy boots, a bone-deep chill, and a sick sensation in the center of his being. The deadline had come and passed without finding Tory.

He was too late. He knew it without a shadow of a doubt. Tory was already dead.

Trudging back to his truck, Zac had just reached the road when the sound of a vehicle had him glancing over his shoulder in surprise. He hadn't heard or seen evidence of a human being in over two hours. Who would be out here as dusk began to creep over this remote area?

There was nothing to see for a minute. Just trees. And more trees. Then a truck pulled out of a side road. Was that the direction of the Henley cabin? His confusion only deepened when he caught sight of the official logo on the side of the truck. It belonged to the sheriff's department.

The truck idled at the end of the road, as if the driver was debating which direction to turn. Finally, it pulled onto the main road and headed directly toward Zac. Planting his hands on his hips, Zac waited for the vehicle to stop next to him, the passenger window rolling down so he could see inside the cab.

"Anthony." Zac frowned in surprise. The last time he'd seen his deputy, the younger man had been headed home to get some rest. There was only one reason he could imagine the deputy being called back into the office. "Did they find Tory?"

Anthony blinked at the sharp question, clearly caught off guard. "I don't think so."

Zac scowled. He was cold, tired, and frustrated. It wasn't the time to wear on his raw nerves. "Then what are you doing out here?" he snapped.

"Looking for you."

"Why?"

"I thought you might want some help searching for Tory."

Zac narrowed his eyes. If it'd been Lindsay sitting behind the wheel, he would have accepted the explanation without hesitation. She was devoted to her job and ambitious enough to go above and beyond the call of duty. Anthony, on the other hand . . .

"No offense, but you rarely volunteer for overtime," he pointed out in dry tones.

The familiar petulant expression settled on the round face, but Anthony managed to keep his resentment out of his voice. "I couldn't sleep. I thought I might as well do something to help."

"Hmm." Zac continued to study his deputy. Did he believe Anthony? Not entirely. Then again, no one knew Pike and the people in the area better than the younger man. For the moment, Zac needed his expertise. "Are there any cabins near here?"

"There's the Henleys' old place." He jerked a thumb over his shoulder. "It's back that way."

"Any other place?"

Anthony pursed his lips, glancing from side to side as he considered the question. "No cabins," he at last told Zac. "But there's an old boathouse near the lake."

Zac felt a surge of hope. He hadn't stumbled across a boathouse during his hours of wandering through the countryside. Perhaps that was the place Tory was being held.

Squashing the certainty that he'd already missed his opportunity to rescue the young woman, he squared his shoulders. "Show me."

Anthony reached down to shut off the engine and climbed out of the truck. "This way," he said, heading into the trees on the opposite side of the road.

Zac quickly caught up to the deputy, his longer strides making it easy to keep pace. "Do you spend time at the Roadhouse?"

"Not really." The man shrugged, angling through the trees with a confidence that revealed he'd been out here more than once. "It's more a place for old people."

Zac studied the man's profile. "You seem to know your way around out here."

"This is public land that they open during deer season. I come to hunt."

It was a reasonable explanation. Many citizens of Pike who didn't have private land used the public acres.

"My dad never taught me to hunt," Zac admitted, more to keep Anthony talking than any genuine interest. "He claimed we had too many chores to waste time sitting in the woods."

Anthony shrugged. "I never had a dad to teach me anything. I came here with my cousin." He pointed toward a spot north of them. "I got a five-point buck not far from here."

Zac turned the conversation to a more pressing problem. "Do you know the Boltons?"

"By reputation." Anthony stopped, glancing around before he headed out again, veering toward the right. "I don't think the son went to school in Pike, but I've seen the older Bolton around town."

"Is he violent?"

"That depends on what you mean by violent." Anthony shrugged. "He's been in a few scuffles. Usually when he's drunk."

"Do you think he's capable of killing someone?"

The deputy took a minute to consider the question, his steps slowing as his breathing quickened. The terrain was angling steadily upward and Anthony wasn't the most athletic man.

"In the heat of the moment, he has a vicious temper," he finally conceded. "But he couldn't plan a murder and keep it hidden."

"Why not?"

Anthony released a humorless laugh as they crested the small hill. "He'd confess everything the first time he went into the bar. When Curly's drunk he never shuts his mouth." Anthony came to a halt, pointing through the trees toward the nearby clearing. "There's the boathouse."

Zac jogged forward, leaving Anthony behind as he hurried toward the weathered building that was shaped like a barn. It was built out of pale gray stones and topped with a rusty tin roof. There were large windows, most of them still intact, and in front there were arched openings for boats to enter. It was perched on the edge of the lake with an old dock that was falling apart.

Reaching the nearest window, Zac peered inside. It was a large, cavernous space that was rapidly filling with shadows, but it was easy to determine that it was empty inside.

No Tory. No mad killer. Nothing but a few rotting life jackets and a stray oar.

"Um . . . boss." Anthony spoke from someplace behind Zac, his voice oddly harsh. "There's something floating out there."

Zac stepped back, his gaze skimming over the silver-gray water of the large lake. It took a few seconds for him to locate what had captured Anthony's attention. Then a bird swooped down, and he caught sight of the dark form that floated facedown in the water.

Shit.

"Call the ambulance," he called out, running along the edge of the lake in search of a boat.

He was too late, but he couldn't stop himself from trying to reach the body.

Chapter 15

It was late when Rachel climbed out of bed and took a shower, but the farmhouse remained silent as she entered the kitchen to make herself a pot of coffee. She didn't know what time Zac had gotten home, but it had to have been after midnight.

Wisely she'd resisted the urge to wait up for him. Not only would he be weary from the hours he'd spent investigating the crime scene, but he needed privacy to decompress from the stress of the night. He'd already called to tell her that Tory had been found floating in the lake, and that she'd been taken to the medical examiner for an autopsy. He had stayed to interview anyone who might have a view of the lake and to search for any tire tracks that might give a clue who had dumped the body. If he'd found anything, she didn't doubt he would have let her know.

Once she had enough caffeine buzzing through her body, Rachel sat at the kitchen table and sorted through the pictures she'd spread over the flat surface. She didn't know why she continued to stare at them. The images had been seared into her mind. And so far her theory that the past might be able to prevent more murders was just that . . . a theory.

Still, there was something nagging at the edge of her mind. Something that she sensed might be important. If she could just pinpoint what it was.

It was past ten o'clock when Zac at last wandered into the kitchen, wearing nothing but a faded pair of jeans. Glancing up, Rachel felt the breath punched from her lungs.

Oh man. He was a mess. His hair was rumpled from sleep, his jaw was shadowed with his morning whiskers, and his eyes were bloodshot, but he'd never looked more edible. Her mouth was dry as sandpaper as her gaze ran over his bare chest sprinkled with golden hair that tapered to a point just above the waistband of his jeans. He was even more muscular than she remembered, with broad shoulders and washboard abs that begged to be explored. First with her fingertips, and then with her lips. Maybe her tongue . . .

"Why didn't you wake me?" Thankfully unaware of her racing heart and damp palms, Zac strolled to pour himself a mug of coffee.

Rachel was forced to clear her throat before she answered. "You needed your sleep."

Turning, he leaned against the counter with a wry smile. "You sound like a wife." He grimaced as she stiffened at the casual words. "Sorry."

"It's okay." She sucked in a slow, deep breath. "I was your wife."

"You'll always be my wife." He lifted a hand to press it against the center of his chest. "Here."

She shook her head. Not in rejection. For the first time

in a very, very long time she didn't wince in pain at the mention of their broken marriage. But now wasn't the time for this conversation. They were in the middle of hunting down a crazed killer. And more importantly, there was a dangerous hunger sizzling through her.

Every instinct urged her to get up and press Zac against the counter. To kiss each inch of his hard, sculpted body. To wrap herself so tightly around him he could never escape.

Lust and good decisions never went together.

"Zac."

"I know." He grimaced. "Rotten timing."

"I—"

She wasn't sure what she was going to say. Thankfully, Zac briskly set aside his coffee and moved to stand next to her chair.

"What were you studying with such intensity when I walked in?" he asked, easing the awkward tension.

Rachel eagerly turned her attention back to the pictures. Murder and mayhem she could handle. Emotions . . . not so much.

"These," she said, waving her hand over the clutter.

He rested his palms on the edge of the table as he leaned forward. "Have you found a connection to the files?"

"Not yet."

He turned his head, obviously hearing something in her tone. "What's bothering you?"

"I've been staring at these pictures for hours."

"And?"

She reached to grab a photo, holding it so he could see the pretty, blond-haired woman with bright blue eyes and deep dimples. Despite being a grainy photocopy it was easy to see her happy, carefree expression.

"And I couldn't figure out why I kept returning to this particular one," she said. "At first I assumed it was because I've seen her before."

"You think you might know her?"

She did. She couldn't pinpoint a name, but she was certain she'd seen her before. "There's something vaguely familiar about her, but that's not what was bothering me."

"Then what is?"

"This picture is different from the others." She waved a hand over the stacks of pictures on the table.

He was silent as he studied the various photos, his brows drawing together as he eventually shook his head. "I'm not sure what's different."

She picked up a random picture. It turned out to be one of Staci Gale. The young woman was walking down the street dressed in a waitress uniform with her hair in a ponytail and her profile tense. As if she was worried, or in a hurry.

"These are all taken from a distance with the women looking in another direction." She waved the picture of the blond-haired woman. "In this one, she's standing just a couple feet away, looking directly into the camera."

Zac sucked in a sharp breath. "You're right. She knew Jude was taking her picture."

"And she was happy about it," Rachel added.

Zac reached out to shuffle through the pictures, his expression impossible to read. "These look like photos a stalker would take," he softly murmured. "But why? He was lovers with Maureen and possibly the others."

"True." She made a sound of frustration. Why did a guy

take stalker pictures when he could have selfies with his lover? Because he never thought of them as lovers? Yes, that made sense. "Maybe I'm looking at it wrong. Or backward," she breathed.

"Backward?"

She waved the picture of the smiling blonde. "I was thinking that this revealed the woman's emotion. But now I wonder if it reveals Jude's." She struggled to put her thoughts into words, glancing toward the image of Staci Gale. "The other women are distant objects. Meaning-less." She returned her attention to the blonde. "This one is . . . real. As if Jude sees her as a human being, not an object. If that makes any sense."

"Perfect sense." Zac pushed away from the table, a surge of energy suddenly humming around him. "We need to discover who she is."

Rachel agreed. She had no idea if locating the blonde in the picture would help in the investigation, but it was a lead to follow. Clues were astonishingly few and far be-tween, considering that Pike was such a small town. Someone should have seen something, right?

With a muttered curse, Rachel shoved herself to her feet, clutching the photo. "I think I might know someone who can help."

"Who?"

She headed toward the kitchen door. "My mother."

Returning to the guest bedroom, Rachel changed into black slacks and a chunky ivory sweater, then gave her hair a good brushing. She left the house by the side door. She wasn't deliberately avoiding Zac . . . Wait, that wasn't entirely true. It wasn't that she didn't want to answer his questions about what she believed she could learn from her mother. She could honestly tell him that she had nothing more than a vague hope DeeDee would recognize the woman. What she didn't want to explain was that she had another purpose in seeking out her mother.

It was a sudden urge that had hit without warning, and one she knew would vanish the moment she gave herself time to consider the consequences.

Driving into town, Rachel pulled into the driveway in front of her parents' home and walked up to the front door. Her hand lifted to knock, only to lower to grab the doorknob and push it open. There was no surprise that it wasn't locked. Even with the murders spreading through Pike the citizens possessed a belief that nothing bad could ever happen in their own homes.

As she stepped into the living room, she heard sounds coming from the kitchen. A second later DeeDee Fisher appeared through the arched opening.

"Rachel." The older woman lifted her dark brows, wiping her hands on the apron that covered her gray slacks and lemon silk shirt.

Rachel closed the front door and lowered her satchel to the floor. "Are you busy?"

"Nothing that can't wait." A tight smile curved DeeDee's lips. "I thought you must have left town. I haven't seen hide nor hair of you."

Rachel sighed at the less than subtle chastisement. "I'm in Pike to work, Mom."

"You're always working."

"I know." She shrugged. "We all cope in our own way."

DeeDee blinked, as if blindsided by Rachel's response. "Would you like a cup of coffee?"

"Please."

Rachel's nerves were already jittery, and the last thing

she needed was more caffeine, but it would be easier to talk to her mother if they were comfortably settled. Pulling the photo from her pocket, she slid off her jacket and tossed it on top of her satchel. Then, stiffening her spine, she followed her mother into the kitchen and took a seat at the table.

With the ease of years of practice, her mother bustled from counter to counter, filling a tray with mugs of coffee, cream and sugar, a plate of muffins and linen napkins. Placing everything on a tray she moved toward the table and slid into a chair opposite Rachel.

"Those just came out of the oven," she murmured, watching in pleasure as Rachel eagerly grabbed two of the muffins off the tray.

"Banana. Yum," Rachel murmured. "My favorite."

DeeDee handed her a mug of coffee and a napkin. "Did you drop by just to chat?"

Rachel consumed one of the muffins before she answered. She hadn't bothered with breakfast and she hadn't realized how hungry she was.

"I do have a question." She took a sip of the coffee, hiding a grimace. Pure sludge.

"About Jude?" the older woman asked.

"About the woman in this photo." Rachel smoothed out the photocopy before sliding it across the table.

DeeDee continued to sip her coffee as she studied the picture. At last she glanced up with a puzzled expression. "What do you want to know about Evie?"

"Who?"

"Evie Parson."

"Oh." The wife of Russell Parson, the owner of the bank where her father worked. The woman that her mother had said was rumored to be having an affair with Jude.

"I thought she looked familiar, but I couldn't place a name with her face."

"I doubt you'd remember much about her. You were still in grade school when she died." DeeDee clicked her tongue, her expression one of pity. "She was very young. Not even forty. I can't say that I ever really liked her, but it was a tragedy."

Rachel leaned forward, her instincts humming. She had been convinced there was something different about Evie Parson, but it was starting to sound as if she was just another victim.

"Do you know how she died?"

"Cancer." DeeDee pursed her lips. "I'm not sure if it was breast cancer or throat. Something awful."

"Oh." It wasn't what Rachel had been expecting. She assumed the death would have been some mysterious accident. But cancer . . . Not even Jude would have been skilled enough to fake a death by disease.

"Where did you get this picture?" DeeDee interrupted Rachel's frustrated thoughts.

"We think it belonged to Jude."

"Really?" Curiosity simmered in her mother's eyes. Gossip was the lifeblood of any small town. "Then the rumors of their affair were true."

Rachel broke off a piece of her second muffin and slowly chewed it. She was missing something. She had to be. "What can you tell me about their relationship?"

"Nothing, really." DeeDee shrugged. "There were whispers that Jude's truck was often parked behind Evie's house when her husband was at work. I also heard that they'd been seen together in Grange. It was no surprise." Her mother looked disapproving. "Russell was at least a dozen years older than her. And to be honest, he has always been a complete bore. Your father admires him, but he's very stern. I don't think I've ever seen him smile, not even at the lavish Christmas parties he hosts. And the way he would speak down to Evie . . . it was no wonder she looked for a bit of fun on the side."

"Did she have a lot of affairs?"

Her mom took a second, as if searching her memories. "I don't think I heard of anyone else. But your father's position at the bank meant that people wouldn't have always shared Evie's indiscretions with me." DeeDee shoved the photo back across the table. "Was Jude carrying this when he died?"

"No." Rachel paused, considering how much she could reveal. The last thing she wanted was to alert the killer that they'd discovered the album. It might provoke him into retaliating. Or changing his strategy. Then again, any information she could get from her mother would help in the search. And with the women of Pike in danger, she couldn't afford not to take any help she could find. "It was left in the Henley cabin."

"Cabin?" DeeDee looked momentarily baffled. "Oh. I forgot about that place."

"Did they have any other properties around town?"

"I couldn't tell you. I didn't really know them that well."

Hmm. Dead end. Rachel returned the conversation back to Jude. He was at the center of the murders. And despite the fact he was dead, he continued to reach out from the grave. If she could understand him, and how he'd chosen his females, then they might have a chance to stop the copycat killer.

Abruptly Rachel recalled Zac talking about the M.E.

report. "Do you know how Jude hurt his shoulder?" she asked.

So far she'd heard Jude described as a bad boy charmer, a misunderstood delinquent, and a petty criminal. She wanted to know if there'd been any indications that beneath the surface he was an actual monster.

Her mom started to shake her head, only to stop as her brows drew together in a faint frown. "Wait. Now that you mention it, I seem to remember he was wearing a cast in a sling when we were young. Grade school, I think. He said he fell out of a tree. I remember because he had all the girls sign it and I didn't want to."

Falling out of a tree was a reasonable explanation. Unfortunately, it didn't offer any help in discovering the true Jude Henley. "Was he ever violent at school?"

"Violent?" DeeDee considered the question. "He probably got into fights. Most of the boys did," she said. "They were always pushing and shoving in the hallways and a few times they threw some punches after school. None of it was serious."

"Violent toward women," Rachel clarified.

"No. Not that I ever heard of." DeeDee hesitated before she wrinkled her nose. "Of course, back then a girl might not tell anyone if someone hurt her. Especially if she was dating her abuser. We didn't discuss stuff like that."

Rachel slowly straightened in her chair, her mouth oddly dry as she met her mom's gaze. This was the perfect opportunity to bring up the second reason she'd driven to her childhood home.

"Is that why you still refuse to discuss painful subjects?" she asked.

Her mom jerked, easily knowing what Rachel meant.

Then, with a predictable determination to avoid the loss that haunted their family, she jumped to her feet. "More coffee."

Rachel reached across the table, grabbing her mom's hand before she could stage a retreat. "Please sit down."

"I just—"

"Please," Rachel interrupted, refusing to release her ruthless grip.

Pinching her lips into a hard line, DeeDee grudgingly lowered herself onto the chair, her back ramrod straight. "There. I'm sitting." She glared at Rachel. "Happy?"

"Not particularly," Rachel conceded in dry tones. "But I think it's time I was honest with you."

"Honest about what?"

"You were right. I do avoid spending time in this house."

Her mother paled, her shoulders squaring as if she was expecting a physical blow. "Because of me?"

Rachel pushed the words past her stiff lips. "Because of Benny."

Chapter 16

DeeDee hissed out a painful breath. "Don't."

Rachel knew she was hurting her mother. Any mention of her younger brother who'd died when he was just four caused the older woman intense agony. As if Benny's death was still fresh and raw. And for eighteen years, the family had tiptoed around the tragedy.

They never discussed what had happened, or how much they missed the bubbly little boy who'd torn through the house with glorious abandon. They didn't visit his grave in Wausau where he was buried next to Rachel's grandparents, or pull out old photo albums to talk about what he might have been like if he'd lived.

The house had been purged of all visible memories, but the emotional ones remained, causing a deepening rot that was destroying the family from the inside out. Unless it was purged, they would eventually shatter beneath the strain.

Dramatic, but true.

"I'm not going to stop," Rachel warned. "Not this time."

DeeDee glanced away, lifting a trembling hand to place it over her heart. "You enjoy hurting me."

"Of course not. That's the last thing I would ever want," Rachel insisted. "You've been hurt enough. We all have."

"Then just let the past be."

The words were depressingly familiar. Her mother had said them a thousand times since the morning they'd awakened to discover that Benny had climbed out of his window in the middle of the night and disappeared.

No one knew exactly why he'd gone into the near blizzard that had swept through Pike. He'd never done anything like it before. Rachel suspected he'd seen a stray dog, or perhaps another animal, and decided to try and rescue it from the cold. That certainly would have been something the kindhearted little boy would have done. Whatever the reason, when they'd awoken the next morning, it was to find an open window and an empty bed.

The entire town had turned out for the search, but by the time they'd found Benny curled up in the corner of the next-door neighbor's garage, it'd been too late. He was gone.

Rachel had felt as if her heart had been ripped out of her chest.

"Allowing the past to be, doesn't mean forgetting the past," she said in a low, husky voice. The tears she'd only been allowed to shed in private filled her eyes.

"No one is forgetting anything."

"Then why have you taken away the memories of my brother?"

DeeDee gasped, her head jerking back so she could glare at Rachel. "I haven't."

"Where are his pictures?" Rachel waved a hand to indicate the recently refurbished living room. "Or the drawings that used to hang on the fridge? Or the baseball mitt that was tossed next to the back door."

DeeDee's jaw clenched, as if she was struggling to keep herself from screaming. Rachel wished she would release a primal cry. Anything to vent the emotions she kept suppressed deep inside.

"I've kept everything that ever belonged to my beautiful boy," she said, each word spit out like a curse.

"Yes." Rachel refused to back down. This confrontation was long overdue. "Locked away in a room no one is permitted to enter."

"It's the only way I can bear the loss."

Rachel clenched her hands in her lap. Her first instinct was to back away from the agonizing subject. It was excruciating. Like ripping open wounds that went all the way to the soul, she acknowledged as her heart twisted with regret. But how could they ever move past Benny's death if they didn't accept that it'd happened?

"I'm sorry, I truly am." The words were thick with regret. "But I can't bear treating my brother like some sort of dirty secret."

With a soft cry, DeeDee surged to her feet, her expression horrified. "Rachel."

"That's how it feels," Rachel doggedly continued. She'd come this far. She wasn't going to stop now. "Ever since we lost Benny we haven't been able to speak his name, except in whispers. And God forbid we laugh and cherish the time we were given to spend with him." She leaned forward, silently pleading for her mother to understand. Although she'd been eight years older than her brother, she'd adored him from the second she held him in her arms. "Like the day his tooth fell out and he accidentally swallowed it. Don't you remember? You tried to comfort him, but I told him that the tooth fairy wasn't going to leave him any money. He was so mad." She chuckled, vividly recalling Benny's flushed face as he stomped his foot and insisted the fairy could find the tooth in his belly. "And the time—"

"Stop. Please."

Rachel studied her mother's tense profile. "Why?"

"It's my fault," the older woman abruptly burst out. "He's gone because of me."

"No." Rachel rose to her feet, moving to place an arm around DeeDee's slender shoulders. "That's not true."

"It is," she stubbornly insisted. "I should have locked his window."

Rachel shook her head. People in Pike didn't lock their doors and windows. And no one could have suspected that Benny would crawl out of his room in the middle of a blizzard.

"It was a tragic accident," she insisted. "No one was at fault."

Her mother bent her head, as if the guilt was too heavy to bear. "You don't understand."

Rachel sighed, wishing she didn't understand. The past eighteen years wouldn't have been nearly so difficult if she hadn't shouldered her own share of remorse.

"I do," she assured her mother. "Why do you think I became a cop?"

Her mother sent her a confused glance. "You said you wanted to help others."

"Exactly. I spent years blaming myself for not finding Benny quicker." She willed herself to share the memories that had haunted her for so long. The hours she'd spent trudging through the snow, her voice hoarse as she called out her brother's name. "I thought if I'd only been smarter, or searched faster, or if I hadn't stopped to talk to my friend . . ." Her voice broke as the memories crashed through her. "And the worst part was, I'd been angry at first. I thought he was playing some stupid game, and that we were all worried for nothing. Then, as the hours passed, I knew it was something awful." She paused to take a deep, steadying breath. "There were so many painful emotions churning inside my heart. They threatened to drown me. And it only made it worse that we swept Benny's memory under the rug. As if we could make his loss disappear if we never spoke about him."

"That's not true."

Rachel ignored the sharp protest. The older woman had been in denial for so long, she no longer realized she was destroying her life.

"I didn't want the bitterness to consume me, so I decided I would become a detective. I couldn't save Benny, but I could at least try to save someone else's loved one."

There was a long silence, as if her mother was trying to process her words. "Has it helped?" she finally asked.

"Yes."

Her mom slowly turned to face her, a heartrending vulnerability in her eyes. "I'm glad."

Rachel grabbed her mom's slender hands, not surprised to discover they were freezing. It had nothing to do with the temperature in the room. She was trembling at being forced to confront the past.

"I want help for you," she said. "And Dad."

"We're fine."

Rachel squeezed her fingers. "You're not."

DeeDee frowned at her daughter's stubborn insistence. "Why are you bringing this up now?"

Rachel glanced away, considering how to explain what had compelled her to share the resentment she harbored at the inability to openly mourn for her brother. It hadn't been one thing, she acknowledged. It was bits and pieces. Spending time in this house and watching the brittle tension between her parents. Walking around town, remembering the places she used to visit. Most of all, being with Zac.

When she'd graduated from high school, she'd been anxious to escape from Pike. She'd thought it was an eagerness to grasp onto her future. She was marrying the man she loved and heading to college to start the first steps in her career. It genuinely hadn't occurred to her that she was running from anything.

"Because being back in Pike has reminded me that being a detective didn't heal all my wounds," she admitted.

"Are you talking about Zac?"

"Yes." Rachel dropped her mother's hands, stepping back. "We were young and made a lot of stupid mistakes when we got married, including my obsession with my career. I didn't realize I was using it as a way to keep people at a distance. Not until too late."

"And now?"

"Now I hope I'm ready to accept the past and look forward to the future," she murmured, still not certain exactly what the future might hold. "And that's what I want for you."

DeeDee bit her bottom lip, something that might have been fear in her eyes. "I don't know."

"Forgive yourself, Mom." Rachel leaned forward,

brushing her lips over her mother's cheek. "It's time to live again."

It was just past noon when Zac pulled into the sheriff's department. Parking in the side lot, he was stepping out of his truck when he caught sight of a uniformed man standing next to a car parked near the dumpster. He paused, watching as the car abruptly pulled out of the lot, almost as if his arrival had frightened away whoever was behind the wheel.

He studied the disappearing car, his brows drawing together as he recognized the driver. Turning back to the man still standing in the shadows of the building, Zac expected to see Anthony. Probably because the younger man had been acting strangely since they'd found Jude's body. Instead it was Greg Barry.

With long strides, he crossed the lot to stand in front of the deputy. "Was that Joe Carr you were talking to?" he demanded.

Greg looked mildly surprised at the sharp question. "Yep."

"What did he want?"

"He said he was here to talk to Anthony." Greg shrugged. "When I told him that he wasn't here, he took off like a bat out of hell."

"Why did he want to talk to Anthony?"

"He refused to say." Greg narrowed his eyes as he sensed Zac's tension. "Do you want me to question him? He might have information about his wife's murder he wanted to pass along."

"I'll take care of it." Zac added a visit with Joe Carr to

his ever-growing to-do list. "What are you doing out here?"

"I was just headed to lunch. Unless you need me?"

"When you're done eating I want you to drive over to Grange and interview Tory's family and neighbors," he told the younger man. "I want to know if Tory mentioned anyone suspicious at work or around her house. Whoever kidnapped her did it in broad daylight. He had to have spent some time tracking her movements to know her schedule at the Roadhouse."

Greg nodded. "Got it."

"Where's Anthony?"

"He left early. He said he had an appointment."

Zac's jaw tightened. If he didn't have a thousand things more important, he would go in search of his missing deputy that second. He wanted to know exactly why Joe Carr would be at the station to talk to him.

But he did have a thousand things more important. He heaved a weary sigh.

"Write up your interview with Tory's family when you get back and leave it on my desk," he told his deputy before turning to head toward the side of the building. He used the keypad to buzz himself in and headed up to his office.

Two hours later he was struggling to concentrate on aerial photos of the lake, trying to discover any hidden cabin they might have missed during their search of the area. It would have been a lot easier if his mind didn't keep returning to the memory of walking into his kitchen that morning to discover Rachel seated at the table.

She'd obviously been working, and was distracted with the photos, but that hadn't stopped his heart from missing a beat and his breath from lodging in his throat. He'd missed her so much it physically hurt. Was it any wonder that having her near was healing a wound that festered deep inside him? Or that he was increasingly desperate to find some way to make sure she never left?

But what about what Rachel wanted? He'd been the one to walk away. Would she ever trust him again? More importantly, did she care enough to try? She had a job she loved, and no doubt plenty of friends. Maybe she was satisfied with her life.

His dark musings were eventually interrupted as the door to his office was pushed open to reveal Monel Jenkins. The middle-aged woman was in charge of the front desk when the deputies were busy.

"There's an Isaac Dowell to see you."

Zac frowned. The name was vaguely familiar. At last he matched it with the mailman who lived next to Curly Senior. "Why?"

"He said he found something."

Zac paused before giving a nod. With Curly still in jail it seemed doubtful he had information about the older man, but he did live across the street from Joe Carr. He might have seen something that made him suspicious. That also might be the reason Joe Carr had come looking for Anthony. Maybe he was hoping the deputy could help him out of trouble.

"Let him in."

Monel nodded, backing out of the doorway. She was quickly replaced by a young man with short, black hair wearing a blue uniform.

"Sheriff." He offered a nervous smile. "I'm not sure if you remember me."

"I remember." Zac leaned forward, his hands flat on the top of the desk. "Are you here about one of your neighbors?"

Isaac seemed baffled by the question before shaking his head. "No, sorry. I haven't really paid attention to whether Curly came back or not. This is the start of hell season for the post office and I'm either working or in bed."

Zac struggled to hide his burst of disappointment. "Why are you here?"

"I found this." The younger man stepped forward to lay a large padded envelope on the cluttered desk.

Shock blasted through Zac. His name was scrawled across the front. Just like it had been on the envelope left in Tory's car. The one with the videotape inside.

"Where did you find it?"

"It was left in Mrs. Wilkins's mailbox," Isaac answered. "I'm not supposed to pick up packages, especially not ones that are missing postage. Folks are supposed to take them to the post office to drop them off. But I saw your name on the front and I decided I would break the rules and bring it to you."

Zac could barely concentrate on what the man was telling him. His focus was locked on the package. As if it were a rattlesnake about to strike.

And that was exactly what it felt like.

"When?"

"Excuse me?"

"When did you find it?"

"On my morning round. Nine? Maybe nine thirty." Isaac was eyeing him with a wary gaze, obviously puzzled by Zac's sharp tone. "My schedule is all out of whack this week. I usually don't pick up in that neighborhood until the end of the day, but we have temporary helpers training for the holiday season so I had one of them take half my route and I took care of the other half. It meant I got done twice as fast."

Zac made a mental note. If this did come from the killer, then any change in routine might have caused him to make a mistake. Something he needed to check out. Later.

"Who else handled the package?" he asked.

"No one." Isaac clenched and unclenched his hands, his expression troubled. "I pulled it out of the mailbox and tossed it into my back seat until I had a chance to run it by. Did I do something wrong?"

Zac ignored the man's obvious desire to be reassured that he wasn't in trouble. Zac didn't have time to worry about anyone's tender feelings.

"What's the address of Mrs. . . ." Zac struggled to recall the name.

"Wilkins. She's an elderly widow who lives on Jefferson Street. I can't think of the number off the top of my head," Isaac said. "It's a yellow house with black shutters."

Zac nodded. He knew the house. And he had a vague memory of an older woman who spent warm afternoons on her porch, tending to several large pots of petunias. She certainly wasn't the killer. So who had left the package in her mailbox?

The obvious answer was the man standing in front of him. No one would notice a mailman carrying around a package. Plus he traveled around town unnoticed, able to keep a watch on people while he remained invisible.

"You didn't think it was odd that she would leave a package addressed to me in her mailbox?"

Isaac shook his head. "Not really. She often leaves me plates of homemade cookies, and at Christmas she knit me a scarf and mittens that she wrapped and put in the box. I assume it's some sort of gift. Or perhaps she had something that needed your help. She's not in very good health so she doesn't leave her house very often."

The explanation was plausible. When he was growing up, his mother often left casseroles on the porches of church members who were ill, or fresh eggs and milk for those she knew were struggling to make ends meet. It was a way of giving without making a fuss about it.

This package, however, he knew was no gift. Just looking at it made his gut burn with dread. The mystery killer was giving him an ulcer.

"Did you mention the envelope to anyone else?"

"No, I didn't think there was anything to mention."

"Keep it to yourself for now."

Isaac shrugged. "Okay."

"And if you come across any more packages addressed to me just leave them where they are and call me."

The man once again looked uneasy. As if he was worried he was in trouble. "Sorry. I thought I was helping."

Zac forced a tight smile to his lips. He didn't want Isaac realizing that he'd gone onto Zac's mental suspect list. If the younger man took off, they might never track him down. "No need to be sorry. I appreciate you bringing the package."

Isaac nodded, but his expression remained tense. "I should get back to work."

Zac waited until the man was nearly at the door before he spoke. "You're not from Pike, are you?"

Isaac halted, reluctantly turning to meet Zac's curious gaze. "No. I transferred here from Green Bay last year."

"What made you want to come to Pike?"

"The usual reason." A wry smile twisted his lips. "A woman."

Zac was caught by surprise. It wasn't the answer he'd been expecting. "You're dating someone in town?"

"No, in Grange. But I couldn't get a job there, so I took one here." He glanced toward the long window that offered a view of Main Street. "It worked out for the best, I suppose. The relationship fizzled and died after only a few weeks. Living here means I don't have to worry about constantly seeing her around town."

"You enjoy living in Pike?"

Isaac grimaced. "It's okay. For now. I'll eventually get bored and move on."

"Back to Green Bay?"

"I was thinking someplace warmer," Isaac said. "The motto of not letting snow or rain or heat or gloom of night keep me from completing my appointed rounds sounds great, but it's not always fun wading through nasty weather."

Zac had grown up on a farm. He had an intimate acquaintance with tunneling his way through several feet of snow in subzero temperatures to feed the cattle and collect eggs from the henhouse. There'd been nothing fun about it.

"True," he agreed with feeling.

Isaac shifted from foot to foot. "I really gotta go."

Zac waved a dismissive hand, waiting for the postman to leave the office and close the door behind him. Opening a drawer, Zac pulled on a pair of latex gloves with a sinking sensation. His mother would call it the heebie-jeebies.

His grandfather would say that someone was walking across his grave.

He just knew that he didn't like it.

Careful not to tear the flap, Zac eased open the envelope. Then, bending forward, he glanced inside, discovering exactly what he'd expected to see.

A VHS tape.

Muttering a curse, Zac grabbed his phone and pressed a familiar number. Seconds later, he was connected to Rachel.

"We have another one," he growled in a harsh voice.

Chapter 17

It was happening.

A shiver raced through my body. Was it too fast? Perhaps. I hadn't been able to savor Tory's death. Actually, any memory of the bitch had been forgotten the moment her body had been dumped into the lake.

A professional therapist would no doubt tell me that I'm escalating. That the bloodlust inside me is like heroin. An addiction that needed a faster, bigger dose each time until I imploded.

I'm not concerned.

It was true that I was overly eager to get my hands on the next victim. Who could blame me? I'd spent what felt like an eternity choosing the perfect women. And then waiting for an opportune moment to strike. It was becoming increasingly frustrating to stick to the rules of the game. Even if I was the one to invent those rules. And I hadn't fully prepared myself for the exquisite rush of beating the women until the life drained from their eyes. It was far more intoxicating than reaching my climax as they struggled beneath me.

But I'm not escalating.

I'm . . . evolving. Yes. That's the proper word.

I could only follow in Jude's footsteps for so long. Eventually I was destined to grow beyond his mediocre abilities, right?

And that evolution included Detective Rachel Fisher.

My blood quickens.

She was never meant to be a part of the game. She has none of the qualities I've been seeking. My prey had specifically been chosen to represent one of Jude's victims. How can I prove my superiority if I don't have a head-to-head competition? Or rather a body-to-body competition. But now that I've added her to my game, why not take it a step further? Why not add her to my list of creations?

Unlike the others, she's an intelligent, beautiful, extensively trained opponent. She will prove that I am truly the master. The Maestro.

Including her, however, will mean moving up my timeline. Something I'm eager and willing to do.

It also means devising a very special surprise for the detective.

She will be the brightest jewel in my crown. One that deserves a properly spectacular death.

Pacing from one end of the hideout to the other, I try to concentrate on the next step in my meticulous plan. I must take care. The sheriff isn't a fool. Certainly not as clever as me, but anyone can make a mistake. And there are things out of my control.

Patience, I whisper to myself.

All good things will come in time.

* * *

Rachel stood next to Zac in his parents' bedroom, shuddering as Zac stopped the tape. The static image caught Jude Henley standing over the woman he'd just beaten to death with the now familiar crowbar. His face was splattered with droplets of blood, and a smile of pure evil was on his lips as he gazed directly into the camera.

Another shudder raced through her. There was a special sort of horror in watching Jude destroy a helpless woman. In part because she knew there was absolutely nothing she could do to stop the monster. And in part because there was another young woman about to be kidnapped and tortured with the exact same savagery.

Without warning, Zac placed an arm around her shoulders, pulling her against the welcome strength of his body. "Are you okay?"

She considered the question. Despite her soul-deep outrage, she managed to leash her emotions. There was only one way to prevent more violence. They had to catch the bastard. And the way to do that was with cool, calm logic. Not tears.

"I'm okay. At least right now." She sent Zac a wry glance. "I have a feeling I'm going to be sick later."

"Me too," he admitted. "Put aside the nightmare aspects of the video. What did we learn?"

Rachel forced herself to glance back at the small television. The late afternoon sunlight slanted through the windows, flooding the room with a golden glow, but she felt cold to the bone.

"She was acquainted with Jude," she said slowly. At the beginning of the tape the girl with a cloud of black hair and big brown eyes had looked happy. As if she was delighted to spend time with Jude. She'd also appeared oblivious to the camera. Rachel suspected she didn't know that she was being filmed. "She called him by name."

Zac nodded. "Unfortunately, he didn't say her name."

Rachel grimaced. It was true. The tape had been shorter than the others. As if Jude had been in a hurry. Or maybe nervous.

"She looked like she'd been anticipating his arrival. She wasn't afraid until he raised the crowbar."

"Yep. She thought she was there for a good time."

Rachel frowned at his words. "This is the first victim who was fully dressed," she said. The girl had been wearing an off the shoulder sweatshirt and leggings. Something that would have been popular in the early eighties. "If they had sex, the girl had plenty of time to pull on her clothes and comb her hair."

Zac stepped closer to the dresser, studying the fuzzy image. "It looks like they're in some sort of shed."

Rachel nodded. The background was lost in shadows, but she could see bare wooden planks on both the floor and wall.

"Maybe a garage," she suggested, pointing toward the open shelves that appeared stocked with numerous boxes.

Zac turned his attention to the girl on the floor who had gone from a vivacious, happy young woman to a motionless, bloody corpse.

"No wedding rings," he murmured.

"She could be divorced."

"Or she might have left them at home."

"True." The woman had been wearing a big, chunky necklace and dangling earrings, but if she'd been expecting her lover, she might have removed her wedding rings.

"Did she look familiar?" Zac asked.

Rachel shook her head. "I don't remember her."

"What about anyone in Rudolf's files?"

Rachel took a moment to mentally shuffle through the cases that Rudolf had considered sketchy. None of the pictures reminded her of the woman on the tape.

"Not unless it was the Jane Doe who was found in the landfill," she finally told him.

Zac heaved a harsh sigh. "There has to be something that can tell us who she was."

Rachel sympathized with his frustration. They had an actual video of the crime. Something any detective would be desperate to get their hands on. Even a cold case detective. But unlike most of her investigations, she didn't have the luxury of time to analyze the video and run endless searches to ID the victim, the location, and the date of the crime.

"She looked younger than the others," she finally said, unable to come up with any other brilliant deductions. "Barely out of high school."

"You're right," he said slowly. "And Jude looks younger. Thinner, with thicker hair."

"Yes." She glanced back at Zac. "I think it's possible this was his first kill. At least the first one he taped. That would explain why the encounter was shorter, and there was no evidence of having sex."

Zac nodded. "I agree."

Rachel turned her thoughts from Jude and the poor girl. There was nothing she could do to change what had happened. Instead, she concentrated on how the tape might reveal who the next victim would be.

"It's odd that the current murderer is choosing his victims in a random pattern," she murmured, speaking her thoughts out loud. "Wouldn't it be more logical to copy Jude's kills in the order they were committed?"

Zac reached out to turn off the television and eject the tape. They'd discovered as much as possible from the past. And the sooner they could get the video to her office in Madison, the sooner her staff could start to process it.

"That's not the only thing out of order." Zac carefully placed the tape in a plastic evidence bag and sealed it shut. "Last time Tory was taken and then the video was left for us to find. This time we got the video first. Unless the killer already has a victim."

Rachel flinched, feeling a physical pain at the thought that there was another woman out there, already in the hands of the monster. How many times would they fail before they brought an end to the madness?

"Maybe the timing of the tape is irrelevant," she said, knowing that she was grasping at straws. Serial killers rarely did anything without a motive. Even if it didn't make sense to anyone but them.

"Or maybe we found the video too early," Zac said, remembering his early question about the timing of the discovery of the package.

Rachel sent him a confused glance. "Too early?"

"Isaac Dowell told me that the envelope was left in a mailbox that usually is last on his delivery route. If he hadn't been training the seasonal postal workers, it's quite possible we wouldn't have gotten this video until tonight, or even tomorrow."

Rachel squared her shoulders. If they had the video before the killer wanted them to see it, they might still have a chance to catch him before he could strike again.

The question was . . . where to start. Turning, she paced

the room, which was stuffed with heavy furniture. There was a lingering scent of starch and vapor rub in the air, reminding Rachel of the nursing home. She wrinkled her nose. Zac was right. The house needed a family before it faded into oblivion.

She impatiently shook her head, returning her thoughts to the only thing that mattered in this moment: stopping the killer. The video hadn't provided any clues. Not that she had been able to . . . Wait. Perhaps there was one obvious clue.

"I want to talk to Mrs. Wilkins," she abruptly announced, spinning back to face Zac. "Her mailbox might have been chosen because it was in a convenient location, but there's a possibility that she might have a connection to Jude."

Zac arched his brows. "You're right. It's at least worth a try." He frowned as a buzzing sound echoed through the room. "Hold on," he murmured, placing the evidence bag on the dresser before he pulled his phone from his pocket. "Sheriff Evans," he answered in clipped tones, pausing as he listened to the caller. "Good," he said, a satisfied expression spreading across his face. "I'll be there in ten minutes. Thanks." He tucked the phone back in his pocket.

"What's going on?"

"I asked Bailey to give me a call when Jacob was coherent enough to answer a few questions," he explained, referring to his cousin who worked at the nursing home. "She just said that he's been more lucid than usual today."

"You talk to Jacob," Rachel suggested. "I'll go see Mrs. Wilkins."

Zac moved toward her, his expression somber as he reached up to cup her cheek in the palm of his hand.

"Be careful."

She tilted back her head, allowing her gaze to move over the face that was as familiar as her own. Perhaps more familiar, she acknowledged, her heart skipping a beat. How many hours had she sat in chemistry class staring across the lab table at the pure lines of his profile? Or watched him sleep with his head in her lap as she studied for an exam? She'd run her fingers through the satin softness of his blond hair, and nibbled kisses down the stubborn length of his jaw. Slowly he'd lift his lids to reveal his green eyes kissed with gold and he would flash his dimpled smile . . .

And she would be enchanted.

Barely aware she was moving, she went onto her tiptoes, pressing a soft, lingering kiss against his lips. "I'm always careful," she assured him.

He sucked in a sharp breath, his hands gripping her shoulders as he tugged her against his hard body. "Rachel."

He returned her kiss with a need that echoed deep inside her. It'd been so long. And no matter how fiercely she'd told herself that she was over Zac Evans, the past few days had stripped away that lie. She was as vulnerable to him as she had been when she was sixteen.

No doubt she should be frightened by the realization. She'd spent years building a life without Zac. Was she really prepared to risk her hard-earned sense of independence for a man who'd walked away?

The dangerous thoughts swirled through her mind even as she arched against him with a blatant yearning. Her mind might be conflicted, but her body knew exactly what it wanted.

Zac.

The image of her ex-husband naked and stretched across the nearby bed seared through her brain. It was shockingly vivid. As if it'd been lurking in the back of her mind since her return to Pike. Or maybe it'd been there for years.

Caught off guard by the sheer intensity of her desire, Rachel stepped back with a shiver.

"We need to go," she whispered.

His jaw tightened, as if he was battling the same urgent need. Then, with a grim effort, he turned and walked from the room.

Zac entered Jacob's private room in the nursing home, finding the older man sitting in a chair next to the window.

He was wearing a pair of pajamas with a thin robe over them, and his face had a stubble of whiskers, as if he hadn't bothered to shave that morning, but there was a sharp clarity in his eyes as he watched Zac's approach.

"What do you want?"

Zac ignored the gruff lack of welcome, grabbing a metal chair from a corner to set it next to Jacob.

"I'm Sheriff Evans," he said, taking a seat.

"I know who you are," the man snapped. "I asked what you wanted."

Zac snorted. The man's blatant resentment meant that Jacob remembered their last encounter. That was a good thing, right? "I have a few questions I need to ask you."

"Questions about what?"

"Jude."

The man winced, his eyes darkening with a genuine pain. "He's dead."

"Yes, this time we can be certain he's dead," Zac agreed.

"Then leave him in peace."

Zac shook his head. "I can't."

"Why not?"

"He's speaking to me from the grave."

Jacob scowled. "What the hell is that supposed to mean?"

Zac leaned back in the uncomfortable seat, folding his arms over his chest. "I have videos of him with women."

"Videos?" Jacob looked momentarily confused, then a sly smile curved his lips. "So? Lots of men like that sort of thing. Did you get off on it, Sheriff?"

Zac held the man's gaze, refusing to react to the taunt. "He wasn't having sex with the women. He was killing them."

A shocked silence filled the small room. "You . . ." The words trailed away, as if his outrage had stolen them. "Liar," he at last hissed.

Zac shrugged. "I can bring the tapes here if you want to see them for yourself. I'll warn you, they're not for the fainthearted."

Jacob shook his head. "There's got to be a mistake."

"No mistake." Zac narrowed his gaze. "How well did you know your brother, Jacob?"

The older man hunched his shoulders. "Well enough."

"If that's true, then you must have suspected he'd been using a crowbar to beat young women to death."

Jacob paled at the accusation, glancing away. "A crowbar," he breathed in a harsh voice. "No. No, no, no. That can't be right. He would never . . ." The older man halted, licking his lips as beads of sweat appeared on his bald head. "Not with a crowbar."

Zac stilled. Jacob's shock at hearing his brother had murdered various women was expected. Even if it was faked. But his stark disbelief at the manner Jude had chosen to kill was setting off Zac's internal alarms. Why would he be more upset by *how* they were murdered than the fact that his brother was responsible for their deaths?

"Is there something significant about the weapon?" he demanded. Silence. Zac leaned forward, placing his elbows on his knees. "Jacob? Jacob." He waited for the older man to glance back at him. "Tell me about the crowbar."

Jacob shook his head, but the words spilled out of his mouth as if he couldn't stop them. "My mother was a beautiful, classy woman. Everyone said so." He glared toward the nearby window. "She was way too good for this backwater place."

Zac hesitated. Was Jacob becoming lost in his mind? He'd known it would be a danger when he confronted the man with the fact that his brother was a crazed killer. Zac grimaced. There was only one way to find out.

"What does your mother have to do with Jude?" he asked.

Jacob jerked his head back to focus his glare on Zac. "She hated it here. She hated the people, the weather, the lack of civilization. And most of all, she hated the funeral parlor. But my dad refused to leave Pike." Jacob's blunt fingers curled around the arms of his chair, clenching so tight his knuckles turned white. "It was his fault."

"What was his fault?"

"Her drinking," Jacob snapped. "She only did it to ease her boredom."

"She was an alcoholic?"

"Don't use that word." A flush crawled beneath Jacob's face, replacing his pallor with a patchy blush. "She wasn't like those people. She was sick."

Zac forced himself to take a second to consider his approach. Clearly this man had been carefully groomed by his mother to see her as a victim. Any hint of disapproval and he would instinctively shut down.

"Okay. She was sick," he said in soothing tones. "What does that have to do with Jude?"

"He made her angry." Jacob's lips pinched together. "He was always a pain in the ass. Even when he was a little boy. The sneaky, whiny brat. If he'd just obeyed the rules, she wouldn't have been forced to punish him."

Zac studied the round face that sagged at the jaws. This man might have loved Jude, but his loyalty was to his mother. Or at least the image they'd carefully portrayed of his mother.

Not surprising. Alcoholism was a family disease, causing dysfunction in everyone in the house. Jacob had accepted the burden of being the protector as well as eventually taking over the family business. Jude had become the scapegoat.

"How did she punish him?" he asked, careful to keep his voice casual. As if they were discussing the weather, not the abuse of a helpless child.

Jacob shrugged. "It doesn't matter. Not now."

"It does matter, Jacob," Zac insisted. "There's a reason Jude beat those women."

Something that might have been regret rippled over the sagging face. Then, Jacob visibly shoved aside any sympathy for his younger brother. "I told you. He was a bad kid. He grew up to be an even worse man."

"She hit him, didn't she?" Zac pressed. The more he could dig into Jude's life and the reason he'd become a serial killer, the more likely he would be to discover who was attempting to follow in his footsteps.

Or at least, that was the hope.

Jacob clenched his jaw. "Are you saying your dad never punished you?"

"Of course he did," Zac admitted. "My dad used a belt on me more than once. But he never left a mark. Or broke any bones." As the words left his lips, a stunning realization slammed into Zac. They'd learned very little from Jude's autopsy. Well, beyond the fact he was dying of a brain tumor. But they did know that he'd been injured when he was young. "What happened to Jude's shoulder?"

Jacob was obviously blindsided by the abrupt question. His mouth parted, then closed, then parted again, giving him the unfortunate appearance of a fish out of water.

"He fell out of a tree," he finally muttered, his gaze darting away from Zac. A sure sign he was lying.

"We both know that didn't happen," Zac chastised. "Your mother hit him."

"No—"

"Yes."

Jacob banged his hand against the arm of his chair, his flush deepening to a dark shade of red. "Jude did it to himself," he rasped. "He was skipping school, stealing money out of Mom's purse. She had to do something to stop him."

Zac ignored the man's bluster. Deep inside, Jacob knew that what his mother had done to her younger son was wrong. But years of indoctrination had made it impossible for him to admit the truth.

"What did she hit him with?"

"Nothing."

"What was it, Jacob?" Zac's tone was hard, demanding an answer. "A crowbar?"

A sound like a wounded animal escaped from Jacob as

spittle formed on the corner of his mouth. "I don't want to talk about this." His hands twitched as he plucked at the thin material of his robe. "Where's the nurse?"

Zac bit the edge of his tongue. As much as he wanted to force the older man to admit that Jude had been beaten by a crowbar, he sensed that Jacob was close to shutting down. Besides, he didn't need the actual words. He could see the truth etched in the man's face.

Jude had been brutally beaten by his mother with a crowbar while she'd been in a drunken rage. Years later, Jude had vented his hatred and resentment toward the woman who should have loved and cared for him by re-creating the painful event. Only he hadn't been satisfied with simply beating his victims. He had to destroy them. Utterly and completely.

It made perfect sense. Unfortunately, it didn't offer any insight into who was currently hunting the women of Pike.

"Tell me about your properties." He abruptly changed the direction of the conversation.

Jacob released a hissing breath, the red fading from his face as he sent Zac a puzzled frown. "Properties?"

"Do you own a home?"

"No. I had to sell my parents' place. I lived in an apartment above the funeral parlor until I came here."

Zac noticed the man didn't refer to the cabin. Was he trying to keep it a secret? Maybe because he'd known Jude was living out there?

"Any other places?" he asked, his tone casual.

"No . . . oh, wait." Jacob furrowed his brows, as if digging through his fuzzy memories. "We have an old cabin near the lake. I tried to sell it a few years ago, but no one was interested."

Zac was willing to believe that the man wanted to sell the cabin. He'd obviously needed the money. And he even believed that Jacob hadn't had any luck in finding a buyer. The collapse of the dairy industry had hit Pike hard. There were few people around who had extra cash to buy an old cabin in the middle of nowhere.

"That's it?" Zac demanded. The current killer had to be hiding somewhere. "Maybe an empty house that belongs to a relative?"

Jacob made a sound of disgust. "You think I would live in a cramped room above the morgue if I had any options?" He paused, his expression suspicious. "Why are you asking these questions?"

"There was a reason Jude returned to Pike." Zac offered a vague explanation. He didn't trust Jacob. He wasn't going to give him any more information than absolutely necessary. "I'm trying to figure out what it was."

"You know why." There was a long silence as a cloud of confusion dulled Jacob's brown eyes. "He came back to die."

Chapter 18

Mrs. Wilkins's house was a one-story home with faded yellow siding, black shutters, and a detached garage located at the end of a one-way street. The lot was long and narrow, with high hedges on each side, offering a sense of privacy. It was just past four in the afternoon and the shadows were already creeping over the sleepy neighborhood, adding to the sense of isolation.

Pulling into the driveway, Rachel climbed out of her SUV and glanced around. Zac had mentioned that Mrs. Wilkins was an elderly widow who lived alone. She assumed that meant she didn't have a job and would be home during the day, making it risky for someone to sneak up to her home and slip in the envelope. Now she could see that the mailbox was next to the street, and nearly hidden by a lavender bush. Anyone could walk by and slide the envelope in without being noticed.

Was that the sole reason this particular address was chosen?

Perhaps.

Rachel turned back to the house, climbing onto the narrow porch, which held a wooden rocking chair and several clay pots that were currently empty. She rapped her knuckles against the metal screen door, a few seconds later hearing the slow plod of footsteps on a creaking floor.

A full minute passed before the inner door was pulled open to reveal a small wisp of a woman with faded red hair that was styled on top of her head. Her narrow face was lined by age, but her dark eyes sparkled with an unmistakable intelligence. She was wearing a pantsuit in a weird shade of rusty brown and leather shoes that had been popular twenty years ago. Rachel suspected that she was a woman who lived on a budget, but refused to compromise on her appearance. She might not be trendy, but she was ruthlessly tidy from the top of her heavily sprayed hair to the tip of her polished shoes.

"Hello."

"Mrs. Wilkins?"

"Yes."

"Hi, I'm Detective Fisher." Rachel displayed her badge. She didn't want to alarm the older woman, but this was official business.

Mrs. Wilkins pushed open the screen door, her expression more curious than concerned. "You're DeeDee's girl?"

"I am." Rachel tucked the badge into her satchel. "Can I have a word?"

"Of course, come in." Mrs. Wilkins stepped back, allowing Rachel to enter the narrow hall. Rachel closed the door, and followed the woman's shuffling steps through an arched opening. "Tea? Coffee?"

"I'm fine, thank you," Rachel said, taking a quick glance around.

They were standing in a small kitchen dominated by a square wooden table that matched a hutch filled with various trinkets that had no doubt been collected over a lifetime. The heavy furniture made the room feel cramped, as if it'd been chosen for a larger house, but everything from the stove to the sink was meticulously scrubbed and there was the scent of bleach in the air.

"Please, have a seat." Mrs. Wilkins hurried to collect the newspaper that had been spread across the table. "I'm afraid the place is a mess."

Rachel settled on a wooden chair as her gaze skimmed over the gingham curtains that had not only been recently washed, but ironed to hang in a perfect, crisp line.

"You wouldn't say that if you could see my apartment," she said dryly.

Setting the newspaper on the counter, Mrs. Wilkins took the time to replace a plastic cover on the toaster before she slid into the seat across the table from Rachel.

"You moved away from Pike, didn't you?"

"Yes, I live in Madison now."

"I suppose most young people prefer a city that has more to offer than this small town." The woman clicked her tongue. "A shame, but I don't blame you."

Rachel shrugged. "It's not that I prefer the city, it just happens to be where my job is now."

"Ah, yes. A detective. Such an interesting career for a woman. And you're so young to be in such a responsible position. I know your parents must be very proud."

Mrs. Wilkins appeared genuinely impressed and Rachel found herself fighting the urge to blush. She couldn't remember anyone telling her that they were proud of her accomplishments. It was surprisingly nice to hear.

"I'm not sure about that, but I do enjoy my job." She met the older woman's curious gaze, suppressing a grimace as she thought about why she was there. "Most of the time."

"Does this have something to do with that dreadful business in the cemetery?"

Rachel wasn't surprised the older woman had heard about what had happened. And not just because Pike was a small town where news spread like wildfire. Even in a city the shocking discovery of a man being shot on top of his own grave would have people buzzing. Soon enough it would be replaced with rumors about the two dead women.

"Yes, I work cold cases," she said.

Mrs. Wilkins tilted her head to the side, eyeing Rachel like a curious bird. "I'm not quite sure why you're here to see me."

"A package was found in your mailbox earlier today."

"Mine?" The woman paused, as if waiting for Rachel to admit that it was a mistake. "Are you sure?"

"According to the postman who works this route."

"Oh, you must mean that sweet Isaac." The older woman smiled, obviously smitten with her mailman. "Such a handsome young man, don't you think? And much nicer than that one before him. What was his name?" Mrs. Wilkins took a second to dredge up the memory from the depths of her mind. "Greg something or other. Barry? Yes, that was it. Greg Barry."

Rachel arched her brows in surprise. "The sheriff's deputy?"

She waved a hand that was swollen with arthritis. "I don't know what he does now, but when he was the mailman he never had time to chat." She leaned forward. "And he was just rude when I asked him to bring me a roll of stamps even though I had the money in an envelope and very clear instructions of what I needed. He told me that it wasn't his job to run errands for every old person in town." She pursed her lips, as if she was thinking of all the nasty words she would like to use to describe her former mailman. "Isaac, on the other hand, is a proper young man who is willing to help a poor widow who lives on her own."

The information didn't seem relevant to the current case, but Rachel pulled out a notepad and pencil from her satchel to jot down Greg's name. He could at least tell her about the neighbors and perhaps if there were any empty houses in the area.

For now, she turned the conversation back to the reason she'd come to this house. "Can you remember for certain that you didn't place a padded envelope in your mailbox?" she asked in gentle tones.

"I don't think so. I haven't started my Christmas shopping and I haven't baked any cookies for Isaac lately." She firmly shook her head. "I think he must be mistaken. There wasn't any package. Perhaps it was Marjorie next door. She has a son who lives in Texas and she's always sending him stuff. Between you and me, most of it the poor boy probably tosses as soon as it arrives. What young man wants old copies of *Reader's Digest* or underpants she bought at the thrift store?"

Rachel didn't have an answer. Mrs. Wilkins offered a sage nod as if Rachel's silence proved her point and continued.

"You might talk to her. Or even Albert Convey across the road. He moved here from Grange a year or so ago. I'm not very well acquainted with him, but he might be the type of man to send out packages."

Rachel obediently jotted down the names, accepting that this woman hadn't been responsible for the envelope. So why was it in her mailbox?

"Did you know Jude Henley?" Rachel kept her tone casual, as if she was making conversation.

"Of course. I knew most of the students in Pike back when Jude was in school."

"Were you a teacher?"

"No, my husband, Bill, was the superintendent until the mid-eighties. I volunteered in the elementary school library." She heaved a sigh. "Bill died a few years after he retired. We never did get to take that cruise we'd been planning."

Rachel set down her pencil and studied the older woman. She wasn't sure what this might have to do with the tape left in Mrs. Wilkins's mailbox, but she couldn't miss this opportunity to discover more about Jude and who might have known he was a killer.

"What can you tell me about Jude?"

"I'm not sure what you want to know."

Rachel didn't know either. She wasn't sure if his past had any bearing on the current killer. Or if they'd recently crossed paths. "I heard he was a difficult kid," she finally said.

Surprisingly, the woman sent her a disapproving frown. "You sound like my husband. He was convinced that Jude was a bad seed."

"You didn't agree?"

"He was certainly in a lot of trouble," Mrs. Wilkins conceded. "That boy was in the principal's office every day. But he wasn't born bad. He was made that way." Her lips thinned to a tight line, as if she was recalling a specific incident.

"Made that way?" Rachel repeated the words. "Do you mean that he was bullied?"

Mrs. Wilkins glanced away, perhaps considering whether or not she wanted to answer the question.

"Yes," she eventually said. "But not by the other kids."

"His dad?"

"His mother."

"Really?" Rachel blinked in surprise. Not that a mother couldn't be capable of violence toward her children. It happened more often than most people wanted to admit. But that there hadn't been whispers that Jude might have been abused.

"Yes. Not that anyone would listen to me, not even my husband." The woman clicked her tongue. "But I could see the bruises on him. Both physical and mental."

Unlike the dearly departed Mr. Wilkins, Rachel believed her. There was a genuine outrage in her voice despite the fact it must have occurred over forty years ago.

"How do you know Mrs. Henley was responsible?" she asked.

"I was helping with detention after school. Jude was in the library working on his homework and I'd stepped into my office to grab my coat and purse. I was in a hurry to leave as soon as the second bell rang. I think I had a hair appointment." She pressed her hands flat against the table, but not before Rachel noticed the faint tremor. The memory had obviously haunted the poor woman. "When I came out I saw Mrs. Henley grab Jude by his hair and shake him so hard his head hit the wall."

"What did you do?"

"I confronted her, of course. The poor kid had blood running down the side of his face." The woman sounded offended that Rachel would even ask. "Mrs. Henley was furious. She threatened to tell everyone that I was responsible for hitting Jude and swore she would sue the school if I said a word. Back then there were no cameras in the library. It would have been her word against mine."

"So what happened?"

The woman's hands curled into tight balls. "While she was busy yelling at me I could smell the alcohol on her breath."

"She'd been drinking?" Rachel grimaced. Mrs. Henley sounded like a real piece of work.

"Yes, I couldn't physically stop her from leaving with Jude." Mrs. Wilkins tilted her chin to a defiant angle. "Instead I called the sheriff as soon as she drove away. I hoped she would be arrested for drunk driving."

"Was she?"

Mrs. Wilkins muttered something beneath her breath. Rachel thought it sounded like "snooty bitch," but the woman's expression was so prim it was hard to believe the words could have come from her pinched lips.

"This was back in the seventies," she said in a louder voice. "Before Rudolf was sheriff. At that time the Henleys had a lot of influence in Pike. Certainly more than me. The law officials didn't want to hear what I was telling them. If they had, it might have prevented the woman from driving in front of a train a few years later."

"Mrs. Henley was driving?"

"It was impossible to say for certain. There wasn't much left of the car." Mrs. Wilkins wrinkled her nose. "Or the Henleys."

Rachel made a soft sound of shock. She'd known that Jude's parents had been killed in a car accident, but she hadn't known they'd been hit by a train. It was a gruesome way to die.

"I suppose not," she muttered.

There was a short silence before Mrs. Wilkins leaned forward, her dark eyes glittering with curiosity. "I try not to listen to gossip, but I did hear that they found Staci Gale's body in Jude's grave."

Rachel nodded. "Yes."

"Such a shame. We all assumed she'd left town. Of course, we also thought Jude was dead. Do you think he killed her?"

The sudden question made Rachel hesitate. This woman might claim a distaste for gossip, but she was no doubt like everyone else in town. Eager to pass along any information whether it was right or wrong. Rachel didn't want the killer knowing the direction the investigation was taking.

"It's one of a number of theories," she vaguely admitted.

The woman heaved a sigh. "My husband did warn me that I allowed my pity for Jude to blind me to his true nature. He was convinced that Jude was dangerous."

"Did he have a particular reason for thinking he was dangerous? Beyond his trouble at school?"

"I always assumed it was because of Destiny."

Rachel frowned in confusion. "Fate?"

"No, Destiny Sykes. Our foster daughter."

"Ah." Mrs. Wilkins was referring to an actual person.

"I wasn't blessed with children, so when Destiny's mother died when she was sixteen we took her in. She didn't have a father, and her grandparents weren't willing to take on the responsibility of a troubled teenager. I suppose I could understand. They had a business in town that kept them busy and we were happy to help."

Rachel impulsively reached across the table to touch the woman's hand. "That was very generous of you."

A sadness swept over the narrow face. "I tried to help. I'm not sure how successful I was."

Regretting the need to dredge up painful memories, Rachel forced herself to continue with her questioning. "Why did you say something about your husband thinking Jude was dangerous? Did he bully your foster daughter?"

"Oh no. Just the opposite," Mrs. Wilkins corrected her. "Although Jude was a year younger than Destiny, the two of them dated her senior year."

Rachel grabbed her pencil and made a note. She should have guessed that Jude hadn't been openly violent. He was far too clever for that. His most potent weapon had been his charm, which he'd obviously honed during his youth.

The fact that he could form an intimate connection with the women before beating them to death with a crowbar only made his murders more horrifying. It was one thing to stalk and kill a stranger, but to woo and seduce a victim before he struck . . . That took a true psychopath.

"Your husband didn't approve of their relationship?" She prompted the older woman to continue her story.

"He was livid." Mrs. Wilkins shivered. "I don't think I'd ever seen him so angry."

"What happened?"

"One night Destiny came home after her curfew. My husband was waiting at the door. There was a terrible argument and Destiny packed a bag and left the house."

Mrs. Wilkins heaved a sad sigh. "I don't know where she went, but a couple days later she was back here and never mentioned Jude's name again. I assume he found someone else to date. He was never without at least one girlfriend."

Rachel stilled. Had Destiny gone to Jude after storming away from the protection of the Wilkinses? And if she had, why had she come back? Had she seen something she shouldn't have? Maybe Jude had revealed the monster that lurked behind the alluring bad boy?

There was only one way to find out.

"Does Destiny still live in Pike?"

Mrs. Wilkins flinched, as if Rachel's words had caused her physical pain. "She died."

"Oh. I'm so sorry." Rachel gave the woman's fingers a small squeeze. "Can I ask what happened?"

"A few weeks after she graduated she got a job at the old drive-in theater working in the food shack. I was so happy for her, but then—" The words broke off on a soft sob. "Then she was gone."

Rachel's mild curiosity was replaced with a sickening sense of premonition. The food shack. That could easily be the background they'd seen in the tape that had arrived that day, couldn't it? Plus, it couldn't be a coincidence that Mrs. Wilkins's dead foster daughter had dated Jude and then just weeks or maybe months after they broke up she was dead.

"What happened?"

"No one knows for sure." Mrs. Wilkins was forced to halt and clear her throat. Her grief for the tragic young Destiny was still raw. "The movie was over and she was there cleaning up for the night when the shack caught fire.

The officials said that it was probably an electrical issue, but there were rumors that the owner of the drive-in set the place on fire for the insurance money and something went terribly wrong."

Rachel dismissed both the accident theory as well as the owner torching the place. When there was a fire people always speculated it was done for the insurance money. "What do you believe?"

"Honestly?" There was a long pause, as if the woman didn't want to say the words out loud. "I fear that Destiny was there with friends doing drugs and that she overdosed. If her friends panicked, they would have done something stupid like burning down the shack."

"Why would you think that?"

"Just a week or so before she died I was cleaning her room and I found a glass pipe between the mattress and box springs." The woman clicked her tongue in disgust. "I knew what it meant. Such a shame. We tried our best."

Rachel gave the gnarled fingers another squeeze. "I don't doubt that for a second."

Mrs. Wilkins sniffed back her tears, firmly squaring her shoulders. "You know, it's odd."

"What's odd?"

"Destiny died around this time of year. I used to visit her grave, but I just can't get around anymore."

Rachel sat back in her seat. She would bet good money that Destiny died either on this date or tomorrow.

"Forgive me for prying into such a painful subject, but do you have a picture of Destiny?"

"Yes." Mrs. Wilkins rose to her feet with a quickness that revealed she was eager to share the memory of Destiny. "I'll be right back."

She was as good as her word. In less than a minute she'd returned to the kitchen clutching a framed eight-by-ten photo that she handed to Rachel.

Studying the picture, Rachel easily identified Mrs. Wilkins in front of the old school building. Her hair was a darker shade of red, and there were fewer lines on her face, but she was wearing a similar pantsuit and clutching the arm of a tall, slender man with a thick mane of dark hair combed from his stern, unsmiling face. Rachel assumed that was Mr. Wilkins. To one side there was a girl dressed in a robe and square cap as if she'd just graduated. She kept several inches between her and the Wilkinses as if to subtly reveal she didn't consider herself a part of the family, and there was a sulky expression on her face.

A face that Rachel instantly recognized.

The premonition was now an absolute certainty as Rachel carefully placed the picture on the table and rose to her feet.

"Thank you, Mrs. Wilkins, you've been very helpful." With a tense nod, she turned to hurry out of the kitchen, her hand already reaching into her satchel to pull out her phone.

Surprisingly, the older woman managed to keep pace with her as she headed down the narrow hallway. "I've enjoyed the chat. I spend too much time alone these days," she said breathlessly. "Be sure and tell your mother that I said hello."

"I will." Too distracted to do more than offer a vague smile, Rachel pushed open the front door and pressed a number on her phone. She was still on the porch when Zac answered. "Hey, I need you to meet me at the old drive-in," she said in grim tones. "As soon as you can get there."

Chapter 19

Risa Murphy was standing in the center of the cramped two-room apartment above the hair salon. She'd just walked through the door after a ten-hour shift at the diner and she wasn't in the mood for her boyfriend's shit. Gerry Sims had been her on-again, off-again partner since they'd graduated high school eight years ago. She was never quite sure why. He'd never held down a real job. He drank, he was addicted to gambling, and he sold prescription pills.

She supposed she kept him around because he was easy. Like an old, comfortable pair of slippers. She didn't have to worry if her bleached-blond hair was hanging in a limp ponytail, or if she'd remembered to put on lipstick, or if she'd packed on enough pounds to go from curvy to plump. She didn't have to try.

Not the most romantic love story, she silently acknowledged, watching as he moved toward her.

Gerry was only a couple inches taller, maybe five-foot-eight, with a thin frame that was just a breath from gaunt. He never wore anything but faded jeans and a white T-shirt. He even wore them to her sister's wedding, despite her protest. His dark hair was long enough to brush his shoulders and his face was thin. Her mother said he looked like a rat, and she couldn't argue. But then again, he had amazing eyes that were so dark they appeared black and a smile that still made her heart flutter.

He flashed that charming smile as he reached to give her ponytail a small tug. "Come on, Risa. What's the big deal?"

She stepped back, her blue eyes narrowing with a silent warning. Her feet hurt, her back ached, and she smelled like stale onion rings. All she wanted was a hot shower and a cold beer before she climbed into bed. Instead, she'd been greeted the moment she'd walked through the door with a demand that she meet with some stranger to deliver a bunch of illegal pills.

"I told you, I don't want to be involved in your crap," she snapped.

The dark eyes flashed with a quick temper. It didn't take much to set off the man. "My crap pays the bills."

Risa snorted. She paid the rent, the utilities, and bought the groceries. Gerry's money went to the massive gambling debt that hung over him like a ticking time bomb.

"I pay my own bills," she reminded him tartly. "And I do it legally."

Gerry's fingers tightened on her ponytail. He didn't like being reminded that he depended on her to keep a roof over his head.

"Waiting tables at a greasy diner isn't anything to brag about."

"Better than being a drug dealer."

"Oh yeah?" His lips curled into a sneer. "Do you think

you get your tips because you're so great at hauling around plates of food?"

She sent him a sour frown. She had no idea what he was trying to imply. "I'm a waitress. That's exactly why I get my tips."

"Bullshit." His gaze lowered to the black knit tee that had the logo of the diner printed on the front. "They like the way your tits look in that tight shirt. And they hope if they tip you big enough they might get to give them a squeeze." His hand moved to cup the heavy weight of one of her breasts.

Risa slapped away his hand. "You're such a pig sometimes, Gerry," she rasped. "I don't know why I put up with you."

Easily sensing he was reaching the end of her tolerance, Gerry visibly regained command of his temper. Then he managed to summon a cajoling expression. "I'm just a pig sometimes," he reminded her. He reached out again, this time to run his fingers down her cheek. "Come on, babe. I need you."

"I don't understand why. You can arrange to do the drop later."

"Because this was the only time the dude could do the deal," he insisted. "It's a new client and he's willing to pay top dollar for the pills. Twice what I usually get on the street. Plus he wanted everything I had."

"Fine, then reschedule your trip to Madison."

The words left her lips before she could halt them. Instantly Gerry's eyes flared with renewed fury. Every Wednesday night he drove to Madison. Not only to pick up the illegal pills he sold, but to make a payment on his gambling debt.

"Are you trying to get me killed?" he demanded, jerking his hand away as if he couldn't bear to touch her. "If I don't show up to pay my debt, Joey is going to put a bullet through my head. And probably yours. Is that what you want?"

She shivered. She'd never met Joey, but Gerry told her that the loan shark had not only threatened to kill him, but that he'd promised he'd destroy anyone that Gerry cared about, starting with his girlfriend.

"God, I hate this."

Something that might have been genuine regret softened her companion's sharp features and he wrapped her tightly in his arms. "Look, this is the last time, I swear, babe."

She stood stiffly, refusing to give in without making sure that he understood she was well and truly at her limit with him. "You've said that before."

He lowered his head, nuzzling the side of her neck in the exact spot he knew would make her knees weak. "This is the score I've been waiting for. If I can convince this guy to let me be his supplier, I can pay off my debts and we can start over. Do you want that ring for your finger or not?"

She pressed her hands against his bony chest. "That's blackmail."

"It's reality. You want some bling, I have to sell enough product to make a profit."

Risa wiggled out of his arms at his blunt words. He knew how much she wanted a wedding. It was another one of those things she wasn't quite sure about. Did she really want to be tied to this man for the rest of her life? In the end, that part didn't matter. She had two sisters who'd had large weddings. Just once, she wanted to be the one in the fancy dress with her hair in curls and everyone in town looking at her as she drove through the streets in a long, shiny limo.

"Fine, I'll do it," she muttered. "But never again."

"You're the best." Gerry turned to scurry across the room to grab a black backpack off the sagging couch, looking more ratlike than usual.

"I mean it, Gerry," she warned, knowing that her words were falling on deaf ears. "The next time you ask, I'm out of here."

"Yeah, yeah." Gerry shoved the backpack into her stiff fingers. "The stash is in here. Get the money up front. Cash only." He dug into the front pocket of his jeans, pulling out a wrinkled scrap of paper. "This is the address."

Risa looked down at the scribbled writing. She frowned as she realized where she was supposed to meet the client. "Are you sure this is right?"

"Of course I'm sure."

"There's nothing there." She lifted her head to study Gerry in confusion. "Not anymore."

"That's the point. Do you think I do my deals in the middle of the town square?"

Of course not, but then again, she didn't want to meet some loser in such an isolated area. "I don't like this," she muttered.

"Christ, I have to go," Gerry snarled, moving to grab his jacket before heading to the door. "Don't be late."

* * *

Rachel parked next to Zac's truck and climbed out of her SUV. The sun had set as she'd driven across town, leaving the area cloaked in darkness. The outer road didn't have streetlamps and the only nearby business was the bowling alley that had been converted into a thrift shop. It ran on a shoestring budget that didn't extend to lights in the parking lot. It made it difficult to make out more than the skeleton frame of the large screen and the rows of small mounds where speakers had been attached to metal poles.

"This place is even worse than I remembered," she murmured as Zac joined her, glancing toward the indoor ice-skating rink that collapsed just behind the drive-in.

"You're not wrong. It needs a good bulldozing," he agreed. "The owner, Claire Kline, lives in Florida and refuses to take responsibility for her property. Eventually I'll declare the place a public hazard and hire someone to clean it out. She's not going to be happy when she gets the bill." A ghost of a smile skimmed over his face, no doubt anticipating the woman's screech of outrage. Then, with a faint shake of his head, he glanced down at her. "So why are we here?"

Rachel pulled her phone out of her satchel, pressing the flashlight app. The soft glow surrounded them.

"Mrs. Wilkins had a foster daughter named Destiny who dated Jude in high school," she told him.

Zac sucked in a sharp breath. "Then it wasn't just a fluke the envelope was found in her mailbox?"

"I don't think so."

"What happened to Destiny?"

"She was working in the food shack at this drive-in late one night when it caught fire and burned to the ground."

"She died?"

"Yes."

Zac glanced back at the darkened lot, his profile hard as he considered what she'd just revealed. "You suspect she was the girl we saw in the tape?"

"Without a doubt. Mrs. Wilkins showed me a picture of Destiny." Rachel recalled the image of the stoic girl keeping a distance between the couple who'd opened their home to her and mentally compared it to the happiness on her face when she'd seen Jude appear. It was tragic, but not that unusual for a teenager. They wanted excitement and danger and romance, not tedious rules they assumed were invented to ruin their lives. Destiny had no idea she was turning her back on the people who cared about her to be with a monster. "It was the same girl."

Zac nodded, reaching beneath his jacket to pull a flashlight off his belt. "Let's have a look around." He aimed the beam of bright light on the ground in front of them. "Be careful. God knows what trash has been dumped out here."

"Whoever placed the tape of Destiny's death in the mailbox had to know about Mrs. Wilkins being her foster mother."

Zac crossed toward the side of the wide lot where there was a flat, barren spot. "Was there an investigation into the fire? Maybe police records?"

"No. There were rumors of arson from the owner and Mrs. Wilkins feared that it was drug related. She didn't have any suspicion it might have been murder."

Zac made a sound of frustration. "So how does the killer know so much about Jude and his crimes?"

"It's possible the killer is from Pike and knew what Jude was doing," Rachel suggested. "Either he spied on Jude, or Jude actually used him as a confidant to brag about his murders."

Zac grimaced. "That would explain the videos. How better to show off his skill in bludgeoning helpless women than to give his admirer a recording of the event?"

"The student and the master," she murmured, referring to the note that had been stuffed in Jude's mouth.

"Over here." Zac focused the flashlight on a splintered piece of wood. Coming to a halt, he bent down to pick it up. "It looks like it was burned."

Rachel nodded. Even in the shadows she could make out the charred end of the board. Had it belonged to the food shack? She shivered at the thought, turning in a slow circle. Even when this place was open it would have been empty once the customers drove away.

"If Destiny was working alone and Jude showed up after closing, there wouldn't have been anyone around to see what was happening," she said.

"Or to hear them," Zac added.

Another shiver raced through Rachel. All the murders were horrible, but there was something especially tragic about Destiny. She was so young. And life had already kicked her in the teeth. It seemed unfair that she would end up in the hands of a violent psychopath. . . .

Rachel frowned, struck by a sudden thought. "Mrs. Wilkins told me that Destiny had just graduated when she got the job here, and Jude was a year younger than her.

He couldn't have been more than seventeen when he killed her."

"Perhaps his trial run as a killer."

"Yes."

Zac dropped the piece of wood. "Now the question is how the current killer intends to copy the murder."

Rachel shrugged. "I hoped there might be something here that would give us a clue."

Wrapping an arm around her shoulders, Zac steered her back toward their waiting vehicles.

"Let's go to the farm and you can tell me what other information Mrs. Wilkins shared with you, and I can tell you about my meeting with Jacob."

Zac grabbed the plates off the kitchen table and headed to the sink. After returning to the farmhouse they'd eaten a fresh salad that Rachel had insisted on making, after she'd vetoed his suggestion for another pizza from Bella's, and discussed what they'd each discovered during the day.

It'd been . . . nice. Not the fact there was a serial killer stalking the streets of Pike. But the sensation that he wasn't trying to catch the bastard on his own.

And beyond the professional advantage of having a trained partner was the personal pleasure of sharing his house with Rachel. He loved her lingering scent in the air, and the sight of her clothes stacked on the dryer, and the knowledge when he woke in the morning she would be in the kitchen with a fresh pot of coffee.

"Well, we know that Jude was abused by his mother."

Still seated at the table, Rachel broke into his rambling thoughts.

Zac nodded, moving to the wine rack he'd installed next to the fridge. "Probably with a crowbar."

"And the abuse might explain why he chose females he had some sort of relationship with instead of strangers," she murmured. "Love and hate must have been a confusing mess in his mind."

Zac grabbed a bottle and pried out the cork. A part of him could feel sympathy for Jude as a child. Being brutalized by his mother had obviously twisted him into a monster. And worse, no one had done anything to stop the abuse. In some ways the entire town of Pike was responsible for failing the young boy. But he didn't have an ounce of pity for the man Jude had become.

And even less for the killer who was following in his footsteps.

"What it doesn't explain is his relationship with the animal who's terrorizing Pike," he said, pouring two glasses of the rich, fruity Merlot. He'd taken time to swing by the local winery that afternoon, knowing it was one of Rachel's favorites.

"Or who might be the next victim." Rachel heaved a loud sigh. "Maybe we should—"

"It's too late to do anything else tonight," Zac interrupted, turning to face her.

She grimaced. "I hate sitting around waiting."

"Me too, but there's no point in wasting energy we might need later." He moved to hold out a glass.

She readily accepted the wine, taking a sip. "I suppose you're right."

Zac pretended to be shocked. "What did you say?"

"I said, I suppose you're right." Her lips twitched. "Just this once."

"I'll take it." He walked to stand beside her. "Let's go into the living room. I have a fire started."

Rachel rose to her feet and together they moved out of the kitchen into the room that was small but cozy with a fireplace surrounded by large stones. There were built-in wooden shelves on one wall that was cluttered with dozens of framed family pictures, and a faded carpet that covered the original planked floor. The furniture was left over from his childhood and had gone from comfy to shabby over the past few years.

Rachel wandered toward the fireplace, absently sipping her wine. Zac studied her profile outlined by the cheerful blaze, a sharp burst of longing twisting his gut into a painful knot. He desperately wanted to move forward and tug her into his arms. Just to feel her pressed against his aching body.

"You never told me what your mother said." He abruptly broke the silence. He needed a distraction before he did something that might destroy their fragile relationship. "Did she recognize the photo from Jude's scrapbook?"

She turned to lean against the mantel. "She did. It was Evie Parson, the wife of Russell Parson."

Zac took a moment to place the name. "He owns the bank where your father works, right?"

"He's retired, but yes, he still holds the majority of the shares. Dad does most of the day-to-day running of the place."

"I've met Russell a few times, but I don't know Evie."

"She died years ago."

Zac wasn't surprised. The women who had the bad luck to attract Jude's attention ended up dead with a depressing frequency. "How?"

"Cancer."

"Really?" Zac hadn't expected that. "Was that what made her different from the others? She died of natural causes? Or did cancer take her before he could kill her?"

"Right now it feels like another dead end." She grimaced. "Sorry. That didn't come out right."

"I know what you mean," he assured her, sensing her fatigue. She obviously needed a break from the case. He didn't blame her. He felt as if he'd been working nonstop since he found Jude's body. "What else did you and your mother discuss?"

She stilled, as if knocked off-balance by the question. Then she widened her eyes, trying to act baffled. "What makes you think we discussed anything else?"

He strolled toward her, his gaze lowering to the stubborn line of her jaw. "I recognized that expression when you left this morning."

"What expression?"

"The one that warns the world you're on a mission and that you'll throat-punch anyone who gets in your way."

"You're making that up." She protested his blunt words.

Zac arched a brow, silently daring her to deny his accusation. They both knew that he was intimately familiar with her various moods. From her giddy joy to frigid anger to sullen disapproval. He'd seen her soft and sated in his arms or so furious she could barely speak. He'd seen her cry and pout and laugh so hard she peed her pants.

She blew out a resigned sigh. "Okay, fine. I decided to confront the elephant in the room."

He studied her pale face, not sure what the hell she meant. "Elephant?"

"Benny."

The name came out stiff, as if she had trouble pushing it past her lips. Probably because she'd so rarely talked about her younger brother. It was a subject he'd quickly learned wasn't up for discussion. Not unless he wanted to be shut out for hours. Sometimes days.

Zac had never pressed the issue. He had plenty of subjects he preferred to avoid. Like the day he'd accidentally walked in on his parents having a nooner in the barn, and the bike he'd stolen on a dare when he was in sixth grade, and the hours he'd spent fantasizing about his math teacher, Mrs. Moore . . .

None of it was as devastating as losing a brother at such a young age.

"Ah. I take it that it didn't go well?" he asked.

"Not at first. As usual, my mom tried to forbid any mention of my brother." Rachel drained her wine and placed the empty glass on the mantel.

Zac wished he'd brought the bottle with them. "What happened?"

"This time I insisted we talk about Benny."

"Good." Zac set aside his own glass, reaching to grab her slender hand. As he expected, it was cold to the touch despite the heat from the fire. "I'll never know how it feels to lose a sibling, but I know you've struggled to accept his death. The wounds were so deep I couldn't reach them."

"I wouldn't let you." She met his gaze with a rueful expression. "The guilt has festered too long. For all of us."

"Did your mom agree?"

She wrinkled her nose. "She didn't actually agree, but

she at least listened to what I had to say. Maybe she'll eventually get the help she needs. I hope so."

Zac felt an unexpected anticipation tingle through him. There had to be a reason she'd confronted her mother after all these years, right? A desire to change the status quo.

Now the question was whether or not he was included in her sudden need to mend broken relationships.

"I hope so too," he murmured. "I don't want you avoiding coming home."

She lowered her head, eluding his gaze. "I've been busy."

"And you've been avoiding coming home," he insisted.

Chapter 20

Rachel spun away from the fireplace, crossing toward the wooden shelves on the far wall. Not in an attempt to reject Zac. Well, not entirely. After all, it was going to take more than one conversation with her mother to alter the habits of a lifetime. But more out of a need to give herself the space to sort through the emotions churning through her.

Ancient guilt. Regret. And a ruthless desire to turn back the clock to grasp the happiness that had once been so effortless.

As if to emphasize her wistful longing, her gaze landed on a silver-framed picture of the Pike High School boys' basketball team. They were wearing their brown and gold uniforms and huddled around Zac, who was holding up a gold trophy with a broad smile.

"Oh. I haven't seen this forever." She sent him a teasing glance. "You look so young."

He strolled to join her, staring down at the picture. "I *was* young."

She ran her finger over the faded image, taking a

moment to place when and where it had been taken. She was fairly sure they'd been at the University of Wisconsin-Madison gym. And that she'd been standing in the bleachers yelling at the top of her lungs while this photo was being taken.

"This is the year both the boys' and girls' teams went to state, isn't it?"

"Yep." He smiled down at her. "You scored thirty-seven points and were voted Most Valuable Player."

She laughed, replacing the picture on the shelf. "I can't believe you remember how many points I scored."

His smile faded, his gaze sweeping over her upturned face. "I remember a lot of things."

"Yeah, me too," she admitted with a soft sigh. "I miss it. I miss us."

He flinched, as if her soft words had caused him physical pain. "Rachel, I'm sorry. I know I made a lot of mistakes—"

"I'm not talking about our marriage," she hastily interrupted. That was not a conversation she wanted to have. Not when a warm glow was burning inside her. A glow created by the blazing fire, the potent wine, and delicious hunger for this man. "At least not right now."

He hesitated, then, seeming to accept her desire to go back in time, he reached up to gently cup her face in his hands. "What do you miss?"

Excitement swirled through the pit of her stomach. She shivered. She hadn't felt this thrill of anticipation in far too long.

"How much fun we had together," she murmured. "Sitting on the porch. Going to the movies." She heaved a bittersweet sigh. "Just holding your hand in the hallway seemed like a monumental event."

His features softened, as if he was recalling those carefree days. "It was simple back then, wasn't it?"

"It seemed that way." She ignored the inner voice that dryly reminded her there'd been plenty of arguments between the two of them, and at least twice they'd called it quits. She wanted to cling to the happy memories. "Teasing each other. Laughing. Kissing. That's what I want again."

His fingers skimmed down her cheek and along the line of her jaw. They felt warm against her skin, sending sparks of heat dancing through her veins. "The teasing or the laughter or the kisses?"

"The uncomplicated fun." She lifted her hands to place them flat against his chest, savoring the solid muscles and the steady beat of his heart. "Do you think we could have that again? Just for tonight?"

"Uncomplicated?" He lowered his head, covering her lips in a kiss that sizzled through her.

Her hands moved to clutch his shoulders as her toes curled in her shoes. Her lips parted, allowing the tip of his tongue to sweep inside. He tasted of wine and desire. A heady blend that clouded her mind with pleasure.

At last he pulled back to regard her with a smoldering gaze. "Like that?"

She arched against him, releasing a shaking breath. "It's a start."

He chuckled. "You were always demanding."

She blinked, struggling to concentrate on his words. Being this close to him reminded her of how addicted she was to the smell of his warm skin. When they first started dating she would wear his letter jacket just to be surrounded by his lingering scent. "Was I?"

His arms wrapped around her, tugging her closer to the solid heat of his body. "You were the one to insist I kiss you the first time."

She had. They'd been standing on her parents' front porch and he'd been about to leave after a peck on the cheek. She'd reached out to grab his arm, impatiently demanding whether or not he ever intended to give her a real, grown-up kiss. He had. And nothing had ever been the same again.

"You were taking too long," she chided, her fingers tracing the broad line of his shoulders.

"You could have kissed me," he pointed out.

Her lips twitched. She wasn't going to admit that she'd been too cowardly to make the first move. Despite the fact they'd been friends forever, the fear of rejection had gnawed at her until she'd lost every shred of courage.

"I didn't want you to think I was easy," she teased.

His eyes darkened with an emotion that shook Rachel to the depths of her soul. He hadn't looked at her like that for a very, very long time.

"I thought you were . . . astonishing." His hands settled at her lower back, urging her against his hardening erection. "I still think you're astonishing."

She reached up to thread her fingers in the short strands of his hair. "Then kiss me."

"With the greatest pleasure."

He lowered his head, but instead of seeking her mouth, he grazed his lips over her brow and down the length of her nose. Next, he nibbled a path up the line of her jaw and dipped his tongue into the hollow beneath her ear.

She made a small sound, something between desire and frustration at the all too brief caresses. Zac chuckled, obviously enjoying tormenting her as he lazily explored each sweep and curve of her face.

Rachel sucked in a ragged breath and swept her hands down his body. Two could play at that game. Grabbing the hem of his sweater, she tugged it upward, wiggling it over his head and tossing it aside to admire the smooth muscles of his chest that angled down to a narrow waist.

A flurry of butterflies danced in the pit of her stomach. Zac had always been the strong, silent type. Preferring to allow his actions to speak for themselves. A trait that could occasionally be aggravating when they were married. He hated discussing his emotions and she too often denied possessing any. It meant they never battled their way through any marital issues. But as she brushed her mouth over the bare skin of his chest, she had to admit that being strong and silent was sexy as hell. Especially the strong part.

She felt him quiver beneath her lips, his fingers biting into her skin as if he was struggling to leash his most primitive instincts. An exhilarating sense of power raced through her at his intense arousal. Whatever else had gone wrong between them, it had never been this.

Flicking out her tongue to taste his warm skin, Rachel moved downward, reaching the stark outline of his six-pack.

She lowered herself to her knees, tilting back her head to send him a chiding glance. "You haven't been eating enough," she said, her hands tracing the prominent bones of his hips. "You need to take better care of yourself."

He sucked in a harsh breath, his eyes dark with need as she efficiently unsnapped his jeans.

"It's not much fun having dinners alone," he growled, hurriedly toeing off his boots to allow her to tug off his jeans. In a heartbeat he was completely naked.

"No," she agreed, although she wasn't really paying attention to his words. She was too busy admiring the sight of his hard male body. He looked as if he'd been sculpted by an artist. Desire blasted through her. "There're a lot of things that aren't as much fun alone."

Unable to resist temptation, Rachel leaned forward to take him into her mouth. Zac cried out, as if the pleasure was too much to contain. And maybe it was. After only a few strokes of her lips he was urging her to her feet so he could hastily peel off her clothes. His movements were frenzied, as if he couldn't wait one more second to have her.

That was fine with Rachel. It'd been too long for a slow, methodical seduction.

She wanted it hot and fast and out of control.

Once she was naked, Zac stood perfectly still, running a heated glance down the length of her slender form. A muscle bunched in the corner of his jaw. Was he battling to restrain his desire? Or was he biting back words he sensed she wasn't ready to hear?

Probably both.

Then, with a muttered curse, he grabbed her by the waist and lifted her off her feet. Rachel smiled in anticipation, her heart thundering in her chest. Expecting him to head for the nearby sofa, she was startled when he instead whirled to press her against the wall. Holding her gaze, he reached down to tuck her long legs around his waist.

"Ready?" he demanded.

She locked her feet together, circling her arms around his neck. "More than," she assured him.

Bracing one hand against the wall, Zac lowered his

head to take her nipple between his lips, using the tip of his tongue to send darts of bliss shooting through her. At the same time, he pressed his erection deep into her welcoming heat.

"Oh . . . yes," she breathed. "I need you, Zac."

"You've got me."

Lifting his head to claim her lips in a fiercely demanding kiss, Zac pounded into her with a delectable rhythm. She clutched him close, her back arching as the friction swiftly rushed her toward a massive release. It was exactly what she needed. Pure physical ecstasy.

Her legs tightened around him, her breath coming in short gasps as her head pressed against the wall. She was so close. A groan was ripped from her throat, and angling his hips to sink even deeper inside her, Zac tipped her over the edge of an explosive orgasm. A second later, Zac cried out as he reached his own climax.

Rachel struggled to catch her breath, feeling as if she'd been flung off the edge of a cliff and was still plummeting to earth.

No doubt she would eventually land. And she might even regret what had just happened. But for now she allowed herself to float in the sense of lethargic joy.

"I'm not sure it was my best effort," Zac murmured, sweeping his lips over her damp brow.

"It felt pretty spectacular to me," she assured him.

"Really?" He pulled out of her, but he didn't lower her to the ground. With a fluid strength, he turned her so she was cradled in his arms, her head against his chest. "I think I could use some practice."

She allowed a slow smile to curve her lips. "Well, practice does make perfect."

He kissed the tip of her nose. "Maybe we should practice in my bedroom."

"Mine's closer."

With long strides he headed across the living room. "Brilliant and sexy," he complimented her in a voice husky with desire. "A lethal combination."

Risa swallowed a whimper as she curled in a tight ball on the floor. She was naked with a blindfold tied around her eyes and her hands and feet bound by a rope that was biting into her raw skin. She didn't know where she was or how long she'd been imprisoned by her captor.

Everything seemed to be a blur. Except for the smell. That was oddly acute. She would never forget the stench of cigarette smoke as her face had been roughly shoved into the carpet. A weird smell of grease from the cloth tied around her eyes. And the scent of fear that clung to her like a shroud.

Or maybe she'd just focused on the smells so she didn't have to concentrate on the brutal assault on her body. . . .

"Damn you, Gerry," she muttered, shutting down the agonizing memory that threatened to overwhelm her.

"Typical," a mocking male voice sent a blast of fear racing through her body. "A woman always blames a man for her problems."

Damn. She'd thought she was alone. Curling into an even tighter ball, she tried to disappear into the filthy carpet. The seconds passed. One. Two. Three. When she didn't hear the footsteps she'd been dreading, she swallowed the lump in her throat.

She hadn't caught a glimpse of her captor. The bastard

had snuck up from behind her while she was standing in the empty lot next to the thrift shop and hit her over the head with something hard enough to fracture her skull. When she'd finally woken up, she'd been blindfolded, bound, and naked. That's when the nightmare had started, but despite the violence of his assault, she never caught so much as a glimpse of him. And even when he'd spoken to her, she hadn't recognized his voice. Then again, she was so traumatized she wasn't sure she would recognize her own mother's voice right now.

"Who are you?" She forced herself to ask the question plaguing her.

"The Maestro."

Risa frowned. Maestro? Was that his name? No. He was just boasting. The prick.

"Maestro of what?" she rasped.

An ugly chuckle echoed through the room. "You've already had a small taste of my talents."

Swallowing the bile that rose to her throat, Risa managed not to vomit. A small but important victory.

"Sure, a real maestro," she muttered. She paused, desperately searching her fuzzy brain for a way to convince the perverted bastard to release her. "I need to go home. I can't be late for work."

There was a momentary pause, as if her words had startled him. Then she heard a rustle, as if he was making himself more comfortable on a chair.

"Trust me, Risa, being late for work is the last thing you need to worry about," he assured her in dry tones.

Terror crawled over her skin, as if it was alive and threatening to devour her. "Why?"

"Why what?"

"Why me?"

"Ah. A good question. You weren't exactly what I desired, but compromises have been necessary." He heaved a loud, dramatic sigh. "It's unfortunate, considering my quest for perfection."

"I don't understand."

"You met the necessary requirements. You have the right appearance. Dark hair, pale skin, a plump ass. And you were easy to lure into my trap."

She sucked in an appalled breath when she realized it hadn't just been bad luck that had led her to crossing paths with this maniac. It'd been planned. Had he been stalking her? Deciding if she would satisfy his sick desires?

For whatever reason, the knowledge that it hadn't been a fluke made it even worse.

"You called Gerry to set up the drug deal," she muttered.

"Of course," he readily admitted. "I knew he was a greedy lowlife who would be willing to put his girlfriend in danger if it meant making a few bucks."

Her lips twisted. Obviously, he knew Gerry. At least well enough to have discovered her boyfriend's lack of morals when it came to money. "How did you know he wouldn't come himself?"

The man released a loud snort. "Everyone in town knows that Gerry spends Wednesday evenings at a private high-stakes poker game in Madison."

She frowned. The creep hadn't done his research as well as he'd wanted her to believe. "No. That's not true. He goes to Madison to pay . . ." The words trailed away as his claim echoed through her mind, touching off alarm bells. Gerry had promised her that he was done gambling after she'd caught him stealing her grandmother's diamond earrings.

He'd sworn that the bundle of money he got from his drug deals was to pay off his final debt to the loan shark and that he'd turned over a new leaf. *Shit.* She was an idiot. A naïve, willfully blind idiot. "He's been lying to me."

A dark, rasping laugh floated through the air, as if her tormentor was well aware he'd just ripped her heart from her chest.

"Are you surprised?"

"That jerk. That fucking jerk," she snarled, anger exploding through her. Not only had the scumbag lied to her, but he'd deliberately sent her into a dangerous situation so he could play cards. Every awful thing that had happened to her was Gerry's fault. "I'm going to kill him."

"Doubtful," her captor drawled.

Shoving away any thoughts of the man who'd disappointed her for the last time, she concentrated on finding a way to escape her tormentor.

"Please, let me go," she begged. "I swear I won't tell anyone what happened."

"Actually everyone is going to know what happened," he said. "At the proper time."

Everyone would know? Her stomach twisted, another wave of bile rising to her throat. "What does that mean?"

"I always tape the coup de grâce. At some point I intend to share with my inevitable fans."

"The coup de what?"

He clicked his tongue, as if annoyed by her stupidity. "Your death."

His words stirred a warning in the back of her mind. She'd heard rumors of a killer in town, but it hadn't actually sunk in. This was Pike, not New York City, and most people assumed that the women who'd turned up dead had been murdered by someone they knew. A husband, ex-husband, boyfriend . . .

"You killed Paige," she breathed, her lips so stiff she struggled to make them move.

"I did." There was no missing the pride in his voice.

"And Tory."

"Yes."

Shudders raced through Risa's body, tears soaking into the blindfold. "Please, no. Please, please, please."

"Save your pleas," the beast chided. "It isn't time yet."

Zac had heard his grandmother tell him to live with a song in his heart. He didn't have a clue what she'd meant. Usually he had a song stuck in his head, not his heart. One that he was desperate to forget.

But waking as the dawn filled the spare bedroom with a rosy glow, Zac suddenly understood.

It wasn't just the night of passion, although that had been glorious. It was the soft warmth of Rachel's body snuggled against him. And her sweet scent that clung to his skin. And the brush of her breath against his cheek.

The sensations completed him in a way he'd taken for granted when he was younger. He'd assumed that loving Rachel would be easy. And that nothing could destroy their relationship. Now he held her close, savoring each second she was near as his heart sang with happiness.

Combing his fingers through her silken hair, he felt Rachel press a kiss to the center of his chest.

"This feels weird."

He released a choked laugh. "Not what a man wants to hear when he wakes up naked with a woman in his arms."

She tilted back her head, her blue eyes shimmering with amusement. "In my head this is still your parents' house. I'm worried they're going to bust through the door and catch us."

Zac wrinkled his nose. He knew exactly what she meant. "You're right. It still feels like my parents' home to me, too. I really need to find my own place."

"In Pike?"

He gazed down at her pale face, suddenly realizing that home had nothing to do with four walls and a roof. It had everything to do with Rachel. He'd rather be in the small, dilapidated apartment they'd shared during college than the fanciest house if it meant he was alone.

"To be determined," he murmured. "Do you plan to stay in Madison?"

"To be determined."

Zac arched a brow. What was she implying? That she was open to a different future? Wanting nothing more than to press her for an answer—or better yet, seduce her into accepting they belonged together—Zac swallowed a sigh. He'd allowed himself to put aside all thoughts of the killer for the night. Honestly, his sanity had demanded a break. But now his sense of duty was nagging at him. It was time to return to the hunt.

"As much as I hate the thought of leaving this bed, I need to get dressed and head into the office," he said with genuine regret.

Rachel nodded, pulling out of his arms and climbing off the bed. Zac's breath hissed between his clenched teeth as he took in the sight of Rachel's slender body. Maybe he should reconsider the urgency of heading to the office. After all, the sun was just cresting the horizon and . . .

No. He slammed shut the mental door on temptation. The people of Pike were in danger. Until he had the killer locked in a cell, nothing else mattered.

Clearly agreeing with his decision to focus on the case, Rachel slipped on a robe and grabbed a brush off the nightstand to pull it through her tangled hair.

"I think I'll do another search of the old drive-in. Just in case we missed something last night."

He slid off the mattress, stretching his deliciously sore muscles. "I called Greg while you made dinner to keep watch on the area. We might not stop the killer from snatching his next victim, but if that's the dump site, then we'll catch the bastard."

Rachel tossed the brush onto the bed. "Speaking of Greg."

"What about him?"

"Did you know he was the mailman before Isaac?"

"Seriously?" Zac tried to recall the man's résumé. He hadn't been the one to hire him, but he'd read through the personnel files of all his deputies. He didn't recall anyone being with the postal service.

"Mrs. Wilkins didn't particularly like him," Rachel continued. "She said he was rude."

Zac frowned. "My deputies seem to have a lot of secrets. I think I should have a word with them," he muttered. It wasn't only embarrassing to think his staff might be keeping vital information from him, but it was potentially dangerous. What if one of them was covering for someone? Or even involved in the murders?

"What else did Mrs. Wilkins say about Greg?" he asked, his tone grim.

She considered for a second, as if reviewing her conversation with the older woman. "Nothing . . ." she started to say, then her eyes widened. "Wait."

"What is it?"

"Something Mrs. Wilkins said." Rachel paced toward the window before turning and heading back to the bed, an electric energy suddenly humming around her. "I didn't pay attention to it at the time."

Zac stepped toward her. "About my deputy?"

"No, she said that her foster daughter's name was Destiny Sykes, and that her grandparents ran a business in town that kept them too busy to take in a teenage girl," she said.

Zac felt a pang of disappointment. He'd been certain that she'd recalled some useful information.

"That's it? Oh . . . shit." The relevance of what she'd just told him hit Zac with stunning force. "Sykes," he breathed, belatedly realizing why the name was familiar. "Sykes Automotive."

She nodded sharply. "Are the Curly boys still in jail?"

"No." Zac clenched his hands. He'd wanted nothing more than to keep the Boltons safely locked away. Unfortunately, the law wasn't created to make his job easy. A damned shame. "I didn't have anything to charge them with beyond trespassing. I had to release them."

"I'm going to have a quick shower and get dressed. Then I think we should check out Junior's apartment."

"It's a long shot," he warned, even as he headed toward the door. As much as he wanted to share a shower with Rachel, he knew they didn't have time for what would happen if he did. They had to get to Curly's place and search it.

"Right now I'll take any shot," she said.

Zac grimaced as he headed out of the bedroom. "That's the truth."

In less than an hour they arrived at Sykes Automotive. It was still early enough that the town of Pike was just starting to wake and a swift glance around the lot revealed just one vehicle. A truck with the name Sykes painted on the side along with a phone number. No sign of Curly or his father.

"I don't think they're open yet," Rachel murmured.

"Someone's here," he said, nodding toward the truck.

Together they climbed out of her SUV and headed toward the front of the shop where the office was located. Zac pounded on the glass door until the same man he'd spoken to when he'd been searching for Curly the first time appeared from the side of the building. He was wearing a clean pair of coveralls with the name Ray stitched on the pocket.

"We don't open—" He bit off his words as he recognized Zac. He didn't appear overly happy. "Sheriff."

"Have you seen Curly?"

"No." The man went from unhappy to downright pissed at the mention of his employee. "And when I do, I'm going to tell him that his ass is fired."

"We need to look in his apartment," Zac said.

"I told you, he isn't here." Ray was clearly annoyed at having his morning routine interrupted. Then, meeting Zac's steady gaze, he heaved a resigned sigh. "Fine. I'll get the key."

Zac and Rachel didn't speak as the mechanic headed

into his office, both watching through the front window as he rummaged through the desk. Although there was no sign of Curly's vehicle, they couldn't be sure that he wasn't hiding in his apartment. Or that he didn't have a woman stashed inside. They had to be prepared for anything.

Ray at last located the spare key and returned to hand it to Zac. "Can you tell me what's going on?" he asked. "Is Curly in trouble?"

"I just need to make sure there's no one in the apartment," Zac said, keeping his purpose vague. He didn't want word spreading around town that Curly was involved with the crimes. Not until he could prove a connection.

Ray frowned, then, glancing from Zac's bleak expression to Rachel, he held up his hands and stepped back. "I'll let you do your thing."

"Good idea," Zac said dryly.

Heading toward the side of the building, Zac cautiously climbed the steps with Rachel just behind him. His attention was locked on the door, acutely aware they were dangerously exposed if Curly decided to start shooting. They'd reached the top step when Rachel grabbed his arm.

"Zac," she hissed, pointing toward the landing. "Blood."

Glancing down, he caught sight of the dark droplets that stained the wooden platform. He reached beneath his jacket to pull his weapon. Rachel moved past him, her gun already in her hand.

"Careful," he breathed, watching as she pressed herself against the side of the building and inched her way to the nearby window.

She nodded, pausing before she cautiously angled her head to see through the glass. Zac stiffened, his finger on the trigger. For a second she stood completely still, as if waiting for something. On the point of demanding what was wrong, Zac realized that the glare of the rising sun, combined with the dirt clinging to the pane, was making it hard for her to see inside. Then, with an audible gasp, she whirled toward him.

"There's a woman on the floor," she said, her voice tense. "I can't tell if she's alive, but she has a blindfold over her eyes."

Zac shoved the key into the lock. It might be more dramatic to knock down the door, but it was faster and considerably less painful to open it in a more mundane manner. "Anyone else?"

"Not that I could see."

She moved to stand beside him, her gun pointed at the door as it swung open. He scanned the shadowed living room, ignoring the unmoving body on the floor as he searched for any hidden assailant.

"Clear," he at last muttered, stepping over the threshold and moving his weapon from side to side as Rachel dashed past him to kneel next to the woman, pressing her fingers against the side of her neck.

Fury pounded through Zac, the memory of dragging Tory's dead body out of the lake still a raw wound. Was he too late? Again? Christ, he couldn't bear it.

A second ticked past, then Rachel glanced over her shoulder, an expression of stark relief on her face.

"She's alive."

Chapter 21

Rachel had traveled with Risa in the ambulance, holding the woman's hand as she woke with a scream of terror. Once at the hospital in Grange, Rachel had stepped aside as a doctor had checked for injuries before a trained nurse arrived with a rape kit to collect any potential DNA left by her attacker.

It was nearly two hours before Rachel could spend a few minutes with the traumatized woman, taking a preliminary statement between Risa's shattering bursts of tears. When it became apparent that she'd pushed poor Risa as far as she could endure, she slipped out of the room and into the long corridor.

She took a deep breath of chilled air that smelled faintly of antiseptic as her gaze searched for Zac. At last she spotted him at the end of the hall, pacing the green and white tiled floor, his shoulders hunched as if carrying the weight of the world on them.

She didn't doubt that was exactly what he felt.

In many ways, Zac was a fantastic lawman. Smart, determined, and methodical. Once he was on the trail of a criminal, he would never give up. And just as importantly, he put his heart into everything he did.

But that heart was also his greatest weakness. He took his position as a sheriff too personally. He didn't have the ability to walk away from the office and put the work out of his mind. She'd seen too many good people burn out.

As if sensing her lingering gaze, Zac abruptly turned, hurrying to stand directly in front of her. "How is Risa?"

Rachel grimaced. "Fractured."

They shared a pained glance. Neither of them would forget the sight of Risa lying naked on the filthy carpet, her hands and feet bound and a rag tied around her eyes.

He finally broke the silence. "I hate to ask, but could she tell you anything about who attacked her?"

"Not really. She said that last night she was sent to the parking lot behind the thrift shop by her boyfriend, Gerry Sims. A spot right next to the old drive-in."

Zac stiffened. "What time?"

"Just an hour after we left the area."

"Damn." His features tightened with the same frustration that burned inside Rachel. They'd been so close to preventing the tragedy. "Was she there to meet her boyfriend?"

"No. She went there for a drug deal," Rachel said, her voice thick with disgust.

Zac arched a brow. "Risa is a user?"

"No. Her boyfriend is a small-time dealer. He was supposedly busy, so he sent her to hand over the pills."

"Charming," Zac drawled in dry tones. "Did she give you the name of the buyer?"

"No. It was all set up by Gerry."

"Could she give you a description?"

Rachel shook her head. "She drove to the spot of the meeting, but as she was getting out of the car someone hit her on the back of the head and knocked her unconscious. When she woke up she was already blindfolded."

"She didn't recognize the voice?"

That had been Rachel's second question. It was hard to believe Risa didn't notice something familiar about her attacker. There weren't that many people in the town of Pike, and unless the monster was a stranger, she'd probably met him at some point. Then again, the poor woman had been brutalized. It would be shocking if she managed to remember anything about the assault.

"She says she doesn't have any idea who it was," Rachel said, keeping her voice low as a nurse passed by pushing an older man in a wheelchair. "I don't want to press her for details. Not until she has some time to process the realization that she's safe."

Zac glanced away. "So did her kidnapper set up the deal to get his hands on her? Or did he just take advantage of a woman alone in an isolated spot?"

"I don't believe in coincidences."

Zac nodded, his expression bleak. "Me either. I'm going to track down Gerry Sims. I want to know who Risa was meeting before I lock him up for a very, very long time."

"He might have asked her to go there deliberately," Rachel pointed out.

At first she'd been infuriated that the jerk had sent his girlfriend to a remote location to meet a junkie without concern for her safety. Who did that? Then it'd occurred to her that Gerry's motives might be more sinister than Risa suspected.

Zac glanced back, his brows arching. "He might be involved with the killings?"

"It's a thought."

He slowly nodded. "Are you going to ride along?"

"I don't think so. I want to stay around here for a while. Risa's parents are coming to pick her up once the doctor signs her release, but I don't want her left alone with a stranger before they get here."

He glanced over her shoulder at the uniformed guard next to the closed door. "She isn't alone."

Rachel shrugged. "Risa is the only one to survive. The killer might be worried she will be able to tell us something that will identify him. And since he's managed to avoid detection for who knows how long, I'm not ready to take any chances."

"Probably a good idea. I'm not sure I trust anyone right now." Zac glanced down at her. "Give me a call when you're done here and I'll come back to pick you up."

She nodded and his gaze lowered to her lips, as if he wished they weren't in a public setting. Reaching up, she touched her fingers to the center of his chest, directly over his heart. "Be careful."

He held her gaze for a long moment, then with obvious reluctance he turned to walk away. She watched his departure, inwardly acknowledging that his butt looked just as fine now as it did in high school. Maybe better.

With a wry shake of her head, Rachel moved to settle in a plastic chair pushed against the wall. She was far enough away from the cop to avoid infringing on his territory, while still easily keeping an eye on Risa's door. No one was going in or out without her seeing them.

It was twenty minutes later when the click of leather

soles against the tile floor had her glancing up. Surprise widened her eyes as she took in the sight of her father approaching. He was dressed for work in his usual blue suit and silver tie, with his hair smoothly combed from his face.

"Dad." Rachel rose to her feet, a stab of concern piercing her heart. It wasn't an accident that the older man was at this hospital in Grange. "What are you doing here?"

He glanced around, as if making sure there wasn't anyone close enough to overhear their conversation. "I stopped by the sheriff's office and they said I might find you here."

"Did something happen?"

He paused, clearing his throat. "I heard about poor Risa."

"Oh." Rachel stared at him in surprise. "Did you know her?"

"Just from the diner." He waved his hand in a vague gesture. "She always seemed like a nice girl. I hate that this happened to her."

"Me too," Rachel cautiously agreed. "It's awful."

"No clues to who's responsible?"

"Not yet."

"Mmm." Wilson rocked back on his heels. "I don't suppose you could tell me even if you did know."

"No." Rachel frowned. "Surely you didn't drive all this way in the middle of the day because you heard about a waitress from the diner being hurt?"

Wilson glanced down, adjusting the cuffs of his tailored jacket. He was like Zac in some ways. He was a man of few words. But unlike Zac, he wasn't just reserved, he was closed off from his emotions. As if afraid they might suddenly explode out of him if they weren't carefully contained.

"Your mother told me that the two of you spoke yesterday," he at last said.

Rachel remained confused. This was hardly the conversation to have in the middle of a public hallway. And she certainly didn't believe he'd taken off work to drive to Grange to have it.

With an effort, she swallowed her impatience. Her father was doing his usual avoidance routine. When she was young and he felt compelled to lecture her on her misbehavior, or inform her she couldn't have something she wanted, he would dance around the unpleasant subject, working up his nerve to finally get to the point.

He would reveal the reason he was there when he was ready, she silently warned herself. And not one second before.

"Yes," she murmured. "I hope I didn't upset her too much."

He considered her words. "She was upset, but I think it was a good thing," he finally admitted.

"Why would it be a good thing?"

"This morning I found her in Benny's bedroom." A wistful smile touched his lips. "It's the first time in years she's allowed the door to be opened."

Rachel pressed her hand against her stomach, not sure whether to be happy or worried. She'd wanted to force her mother out of her protective bubble, but she had no idea what would happen if she managed to succeed. "What was she doing in there?"

"Sitting on the bed, holding his baseball mitt."

"Was she crying?"

"There were tears on her cheeks, but there was a smile on her lips. As if she was letting herself remember our precious boy."

Rachel reached out to grasp her father's hand. "Maybe this is a beginning."

He nodded, a hint of regret in his eyes. "I should have said something to her a long time ago."

"Why didn't you?"

The older man grimaced at her direct challenge. "It was easier to ignore our grief than to share it. I've never been good with the emotional stuff."

Well, that was the understatement of the year, she silently acknowledged. Then again, she'd already conceded that she wasn't Miss Chatty when it came to expressing feelings. They all needed to do better.

"I get that," she murmured.

He gave her fingers a small squeeze. "Things are going to change, I promise."

"Good." She paused, studying his still-handsome face. "Is that why you're here?"

Tugging on her hand, he pulled her down the hallway. Rachel could clearly see Risa's door, but they were far enough away from the cop on guard duty to prevent him from overhearing their conversation.

"Not entirely," he admitted.

She resisted the urge to glance at her watch. "What is it?"

"Your mom also told me that you brought over a picture of Evie Parson."

Rachel sucked in a sharp breath as anticipation burst through her. This was it. This was why her father had left his office and driven all the way to Grange.

"Yes. We found it in the Henleys' cabin. We assume it belonged to Jude."

"Probably."

She studied the older man's expression, which was giving nothing away. "Do you know something?"

His jaw clenched, an unexpected heat staining his cheeks. "I hate spreading gossip. Especially when it involves the bank."

She nodded. It wasn't just words. Her father never, ever talked about his work, or the employees at the bank. Much to her mother's annoyance.

"A good business decision," she said, well aware that a part of her father's success was due to his ability to keep his lips shut. No one wanted their financial information spread around town.

"Exactly. But now . . ."

"Dad?"

Wilson clenched and unclenched his hands as if struggling against a powerful force. "I don't know if the past has any bearing on what is happening in Pike, but I won't allow my loyalty to Russell to put my daughter in danger."

Rachel arched her brows, as surprised by his insistence on putting her before his employer as by the implication that the owner of the bank might have some bearing on her case.

"What does Russell have to do with Jude?"

"One night Russell called and asked me to come to his house." His gaze moved over her shoulder, as if he was peering into the past. "I remember it was late because your mother was annoyed I had to leave during our favorite television show. When I got to Russell's house I discovered that he'd been drinking."

"Was that unusual?"

"Very. He might have a glass of wine when we went out to dinner, but he never overindulged."

Rachel didn't doubt that. Russell Parson had always been a grouch. Her mom said he could suck the joy out of the room the minute he entered it. She wasn't wrong. On the rare occasions he'd come to her parents' house she'd done her best to be elsewhere.

"Had something happened to upset him?" she asked, not revealing her opinion of the older man.

"Evie had just confessed that she was pregnant."

Rachel waited. When her father didn't speak she shook her head in confusion. "He didn't want children?"

"He couldn't *have* children." The color staining her father's cheeks darkened. "He'd had a vasectomy after he'd divorced his first wife."

"The baby wasn't his," Rachel breathed. Now the story was getting interesting. "Jude Henley?"

"That's who Russell suspected, although Evie refused to name the father," Wilson conceded.

She stored the information in the back of her mind. "Why did he call you?"

"It was too late to have an abortion. I believe she was over five months along, and I doubt Evie would have had one anyway." He stopped to clear his throat, as if trying to get rid of a bad taste in his mouth. Rachel didn't doubt her father had been appalled to be forced into the middle of the sordid argument. "She did, however, agree to give the baby up for adoption. She decided to travel to her grandmother's home in Chicago until the child was born."

"What did he want from you?"

"To drive her to Chicago."

Rachel frowned. Hauling a pregnant wife to Chicago went well above and beyond her father's duties at the bank. "Why?"

"Russell wanted to make sure she didn't see Jude before she left town." He shrugged. "I think he was afraid that Jude might convince Evie to take off with him."

Rachel felt as if something nasty was crawling over her skin. She'd never liked Russell Parson. Now she liked him even less. It was understandable that he'd been angry about the affair, but why not divorce Evie? Instead he'd demanded she get rid of the child, at the same time controlling her like she was a possession, not a wife.

And what about Evie? Talk about poor taste in men. A manipulative creep and a serial killer.

"There was nothing to stop Jude from following her to Chicago, right?" she asked. "I mean, you weren't going to stay and babysit her for the next four months."

His lips twisted. "You're assuming Russell was thinking clearly. I assure you he wasn't."

Rachel wasn't so convinced. She wouldn't doubt that Russell had someone spying on his wife during her time at her grandmother's house.

"Did you drive her to Chicago?" she asked.

A visible shudder raced through her father. "Yes, the longest trip of my life."

"Did she say anything about the baby?"

"She didn't say a word the entire drive. She just stared out the window. I don't know if she was in shock or if she was hoping Russell would change his mind and follow us to take her home." Wilson heaved a deep sigh. "In the end

I left her at her grandmother's house, and four months later she returned to Pike. She was never the same."

"What do you mean?"

"She was . . ." Her father struggled for the right word. "Withdrawn. As if a light inside her had been stolen. And maybe it had." Another deep sigh. "She gave up her child just days after the father of the babe had died. Or at least after we thought Jude was dead. It was too much for her."

Rachel's interest in Russell and Evie was forgotten as she allowed her father's words to sink in. "She had the baby at the same time that Jude died?"

Wilson considered his answer, as if he could sense the vital importance of her question. "Yes," he at last said with a forceful nod. "I remember thinking that Russell must be relieved that the man wouldn't be around to bother Evie when she returned to town." He stopped, a sick expression crossing his face. "Isn't that awful?"

Rachel turned away, her mind whirling. Obviously it was conceivable that Evie giving birth and Jude faking his death had nothing to do with each other. Or maybe Evie's decision to give up the baby and stay with her husband had prompted Jude to start over somewhere else. New name, new life.

But the possibility that Jude had chosen to take the baby and disappear seared into her mind.

"The master and the student," she whispered.

"Excuse me?" Her father intruded into her wild imaginings.

She whirled back to face him. "What happened to the baby?"

He blinked at her harsh tone. "I guess it must have been adopted."

"If there was an adoption, there will be paperwork I can follow," she said, speaking more to herself than her father. Then she sent him a searching gaze. "Who else knows about this?"

"No one," he assured her. "Evie is dead. Jude is dead. At least he is now. And neither Russell nor I ever spoke a word about that night." He lifted his arm to glance at the expensive watch wrapped around his wrist. A gift from his employer. "I have to get back to the bank. If you could keep this as discreet as possible, I'd appreciate it."

"I'll do my best," she promised. There was no need to open old wounds unless absolutely necessary. Then again, the truth always had a way of coming out. One way or another.

Unexpectedly her father leaned down to brush his lips over her cheek. "Come for dinner soon," he urged. "We miss you."

A poignant sense of longing settled in the center of her heart. She'd spent so long avoiding her parents she hadn't allowed herself to realize just how much she missed them. It would be nice to spend a few stress-free hours in their company.

"I will," she said. "I promise."

She stood in the center of the hallway watching her father disappear through the far doorway. Once he was gone, she reached into her satchel to pull out her phone. Pressing the top number on her favorites list, she waited to be dumped into voicemail.

Chapter 22

Zac was once again in the basement beneath the courthouse, sitting in the cramped holding cell. Across the narrow table Gerry Sims slouched in his chair, his thin, sullen face framed by lank hair that fell to his shoulders. His jeans and tee were wrinkled as if they'd been slept in and there were dark circles beneath his sunken eyes.

Worry for Risa? Or burned out from drugs? Zac was betting on the drugs.

"This is bullshit," the younger man muttered.

"So you've said." Zac curled his lips. "Repeatedly."

Gerry scowled. "I told you, I was out of town last night. I have no idea what happened to Risa."

"And you care even less."

The man flinched, as if he wasn't used to being called out for his sleazy behavior. And he probably wasn't. Gerry Sims was a typical bully. He surrounded himself with people whom he could easily intimidate.

"You don't know what you're talking about."

Zac forced himself to lean back in his seat, folding his arms over his chest. He'd changed into his official uniform, complete with his badge and weapon, before having

Gerry brought in. He wanted the younger man to understand this wasn't just a casual questioning. His future was never going to be the same.

"You're right," he drawled. "I don't know if you're just a low-life creep who pressured your girlfriend into the clutches of a serial killer." He deliberately paused. "Or if you're the killer."

The sullen expression slid off the narrow face as Gerry absorbed the implication in Zac's words. "What did you say?"

"I'm sorry. Am I not being clear?" Zac narrowed his eyes. "I think it's very likely you murdered Paige and Tory. And last night, you tried to kill Risa."

"That's . . . that's crazy," the man stammered, his skin paling to a disturbing shade of ash. "If I wanted to hurt Risa, I could have done it any time. Why would I kidnap her?"

Zac shrugged. "If she died in her apartment, you would be the first suspect. Not even you are that stupid."

"No. I would never hurt Risa." Leaning forward, Gerry glared at Zac. A barely suppressed violence vibrated around his skinny body, revealing an explosive temper.

Zac frowned. Not exactly the disposition of a serial killer. At least not one who seemingly plotted and planned with meticulous detail. That didn't mean, however, that the man wasn't involved.

"I loved her."

Zac snorted. "You loved her enough to manipulate her into dealing drugs."

"It was just a one-off. I was . . ." He cut off his words, no doubt realizing he'd just incriminated himself. "Busy," he muttered.

"Busy where?"

Gerry glanced away, his hands balling into fists. Was he silently weighing the risk of revealing his illegal activities against the fear of being charged with murder? Whatever his inner debate, he finally answered Zac's question. "I was in Madison."

"Doing what?"

"Hanging with my friends."

"Not good enough."

There was another flare of anger in Gerry's eyes, but he managed to control his urge to lash out. "I was at a private poker game. I have a dozen witnesses," he spat out. "Happy?"

Zac calmly reached for the notebook and pen lying in front of him. Sliding it across the table, he held Gerry's fierce glare. "Write down their names."

He jerked, as if blindsided by the request. "No fucking way. They're not the kind of guys who are going to talk to cops."

"That would be a shame. At least for you." Zac narrowed his eyes. "Right now you're my prime suspect for three murders and an attempted murder. You'll never see the light of day again."

"Screw that." Gerry jutted out his chin. "You're just trying to scare me."

"Am I?" Zac allowed a humorless smile to curve his lips. "You're the one who sent Risa to that isolated spot last night and supposedly disappeared out of town. You're the only one who knew what time she'd be there. And you were the one who didn't bother to report her missing when she failed to come home. Do you want to explain that to a jury?"

"Shit." Gerry grabbed the pen and scribbled down a list

of names. Then, tossing aside the pen, he shoved the notebook toward Zac. "Track them down if you want. It's your funeral."

Zac didn't bother glancing at the notebook. He'd have one of his deputies check with the witnesses. Instead he kept his gaze locked on the younger man's wary expression.

"Who was Risa supposed to meet?"

Gerry hunched his shoulders. "I don't have a name."

"You really are a piece of work." Zac didn't bother to hide his disgust as the image seared through his mind of a naked, broken Risa left like trash on the floor. "Your girlfriend was kidnapped, brutalized, and nearly murdered, but you're worried about protecting your junkie."

Gerry flinched, as if Zac had managed to strike a raw nerve. "Dammit. I don't have a name. If I did, I'd give it to you."

Zac frowned. Did he believe the loser? Not really, but he'd play along. "If you didn't know who was buying your merchandise, then how did you set up the deal?"

"It was Curly."

Zac slowly leaned forward. Now things were getting interesting. "Curly Bolton?"

"Yep."

"Senior or Junior?"

"Junior."

Zac tapped his finger on the table, trying not to get ahead of himself. It was no shocker that Curly would be looking for some drugs to purchase. And they hadn't determined for sure that the drug deal was related to Risa's kidnapping. But he wasn't going to ignore the fact that the younger Bolton's name kept popping up in his investigation.

"Risa was supposed to meet him last night?"

"No."

Zac's breath hissed between his clenched teeth. Was this idiot playing games? If so, he was going to discover that Zac wasn't in the mood to be jerked around.

"I'm losing my patience," he rasped.

Gerry leaned back, lifting his hands as he sensed that Zac was on the edge. "Look, I was in the bar waiting for Risa to get off work a month or so ago—"

"Which one?"

"The Bait and Tackle." Gerry sent Zac a chiding frown at the interruption before continuing his story. "Curly was sitting next to me moaning about his shitty job and the shitty pay. I told him he could earn some extra cash if he could help move my product. A . . . finder's fee."

Zac silently acknowledged that just a week ago, having this sleazebag admit to selling drugs would have been big news. Now he barely considered the pending case. Oh, he was going to arrest the bastard. Rachel had already gotten permission from Risa to search the apartment. He didn't doubt for a second he was going to find enough drugs to charge Gerry with trafficking.

"Did Curly agree to your offer?"

"Not at the time." Gerry shrugged. "In fact, I'd forgotten all about our conversation until yesterday afternoon."

"What happened?"

"He sent me a text to say he'd met some dude who was having a party at the lodge," Gerry explained, referring to the old Elks Lodge. It'd once had a restaurant and dance floor that was packed on Friday and Saturday nights. Now it was rented out for family reunions, wedding receptions, and the occasional bachelor party. "He said that his usual supplier had crapped out on him, and since this was short notice he was willing to pay top dollar for fifty oxy. He told me the time and place for the meeting and that was that."

Zac frowned. Gerry Sims obviously wasn't over-burdened with brains, but it was surely Drug Dealing 101 to avoid meeting some mysterious buyer at an isolated location? Not only was it a good way to get robbed, but there was every chance it might be a sting.

"And it never occurred to you that the entire setup was a little sketchy?" he asked in disbelief.

"I wasn't thinking about anything but the money," Gerry muttered, looking embarrassed. "I'm in debt up to my ass."

"And it wasn't you in danger, right?" Zac said dryly.

"I didn't know." With a loud huff, Gerry threw himself back in his chair, the sullen expression returning. "I swear I didn't know."

With an abrupt motion, Zac rose to his feet and headed for the door. Gerry wasn't going anywhere and Zac had more important matters to concentrate on. If he had more questions, he knew where to find the creep.

Stepping into the dark hall, Zac motioned toward the deputy patiently waiting near the staircase.

"Lindsay, give our prisoner his phone call and then lock him up. I'll deal with the paperwork later." He frowned as he considered the numerous tasks that were piling up at an alarming rate. First he wanted to pick up Rachel from the hospital in Grange. He'd received a call from her while he was in the holding cell. He assumed Risa's parents had arrived and she was ready to leave. He needed to search Risa's apartment, as well as track down her missing car. And most importantly, he needed to find Curly Junior. "Where are Greg and Anthony?"

Lindsay had the harassed expression of a person who was doing the job of three. "I haven't seen them today."

"Great." Zac added tracking down his missing deputies to his list. "I'm going in to pick up Rachel and then head up a search for Curly Junior. Call me if you need anything."

Rachel sat beside Zac as he drove through Pike. He'd picked her up from the hospital in Grange and they were headed toward the trailer park.

"A child," he muttered, his hands tightening on the steering wheel.

"Born twenty-eight years ago," she said. She'd spent the drive filling Zac in on what her father had revealed. "I have my office trying to track down the adoption papers."

"It might explain why Jude decided to disappear," Zac said, slowing as he pulled into the entrance of the park. "He couldn't pretend to suddenly appear with a child just after his lover returned to town from an extended absence." He grimaced. "Then again, could a serial killer really care enough about a child to want to turn his back on his life to raise it?"

It was a question Rachel had considered while she'd been waiting for Zac to arrive at the hospital. "I doubt he could love the baby, but he might have seen it as a potential audience."

Zac sent her a startled glance. "An audience?"

"Most serial killers are egomaniacs." A shudder raced through Rachel. It was horrible enough to recall the tapes that had captured the brutal beatings. It was even worse to imagine that Jude had used them as trophies to celebrate his evil deeds. "They think they're above regular mortals. And like anyone with an oversized ego, they crave an audience to admire their brilliance."

Zac slowed to a crawl as they turned onto the narrow street that would lead to Curly Senior's trailer.

"True." He shook his head. "It's not like they can brag about their kills at the local bar."

"Plus, if you had a kid, you could train it to keep your secrets while convincing them you're some sort of god, controlling who lives and dies," she murmured, speaking her thoughts out loud.

It was remarkably easy to believe a demented madman could enjoy the unconditional adoration only a child could offer. "The master."

"Creating a monster just like Dr. Frankenstein."

Zac pulled to a halt a few trailers away from Curly's place. Clearly he didn't want to alert the Boltons the cops were looking for them, although it was obvious even from a distance that there weren't any vehicles in the driveway.

"And just like Dr. Frankenstein, the monster turned on the creator, ultimately destroying him," Rachel added.

Zac unhooked his seat belt, turning to face Rachel. "Okay, let's consider the possibility. Jude learns that Evie intends to give up their child."

Rachel nodded, picking up the thread of the hypothesis. "He plots to fabricate his tragic death, along with help from his older brother, and disappears from Pike."

"I assume he managed to meet with Evie at some point to take the child and then vanished like a ghost."

Rachel started to nod. That had been her first thought as well. Then she hesitated, struck by a sudden thought.

"Or maybe he didn't raise the child," she said slowly. Would a serial killer really want the burden of being a full-time dad? "Maybe he paid someone else to do it."

Zac's eyes narrowed. "Someone like Curly Junior's mom?" he suggested. "Senior did have doubts about whether the kid belonged to him."

"It's possible."

Zac was silent for a moment, as if considering the various implications of what they'd discovered.

"Jude could have visited the kid and shared his dark deeds," he finally said. "Or even taken him in during the summer. It would give him the chance to teach his heir the tools of the trade."

Rachel tried to imagine Jude raising a child. Even if it was as a part-time parent, it was remarkably difficult. Probably because it was hard to accept a ruthless monster had the capability to consider anyone but themselves.

"How did he survive?" she demanded. "It's one thing to support yourself. But if he had to pay for a child, he had to make money somehow."

Zac shrugged. "It's not that hard to work off the books," he told her. "There are lots of people who prefer to pay for services in cash to avoid taxes. Not to mention the fact he had already developed his skills in petty theft and dealing drugs. And if he lived out of a camper or RV, he could move around without attracting notice."

The breath was squeezed from her lungs at his words.

He was right. And better yet, her cold case might actually help them track down the killer. "Yes."

"What is it?"

"I have a register of the campers who were staying at the Devil's Lake State Park at the time Kim Slade disappeared." A tight smile curved her lips. "It might be worth checking into them. We might be able to discover the fake name that Jude used after leaving Pike, and what he called his child."

Zac nodded. "I think I'll do a sweep of the local campgrounds. It could be that Jude's child is using the same technique. But first . . ." He shoved open the door of his truck and jumped out. "I'm going to have a quick look around Senior's trailer. I want to see if they're hiding inside."

Rachel remained in the truck, wanting to keep watch. She had a full view of the trailer, along with the street. She didn't want the Boltons trying to sneak out a window and disappearing. Or worse, returning home and catching Zac off guard.

Jogging along the sidewalk, Zac darted between the narrow yards. Then, reaching the trailer he peered into the windows as he made a slow circle. At last he headed back to the truck and climbed in.

"The place is empty. Let's check out the bars."

About to agree, Rachel blinked as the loud rattle of an engine captured her attention. She glanced out the front windshield as a flash of a vehicle zoomed down the street at the end of the park.

"Wasn't that Curly Senior's truck?" she demanded.

With a curse, Zac pulled on his seat belt and whipped his truck in a tight U-turn. Then, with a surprising caution, he headed toward the entrance. They were going to miss the opportunity to cut off the man.

"Aren't you going to stop him?"

Zac shook his head, his gaze trained on the truck that swerved out of the park with a squeal of its tires.

"I want to see where he's going."

Chapter 23

I'm restless. Why? I'm sure a part of my anxiety is the fact I didn't complete my creation. A coitus interruptus. Or whatever you call a serial killer being denied his final blow. It's enough to make anyone twitchy. And then there's the fact that Risa is still alive. I've been careful. But no one is perfect. Not even me. There's the faintest risk that the bitch noticed something that might reveal my identity.

The energy humming through me, however, has nothing to do with the unfulfilled desire or a fear of being exposed. Risa was always a less than adequate choice to satisfy the requirements of my game. There are others who could easily replace her. And I'm certain she is too terrified to say shit about what happened to her. By the time she finds her nerve, she will be dead.

One way or another.

None of that is responsible for my buzz. It zaps and sizzles through me like champagne flowing through my blood. And it is just as intoxicating.

Finally, I understand.

I wasted so much time on my stupid pride. I wanted to

prove I was the best. Far better than my mentor. And my obsession somehow stole the joy that I had so desperately been seeking.

Oh. I'd found pleasure. Delicious pleasure. And following in the footsteps of my teacher means that I was allowed to practice and hone my talents. But like any great artist, my style will be my own.

Not cautious. Not timid. There won't be endless plotting and planning and then wasting the effort on an inferior specimen.

Jude Henley will be a footnote in history. Just another savage beast who hunted and destroyed the most vulnerable.

I will be more. A legend. A killer who captured a tigress and turned her into his masterpiece.

Zac maintained as much distance between his vehicle and the truck in front of him as he dared. The last thing he wanted was to allow Curly to disappear. Not when Zac suspected he was headed to meet his son. Why else would he have left town to weave through the dirt-packed roads that led to the middle of nowhere? Then again, he didn't want to spook the older man. If he realized he was being followed, he would lead them in circles until they gave up.

Seated next to him, Rachel leaned forward to peer out the front windshield, her eyes narrowed.

"He's going to Jude's cabin." She broke the silence, her body vibrating with the tension that flowed through her.

Zac glanced to the side, catching sight of the turnoff that would eventually lead to the Roadhouse as they bounced past. He'd been so focused on his prey that he'd barely noticed where they were headed. Now he hastily pressed on the brake as he watched Curly's truck whip into the hidden driveway.

Parking his vehicle at the side of the road, Zac pulled his weapon and climbed out. A second later Rachel was standing beside him, her gaze scanning the thick woods that lined the narrow lane.

"I'll keep watch," she assured him.

Zac nodded. He hated to leave her on her own, but they couldn't both risk walking into a trap. If he didn't come out, he wanted to be sure someone would come looking for him. And besides, she was a trained law official. This was literally her job.

Stepping between the nearest trees, Zac cautiously made his way to the back of the cabin. The last time he was out there, they'd discovered there was no lock. He'd intended to mention the lack of security to Jacob, but he'd had a few other things on his mind.

Silently climbing the steps, he entered the kitchen and moved toward the opening where he could hear the heavy tread of footsteps.

"Curly. Curly!" the older Bolton called out. "You in here?"

Waiting to make sure there was no answer, Zac stepped into the front room. "Looking for someone?"

The older man leaped backward, flapping his arms. He looked like a bird awkwardly trying to take flight. "Shit." Realizing that Zac wasn't the ghost of Jude Henley, Curly pressed a hand to his chest. "You scared the crap out of me. You shouldn't sneak up on an old man like that. What if I had a heart attack?"

Zac took a slow survey of the older man. He looked even

more gaunt and his hair was standing straight up, as if he'd been running worried fingers through it. His imposing nose twitched, no doubt sensing danger.

"That would necessitate having a heart," Zac drawled.

Curly blinked. "What?"

Zac shook his head. Sarcasm was lost on this man. "Never mind." Holstering his weapon, Zac folded his arms over his chest. "You just don't learn, do you?"

"I don't learn what?"

"Ah, that question covers such a vast territory," Zac retorted in dry tones. "But I was referring to the fact that I just arrested you for trespassing. And yet here you are."

The familiar sullen expression settled on Curly's thin face. "I'm not trespassing."

Zac arched a brow, waving a hand to indicate the space around them. "You broke into a cabin that doesn't belong to you. That's the definition of trespassing."

"I mean I'm not here to stay. I'm looking for . . ." The words came to an abrupt end as Curly snapped his lips shut.

"Looking for what?"

There was a long pause. "My wallet." Curly finally managed to come up with a lie. "I think I might have left it here when I was so rudely hauled off to jail."

"You were taken to a holding cell." Zac corrected the man. "And I'm fairly confident that if I searched you, I would find your wallet in your back pocket."

Curly cleared his throat. "Did I say wallet? I meant—"

"You know what I think?" Zac sharply interrupted.

"Don't know," Curly muttered. "Care even less."

"I think you're here looking for your son," Zac continued, watching the man's eyes dart from side to side. Either he was thinking about making a run for it, or he was worried Junior was hiding nearby and about to do something stupid.

"Why would I be looking for him?"

"Because we found a kidnapped woman tied up in his apartment."

"What?" Curly tried to act shocked. Instead, he looked sick to his stomach. "I don't know what you're talking about."

Zac stepped closer, towering over the man as he glared at him in frustration. "Do I look like I'm in the mood to be jerked around?"

Curly's hands clenched as if he was resisting the urge to throw a punch. Zac didn't doubt the man was handy with his fists, but luckily for him, he managed to control his angry impulse.

"I'm telling you I don't know," he finally growled. "Curly and I spent the night drinking at my trailer until we both passed out. I woke up an hour or so ago and couldn't find my wallet. I had a wild hunch it might be out here. Nothing to get your panties in a twist about."

Zac rolled his eyes. The man had to be a terrible poker player. "And your son?"

"He's still passed out."

"At your trailer."

"Yep." Curly licked his lips, no doubt realizing that Zac could easily check the truth of his claim. "Course he did mention the need to check in with work. He's missed a couple of days, so . . ." The words trailed off with a shrug.

Zac held his wary gaze, allowing a tense silence to draw out before he spoke. "Accessory. To. Murder."

"What?"

"You keep lying to me and I'm going to charge you with accessory to murder."

The man made a choked sound between fury and fear. "Curly didn't do nothing."

"If you truly believed your son was innocent, you wouldn't be giving him a fake alibi."

"Are you kidding?" Curly sent him a frown of pure disbelief. "You've been pestering us since the trouble started in Pike. It's obvious you want to pin the crime on one of the Boltons. Doesn't even matter which one of us takes the fall. Just like every other sheriff we've had. Too lazy to find the real criminal so you blame it on some poor slob who doesn't have the money to fight back."

Zac ignored the practiced spiel. The man had obviously used it a dozen times to try and get out of trouble. "Shut up."

"Hey."

Zac took another step forward, forcing the man to tilt back his head to meet Zac's glare. "This isn't a joke, Curly. Someone is murdering the women of Pike."

"It ain't me," he protested. "Or my son."

Zac's lips twisted as he silently noted that Curly was anxious to protest his own innocence first. "How can you be so sure that Junior isn't involved?"

"I know him." Curly planted his hands on his hips, visibly warning Zac he wasn't going to be swayed. "He may not be the brightest bulb, or the hardest worker, or even the most honest man. But he's not a killer. I've never even seen him kick a dog."

"That's your proof? He doesn't kick dogs?"

Curly spat out a curse. "Why does he need proof? This is police harassment."

Zac leaned down until he was nearly touching Curly's large nose. "Listen very carefully." His words were barely above a whisper. He'd found over the years that a softly spoken word was far more threatening than a shout. "Both you and your son worked for the Henley family, which meant you were familiar with the morgue where the first victim was found." He watched Curly flinch. "You admitted you knew that Jude was in town shortly before his death, and I'd bet good money your son knew more about him than you're willing to admit."

"He didn't." Curly fiercely denied the accusation.

Zac ignored him. "Now a woman was found in Curly's apartment. A woman who was lured to an isolated location to be kidnapped by a text sent by your son."

"What text?"

Zac hesitated, then shrugged. The information was bound to come out. Gerry wasn't the sort of guy to keep his mouth shut. "A drug deal with Gerry Sims," he said.

Curly jerked, his brows snapping together. "That's bull-shit."

"I've seen the text."

"No way," the older man insisted. "Curly isn't into that stuff. Not anymore. And even if he was, he wouldn't use Gerry. Everyone in town knows that the bastard weights the scales and passes off fake pills."

Zac frowned. He believed Curly. At least about Gerry Sims being a sleazebag. But that didn't change anything. "Your son wasn't interested in the pills. He wanted the girl."

"No." Curly stomped his foot like a child, his face flush-ing with emotion. "No, no, no. This is insane."

"Where is he?"

"I don't know."

"I'll ask you once more." Zac glared down at the stubborn fool. "The next time we talk you'll be sitting in a jail cell."

"I'm as serious as a heart attack," Curly snarled. "I don't know where my son is. That's why I'm here. Looking for him."

Zac's breath hissed between his clenched teeth. The past week had rubbed his nerves raw and this man wasn't helping. Zac didn't know if he was being deliberately annoying or if it just came naturally, but the fact that Zac hadn't given him a good shaking was nothing short of a miracle.

Sucking in a slow, deep breath, Zac calmed his temper. "When was the last time you saw him?"

Curly hunched his shoulders, sending Zac a sour frown. "After being unlawfully detained we decided it would be best to lie low for a while. I said we should go to the trailer. My rent is paid until the end of the month. Might as well get my money's worth."

"And?"

"And I went home." The older man glanced away, shifting his feet. "Curly had a few things to do before he came over."

"What things?" Zac waited, but the man refused to meet his gaze. "Curly?" he at last snapped.

Curly grudgingly answered. "He was going to his apartment to pick up the few things he'd left behind. He knew he'd worn out his welcome at the auto shop and he didn't want them thrown in the street."

Zac didn't react to the explanation, although he did force himself to consider the possibility that Curly was telling the truth. It would be blind stupidity to jump to conclusions without hard facts. And if Junior had gone to his apartment to collect his belongings, there was a chance that the killer had been caught off guard by his return. Or maybe he'd been waiting for the younger man to arrive. The killer could have knocked out Curly and used his phone to set up the meeting with Gerry Sims.

Of course, that didn't explain where Curly was now. Or how the killer had known that Gerry had suggested Curly call him if he wanted to score some extra bucks. "Or more likely to set up a meeting with his next victim," he said.

"Don't say that," Curly rasped. "He was going to get his stuff. Nothing else."

"Then where is he?"

The man's defensive expression crumbled, leaving behind a vulnerable old man terrified for his son.

"He never showed up," Curly admitted. "When I didn't see him by dinnertime last night I started calling. He never answered his phone." His hands clenched and unclenched, a visible indication of his inner anxiety. "Then today I heard there was a woman found at his apartment and I freaked out. I was afraid something must have happened to him."

Zac glanced around the empty cabin. He was willing to accept Curly's explanation. For now. "Why did you come here?"

"I've tried his friends and the local bars." Curly shook his head in a helpless gesture. "I didn't know where else to look."

"What about girlfriends?"

"Nah . . . Wait." Curly fell silent, his gaze distant as if he was searching his mind for something. A seemingly difficult process.

"You thought of someone," Zac impatiently prompted.

"Tara." He glanced at Zac as if he should instantly know who he was talking about.

"Who's Tara?"

"Tara Mitchell. They've dated off and on since Curly came to Pike." Something that might be hope flickered in the man's sunken eyes. "If he was in trouble he might go there."

"Where does she live?"

"I don't know where her house is. But she's a beautician . . . or whatever you call them nowadays . . . at the Golden Shears. I suppose that's where she would be this time of day."

Zac hissed at the unexpected words, a sudden urgency pounding through him. That couldn't just be a coincidence, could it?

"Go home," he ordered in harsh tones, crossing toward the front door. He paused to glare over his shoulder. "And don't even think about leaving town."

Curly scowled. "Just find my boy."

Zac left the cabin before the older man could see his expression. He had every intention of finding Curly Junior.

And locking him away for the rest of eternity.

Jogging through the trees, Zac angled toward the general area he'd left the truck. "It's me," he called out as he neared the road. They were all jumpy. He didn't want Rachel wondering if he was a bad guy. Not when she was holding a loaded gun.

He stepped out of the woods, not surprised when Rachel hurried to stand in front of him. She was anxious to discover what he'd learned.

"Well?"

"Curly claims that Junior disappeared after I released

them yesterday," he said in clipped tones. "He hasn't seen or spoken to him since then."

Rachel grimaced. "Helpful."

"It's what I'm starting to expect." Zac shook his head in disgust. "One step forward, a dozen backward."

She tilted her head, studying him with a curious expression. She could obviously sense the tension that was humming through him like an electric current. "Now what?"

"We head back to Pike," he said, leading her toward the truck. "Curly has a girlfriend who works at the Golden Shears."

They both climbed into the vehicle and Zac started the engine.

"You think she might know where he is?" Rachel asked.

"Even if she doesn't, I want to talk to her." Zac stomped on the gas, sending the truck lurching forward.

Rachel wisely grabbed her seat belt and pulled it across her body. Even if he wasn't driving like a maniac, the road was one long series of potholes. He needed to have a word with the county commissioner.

"Why do you want to talk to her?"

"Risa Murphy's apartment is above the beauty shop."

Chapter 24

They'd reached Pike by the time Zac had finished repeating his conversation. Rachel silently considered what they learned. It didn't seem like much on the surface.

They confirmed that Curly Junior had intended to go to his apartment. And that he was currently missing in action. At least as far as his father was concerned. That put him at the top of the list of suspects.

What they didn't have was any sort of physical evidence that would prove the younger man was guilty.

Zac parked the truck across the street from the two-story brick building. On the lower floor there was a large window painted with letters spelling out GOLDEN SHEARS, and a glass door. The second floor had much smaller windows that were currently opened despite the chill in the late afternoon air, allowing a blast of heavy rock music to spill onto the street below.

Rachel tried to ignore the noise, turning to glance at the man standing next to her. "Do you mind if I do the questioning? I might be able to make a connection with her."

Zac nodded, his eyes narrowing as he glanced toward

the outside stairs that led to the upper floor. "I'm going to check out Risa's apartment. Sounds like someone's inside. I want to know who it is."

"Gerry?"

"There's no way he could have got bonded out yet."

Rachel shook her head in disgust. "Whoever it is, they clearly aren't concerned about Risa being kidnapped and brutally raped."

"Real gems," Zac muttered, crossing the street and angling toward the end of the building.

Rachel followed, veering off to push open the glass door. Instantly she was drowning in the scent of ammonia, peroxide, and hairspray. She blinked, her eyes watering. This place was in serious need of a ventilation system.

Glancing around she took in the individual sinks built into one side of the long space with hydraulic chairs. The entire wall was made of glass that reflected the shelves on the opposite wall, which were stocked with various bottles of shampoo, conditioner, nail polish, and sparkling hair ornaments.

There were only a couple customers in the chairs, both of them getting haircuts. A third woman turned from a cash register at her entrance. She was short, with a plump face and smiling brown eyes. Her dark hair was cut short and tipped with a bright purple dye. She was wearing a loose dress that did nothing to conceal her large baby bump.

"Rachel?" The woman crossed the linoleum floor, a smile of genuine pleasure on her face. "Rachel Fisher? It's Cate."

It took a second for Rachel to place the name. It'd been a lot of years since she spent time in Pike. Her recollection of childhood friends had faded. Finally, she placed the name with a memory. Cate Hagood—or whatever her married name was—had been a couple years younger than Rachel, but they'd been on the same basketball team. They'd spent endless hours after school practicing in the gym. "How are you?"

"Fat." Cate ruefully touched her swelling belly. "And getting fatter by the day."

Rachel felt an unexpected pang of envy. Not at the pregnancy. She wasn't ready for a baby. In fact, she wasn't sure she'd ever be ready. But there was an unmistakable happiness that literally sparkled around her friend. As if she couldn't contain her joy.

"You're glowing," Rachel said, a smile curving her lips despite the grim reason she was there.

This was what she wanted—a bubbling, infectious contentment. And when she got it, she was never, ever letting go of it again.

"That's one word for it," Cate said dryly. "We don't usually take walk-ins, but if you want to wait a few minutes I can work you in after I comb out Ruth."

Cate nodded toward the two old-fashioned dryers at the end of the room where a reed-thin older woman was seated with a dozen curlers wrapped tightly in her steel gray hair.

"Ms. Caufield?" Rachel asked, studying the familiar face that was deeply wrinkled from years of scowling at the kids in her classroom.

Ruth Caufield had been an English teacher at Pike High School since the Stone Age, bludgeoning them with Shakespeare, Poe, and Hemingway until reading the classics became a misery, not something to be treasured. A pity.

"One and the same," Cate muttered.

"She hasn't changed at all."

"Evil doesn't age."

Rachel's lips twitched. She remembered why she enjoyed spending time with Cate. Then, with a shake of her head, she tucked away her old memories. It was time to concentrate on the present.

"I'm not actually here to get my hair cut, although I should probably run by before I leave town," she ruefully acknowledged.

Cate looked confused. "Do you need some hair products? We carry several of the top brands."

"No, I'm looking for Tara Mitchell."

"Oh." Cate started to wave her hand toward one of the nearby sinks only to discover it empty. "She was here a minute ago. She's probably in the break room. You can go on back if you want."

"Thanks."

"Give me a call when you want that trim," Cate called out as Rachel headed toward the long curtain that covered the opening in the back wall.

"Will do," Rachel promised.

Pushing aside the thin material, Rachel made her way down the hallway, past the bathroom on one side and the storage room on the other. She entered the open area at the end, her nose wrinkling at the smell of stale coffee, perfume, and tuna fish. It wasn't just the front shop. The entire building could use a good ventilation system. She glanced around the small kitchenette with a sink, microwave, and coffee maker.

A young woman was seated at a kitchen table that was shoved against a wall, her head bent down as she studied the phone clutched in her hand.

"Excuse me," Rachel murmured.

The woman jerked up her head, revealing a pale oval face that appeared shockingly young. It might have been the large blue eyes or the smattering of freckles, but Rachel found it hard to believe she could be much more than eighteen years old.

"Hey, this is a private area." The girl frowned, tossing back her long, bleached-blond hair. "The public bathrooms are back down the hall."

Rachel stepped forward, reaching into her satchel. "Tara Mitchell?"

"Who are you?"

"Detective Fisher." Rachel pulled out her badge to flash it toward Tara.

"Shit." The image of youth was marred by the jaded anger that hardened the girl's features. She was older than Rachel first suspected. "Why won't you guys leave me the hell alone?"

Rachel tucked away her badge, wondering how often Tara had to deal with the law. She made it sound like a regular occurrence.

"I'm looking for Curly Bolton."

"Yeah, you and everyone else," Tara muttered, tossing her phone on the table as she slouched in her chair. "I don't know where he is."

"Okay. When was the last time you spoke to him?"

"It's been weeks."

"Really?" Rachel arched a brow. "Now, why do I think you're lying to me?"

"I don't know." Tara blushed, but her expression remained defiant.

Rachel felt a stab of unease. The girl obviously had no fear of her casual lover.

"Curly and I haven't dated in forever."

"I'm not asking about a date, I just want to know the last time you called or texted each other."

The girl's hand darted toward the phone, covering the screen. Rachel didn't have to be a genius to suspect she'd been texting Curly just before Rachel had walked into the room.

"Like I said, it's been forever."

Rachel ground her teeth, biting back the urge to tell the girl that she was an idiot to protect the guy. She had no proof that Curly was involved in the killings. Or that he was a danger to Tara.

All she could do was try to convince the girl it was in her best interest to cooperate with the investigation.

"I think I should warn you that we're pulling Curly's phone records," Rachel said, not bothering to admit that they hadn't gotten the warrant yet. She had no doubt they would have it soon enough.

The girl sent her a venomous glare. "That's illegal."

Rachel's lips twisted into a rueful smile. So much for connecting. "I'm a detective investigating three murders in this town. I can do whatever I want."

"I hate cops."

"When was the last time you talked to Curly?" Rachel forced a sharp authority into her tone.

Tara glanced down, her shoulders slumping. "He texted me yesterday."

"What did he want?"

"He said he and his dad were being hassled by the sheriff." She reached up to twine a blond strand of hair around her finger. Rachel sensed it was a nervous habit. "He didn't want to stay at his apartment. I'm guessing he's decided to quit his job. Big shock. And he didn't really want to stay with his dad. The two of them don't always get along. He was wondering if he could stay with me."

"What was your answer?"

"I said he could stay for a few nights. Just until he found something else." She shrugged. "I like my space."

"Did he stay with you?"

"No. He never showed up."

Rachel frowned. That was two people who'd been expecting Curly last night. Was it a deliberate attempt to throw the cops off his track?

"Did it worry you that he didn't come by?"

"Not really." Tara lifted her head to reveal the expression of a woman who'd been disappointed by the men in her life. "The jerk has a habit of making plans he doesn't keep. I assumed he got to his apartment and found a stash of beer he'd forgotten and spent the night getting toasted."

"He didn't call or text you?"

"Nothing." Tara's sharp laugh echoed through the cramped room. "Bastard."

"If he didn't come to your house, where else would he stay?"

"Take your pick." Tara's tone was bitter as she waved her hand in a vague gesture. "He's slept his way around town."

Rachel studied the younger woman. Obviously she wasn't stupid. At least she knew that Curly wasn't prime boyfriend material. That didn't mean, however, she wasn't in danger.

There was a thumping from above their heads, loud enough to rattle the coffee mugs piled in the sink. Presumably from the music being played at a deafening level. She doubted that Zac had given in to his impulse to beat information out of whoever was up there. As much as he might want to.

"Do you know Risa Murphy?"

Tara looked confused by the abrupt question. "We went to school together. We're not friends or anything. Why?"

"She has an apartment above the shop."

"So?"

"Did you happen to notice anyone hanging around over the past few weeks? Maybe sitting in their car, watching this building?"

"No." Tara surged to her feet, snatching the phone off the table. "I come here to work and then I leave. I don't have time to stare out the window."

Rachel sensed that she'd gotten all she could from the girl. At least for now. If Curly was still missing tomorrow, they might think about putting a trail on her. Just in case she was kind enough to lead them to the missing man.

"If Curly contacts you, I need you to let me know." Rachel reached into her satchel and pulled out a business card, pressing it into Tara's hand. "And—" She bit off her words. "Be careful."

Unimpressed with Rachel's vague warning, Tara angrily shredded the business card and tossed the pieces on the floor. "I'll tell you what I told the last cop. I'm not a snitch."

On the point of turning away, Rachel glanced back at the defiant girl. "What cop?"

"The one that was here an hour ago."

Rachel studied Tara, briefly wondering if she'd mis-heard. Then she recalled the girl's words when she'd first entered the break room.

Why won't you guys leave me the hell alone.

"A local cop?" Rachel asked.

"I guess."

"Did you recognize him?"

"Idiots in uniform all look the same to me," Tara sneered, trying to act tough.

Rachel ignored the deliberate provocation. "What did he ask you?"

"He wanted to know where Curly was." She hesitated, as if deciding whether to reveal the rest of their conversa-tion. Then she sniffed. "And he offered me fifty bucks for a recent picture of him. I'll admit it. I took the cash. Why not? God knows I need the money."

Rachel blinked, trying to process what Tara was telling her. "He offered you money?"

"That's what I just said. I gotta get back to work." Tara shouldered past Rachel, her rebellious expression visibly daring Rachel to try and stop her.

With a grimace, Rachel used the narrow back door to leave the salon and rounded the side of the building to head toward the truck where Zac was waiting. She didn't want anyone seeing her expression.

As if to prove her point, Zac frowned as she climbed into the passenger seat. "Did she tell you where Curly is?"

"No." Her voice was clipped. "But I think you should check out your deputies."

Zac stilled, his fingers gripping the steering wheel. "Why do you say that?"

"Tara said that some man in a uniform came earlier to interview her and offered her fifty dollars for a recent picture of Curly Junior."

"She didn't give you a name?"

Rachel rolled her eyes. "All she gave me was attitude. But I believed her when she said there'd been someone there pumping her for information. And that she'd taken the fifty bucks."

"Shit." Zac started the engine. "I don't know what's going on, but my chat with Anthony is severely overdue."

"If you don't mind dropping me at the courthouse, I'd like to check in with my office," Rachel said as Zac pulled away from the curb and drove toward the center of town. "I want to know if Evie Parson ever signed official adoption papers."

In less than ten minutes they were pulling into the side parking lot. "I don't know how long this will take," Zac warned. "I'll meet you at the farm later."

Rachel opened her door and jumped out, glancing back at Zac's hard expression. "I didn't ask. Who was in Risa's apartment?"

"Gerry's cousin, Dale Sims. He claimed that Gerry had called and asked him to clear out his things. He also claimed that he had no idea it was a crime scene."

"Yeah, right." Rachel shook her head, not surprised that Gerry would have a relative willing to destroy evidence for him. Or that he would be stupid enough to play loud rock music while he was doing the deed. "Did you get anything out of him?"

"Does a headache count?"

She smiled wryly. "See you later."

Chapter 25

Zac felt like he was driving around in circles. Probably because he was. He'd already gone by Anthony's house, his mother's house, the various bars, including the Road-house, and was about to admit defeat when he decided to take the outer road on his way back to the town square. His impulsive decision looked as if it was going to pay off as Zac caught sight of the uniformed man standing at the edge of the abandoned drive-in.

Whipping his truck into the parking lot of the thrift shop, Zac switched off the engine and unzipped his jacket. Next, he removed the holster strap that kept his weapon in place. He wanted to be able to draw the gun quickly if necessary. Once confident he was prepared, Zac stepped out of his truck and followed the broken sidewalk to approach his deputy from behind.

He'd nearly reached the man with his back turned toward the street when Zac belatedly realized it wasn't Anthony. If he'd been paying closer attention he would have noticed the figure was too tall and slender. Zac muttered a curse, but he continued forward. It was possible that Greg would know where his fellow deputy was.

"Greg." Zac stepped next to the man. "What are you doing here? I told you we didn't need surveillance any longer."

The younger man jerked in surprise, swiveling his head around as he stuffed his phone back in his pocket. He'd obviously been texting with his friends instead of doing his job.

"I thought whoever kidnapped Risa might have left behind a clue." He cleared his throat, as if embarrassed to be caught wasting time. "I wanted to check out the location before it was dark."

Zac swallowed a sigh. If he decided to remain the sheriff of Pike, he was going to have to consider his staff. Starting with firing his current deputies and hiring new ones. Well, he would definitely keep Lindsay. She was obviously competent and self-motivated. But the others? No way.

"Have you seen Anthony?" he asked, trying to keep the sharpness out of his voice.

Greg paused, considering the question. "Not today. I don't think he's been into the office. Why?"

"I have a few questions for him."

"Is something wrong?"

Zac started to ignore the question. He didn't want anyone to alert Anthony that he was under suspicion. Then again, who better than Greg to tell him if his deputy had been sneaking behind his back?

"He's been acting . . ." Zac struggled for the right word.

"Weird?"

"More weird than usual."

Greg turned to directly face him, blatant curiosity on his face. "What's he done?"

Zac considered his answer. He didn't want to give too

much away. "I've seen him entering crime scenes when he shouldn't have been there," he finally revealed. "And this afternoon I discovered that a uniformed man offered a potential witness a bribe."

Greg appeared genuinely shocked, his eyes widening. "A man in a sheriff's uniform?"

Zac shrugged. "That was the implication."

"Was the bribe for information?"

"For a recent picture of Curly Junior."

"Seriously?"

"I couldn't be more serious."

Greg stared at him, as if having trouble accepting what Zac was telling him. Then he gave a slow shake of his head. "I don't understand. What do you think he's up to?"

Zac ground his teeth. What did he think Anthony was up to? He didn't have a good answer. All he knew for sure was that he had to make absolutely certain the deputy wasn't somehow involved with the killer. That vague fear was giving him an ulcer.

"I don't know. But if he did offer a bribe, he will most certainly be fired and quite likely charged with tampering with an ongoing investigation," Zac said in harsh tones. "If not worse."

"Damn." Greg looked vaguely sick, as if he was deeply disturbed by Anthony's behavior. "I didn't want to say anything, but . . ." The words faded as Greg grimaced.

"If you have information, Greg, now's the time to share it," Zac snapped.

Greg glanced down, drawing in a slow, audible breath. "Okay. Over the past week I've been watching Anthony."

"Why?"

"Like you said, he's been acting a little sketchy."

Zac didn't know whether to be relieved that Anthony's strange behavior wasn't a figment of his imagination or terrified the killer had been hiding beneath his very nose.

"Be more specific," he commanded.

"Well for one thing, I came into the office and I found him taking pictures of the files."

"What files?"

"Staci Gale and Jude Henley."

Zac frowned in surprise. He'd assumed Greg would reveal that Anthony had been snooping through the latest murders. Perhaps keeping track of the ongoing investigation. For himself, or for a partner.

Why would the deputy be interested in Staci Gale? Or even Jude? Unless the killer was using the files to duplicate the old murders?

Zac shook his head. None of it made sense. "Did you ask him why?"

"Of course."

"And?"

"He said he was going to question Jacob Henley at the nursing home and he wanted the background information." Greg shrugged. "I thought it was odd at the time."

More than odd, Zac silently conceded. He'd never directed Anthony to question Jacob Henley, and even if he had, the deputy wouldn't have considered the possibility that he might need additional information. Being prepared wasn't his style.

Zac mentally added the pictures of the files to the mounting evidence against Anthony.

"Anything else?" he asked.

Greg shifted nervously from foot to foot, as if trying to decide whether or not to share what he'd seen.

"When I drove to work this afternoon I saw his car parked in front of the Golden Shears," he at last said, the words rushed as if he was trying to get them out as fast as possible. "I thought he was there to search Risa's apartment. But now . . ." He sent Zac a worried glance. "That's where Tara works, isn't it?"

Zac's lips parted, then he abruptly froze, the breath squeezed from his lungs. He hadn't said Tara's name, had he? Which meant there was only one way Greg could know that she was the one who'd been bribed.

From the night he'd found Jude Henley on top of his grave with a bullet in his brain he'd felt as if he was being led through a maze by a master manipulator. Every corner he took led to another corner, or worse, a dead end. But he'd accepted that being an investigator meant being one step behind. The perp would always be in control of the situation since he or she was the one committing the crime. Especially with a serial killer. The murderous bastard had no doubt schemed and plotted and planned the deadly spree for years, while Zac was desperately trying to catch up.

Failing to have predicted who might be the killer or even the next victim was frustrating, but understandable. Being completely oblivious to what was happening in his own office was . . . unforgivable.

Suddenly he thought about Greg's reaction when he'd first arrived. He'd assumed the younger man had been startled because he'd been caught texting with his friends while he was on duty. Now Zac suspected something far more nefarious.

"Boss? Is everything okay?"

Sensing Greg's curious gaze, Zac forced himself to

clear his tangled thoughts. The time for regrets would be later.

After the killer was caught and rotting in jail.

"Of course." He placed his hands on his hips. Close to his weapon. "Although I wish I'd known more about Anthony."

"I'm sorry." Greg continued to study Zac, as if he suspected the churning anger just below the surface. "I should have said something sooner."

"Yes. Why didn't you?"

Greg licked his lips. Was he nervous? Or giving himself time to come up with a logical lie? Maybe both.

"To be honest, he's not very competent," Greg finally said. "I was afraid if you fired him, he might not get another job."

"We're investigating a potential serial killer and you were worried about Anthony's employment status?"

"It seems stupid now." Greg coughed, shifting from foot to foot. "Well, I should get back to the station."

"Before you go. Can I see your phone?"

Greg blinked. "My phone? Why?"

Zac held out his hand. "I just want to check something."

Greg stepped back, his hand slipping into the pocket of his jacket as if protecting the phone. Or maybe reassuring himself that it was still there.

"This is my personal property."

"I'm aware of that." Zac narrowed his eyes. "Do you have something to hide?"

Greg's eyes darted to the side, as if seeking inspiration. A second, and then two, ticked past before his tension eased. He leaned forward, as if about to share a secret between buddies.

"There are private photos on here. The sort my girlfriend wouldn't be happy with me sharing." He sent Zac a wink. "Not with anyone."

If Zac hadn't been infuriated by the younger man's deceptions, he might have admired his slick ability to lie on cue. It wasn't a talent everyone possessed. "I'm afraid that I'm going to have to insist."

"Why?"

Zac snapped his fingers. "The phone, Greg."

The charming expression crumbled, revealing a sullen anger that Greg had been careful to keep concealed. "I don't have to give you anything," he snarled. "Screw my job. It doesn't pay shit anyway."

Zac stepped forward. "This is no longer about a job," he warned in dark tones. "We can do this here or we can do it at the station."

"Fine. You wanna throw your weight around, then . . ." The man's words faded as he glanced over Zac's shoulder. "What the hell do you want? I told you we could meet later."

Zac snorted, not about to be distracted. The deputy had already managed to fool him once. It wasn't going to happen a second time.

"Nice try," he muttered, wrapping his fingers around the holster of his gun.

He was fully prepared for Greg to try and escape. Either shoving him aside or taking a swing at him. What he wasn't prepared for was the blow that landed on the back of his head. Shocked by the agony that burst through his brain with titanic shockwaves, he stared at Greg in disbelief.

The man was working with a partner. Who? The serial killer? Or was Greg the killer and he had a sidekick?

His mind was already growing fuzzy when the second blow sent him to his knees, a ringing in his ears making him fear his skull was cracked.

"Let's go," he heard someone mutter.

There was the muffled sound of footsteps, but Zac was incapable of stopping them. He couldn't even manage to shout for help. The agonizing pain made it impossible to think clearly. Besides, he had other things to worry about. Sensing his body swaying forward, Zac struggled to lift his arms. Why were they so heavy? They felt like cement blocks.

"Shit," he rasped, his hands still at his sides as his face hit the ground.

Seconds later a gaping darkness sucked him into oblivion.

Rachel used Zac's office to make her calls. She enjoyed being surrounded by the worn furnishings and scent of leather. It reminded her of the afternoons she'd spent in this room chatting with Rudolf. Unlike her parents, the former sheriff had been fully supportive of her decision to become a cop.

Of course, it wasn't the older man's scent that hung in the air, or his handwriting on the various notes tossed across the desk. That was all Zac.

Lowering her phone, Rachel finished writing on the pad she had in front of her.

So far she'd discovered that there were no official adoption papers that listed the birth mother as Evie Parson. They'd even tried under Evie's maiden name, Mills. Her staff had also run background checks on the registered visitors at Devil's Lake the night Kim Slade had gone missing. Most had been easily crossed off the list. But there'd been one name that they were still trying to track down. A John Wilson who'd rented a cabin along with his son, Jacob.

Jude Henley and his son?

It was possible. At least it was a lead that could be followed.

She was contemplating her next steps when there was a buzzing sound from the nearby intercom. Glancing toward the monitor mounted on the wall, Rachel could see a young woman standing outside the courthouse. There was a second buzz, and the woman disappeared from view.

Dismissing the interruption, Rachel was reaching for her phone when there was the sound of footsteps in the reception area and the door to the office was abruptly thrust open. She turned her head, watching as Bailey stepped over the threshold. The younger woman came to a halt as she saw Rachel sitting behind the desk.

"Oh, I was looking for Zac."

Rachel rose to her feet, studying the intruder. Bailey was wearing a heavy jacket, but beneath it she could see she was still wearing her work scrubs, and her brown hair was starting to escape her ponytail. She looked like she'd had a bad day. One that was only getting worse.

"I'm sorry," Rachel said. "He's not here at the moment."

"Damn. I was hoping . . ." Bailey bit her lip, clearly struggling to control her emotions.

Rachel rounded the desk. "If this is an emergency, I can track him down."

"No." Bailey shook her head. "I know he has a lot on his plate."

"I'm not the sheriff, but maybe I can help," Rachel offered. She didn't have the authority to take Zac's place.

Not when it came to enforcing the law in Pike. But she could potentially offer advice.

"Okay." Bailey closed the door, moving to the center of the room. "But I'd like to keep this between us. We're trying to keep this quiet."

"We?"

"The nursing home."

Rachel hid her regret at offering her help. Was this some sort of workplace complaint? Or worse, a charge of abuse by one of the patients? She wasn't going to be able to give any assistance if that was the case.

Swallowing a sigh, she forced herself to meet Bailey's worried gaze. "Has something happened?"

"It's Jacob."

Rachel's reluctance was shattered beneath a surge of sharp-edged interest. "Jacob Henley?"

"Yes."

Rachel frowned, not certain why Bailey would be looking for Zac. "Is he hurt?"

"I don't think so." Bailey visibly shivered. "I hope not."

"Bailey." Rachel moved to stand next to the woman. "Please tell me what's going on."

Bailey hesitated, as if wondering whether or not to trust Rachel. Then she released a harsh sigh. "He's missing."

"Missing from the nursing home?"

"I mean he's not exactly missing," Bailey hastily corrected, as if she'd been frightened by the sound of the words being spoken out loud. "We're not a prison. And he isn't on a locked ward. Not yet anyway. He can come and go from his room whenever he wants."

Her explanation did nothing to temper Rachel's unease. Was it possible that Jacob had simply wandered off? Of course. Especially after being informed his brother was not only dead, but a potential serial killer. He must be rattled by the knowledge Jude was a cold-blooded psychopath.

"Does he often leave the home?"

"Not really, but when his mind is clear he occasionally takes a walk around town. He's not supposed to leave without checking with the floor nurse and having a companion go with him. We have private caregivers who can be hired to take on extra duties."

"How long has he been gone?"

Bailey looked sick. "No one knows for sure. He was at breakfast, but he missed lunch. That's when we started looking for him."

Rachel glanced toward the large, old-fashioned clock on the wall. If he'd left the nursing home around nine o'-clock, he'd been missing over seven hours.

She returned her gaze to the younger woman. "Don't you have some sort of security to keep residents from wandering away?"

"Of course we do. Anyone coming in or out has to be buzzed through the front door. But the residents can go into the back garden through the patio doors. They're not locked from the inside."

"Is that how he got out?"

Bailey flinched before giving a jerky nod. "We checked the security video when we couldn't find him in the facility. He squeezed his way through the hedges. No one has ever done that before."

Her defensive manner warned Rachel the younger woman assumed that she was accusing the home of negligence. She paused, forcing herself to soften her tone. The various protocols of the nursing home really didn't interest her. She was confident they did their best to protect their residents.

All she wanted to know was if Jacob had drifted away in a cloud of confusion, or if he'd been intentionally lured away. "He was alone?"

"He was. And he seemed to be in his right mind," she hastily added. "In fact, he seemed to be on his way to an appointment or something."

Rachel studied her in confusion. That was an odd assumption. "Why do you think he had an appointment?"

"He was wearing his best dress shirt and slacks," Bailey explained. "And he was glancing at his watch as he walked across the back garden. As if he was checking the time."

A bad feeling settled in the pit of Rachel's stomach. The man was living in a nursing home. If he had any appointments, he would have simply informed the nursing staff and they would have arranged for transportation. Or even for a companion to accompany him. There wouldn't have been any need to sneak through the hedges.

So where was he going? And more importantly, was this the first time he'd snuck out? Maybe he'd been using his secret exit to come and go without anyone noticing since he first arrived. His younger brother had obviously been a cunning master of manipulation. Was it possible Jacob was equally talented?

"Has anyone been to visit him lately?"

Bailey considered the question before giving a shake of her head. "I don't remember anyone. Just you and Zac."

"What about calls?"

"Not that I know of—" Bailey's eyes widened as if she'd suddenly remembered something. "Oh."

"What is it?"

"In the video he had an object in his hand. It looked like a phone, but as far as we know he's never used one. At least not since he moved into the home." Bailey shrugged. "He never called anyone and he never received any calls. I always thought it was sad for him to be so alone."

A burst of impatience exploded through Rachel. She didn't know why Jacob was out prowling the streets. It seemed unlikely that he was searching for his prey. Or even that he was working with the killer. His increasing dementia would make him too untrustworthy to keep a secret.

No, she was guessing that he was just another victim.

Whatever the reason, she wanted to be out there looking for him.

"Do you want to file a missing person report?" she asked.

Bailey paled, shaking her head. "We'd like to keep the search unofficial for now. Technically Jacob isn't missing. We just want to make sure he's okay."

Rachel moved back to the desk, grabbing her jacket off the back of the chair. "Where have you searched?"

"The town square. That's where he usually goes," Bailey said. "He likes to sit in the park."

"Anywhere else?"

"A few times he's gone to the diner. He likes their apple pie."

Rachel arched her brows, wondering if it was the same diner where Risa worked as a waitress. Something to consider.

Thankfully unaware of Rachel's dark thoughts, Bailey snapped her fingers. "Oh, and he goes to the cemetery on special holidays to visit his parents' graves."

"Do you have anyone looking there?" Rachel grabbed her satchel and looped it over her shoulder at an angle.

"Not yet."

"You go to the diner, I'll check out the graveyard." Rachel herded the younger woman out of the office, anxious to locate the missing man. "I'll call Zac. I'm sure he'll join the search as soon as he can." She reached into her satchel to pull out a business card, shoving it in Bailey's hand. "Here's my number. Call me if you find Jacob."

Bailey released a shaky sigh, clearly relieved to have the responsibility for the older man handed off to a professional. "Thanks."

They moved through the narrow hallways of the courthouse that was closing up for the night, heading out the front door.

"No problem." Rachel stopped to watch Bailey hurry toward her car, which she'd parked in the loading zone. Once the woman was driving away, she pulled out her phone and pressed the top speed dial. Seconds later she was dumped into voicemail. "Zac. Jacob Henley is missing from the nursing home. I'm headed to the cemetery to look for him."

Chapter 26

Zac had always been a morning person. Probably because he'd spent his childhood waking at the crack of dawn to help his dad with the chores around the farm. Even when he'd left Pike to go to college he'd jumped out of bed before his alarm went off.

So why was he struggling so hard to wake up now? And why did he feel like he was riding a wild bronco? And most importantly, why did his head feel as if it was about to explode?

Reluctantly forcing open his eyes, he found himself staring into a round face just an inch from his own.

"Boss. Boss." The frantic word was repeated over and over as rough hands gripped his shoulders. Suddenly he was being shaken hard enough to make his head roll side to side.

Each movement sent fireworks of pain shooting through his brain.

"Stop that," he hissed between clenched teeth.

Anthony heaved a sigh, pulling back to study Zac with a worried expression. "Do you need an ambulance?"

Zac lifted a hand to touch the back of his head, the

fragmented memories painfully snapping back into place to form a clear image. He'd been confronting Greg and then he'd felt a massive blow from behind that had knocked him out. Cautiously he touched the large lump that had formed while he'd been unconscious.

He grimaced. He probably needed an ambulance. Or at least a trip to a doctor to make sure his skull wasn't fractured. Instead he forced himself to his feet, reaching out to grab his deputy's arm as his knees threatened to buckle. "No, I don't think so."

The younger man frowned. "Are you sure? You were out cold when I found you."

Zac forced himself to lower his hand and take a step back. He'd allowed himself to be fooled by Greg. It wasn't happening again. For all he knew, Anthony was the one who'd snuck up behind him and whacked him on the head.

"What are you doing here?"

"My uncle Sal called me to say he saw you passed out at the old drive-in." Anthony shrugged. "I thought he must be drunk, but I drove out here to check. Did you fall?"

Zac glanced toward the nearby road. How long had he been out? There was still enough light to see, but there were shadows beginning to creep in. It couldn't have been long. A half an hour at the most.

"No, I was attacked," he admitted in clipped tones.

"Seriously?" The deputy appeared genuinely shocked. "By who?"

"Greg Barry." He touched the lump again, studying Anthony. "And his partner."

Searching for any hint of guilt or unease, all Zac could see was an unexpected fury on his companion's face.

"That bastard," the deputy spit out. "He's gone too far this time."

Zac narrowed his eyes. "This time?"

There was the sound of a honking horn as a car drove by. Zac assumed it was one of Anthony's numerous friends.

"Let's get off the street," the younger man muttered, leading Zac toward the SUV parked next to the curb.

Zac hesitated. He still didn't know the identity of Greg's partner. Anthony would be the obvious suspect. But then again, why would he show up to help him if he'd been involved? He could have left Zac lying on the ground. Or even finished him off while he was still unconscious. At last he shrugged and followed the deputy to his vehicle. He wasn't going to let his guard down again.

And besides, he wanted to hear what Anthony had to say.

Once they were in the SUV, Zac turned to press his back against the passenger door, his hand hovering near his weapon. "What did you mean about Greg?"

Anthony reached into the jacket of his uniform and Zac's fingers curled around the hilt of his gun. This time he was going to shoot first and ask questions later. Anthony pulled his phone out of his pocket.

"I think he's responsible for this." The deputy concentrated on his phone, his brow furrowed until he finally held it out so Zac could see the screen.

Zac cautiously leaned to the side, his gaze moving to the phone. "What is it?"

"A website dedicated to the Pike Phantom."

"The Pike what?"

Confused, Zac studied the garish headline splashed across the top of the site. ARE GHOSTS KILLING THE CITIZENS OF PIKE?

"It's a stupid name," Anthony said, scrolling down the page. "But the site has been sharing information on our investigation. The sort of information no one outside our office should have."

Zac abruptly reached out to stop Anthony's scrolling, pointing toward a blurred picture. "That's the morgue at Henley's Funeral Parlor."

"Yep, it was a live feed." Anthony pressed on the picture and it started to flicker as if it was alive. It was focused on the gurney where they'd found the body of Paige Carr. "See? It claims to show the spirit of the dead who still roam the funeral parlor."

Zac cursed in disbelief. "Who put a camera in there?"

"I heard about the site and when I saw the video I went back to the morgue to check it out."

Was that when Zac had seen Anthony leaving the funeral parlor as he was driving past? *Crap.* He wished now he would have stopped and demanded an explanation. "And?"

"It took some searching but I eventually found a small camera taped beneath one of the rolling trays."

Visualizing the room as they'd left it, Zac recalled the silver trays that held surgical equipment. It would have been simple to place a tiny camera under one and arrange it to capture the gurney.

"Why didn't you come to me with this information?" he growled.

Anthony's expression hardened with a strange hatred. "Because I suspected it was Greg."

"Really?" Zac sent him a curious frown. "Why would you suspect him?"

Scrolling farther down the website, Anthony halted at

the shadowed picture of a man stretched next to a grave, blood dripping down the side of his face. "This is from the official crime scene photos he took after we found Jude Henley's body." Anthony did more scrolling. "There are pictures of the cabin where Jude had been living. And these are from the file I saw on Greg's desk." Anthony tapped on pictures of official police reports, enlarging them so Zac could read the typewritten words. "Staci Gale," he breathed.

Zac ground his teeth. Greg had virtually confessed his sins. He'd just made sure to make Zac believe that Anthony was the one who was guilty. "That was even more reason to come to me if you truly thought that Greg was responsible for this website," he chided.

"I didn't have any proof. Greg has talked his way out of trouble too many times. I wasn't going to let him squirm out again."

Zac wasn't satisfied. "Did you ever consider the possibility that he was the killer?"

"Greg?" Anthony blinked, as if dumbfounded by the mere suggestion. "Naw. He's a sleazebag, not a psycho."

"You're sure? Absolutely sure?"

Anthony parted his lips, but catching Zac's fierce gaze, he gave a reluctant shake of his head. "No."

"You should have come to me."

"Easy for you to say." Anthony lowered the phone, scowling out the front windshield. "Greg was your golden boy and I'm the fuckup. Who would you have believed? It sure the hell wouldn't have been me."

Zac stiffened at the accusation. Was Anthony wrong? Nope, he was forced to acknowledge. Greg hadn't been a perfect deputy, but Zac had believed he could depend on the younger man. Anthony, on the other hand, barely bothered to deal with the most routine duties.

Plus, Anthony had been sneaking around and acting in a suspicious manner since Jude's body had turned up. First being seen at the funeral parlor when he shouldn't have been there and then showing up at the cabin when Zac had been searching for Tory. Not to mention the fact he was never at the office when he was supposed to be.

"The truth would have come out," Zac protested.

"Not before I was fired," Anthony said in bitter tones. "It's always been the same. Greg was the kid all the teachers loved, but behind their backs he would terrorize the younger kids and sneak into the girls' bathroom."

"You were friends?"

Anthony made a sound of disgust. "Not hardly. I don't like two-faced jerks who lie and cheat and bully people, then blame it on someone else."

Zac grimaced. That was exactly what Greg had done. "Yeah, I get that."

"He was even worse as he got older," Anthony continued, turning his head toward Zac as he warmed to his subject.

"How?"

"His first job was working at the farmers' co-op."

Something about the words nagged at Zac. It took a second to realize what was bothering him. "With Joe Carr?"

"Probably. I heard he was caught stealing anhydrous ammonia and selling it to a meth lab in Grange."

Zac arched his brows. Stealing anhydrous ammonia wasn't like pocketing a few screwdrivers or even money out of the till. The gas was tightly regulated, not only because it was used in the illegal drug trade, but because it could be dangerous to transport. Greg had either been desperate or an idiot.

"Why wasn't he arrested?"

"They didn't want to make a fuss." Anthony's lips twisted in anger. "Greg agreed to quit and they covered it up. I wouldn't doubt he was asked to leave the post office."

Zac released a harsh sigh, belatedly recalling Mrs. Wilkins's complaint about Greg. He'd dismissed it when Rachel had told him about her meeting with the older woman. Now he realized that Greg's familiarity with the postal route would have given him the perfect opportunity to leave the package with the videotape in Mrs. Wilkins's mailbox. Plus, he would have known Joe Carr, and his pretty young wife, Paige.

Zac frowned as a memory suddenly surfaced. "I saw him in the parking lot talking to Joe Carr. He claimed Joe was there to see you."

Anthony lifted his phone, pointing toward the website. "He was probably getting pictures of Paige for his site. There are a dozen of them on here. From the time she was just a kid until a few days before she died. They had to have come from someone who could get ahold of her private belongings."

"You think Joe would sell photos of his dead wife?" Zac's voice was sharp.

Anthony shrugged. "He's got a daughter to raise on his own. Every penny would help."

With an effort, Zac shoved aside his revulsion. He didn't have the time or the energy to judge others. He instead turned his attention to Greg's other victims.

"So why would he buy pictures of Curly Junior from Tara?"

"He's the leading suspect on the chat boards," Anthony said. "I'm sure Greg wanted to add a few photos to stir interest."

Zac released a hissing breath. "I suppose everyone in town knew about this website but me?"

Anthony shrugged. "Not everyone. Most of the people who are active on the site are from other places. A lot of them from other countries. But probably a few in the area have seen it."

Zac struggled to leash his anger that no one had said anything to him. He knew Pike. Most people tried to see the best in their fellow citizens. And while everyone was willing to indulge in a little gossip, and what they would have seen as harmless speculation, no one wanted to accuse someone and get them in trouble. Especially not with the law.

He settled back in his seat. "Why would Greg go to such an effort to make the website?"

"Money." Anthony slid the phone back into his pocket. "He built up a huge following and then created a store on the site to sell merchandise. A Pike Phantom T-shirt can be yours for twenty-four dollars and ninety-nine cents." Anthony's lips twisted. "I bet he's making a killing."

Zac flinched at the unfortunate word. On the surface it sounded as if Greg was simply taking ghoulish advantage of the situation. But there was always the possibility that he'd created the Pike Phantom not only to make a few easy bucks, but to satisfy an inner demon.

Right now, anything seemed possible.

"Someone was with him today." Zac reached up to

touch the back of his head. It continued to throb. Like a nagging reminder he'd been careless. "Who would it be?"

Anthony paused, perhaps searching his mind for a name. At last he gave a lift of his shoulders. "I don't know."

"Now's not the time to keep secrets, Anthony," he warned.

Anthony lifted his hands. "I swear I don't know. I've never seen him hanging with anyone in particular. I assume everyone else in town thinks he's a pile of horseshit."

"Does he have any brothers?"

"I don't really know anything about his family."

Sensing that he'd hit a dead end with Anthony, Zac reached into the pocket of his jacket, relieved to discover he still had his phone. Pulling it out, he was prepared to call Rachel when he noticed a text from her flashing on his screen.

"Damn," he rasped, grabbing his seat belt and locking it in place. He wasn't sure his fuzzy brain had cleared enough to drive. Besides, he didn't want to waste a second. "Let's go."

The deputy fumbled to grab his keys and start the engine. "Go where?" he demanded when he finally screeched away from the curb.

"The graveyard."

I smile as I watch Detective Rachel Fisher ease her truck through the narrow gate into the cemetery. After an afternoon of endless frustrations is my luck finally changing for the better?

Pulling my vehicle around the corner, I park and glance toward the man seated beside me.

Jacob Henley.

The older man is looking rough around the edges, I acknowledge. Not my fault. Well, not entirely.

Jacob was fresh as a fucking daisy when I picked him up a couple of streets away from the nursing home. But while I'd gained his trust over the past few days, I can't risk having him attract unwanted attention. I have to keep him . . . compliant.

It was easy to spike a soda with a slurry of drugs, but I didn't anticipate that it would take the damned nursing home so long to call out the hounds to look for him. I've been forced to keep medicating the man until drool was running down his chin and his eyes were blankly staring down at his seat belt.

Now I forget the hours of frustration. I have Detective Fisher in my sights, and best of all Jacob Henley will finally be worth the effort I've put into him.

Leaving the engine running, I reach out to shake my companion out of his stupor. "Uncle."

"Hmm?" Jacob lifts his head to glance around in confusion.

"It's time."

"Dinnertime?"

"No, dinner will be later."

The man sticks out his bottom lip like a petulant child. "I'm hungry now."

I reach out to calmly slap him across the face, hard enough for the crack of my palm connecting with his cheek to echo through the car.

Jacob's head jerks back, his hand lifting to touch his reddened skin. "Ow."

I lean toward him. "Do I have your attention?"

The watery blue eyes blink, his heavy jowls making him look like a pig. "Who are you?"

"You know who I am."

He studies me, still blinking. Then he draws in a harsh breath. "Jude?"

The name snatches the air from my lungs. The light is growing dim, and the man is half mad even without the drugs, but I suddenly wonder if he can see something of my father in my face. The line of my jaw. Or the shape of my eyes. No one else has ever seen it. The thought that this man has noticed the family connection is oddly comforting.

I don't want my father back. Not after I went to the trouble of putting a bullet through his rotting brain. But it does please me to think that a part of him remains. In me.

"Jude's dead," I remind the idiot. "We're here to have our revenge against those who murdered him. Remember?"

There is a slow, hesitant nod. "Yes."

"Good." I slip out of my vehicle and round the hood to pull open Jacob's door. Unlatching the seat belt I grab his arm and give it a tug. "Come with me."

Jacob manages to climb out, his movements sluggish as I urge him toward the line of cedar trees that mark the edge of the graveyard.

He glances around in confusion. "Why are we here?"

"We need to lure our prey to a more secluded location."

He shuffles forward at a painfully slow rate, his shoulders hunched. I've seen a sloth at the zoo who looks just like him. Except the sloth probably had more brains.

"What?"

I click my tongue with impatience, shoving him through the trees and into the cemetery. "We can't do anything on a public street. We need to get the enemy back to the funeral parlor."

"Oh."

"You got it? You're going to be the bait."

Jacob scowls, as if sensing the mockery in my words. "I'm not stupid."

"Matter of opinion," I whisper too low for my companion to hear. Then I point toward a slender form stepping out of a tan SUV and glancing around. "There."

Jacob stumbles to a halt, his brow furrowed in confusion as he studies Rachel Fisher. "That woman killed Jude?"

"She was involved." The lie falls smoothly from my lips.

"She came to the nursing home. With the sheriff." Jacob shakes his head, as if trying to rid it of the fog of drugs. Or maybe it was his dementia creeping in. "They said terrible things about my brother."

"Yes." I smile. It's all so simple. "They were there to deceive you."

"Why?"

"To make you believe that Jude was a monster."

Jacob releases a shaky sigh, the spittle still running down his chin. "I knew it was all lies. I knew it."

"We can't let them continue to tarnish Jude's memory." I lean forward to whisper directly in his ear. Like the devil himself. "She must be punished."

"Yes."

"But not here. At the funeral parlor."

"Okay." Jacob starts to turn, as if he's about to head for his old place of business.

"No," I snap, grabbing his arm to shove him farther into the cemetery while I remain in the shadows of the trees. "First you have to get her attention."

Jacob stands like a lump, his face slack. "How?"

I force myself to count to ten. How can a man with my cunning and ruthless ambition come from such weak bloodlines?

It is unimaginable.

"Walk around," I snap.

Jacob frowns, but slowly begins to amble from gravestone to gravestone. I grimace. He looks like a drunken zombie. And worse, dusk is starting to thicken around us. Soon it will be too dark to see anything. Just as I'm about to tell the idiot to wave his hands or jump up and down, the woman across the graveyard finally notices him.

"Jacob?" she calls out, taking a step toward the man walking in circles. "Jacob! It's Detective Fisher."

"Come back," I hiss in urgent tones. "We have her attention. Now we have to lure her into our trap."

Chapter 27

Rachel muttered a curse, turning to jump into her SUV and back out of the cemetery. She hadn't intended to spook Jacob. She just wanted to catch his attention so he didn't wander away.

This was why she never liked working at the nursing home, she ruefully acknowledged, turning onto the street and heading in the direction that Jacob had disappeared. She didn't have the necessary patience.

Now she was forced to track down the man before he became lost in the darkness. Whatever his reason for roving the streets of Pike, she couldn't be sure he could find his way back to the nursing home before the temperature dropped below zero.

Keeping the SUV to a mere crawl, Rachel scanned the sidewalk for any sign of Jacob. He couldn't have gone very far. Not even if he was in a hurry to get away.

She reached the end of the block with no luck and was about to backtrack to make sure she hadn't missed the man in the shadows that were thickening when she realized how close they were to the Henley Funeral Parlor.

If Jacob was confused or even trying to get away from

her, that seemed like the logical location for him to head toward. It'd been his home for years.

Maintaining her frustratingly slow speed, Rachel turned the corner and drove the two blocks to the long brick structure set away from the street. There'd been no sighting of Jacob, but as she pulled into the parking lot she noticed the front door was open.

Jacob had to be inside. Who else would have the key?

Not that she was about to take any chances, she acknowledged, pulling out her phone to send a quick message to Zac. She hadn't heard back from him, so she assumed he was busy, but she wanted someone to know where she was.

Then, shoving the phone into the pocket of her jacket, she touched the hilt of her gun, reassuring herself that it was holstered at her hip. Accepting that she was as prepared as she was going to get, she slid out of the SUV and made her way to the portico.

"Jacob?" she called out, halting at the open door to peer inside.

It was too dark to make out more than the large reception area. She thought she could see the outlines of several padded chairs pressed against the walls along with a couple of low coffee tables. And there was something in the center of the room.

Another chair?

Yes. But what was that on top of it? It was tall and slender. . . .

Without warning a light from a side room was switched on. A soft glow spilled into the reception area, allowing Rachel to see the shadowy object.

A gasp was wrenched from her throat as she realized it was a person.

Rachel battled back her fierce instinct to rush forward. It didn't take a trained professional to know the whole situation screamed trap. Instead she clenched her muscles, allowing only her gaze to move over the room.

It reminded her of a theatrical tableau. As if everything had been frozen in a precise moment in time. Making sure there was no one hidden in the corners, Rachel concentrated on the man in front of her. And it was a man. She was certain of that despite the burlap bag that had been wrapped over his head.

He was wearing a torn T-shirt and wrinkled jeans and a pair of sneakers that looked vaguely familiar. Not that it mattered at the moment. Her attention was focused on his arms, which were wrenched behind his back as if they were tied together, and the shackles that were locked around his ankles. Her gaze skimmed back up the slender body, belatedly noticing the rope tied around the man's neck. It was nearly hidden by the burlap bag.

Rachel tilted back her head, her eyes following the rope that was stretched from the man's neck to the large chandelier that hung from the center of the ceiling.

Her breath hissed between her teeth as she reached for her gun. At the same time she took a step backward. She went from a suspicion that this might be a trap to an absolute certainty.

Which meant that she had to get out of there and call for backup. She wouldn't be able to save anyone if she ended up another victim.

She had reached the door when the intercom that was

installed on the nearby wall crackled and popped. A second later a disembodied voice floated through the air.

"Stop."

Rachel came to a halt, lifting her weapon and pointing it toward the opening where the light was entering the reception room.

"Who's there? Show yourself."

A chilling laugh floated out of the intercom. "You're not in control of this game. I am."

Rachel licked her dry lips, squashing the tide of fear that threatened to cloud her mind. If she ever needed to think clearly, this was the moment.

She sucked in a deep breath, concentrating on the man in front of her. His shoulders were slumped and his head drooped forward, as if he was exhausted. That suggested he'd been there a while. It had to be the work of the serial killer, right? But why? Until now he'd chosen young women. And there'd been no sign of strangulation during the autopsy. They'd all been brutally beaten.

Was it possible that he'd accidentally stumbled across the identity of the killer and was being punished? No, that didn't make sense. The killer wouldn't risk being exposed. If someone had learned who he was, he'd make sure they were dead before they could share the information.

This looked more like . . .

"Are you just going to stand there, Detective Fisher?" The voice interrupted her scattered thoughts, drawing out her name as if he was savoring it. "I've been waiting for you."

Waiting for her? Did he mean her in particular? Rachel jerked, a violent shiver racing through her as she recalled catching sight of Jacob standing at the edge of the cemetery. She'd been searching for him so it hadn't seemed suspicious for him to be there. Or even to follow him to this funeral parlor. And despite being nervous this might be a snare, she hadn't considered the possibility that she was the intended victim.

Obviously a mistake.

"Who are you?" she called out.

"You can call me Maestro."

She grimaced. She should have known he would have some egotistical nickname for himself. In some ways serial killers were tediously predictable.

"What do you want?"

"I told you in my note. I'm here to prove my superiority."

"Fine." She kept her gun pointed at the opening, but she continued to scan the reception area from side to side. She didn't want anyone or anything catching her by surprise. "Come out here and prove it."

There was a low chuckle. "That's not how the game is played."

"Give me the rules," she called out, attempting to keep the killer distracted as she reached into her pocket for her phone.

"Very well. You try to step out of this building and someone dies." There was a pause before the voice continued. "And no calls, Detective Fisher," he snapped. "That's cheating."

Rachel cursed, pulling her phone out of her pocket. Obviously, she was being watched. Which meant there was no way she could gain the upper hand. If she did what the killer wanted, she had no doubt that she would die, along with the poor man on the chair. There was no way to win.

"I'm not playing your game."

Lifting the phone, she started to press nine-one-one, but even as her thumb touched the screen there was a loud scraping sound. Rachel whirled toward the opening across the room, pressing her back against the wall to make sure no one could sneak up on her. Expecting someone to enter the reception area, Rachel frowned when there was another loud scrape.

What was that?

It wasn't until the chair in the center of the room was abruptly jerked to the side that she realized that there'd been an unseen string attached to the leg. Fishing line? Nylon rope? It was strong enough for the chair to be yanked from beneath the man while remaining invisible in the shadows.

"No!"

Rachel raced forward as the man dropped with shocking force, the rope snapping tight around his neck. Overhead the chandelier swayed, the crystal pendants smacking together. The sound was unnaturally loud, almost masking the more ominous groan of the ceiling that hadn't been constructed to take that much weight. She was still a few feet away when the plaster cracked and pulled away, allowing the chandelier to fall.

The body hit the floor with sickening force, followed by the chandelier, which promptly smashed into a thousand pieces, spreading broken glass and twisted bits of metal over the marble in a shattered mosaic.

Ignoring the carnage, Rachel continued forward, dropping to her knees beside the unmoving form. She reached to grab the rope, battling against the knot to loosen it enough to tug it off the man's head. It was a painfully slow process. The rope was thick and surprisingly rigid, plus the burlap bag kept getting tangled. At last she grabbed the hem of the bag and yanked it up and over the man's head, taking the rope with it.

Tossing aside the rough material, Rachel gazed down at the pale face, its several bruises revealing he'd taken a beating before being strung up. But even with the discoloration and swelling it was easy to recognize him.

Curly Junior.

She didn't have the chance to be shocked. She had, after all, nearly managed to convince herself that this man was the lunatic stalking the women of Pike. Right now all that mattered was whether or not he was still alive.

She pressed her fingers against the side of his neck, searching for a pulse. At first she felt nothing, then, as she pressed harder, she could detect a faint, unsteady beat beneath the tips of her fingers.

"He needs a hospital," she called out.

"You failed, Detective Fisher." The voice floated from the intercom, a smug satisfaction in his tone. Clearly, he wasn't concerned whether or not Curly was dying. He'd meant to kill him. He was just a part of the game. Just as she was. "Lucky for you, that is only round one. You have another opportunity. Will you or won't you succeed?"

There was the distant sound of a door opening and Rachel reluctantly glanced through the opening to peer down the narrow hallway. In the dim light she could see that the door at the end of the corridor was open. As if inviting her in. A chill snaked down her spine.

The logical choice was to escape the funeral parlor and call Zac. Not only did Curly need medical attention ASAP, but only an idiot would take on a crazed killer without backup. But the knowledge that there were most certainly more victims made her hesitate. The killer had proved he had gone to great lengths to prepare for this moment. Curly must have been kidnapped when he returned home. Perhaps because the killer wanted the use of his apartment to fulfill his psychotic need to walk in Jude's footsteps. Or because he'd already planned to use him as a pawn in his game. How many other people could be hidden around the sprawling building?

She couldn't walk away knowing she was condemning innocent victims to death.

Holding her gun at her side, she slipped her phone back in her pocket and slowly straightened. She'd sent Zac a text to tell him where she was. Sooner or later he was going to come searching for her, right?

She could only hope that it was sooner, not later.

With an effort, she walked across the marble floor, the glass crunching beneath her shoes and her heart thundering in her chest. Inanely she was reminded of when she was very young and her father had taken her to a traveling carnival. She'd begged to go into the fun house and he'd eventually relented, giving her the ticket necessary to pass through the front door.

The place had terrified her. The tilted floors, the loud music, the flashing lights that were reflected in distorted mirrors. She was desperate to escape. There was a sense of being out of control that had touched a fear deep inside her.

She felt the same sensation as she inched her way down the hall. A sickness in the pit of her stomach and a weakness in her knees. This time, however, she wasn't a child, she sternly reminded herself. She was a detective who was fully capable of dealing with any situation.

"What do you want from me?" she called out, keeping

her steps painfully slow. The more time she could prolong the sick game, the more time she had for Zac to get there.

"A challenge. So far my . . . creations have been disappointing. I hope you can offer more entertainment value."

Her jaws clenched at his mocking dismissal of the women he'd murdered, but she bit back her words of loathing. She refused to give him the satisfaction of knowing she was disturbed by his crimes. Not when she sensed that was exactly what he wanted.

"Did you shoot Jude?" she instead asked.

"Of course."

Rachel cautiously passed by a closed door, still headed toward the end of the hall. "Why?"

"He was no longer any use to me."

"He was your father."

There was a startled silence. He obviously hadn't expected them to figure out his connection to the older man.

"Yes."

"And Evie Parson was your mother."

"Very good, Detective," he rasped, sounding annoyed.

Rachel allowed a humorless smile to touch her lips. They'd been on the right track. A shame they hadn't been quicker to figure out the identity of the son.

"Did you know your father was a killer?"

"Naturally," he drawled in sneering tones. "Even as a young child he would tell me stories about his kills. He was very proud of his accomplishments and later we worked on our masterpieces together. You could say he molded me into a perfect killing machine."

She continued forward, her mouth so dry she could barely speak. "So why shoot him?"

"It was time for me to become my own man. Plus, I

wanted to prove I was the superior artist. What better way than to re-create my father's murders?"

There was no mention of the brain tumor. Did he know his father was dying? Rachel considered what little she knew about Jude Henley. He seemed the type to want to keep his illness a secret. His pride wouldn't allow him to appear weak, especially not in front of his son.

"That doesn't explain why you killed him."

"He tried to interfere. He claimed he didn't want me to follow in his path." A shrill laugh echoed through the intercom. "I knew he feared I would create masterpieces that would make his own appear to be the work of an uninspired has-been."

Had Jude tried to prevent his son from becoming a serial killer? Was he capable of remorse?

Rachel shrugged. It didn't matter what his reasons. She was more interested in what he did during the years he'd been away from Pike.

"How many women did Jude murder?" she asked.

"He claimed it was twenty-five, but he only has videos of twenty-three."

Twenty-five? Shock jolted through Rachel. She knew the number would be high. Jude had managed to avoid being caught for far too long. But the thought of so many dead women was nauseating.

"Including Kim Slade?" she managed to ask.

"Who?"

"The woman who was camping with her boyfriend at Devil's Lake State Park."

"Ah, yes. I was there for that one." He paused, as if savoring the memory. "She screamed for hours."

Rachel's breath hissed between her clenched teeth. Kim

Slade had only wanted to spend the weekend camping with her boyfriend. A simple pastime. She hadn't deserved to be snatched by a violent monster and his monster-in-training.

"Where is she buried?"

"Do you really want to know?"

"Yes."

"Survive the game and I'll tell you."

Reaching the end of the hallway, Rachel found her steps faltering. She shoved away all thoughts of Jude and his evil killing spree and concentrated on what was ahead of her.

Once she stepped over the threshold, the next part of the twisted game was going to begin. She couldn't risk being distracted. She took a brief second to gather her courage, and then grimly moved through the opening. As much as she wanted to draw this out to give Zac time to arrive, she couldn't be sure that she wouldn't lose her nerve completely.

It was now or never.

Once inside, she pressed her back against the wall and swept her gaze around the space. There was a lamp in the corner that was switched on to offer a soft glow, revealing a room that wasn't as large as the reception area, but still big enough for the short pews that faced a small dais where she assumed a coffin was usually placed.

A viewing room? Not that it mattered. There was no coffin in the center of the dais tonight. Instead there was another padded chair with a man standing on top of it. Like poor Curly his hands were bound behind his back and his legs were shackled together. And once again, there was a burlap bag over his head with a noose wrapped around his neck. This time the rope was attached to the open wooden rafter overhead.

Which meant that if the chair was pushed away, the ceiling wasn't going to collapse. And whoever was standing there was most certainly going to end up with a broken neck.

Lowering her gaze back to the man, she was judging the distance to reach him when she belatedly noticed what he was wearing. Rachel gasped, a white-hot fury replacing the fear that had been cramping her stomach.

She recognized those brown slacks and the heavy jacket with the sheriff badge sewn on the sleeve.

"You bastard!"

Without giving the killer the opportunity to fulfill his perverted fantasy, she was rushing forward, knocking her hip painfully on one of the pews.

"Stop." The voice shouted through the intercom.

She ignored the angry command. Her only thought was reaching Zac before he could be hurt. Still a few feet away, she heard the sound of scraping. The same sound she'd heard just before Curly's chair had been jerked from beneath him.

She was too far away. She knew it with absolute certainty. There was no way that she could stop Zac from dying.

A primal cry was ripped from her lips. The thought she might lose the only man she'd ever loved was too brutally painful to even imagine. But even as she prepared to make a futile leap toward the chair, a movement out of the corner of her eye captured her attention. It was something on the polished wood floor.

Rachel was momentarily confused. Then, her heart

missed a beat when she realized that it was the line that had been tied to the leg of the chair. Whoever was pulling it was located behind the curtain on the far side of the room.

Hope surged through her as she scrambled to step on the line, pressing it against the floor with her weight as she lifted her gun and fired in the direction of the curtain. The bullet lodged in the floor just in front of the hidden opening, sending up splinters to smack against the velvet material. She wasn't going to blindly fire at her tormentor. Not when she couldn't be sure there wasn't another victim concealed in the shadows.

But the sound of gunfire had thankfully accomplished what she wanted. The tension on the line eased as whoever was holding the other end dropped it. At the same time, there was the echo of running footsteps.

Cautiously Rachel reached down to grab the line and backed her way toward the dais. She kept her gun pointed at the curtain as she moved. She wasn't going to let down her guard. Not until Zac was safe.

Her heels hit the platform and she quickly turned to climb onto the chair. Then, holstering her gun, she reached up to loosen the knot on the noose. It was easier than the first one, or maybe she was getting better with practice, she acknowledged with grim determination.

Once the rope was loose enough, she grabbed the bottom of the burlap bag and pulled it over his head. Expecting to see Zac it took a second for her to realize she was staring into the face of Greg Barry. His hair was tangled and his face was bruised and there was a piece of silver tape stuck over his mouth, but there was no mistaking it was Zac's young deputy.

Relief blasted through her. Not only because Zac hadn't been hurt, but she could cling to the hope that he was on his way to the funeral home. Jumping off the chair, she was debating the best way to help the deputy down while he was still shackled when the killer's voice returned.

"Better, Detective Fisher. You win this round. Time for round three." There was the sound of shuffling before a raw, painful scream vibrated through the intercom. "Uncle Jacob is waiting for you."

Chapter 28

Zac was clenching his teeth. Pike was a small town with minimal traffic even during rush hour, but the outer road in front of the old drive-in was on the opposite side of town from the cemetery and there were several streets closed to lay a new water line. They had to backtrack twice to find a way to get around the area. Plus, Anthony drove like his vehicle would explode if he went over twenty miles an hour.

"Finally," he muttered as they turned onto the street where the graveyard was located. He didn't understand his urgency to reach Rachel, but it thundered through him with a driving force. "I've driven across Chicago in less time."

"I've been thinking," Anthony abruptly announced. "It can't be Greg."

Zac blinked in confusion. "What can't be Greg?"

"You asked me if I had considered whether or not Greg was the killer," Anthony said. "I just remembered it couldn't be him."

"How do you know?"

"I bowl on a men's league in Grange. I was there the night that Paige Carr was killed."

"Is Greg on your team?"

"No. But he bowls on another team in that league."

Zac smacked his fist against his leg. Every time he thought he might have a genuine lead on the killer, something came along and destroyed his theory.

"You're sure he was there?" Zac demanded.

Anthony's fingers tightened on the steering wheel, as if he was considering the pleasure of throttling his fellow deputy. "He was working on a seven hundred series and he made sure everyone in the place knew it."

"He couldn't have left early without you noticing?" Zac pressed.

A smart killer would make sure he drew a lot of attention if he was establishing his alibi before quietly disappearing.

"He was at the bar flirting with the waitress when I left."

"Damn."

"Yes," the younger man agreed in dry tones. "I wanted it to be him."

The vehicle slowed as they neared the entrance to the cemetery. Zac leaned forward, his gaze scanning for some sign of Rachel even as he considered what he'd just learned.

If Greg was scratched off the list of potential killers, then who remained?

"Curly Junior seems to be the most likely suspect," Zac murmured, hoping if he spoke his thoughts out loud they might start to make some sense. "But why would he take Risa to his own apartment? Even if he was compelled to fulfill some creepy replication of the murders, he was taking a risk."

"Maybe he meant to dump her somewhere else, but you interrupted him," Anthony retorted.

That had been Zac's first thought. At least until Lindsay had searched the place and reported back to him.

"It's possible, but there was nothing in the apartment that would connect Curly to the killings. No old tapes, no pictures of the potential victims, not even a crowbar," he said, not bothering to add that he didn't think Curly had the mental skills to meticulously plan the murders.

It was one thing to take a crowbar and beat a woman to death. It was another to hunt down your victims, arrange to kidnap them, murder them, and then leave their bodies in specific locations. All without being caught. Lost in his dark thoughts, Zac was distracted by the sound of his phone buzzing. He lifted it to glance at the text that flashed across the screen. He frowned as he read it, relieved to hear from Rachel, but concerned that she was alone. "That's Rachel. She followed Jacob to the funeral parlor." He sent his deputy and impatient glance. "Let's try to get there at a speed faster than a grandmother can walk."

Anthony drove past the graveyard, his foot pressing on the gas so they went from a sluggish roll to a crawl. Zac swallowed a sigh. It was better than nothing.

"Did you ever suspect Jacob?" Anthony asked.

"As the killer?"

The deputy nodded, turning the corner. "He gives me the creeps."

Zac silently agreed. There was something creepy about Jacob Henley. And not just because he'd spent his life as a mortician. Someone had to do it. It was the coldness in his eyes and the bitterness that stewed around him. Like a flabby viper waiting to spew his venom on anyone who crossed his path. But the short amount of time he'd spent with the older man had revealed a fragility he didn't think could be faked.

"I'm pretty sure he's physically incapable of kidnapping a young, healthy woman. Plus, the nursing home would have noticed he was missing." He shrugged. "Since Rachel is on the chase for Jacob, they obviously have some sort of security system in place to monitor the residents."

"Surely it can't be old man Bolton?"

"Doubtful."

"So who?" They shared a frustrated glance before Anthony pulled into the graveled lot and parked next to Rachel's SUV. The deputy turned off the engine as Zac unhooked his seat belt and shoved open the passenger door. "It's like the Invisible Man is going around snatching women off the streets of Pike."

Zac had one foot out of the vehicle, his gaze already focused on the open front door of the funeral parlor, when Anthony tossed out the casual words. He froze, something about what the young man said niggling at the edge of his mind.

That had been his first impression of the killer. A man who could move around Pike without being noticed. He'd even considered a potential suspect because . . .

"He's invisible," he whispered.

"What's wrong?"

"I know who it is."

"Who?"

Zac continued out of the vehicle, anxious to find Rachel so they could get Jacob back to the nursing home. He had every intention of pulling his suspect into the station tonight to question him. But as he parted his lips to answer Anthony, the sound of gunfire reverberated through the parking lot.

"Shit." Zac grabbed his weapon, turning toward the funeral parlor. There was no doubt that the shot had come from inside. "Call the state police. Tell them we have an active shooter. And ask for reinforcements from Grange," he snapped.

"Then what?" Anthony's voice was shaky but surprisingly determined.

Zac took a second to consider how to enter. He had no idea who was inside, but he had a nasty suspicion that the killer had lured Rachel into an ambush. If he was going to get to her, he couldn't fall into the same trap. Somehow he had to catch the killer off guard.

"Go to the front door," he told his deputy. "Don't actually enter the building until you have backup, but make sure you are loud enough to attract attention."

"Okay."

Staying at the edge of the lot, Zac crouched low and hurried toward the back of the building. If he could get inside without being seen, he was confident he could get to Rachel.

He just had to make sure he got there before it was too late.

Rachel helped Greg off the chair, leaving him curled in a ball on the dais. She didn't have time to comfort him. Or even to try and deal with the shackles around his wrists and ankles. The scream she'd heard meant that there was another victim. She had to get to them before the killer could take the game to the next level.

Crossing the carpeted floor, she used her gun to part the curtain, peering into the shallow alcove. Empty. She stepped through the velvet fabric, glancing around the shadowed space. The killer couldn't have just disappeared, she assured herself, reaching out to run her hand over the paneled wall. After what felt like an eternity, but was probably just a few seconds, her hand wrapped around a small handle. She pushed it down and a portion of the paneling swung open to reveal a plain hallway that was obviously a way to move the body into the viewing room.

Her feet felt as if they were encased in cement as she grimly moved through the narrow opening. She needed to keep herself distracted if she didn't want to lose her nerve.

"Did you kidnap Paige behind the Bait and Tackle?" she called out, assuming there was an intercom set up in every area of the building, just as she assumed she was still being watched.

She was right. There was a crackling sound before the killer was answering her question.

"Yes. I had intended to wait another week and grab her when she went to the grocery store. She always leaves her daughter with her mother when she goes," he told her, revealing that he'd spent enough time watching Paige that he'd memorized her movements. "But then I overheard her arguing with her husband and I couldn't resist temptation. It's those little details that confirm my true talent."

She frowned, not sure what he meant. "What detail?"

"Really?" The killer clicked his tongue loud enough for her to hear it through the intercom. "You call yourself a detective?"

"I'm not as clever as you," she said, slowly moving

forward. She couldn't see any openings, but she assumed the hallway led somewhere.

"True. No one is," the man drawled. "You see, my father had a preference for choosing women who were angry. Usually with a man."

Rachel felt a small surge of satisfaction. Maybe she wasn't such a bad detective. She'd sensed the women's relationships with the men in their lives was important. Of course, she didn't know why it mattered.

There was one way to find out.

"Why did he want angry women?"

"Who can say?" The killer didn't sound as if he cared one way or another. "A psychologist would probably claim that he was punishing his bitch of a mother who made his life a living hell. Or striking out at my mother who refused to leave her husband and threatened to hand me over to strangers. Or it's possible he just hated rejection. Personally, I think he was terrified of women. That's why he had to subdue them. And eventually destroy them. It was the only way to prove he wasn't a spineless coward."

Rachel was startled by the man's insight into Jude's motivations. It was obvious to her that the killer had spent a lot more time considering his father and what had turned him into a monster than he wanted to admit. Not surprising. The fact that he'd returned to Pike in an effort to prove he was the better serial killer revealed his obsession with Jude Henley.

The ultimate father/son dysfunctional relationship.

Rachel continued forward, her gun pointed in front of her even as she glanced over her shoulder. She wasn't going to let anyone sneak up on her from behind.

"What about Tory?" she demanded, determined to keep the killer talking. "How did you kidnap her?"

"She was pathetically easy. She always went out for a smoke at the same time every day she worked at the Roadhouse. An idiot could have snatched her."

Rachel ground her teeth. He talked about Tory as if she was an object he'd shoplifted, not a flesh and blood woman who'd had people who loved her. But there was no point in protesting. A serial killer was too self-absorbed to care about their victims.

"Where did you take her?" she instead asked.

"Ah. I was too smart to use Jude's cabin," he said. "There was always the chance you would look there. I found an old cellar at an abandoned house. We were far enough away from the neighbors to avoid anyone hearing her screams."

Rachel ignored his deliberate attempt to stir her anger. She was running out of hallway and all she could see was a blank wall ahead of her. It wasn't until she reached the end that she realized there was a narrow opening on the side. She halted, staring at the steel ramp that led into the dark basement. Was this how the coffin was moved down to collect the embalmed body? She'd assumed there'd be an elevator or something.

She hesitated. The ramp appeared sturdy enough, but there were no walls on either side. She would be completely vulnerable. Crouching low, she stepped through the opening, placing her foot on the rubber pad that lined the steel.

"And Risa?"

The intercom was turned off with an audible click and the voice floated from the darkness beneath her.

"I was having a drink at the bar and I overheard Gerry and Curly talking about setting up a drug deal," he told her, his voice sounding different in person. Did she recognize it? She grimaced. Right now she was too tense. "It wasn't the elegant plan I'd hoped for," he continued, "but it was functional and I was in a hurry."

Careful to keep her balance, she inched her way down the steep incline, surrounded by a blanket of darkness.

"Why were you in a hurry?"

"Because of you, Detective Fisher." There was a soft chuckle before the overhead lights were flipped on. "I wanted you. So all the rules of the game were thrown out the window."

Rachel instinctively leaped off the side of the ramp as she was temporarily blinded. She crouched low, her gun pointed toward the center of the room. Blinking, she desperately strained to make out the figures that were blurry outlines.

As her vision cleared, she could see she was in the open embalming room with its dusty countertops and strange machines and a large drain in the center of the cement floor. She shivered. The place had been creepy enough in the daylight. At night it was downright terrifying.

Jacob was standing in a weird position with his mouth hanging open and his bald head with its liver-shaped birthmark coated in sweat. Behind him was a shorter man who had his arm around Jacob's neck, bending him backward with a gun pressed to his temple.

"Isaac," she breathed, her mouth dry as her gaze skimmed over the short black hair and bland features that were so easily forgotten.

He smiled, his gray eyes smoldering with a fierce

pleasure. As if he'd imagined this moment over and over. "Surprise!"

"What's happening?" Jacob weakly struggled against Isaac's choking grip, his flabby body quivering with fear. "I don't understand."

Rachel remained next to the ramp. If Isaac decided to shoot in her direction, she could duck under the steel structure and hope it would deflect the bullet. It wasn't perfect, but for now it was all she had.

"Why don't you let him go?" she demanded, nodding toward the older man. She wasn't trying to be a hero, but there was no way to take out Isaac without hitting Jacob.

Besides, she might not personally like Jacob Henley but he was an innocent hostage. She would try everything possible to ensure he survived the night.

Isaac's sharp crack of laughter reverberated through the basement. "Why would I let him go? We're having such a nice family reunion, aren't we, Uncle Jacob?"

Jacob's face changed to a dangerous shade of puce as he struggled against the arm locked around his throat. Was he having a heart attack?

"He's done his job," she snapped. "He led me here."

Isaac sent her a mocking smile. "Actually his job was supposed to be keeping your lover occupied."

"Zac?"

"Don't worry, I made sure he won't be interrupting us."

Her heart squeezed with fear. "What did you do to him?"

The amusement in the gray eyes vanished. As if someone had flicked a switch inside him. The mild-mannered, forgettable postman was gone, and in his place was a cold, ruthless killer. Like a snake shedding his skin. "We're discussing me."

"Yes." She struggled to breathe as an ominous promise of pain slithered through the air. This was the truth of Isaac. And what those poor women must have seen before he beat them to death.

Isaac silently stared at her, as if trying to decide whether or not to continue with the game or simply kill her. Then he shrugged, the sneer returning to his lips. "As I was saying, Jacob was intended to keep the sheriff busy, chasing him around town. When that didn't happen, I decided to use him as a lure to bring you into my lair. That's what makes me a genius. I can create magic no matter the challenges."

She cleared the lump from her throat. "How did you get Jacob out of the nursing home?"

"I deliver the mail. I started chatting with Jacob as soon as I arrived in town, although I didn't reveal my true identity. Not until a couple of days ago."

Of course. Rachel silently chided her carelessness. It was so easy to overlook the obvious. She'd asked Bailey if Jacob had any visitors, but the woman hadn't considered the people who came and went on a daily basis. Doctors, janitors . . . postmen.

"You gave him the phone?" she asked, covertly glancing around the room.

It wouldn't be long until Isaac grew tired of toying with her. He would shoot Jacob in the head, just like he shot his own father, and then he would come for her. Under normal circumstances she would assume she had better than average odds to take down the perp. She was a trained marksman who rarely missed her target. But she had no idea what traps might be lurking in this freakish fun house. Isaac had obviously taken time and care to arrange this encounter. If she miscalculated, she would be dead.

She had every intention of making it out of there alive.

"Yes, I pretended I had a package he needed to sign for and took the phone to his room. I told Jacob I was searching for the person responsible for killing my father and that once I found him, I would send a text for him to join me in our revenge." Without warning, Isaac whacked Jacob on the side of the head with the muzzle of his gun. "He was ready and eager to help, weren't you?"

Jacob cringed in pain, tears trickling down his pudgy cheeks. "I want to go home."

"You are home." Isaac waved his hand around the embalming room. "A perfect end to your miserable life."

He was spiraling. Rachel could see it in the feverish glitter in the gray eyes and the twitch at the corner of his mouth. He was already visualizing the splatter of his uncle's brains before he satisfied whatever sick obsession he'd developed with her.

"No!" She lifted her gun, her fingering hovering over the trigger.

Isaac laughed, easily sensing her hesitation at the risk of hitting Jacob. "You can't save everyone, Detective Fisher."

Rachel squared her shoulders, her eyes narrowing. She'd failed her brother, but she wasn't going to fail this time.

The only way Isaac was getting out of this morgue was in cuffs or a body bag.

* * *

Heading toward the funeral home, Zac grimly focused on what he needed to do to get inside without alerting anyone he was there. Later he would be furious at the knowledge that Rachel was alone with a serial killer. Right now, he needed a clear mind.

He was hurrying past the long garages when something niggled at the edge of his mind. He came to an abrupt halt. What had Curly told him? That there was always a key left hanging in the garage? He veered to the side, pushing open the door. He didn't dare risk flipping on the light. Instead he blindly ran his hand down the wall, eventually finding the key hanging on a small hook.

Grabbing it, he darted out of the garage and around the side of the funeral parlor, heading toward where they'd entered the morgue when Paige's body was discovered. He held his gun in one hand, using the key to unlock the door, and silently pushed it open.

With an effort, he forced himself to pause and listen. He wasn't going to help Rachel if he stumbled into a trap. At first all he could hear was muffled sounds in the distance. Someone was inside, but it was impossible to tell where they were. Then, as he stepped into the small storage area, he managed to pinpoint the direction of the voices. They were coming from the basement.

Moving toward the narrow flight of stairs, Zac made his way down the steps, his back pressed against the wall. Once at the bottom, he leaned forward, peering into the embalming room. What he saw made his heart swell with relief.

Rachel was standing across the embalming room with

her gun pointed at the two men with their backs turned toward him.

Isaac Dowell and Jacob Henley.

At first glance it was difficult to determine why Rachel hadn't pulled the trigger. He could see the weapon in Isaac's hand. Then he realized that the younger man was using Jacob as a shield. She didn't want to fire and risk injuring a hostage.

Zac didn't hesitate. He was going to do whatever necessary to protect his wife. Raising his weapon, he fired a shot into Isaac's shoulder. As he'd hoped, the impact of the bullet forced Isaac to drop his own gun as he cried out in pain.

Almost as if she'd been expecting him to appear and offer a distraction, Rachel was leaping forward, tackling Isaac to the ground. Then, before the killer could react, she had him flat on his back with her knee in the center of his chest, and her gun pointed in his face.

Zac strolled forward, his own weapon aimed at Isaac's head. One wrong twitch and he was putting a bullet in the monster's brain. Belatedly realizing that there was someone else in the basement, Jacob glanced over his shoulder. His face paled, as if he was terrified of Zac, then with a shrill scream he waddled toward the nearby cooler and slammed shut the door.

"Fucking coward," Isaac growled. "Just like my father."

Zac ignored the man squirming on the floor. Later he'd try to figure out if he should have seen the clues sooner. Or if there'd been anything in Isaac's features that resembled Jude Henley. At the moment his concentration was locked on Rachel's pale face. "Are you okay?"

She sent a taunting smile toward Isaac. "Better now."

"Bitch. When I get out of jail I'm going to hunt you down and beat you until your screams make me climax in bliss."

Isaac reached up, as if intending to wrap his hands around Rachel's throat. Zac's fingers tightened on the trigger, but he managed to resist the temptation to put an end to the monster. He wanted Isaac to live a very long time, in a very small cell, knowing that he would never get out.

Stepping forward, Zac lifted his foot and slammed it down on Isaac's head. There was a dull thud as the younger man's skull connected with the cement floor and his eyes rolled back in his head. They stared at the killer in silence, making sure he was unconscious before Rachel slowly rose to her feet.

"I knew you'd come," she whispered.

"Always." Zac wrapped his arms around the woman who had owned his heart since he was sixteen years old. "Always. Always. Always."

Epilogue

Two weeks later

The funeral for Staci Gale was a small private affair held beneath an ancient oak tree in the back of Pike Cemetery.

Standing next to Zac, Rachel watched as Lynne Gale Jansen and her father tossed flowers onto her mother's coffin before Kir was urging them away from the open grave. The day was sunny, but there was a sharp edge in the wind that made the handful of mourners anxious to head toward the Jansens' new home and the waiting buffet lunch.

As they passed, Lynne reached out to give Rachel's hand a quick squeeze of gratitude. As painful as it was for Lynne to accept her mother was dead, she had confessed that there was a part of her that found comfort in the knowledge that Staci hadn't simply walked away from her family.

Zac wrapped his arm around Rachel's shoulders as they walked in the opposite direction, heading toward his truck, which he'd left parked near the tree line. Rachel had driven in from Madison that morning, meeting Zac at the courthouse just in time to make it to the funeral.

"Did you have a chance to talk to Dr. Gale?" she asked, referring to Lynne's father.

Since the night they'd captured Isaac Dowell both she and Zac had been crushed with work. The killer might be safely behind bars at the supermax prison in Boscobel, Wisconsin, but Zac had been busy collecting the necessary evidence. They were still looking for the rest of Jude's tapes, as well as trying to discover who Isaac had been before taking on the identity he'd used in Pike. Zac had also been meeting with the prosecutor to determine the criminal case against Greg Barry.

She'd been concentrating on the carnage Jude Henley had left in his wake, requesting that her office dedicate themselves to pulling the various case files that matched the victim profiles for the past twenty-eight years. A daunting task.

"Dr. Gale came into the office this week," Zac murmured, pulling open the passenger door of his truck. "He remembered that he'd hired Jude to work on the plumbing at his house not long before Staci supposedly walked away. I didn't say anything to him, but I assume Staci probably had a brief fling with Jude, and he used their relationship to lure her to her murder."

Rachel climbed into the truck and settled against the leather seat. "The Henley men have caused a lot of damage in Pike."

"Not just Pike," he reminded her.

She grimaced, thinking of the giant stack of files in the back of her SUV. "True."

Closing her door, Zac hurried around the front of the truck. This afternoon he was wearing a pair of black dress pants with a dark trench coat, emphasizing his golden beauty. Even with his blond hair tangled from the wind, and a lingering shadow beneath his green eyes, he looked like her old Zac. Strong, determined, but with his easy charm back in place. She'd feared the grim tension might have destroyed it forever, but now she felt her heart flutter with a familiar excitement.

Two weeks was too long to be away from this man.

He slid behind the steering wheel and started the engine. "How's your investigation going?"

She sighed as they bumped over the frozen dirt path toward the road. "Slow, but that's the usual pace for cold cases. Thankfully, the pictures we found in Jude's scrapbook should at least help us match any missing women to his potential victims."

His fingers tightened on the steering wheel. "Does that mean you're headed back to Madison today?"

"Actually . . ." She deliberately allowed the words to trail away.

He waited until he'd merged with the traffic and headed toward the courthouse until he prompted her for an answer. "Actually what?"

"I've discovered that trying to identify and locate the rest of Jude's victims is going to take a considerable amount of time."

Zac visibly shuddered. It wouldn't matter how many times they discussed the heartless monster, they would never think of him without a chill of horror. "If Jude was telling the truth to his son, then there's almost twenty-five dead women out there who all deserve a proper burial."

"My supervisor agrees," Rachel said, smiling as she recalled her conversation with the chief of her department. Rachel had gone into the meeting with facts, statistics, and a list of rock-solid reasons that she should be allowed to do her job from someplace other than her office. It'd taken some negotiating, but she'd ultimately succeeded. "She also agreed to allow me to work remotely."

Zac turned onto Main Street. "What's that mean?"

"Most of my time will be spent either traveling around the state interviewing witnesses and reviewing evidence." She studied his strong profile. "Or I'll be in Pike completing the case files for the women we've already linked to Jude. I can set up my office wherever I find it the most convenient."

She felt his body tense as he absorbed what she was telling him. "Where will you stay?" he demanded. "Your parents'?"

Rachel instantly shook her head. She'd been busy, but she'd invited her parents to visit her in Madison. It'd been nice to have an evening out in an unfamiliar setting and she'd been happy to see that her mom and dad were able to have a conversation without sniping at each other.

"Things are getting better between all of us," she assured Zac. "We even plan to visit Benny's grave next weekend. But there's no way I could live with them. We'd drive each other nuts."

He sent her a quick glance. "You can't stay at the psychedelic motel."

"No." She deliberately paused, the sense of anticipation snapping and sizzling through her. It was like waiting for him to invite her to the prom all over again. "Lynne offered me her father's house. He's getting ready to go back to Florida and it will be empty."

His brows snapped together before he was forced to

return his attention to the road. "Do you intend to accept her offer?"

"Do you have another suggestion?"

"Yes. Stay with me."

Her heart did more fluttering at the fierce urgency in his tone. It was easy to assume when she was packing up her belongings in Madison that he'd want her to stay with him. But it was another thing to sit next to him, waiting to hear the words.

"At the farm?" she asked, recalling that he'd talked about selling the place.

"Anywhere." He shrugged. "The farm. Or I can find a house in town if you prefer. I don't care if we live in a tent as long as we're together."

She released a shaky breath. That was exactly what she needed to hear. "What about you?"

He sent her a puzzled glance. "What about me?"

"You're the interim sheriff. Do you plan to make it a full-time occupation?"

The question wasn't intended to force him into a corner. She was no longer the insecure young woman who had to throw herself into her career to prove herself worthy. She was still ambitious, but it'd been tempered with the desire to have more than just a job in her life. Her question was nothing more than curiosity.

Whatever his decision for his future, they would make it work. Together.

He slowed and pulled into the parking lot next to the courthouse. "You know, I'm thinking I might stick with this sheriff gig. At least for now. I like helping the citizens of Pike. And when there's not a serial killer on the loose, it's not a bad job." He paused, a mysterious smile curving his lips. "Of course, my most important plans for the future involve scheduling a second honeymoon."

She blinked. "A second honeymoon?"

He put the truck in park and turned to meet her narrowed gaze. "Yep."

"There're two problems with that."

He pretended to be baffled by her words. "What problems?"

"You never had a first honeymoon, so you can't have a second one," she said dryly.

Their marriage had been a small, quiet ceremony followed by a move to Madison to attend college. There had been no time or money for any sort of getaway.

"I'm intending to stretch it out a couple of weeks to include a first honeymoon swiftly followed by a second honeymoon," he explained.

"Ah." Her lips twitched. "And where are those honeymoons going to take place?"

He considered the question. "My preference is a secluded beach house with plenty of tropical drinks and not one serial killer in sight." He studied her with a blatant desire. "Of course, my wife will have an opinion on where she'd like to go."

Her mouth went dry. Two weeks in a secluded beach house with Zac sounded like paradise.

"And that's your next problem." Her voice was a low rasp.

He leaned toward her, brushing her hair away from her cheek. She trembled at the soft caress.

"Listening to my wife's opinion is a problem?" he teased. "That sounds like a good thing."

Her stomach clenched. This was the Zac she'd tumbled

into love with. Charming, gorgeous, utterly focused on her.

"You don't have a wife."

His fingers drifted down her jaw, his thumb brushing her lower lip. "I'm working on it."

"Are you?"

The gold flecks in his eyes shimmered with need. "I'll admit that it would be easier if she would agree to spend some time with me."

She leaned toward him, pressing a light kiss to his lips. "Are you done for today?"

She heard a low growl rumble in his chest. "Lindsay is training my new deputies and Anthony is out on patrol," he told her. She had yet to meet the latest members of the sheriff's office, but she had every confidence that they would be an improvement over Greg. And Anthony had surprised her by being suspicious of his fellow deputy when no one else had noticed anything strange. He was at least trustworthy. "I'm officially off duty."

"Then why don't we swing by Bella's and get some pizza and a bottle of wine and you can start convincing me to be your wife."

Abruptly straightening, Zac shoved the truck back into gear and squealed out of the lot.

"I thought you'd never ask."